MEN I'VE LOVED
BEFORE

ADELE PARKS

MEN I'VE LOVED BEFORE

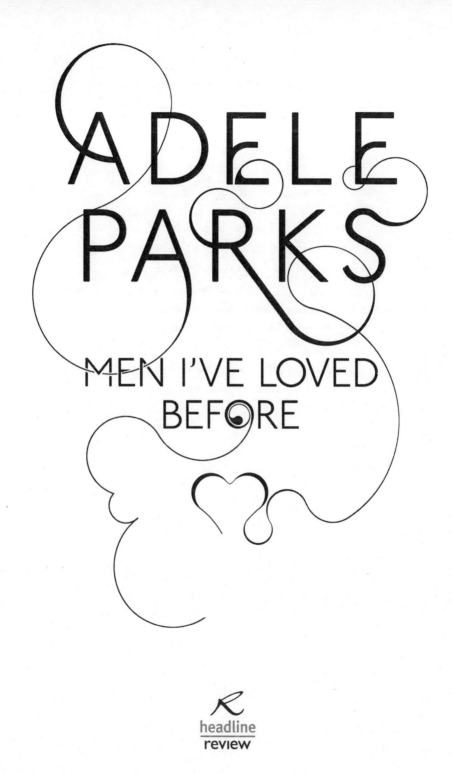

R
headline
review

First published in Great Britain in 2010
by HEADLINE REVIEW
An imprint of HEADLINE PUBLISHING GROUP

1

Cataloguing in Publication Data is available from the British Library

ISBN 978 0 7553 7125 9 (Hardback)
ISBN 978 0 7553 7126 6 (Trade paperback)

Typeset in Monotype Dante by Ellipsis Books Limited, Glasgow

Printed and bound in Great Britain by Clays Ltd St Ives Plc

Headline's policy is to use papers that are natural, renewable
and recyclable products and made from wood grown in sustainable forests.
The logging and manufacturing processes are expected to conform to
the environmental regulations of the country of origin.

HEADLINE PUBLISHING GROUP
An Hachette UK Company
338 Euston Road
London NW1 3BH

www.headline.co.uk
www.hachette.co.uk

For mothers and daughters everywhere.
Especially my mum Maureen, my Nana Mary
and my Nana Finn.

With love.

1

Nat picked up her BlackBerry. Its smooth, cool, shininess was instantly soothing; once again she ran through the 'Birthday To Do List'. It wasn't that she was a neurotic controlling type, she told herself; it was just that it was important to her that Neil's birthday was absolutely perfect. Actually, she was a neurotic controlling type but luckily her husband rather liked it in her, he recognised that her organisation skills propped up his tendency towards the chaotic.

1) Confirm cake has been delivered to restaurant. Check.

She'd already called the Bluebird restaurant and verified that the moist chocolate cake with lavish marshmallow stack had safely arrived in the kitchen. It had been delivered by a neighbour of her parents who, coincidentally, had been coming into town to see a new exhibition at the Tate Modern and (according to her mother) really didn't mind making the diversion to drop off the cake. It was true people tended to like doing things for Nina. It had taken some negotiation to convince the restaurant chef to allow Nina's homemade cake into his inner sanctum in the first place. But Natalie was very persuasive when she needed to be and she considered her husband's thirty-fifth birthday such an occasion. Neil would not think his birthday complete without a cake baked by his mother-in-law.

The Bluebird restaurant on the King's Road in the heart of Chelsea was undeniably stylish, but the obvious sophistication and daring modernity was not at all intimidating because some clever interior designer had chosen warm, rich colours and subtle lighting which created a relaxed and intimate ambiance. Nat had thought it the perfect place for cocktails and dinner with friends. Neil would appreciate the modern British menu; he always had to stop off at the chippie if they ate at a nouvelle cuisine restaurant or at a sushi bar.

While she'd been on the phone, Nat had also checked that the reservation was for 7.15p.m., *not* 7.30p.m. She'd once read a tip in a magazine about how to ensure great service in a restaurant and she'd been struck by the suggestion of making a booking for quarter past or quarter to the hour, as the vast majority of the general public arrived at restaurants on the hour or half past. Nat had never bothered to follow the tip before, but tonight she was keen that everything (including service) was heavenly.

2) Confirm time of reservation. Check.

Whilst on the phone she'd also changed the reservation for eight people to six. Neil's brother's wife, Fi, had called this morning to cancel – again. Babysitting issues – again. Nat was disappointed, for herself and especially for Neil. She knew he'd have loved to have had his big brother there tonight, not least because Ben was always rather good at discreetly mediating between Tim (Neil's oldest friend) and Karl (Neil's most fun friend). Despite the fact that Neil, Tim and Karl saw each other socially at least once a week, from what Nat had witnessed over the past seven years, it was clear that, other than a deep and enduring affection for Neil, Neil's best mates didn't have that much in common. Neil appeared to be unaware of the slight tension and tussle of their being a threesome, or at least he did a damn good impression of seeming so. He was happiest when everyone just got along.

After Nat had informed the restaurant about the alteration to the number of guests she was expecting, she'd also made sure that the sommelier's selection still included Chenas Cuvée Quartz, Piron & Lafontthe. She was quite nervous about her pronunciation of the wine's name but the last time she and Neil had visited Bluebird (well, the only other time, in fact) he'd commented how much he liked the wine and she'd taken note of it so she could try to track it down in a supermarket.

3) Confirm availability of Chenas Cuvée Quartz. Check.

She could almost feel the maître d' rolling his eyes in exasperation through the telephone. No doubt he thought she was horribly painful and was probably contemplating instructing the kitchen staff to spit in her soup. Nat didn't care. All she cared about was giving Neil a great night. Nat never got so excited about her own birthdays; actually she preferred to ignore them altogether, that date wasn't much cause for celebration, but Neil's birthday was something special. The day Neil came into this world was really important, at least to her. Not that she was given to saying such sloppy things; she preferred to show her feelings through her actions. That's why she wanted tonight to be wonderful.

The sun had cooperated, which was a bonus. It had been a hot and hazy day, the warmth still snuggled in the London pavements and brickwork and in the smiles of people who spilled outside pubs, beer bottle and fag in hand. Nat loved the lively sun-induced chatter that erupted between strangers, she loved the brightly coloured clothes that, like butterflies, could only be spotted in London for a fleeting summer moment, and she loved blasts of the smell of suntan lotion on warm skin. Despite Neil's birthday landing in late August, there was never an absolute guarantee that they'd enjoy sunshine on the day. The likelihood of a British BBQ summer was about parallel to actually spotting a UFO or that of a woman over forty being compli- mented on her beauty without the compliment being accompanied by the deadening caveat, 'for her age'. Nat remembered Neil's thirty- third birthday with horrible clarity. She'd arranged for them to enjoy a gourmet picnic in their local park, Ravenscourt; they'd practically had to use the hamper as a lifeboat because of flash floods. Then there was the year that she'd thought it might be fun to go to Brighton and eat fish and chips on the front. In her mind she'd imagined them wandering, hand in hand, along the pier. She'd expected bare, sun- kissed shoulders and flip-flops. In fact they'd needed to wear wellington boots as they bravely strode along the pebbles and, ultimately, they were driven back inside the hotel because of the bitingly cold sea wind. Still, the hotel had been cosy, there were compensations. Nat started to think fondly of the fireside loving they'd enjoyed in their Brighton suite – which brought her to item four on the 'Birthday To Do List'.

4) Wear matching underwear.

Nat reached into her underwear drawer, rummaged around and then pulled out a flesh-coloured bra and knickers set which was edged with cream lace. Perfect. Dressy enough to show that she'd made an effort but comfortable and wouldn't show through her blouse. Check.

Natalie wanted to look her best. Dressing up was fun and she always believed preparing for a night out was part of the joy of the event. During her lunch hour she'd dashed to the hairdressers for a blow dry and last night she'd squeezed in a quick visit to the local beautician and undergone the masochistic act of having a bikini and half-leg wax. She'd thought longingly of the wonderful pampering treatments on offer. She'd have loved an Indian head massage or a rehydrating facial but Nat was aware that no matter what beauty miracles might be achieved through an hour in the floatation tank or a quick rub-down with hot stones, Neil would be more impressed by a tidy vadge and, after all, it was his birthday.

Despite the fact that Nat had an important and nerve-wracking meeting with her boss in the morning she'd slipped out of work at exactly 5p.m. today; an unusual occurrence as Nat loved her job at the world's largest pharmaceutical company and often worked much longer hours than those specified on her contract. She was happy to run the extra mile whenever asked (or even without being asked) as she believed what she did was life-changing and contributed to society at a profound level. Although, obviously, this was not an opinion she often voiced as she was aware that doing so would, at best, make her sound self-consciously worthy (which was unfashionable) and at worst make her sound self-congratulatory and smug (which was unattractive).

She'd dashed home to shower, slather her body in moisturiser and pull on a fresh outfit. Home was a modest but stylish two up, two down terraced home in Chiswick, west London. Nat and Neil both loved living in Chiswick, a leafy, villagey sort of place, awash with bistros, trees, arty types and, less romantically but quite certainly, stuffed with commuters, Starbucks franchises and estate agents. They embraced both aspects of Chiswick life, the cool chic and the convenience. Proud and thrilled to have got on the property ladder at all, they were both delighted to be living in such a desirable part of London. They'd chosen to live in Chiswick because it was so convenient for both of their places of work. Nat's office was in Brentford, less than three miles west of Chiswick, and Neil's office was right next door to Goldhawk Road tube station, just two miles east. Neil had argued that the extra they spent on rent was offset because they barely had any commuter costs, they could even walk to work, he'd said somewhat optimistically. They rarely did so, they usually opted to stay in bed for an extra ten minutes and catch the bus. His figures didn't add up but Nat also desperately wanted to live in Chiswick and so was prepared to pay the inflated rents if they had to.

They had rented the house from the relative of an elderly woman who had been seeing out her days in a residential home. She died six months before their wedding and her relatives, keen for a quick sale, gave Nat and Neil first refusal on the property and offered it at a knockdown price. Nat and Neil had snapped it up; after all, for months they had been imagining and speculating as to what they would do with the property if it was theirs. As soon as they had the deeds, they started to strip the pink flowered wallpaper and painted the walls in taupe and beige shades. They ripped up the tatty carpets and varnished and polished the floorboards that secretly lay below. They painted the front door an imposing black and Nat spent a week online choosing a new knocker and letter box. Instead of a conventional wedding list, they asked their guests if they'd mind giving B&Q or Ikea vouchers, and before their first anniversary they had the kitchen and bathroom replaced. They had potted plants on the window sills and blinds rather than curtains in every room. They had their perfect home.

They lived in a small, thin road, south of Chiswick High Road. True, they could always hear the A4 traffic whiz or chug by (the speed of the traffic was time-dependent, but it was safe to say there were snarls during most daylight hours) yet the noise was more than compensated for by the fact that they were a short walk away from Ravenscourt Park, if they ever craved greenery, a stone's throw away from countless trendy bars and cute chichi shops, if they ever needed to buy anything pretty, tasty or luxurious, and for Nat, the best thing of all about Chiswick was that it was nestled right next to one of the long, lazy loops of the River Thames. She often dragged Neil out of bed on a Sunday morning so that they could amble along the Chiswick Mall, a road lined with elegant and shockingly expensive houses, which had the pleasure of overlooking the Thames. The houses ranged in style from Georgian to gingerbread; the thing they had in common was that all the residents enjoyed tremendous views of the river.

She had hoped to meet Neil at home this evening so that they could go to the restaurant together. Truthfully, she had thought that maybe, somewhere between applying the body moisture and picking out what she'd wear tonight, they might have the opportunity to make love. It wasn't that Nat was expecting to swing from the chandeliers on this hot evening; she would have been extremely content with something more straightforward, something satisfying in the missionary position, perhaps. Neil invariably left his office the moment the clock struck five. He loved his work too, he worked as a video games designer, an ambition he'd had since he was a kid and discovered Pac-Man and Donkey Kong in a seaside arcade when he was on a family holiday in Blackpool, but he never saw the need to linger in the office. He could play games at home and call it research. Nat had thought he'd be home early enough for them to enjoy some lovely birthday sex and still get to the restaurant on time. Sex before the birthday dinner was preferable to sex after the birthday dinner because the important meeting with her boss tomorrow meant that Nat wanted to avoid a very late night if at all possible.

Nat was aware that it was a thin line between being organised and squashing all artless and joyful spontaneity. Everyone knew spontaneity was a great thing to have in a relationship – in a personality, come to that – so she really wished that she didn't think through every last detail with such precision but she found she couldn't help herself. She was such a worrier. She had responsibilities, lots of them; responsibilities to her husband, to her boss, to her family, to her friends and to the maître d' who was expecting them at 7.15p.m. precisely. She found that careful planning minimised the opportunity for disaster and disillusionment. However, extensive planning could not cancel *all* risk of disappointment, as was proved when Neil called her and said she was not to expect him home as Karl had insisted that they go for a birthday drink straight from work, to kill the time between work finishing and their reservation at the restaurant.

'Do you mind?' asked Neil with concern. He was aware that Nat liked to plan things and he didn't want to mess up anything she might have arranged.

'Not at all. It's your birthday. The important thing is you have fun,' Nat replied honestly. She didn't think it was fair to say she was lying on their bed in her scanties; what would Karl do with himself when Neil made a dash from the pub?

'You're sure?'

'Certain. I'll see you there. Has Karl arranged to meet Jen there too?'

'Dunno, I'll ask him.'

'Do. You know what he's like, he might just have a beer too many and forget that he has a girlfriend who is supposed to be joining us.' Nat had introduced Jen to Karl about this time last year and she tended to feel responsible for their relationship staying on track; quite an undertaking as Karl was a consummate flirt and Jen was an absolute romantic. Neil often said that they were all grown-ups and that Nat shouldn't feel she had to manage them but she couldn't shake the habit.

'Will do,' said Neil. He glanced towards Karl, who was at the bar ordering drinks. Karl was chatting up a very beautiful redhead but Neil decided there was no point sharing this information with Nat, it would stress her out. Best thing he could do was go and drag his mate back to the table. 'Better go. Love you, see you there. Thanks so much for arranging tonight, Nat. I'm really looking forward to it,' he added sincerely.

'You're welcome. Love you too.' Nat hung up and considered how she could best use the unexpected hour she now had to herself. She could tie the helium balloons to the bedposts, at the moment the balloons were just drifting around the house willy-nilly, or she could reread her notes for the morning meeting, or she could paint her fingernails. She decided that she would reread her notes and then arrange the balloons. Neil would be so excited when he saw the thirty-five balloons (various shades of blue and purple) as he was such a big kid. So there wasn't to be birthday sex, at least not yet. That probably meant they'd have to miss out or she would have to stay up late. Nat put the issue to the back of her head and reached for her laptop. Oh well, Nat thought to herself. After all, sex isn't everything.

2

Neil clawed through the fuzzy mess that was his mind and tried to grab on to the point his friend, Karl, was making.

'Say that again.'

'A man can never hope for, think about or indeed actually have too much sex. Sex is *everything* it's cracked up to be and more,' Karl said with absolute, unwavering conviction. Then Karl closed his eyes and pursed his lips. He probably wanted to communicate certainty and confidence, but Neil thought his mate had only managed cool and smug. Karl liked to play the sage, even when he was pissed – especially then. Yet Neil and Tim had to grudgingly admit that Karl could afford to be cool and smug because, as his freshly relayed story about his recent antics with a Dutch air hostess proved, he was clearly still enjoying the sort of sex that *is* everything, although admittedly not always with his girlfriend, Jen.

Sex is *everything* it's cracked up to be and more. How profound was that? Neil stared at his empty wine glass, probably his fifth empty wine glass that evening, and two pints before that. The empty glass provided the answer to his question: his mate was *deeply* profound.

'You're right. It's bigger than football and even video games by a long shot,' Neil agreed with drunken enthusiasm. He nodded his head so vigorously that his eyes disappeared, up and away, somewhere behind his forehead. His smile was slack and accepting but, even through his drunken haze, Neil recognised a prickle of discomfort spike his conscience. By agreeing with Karl he was tactically condoning his illicit affairs, but in fact he didn't agree with Karl's behaviour. Besides, Neil knew that Nat would be disgusted if she got so much as a whisper of Karl's exploits and he knew she'd want him to be dismayed by Karl's vulgar, careless bragging. And so he was. Appalled by it. Mainly. But the horrible truth was, he was also just a tiny bit curious and a smidgen envious.

Neil and Natalie had been married five years now and in all that time Neil had been completely and utterly faithful in deed and mostly faithful in thought. Naturally, after years of sex with the same woman (usually in the same bed, at the same time of the week, initiated in the same break between TV programmes) it tended not to be the sort of sex that could be described as *everything*. Neil found that he often stole some illicit, gratuitous pleasure from listening to Karl's stories. Neil sneaked a look at Tim, who had been married to Alison for three years. Were they still having the *everything* sort of sex?

Tim was trying to look bored with Karl's conversation; he hadn't had a drink and so could not find it in him to indulge Karl's loutish conceit. In the past there had been occasions when he, too, had enjoyed living vicariously through Karl's escapades but now it all seemed infantile; he was simply irritated by it. He would have liked to tell Karl that he was spouting crap but it was Neil's birthday and to celebrate the fact they were here at the Bluebird restaurant on the King's Road in posh Chelsea and so it would seem rude; dissent would hinder the digestion of the gorgeous grilled organic rib-eye steak. Besides, a condemnation of what Karl was saying might reveal that he was not having the *everything* sort of sex and he'd rather stab himself in the eye with a steak knife than admit as much to Karl.

Karl and Tim had always been furtively competitive. Tim knew it was something to do with the dynamics of their respective relationships with Neil but he couldn't put his finger on exactly what (not without sounding gay) and he'd rather admit to Karl that he wasn't having the *everything* sort of sex than say something that might make him sound gay. Neil and Tim were each other's oldest friend. They'd been buddies since primary school.

They'd grown up on the same sprawling housing estate, just a few miles south of Nottingham town centre, in identical, modest 1970s semis. Houses that Tim's mum and Neil's parents still lived in, although both families had since added a porch and Neil's parents had gone the whole hog, they'd built an extension which provided a fourth bedroom. They had been able to afford this at just about the time Neil, his brother and sister had left home, rendering the longed-for extension useless except for every other Christmas when Neil and his siblings, their spouses and families visited home for three tense days of overeating and mild squabbling. Neil had once told Tim that he didn't mind Christmas squabbles; he believed them to be inevitable. He thought of his family as a very close family and he was pretty sure that things like his mother's continual insistence they all eat just one more mince pie, his sister's doggedness that they opened their Christmas presents in size order, his father's resolve that they each discuss (at tedious length) the route they chose to travel home (and then all alternatives!), and his brother's competitive nature, which sprang like a well throughout charades, monopoly and even when answering the quiz questions in the crackers, were all signs of their closeness. Families were supposed to be comfortingly habitual; that was the point of them.

Neil and Tim had attended the same small and earnest primary school and the same sprawling and indifferent comprehensive. At both institutions they had frequently stood side by side, silently encouraging and supporting one another whenever they faced their headmaster or mothers (after being caught in the inevitable scrapes that kids are caught in) and then, as teenagers, when they'd faced down Dave-built-like-a-brick-shithouse and his gang of thugs (both of them refusing to hand over their lunch money which was a stand neither could have made alone). They went to separate universities, Tim studied mathematics at Bristol and Neil studied computer graphics at Cardiff, but they called and visited one another frequently throughout those three years and then after graduating they moved to London and shared a dingy flat and numerous cheap curries. For nearly three decades now they'd stood shoulder to shoulder for various team photos, at bars, in ski lifts, before exams and job interviews and at the altars where they'd been each other's best man. There was no doubt that Tim was Neil's *oldest* friend but at the risk of sounding like a girl, Tim could never shake off the nagging feeling that Karl was Neil's *best* friend.

Of course Neil and Karl both worked in video games, they had that in common, Neil as a designer, Karl as a marketer. This instantly transformed them into hipper types than Tim could ever hope to be. Tim was a computer programmer. He liked his job well enough, it paid nicely but it hadn't been a childhood ambition, he wasn't passionate about it like Neil was about his work. Neil had always been mad about video games and manga illustrations and superhero comics and all sorts of other cool stuff. Since Neil had been a teenager he'd been determined to become a games designer and he didn't give a damn that career advisers, teachers and such were forever telling him there was no real money in it.

Neil and Karl had met twelve years ago at an industry event but cut the seminar to go to a lap-dancing club. Tim had had no idea that Neil had ever wanted to visit a lap-dancing club; he probably hadn't wanted to until Karl had suggested it. It turned out Neil also wanted to go snowboarding in Le Corbier, quad biking in the Cadiretas Mountains and mud wrestling with naked girls in Bratislava. Everything Karl suggested was fun, enticing and irresistible; everyone found this to be the case. Especially women. Karl was sickeningly successful with women. The mystery was, Karl wasn't actually that good-looking. He was trendy and had an expensive haircut (artfully sculpted to look as though he'd just got out of bed and never gave styling any thought) but it had long since occurred to Tim that all of Karl's features just missed being extremely handsome by a smidgen. His eyes were blue and he had thick, long lashes (the type that girls craved) but the eyes were small and too close together, his top lip was disproportionately thin in comparison to the bottom one, he had a fine nose but it was a fraction too long and gave the illusion that it was about to crash into his chin. He was tall, which was a plus, but he hadn't bulked out in his thirties as most men did and he'd been described as lanky as a teenager and it was just as accurate a description today. And yet, charismatic Karl was and always had been a colossal hit with women, with his bosses, with his mates, with footie refs, even with the men who came to install his cable or read his meter.

It was sickening, really.

When he burst into any room or gathering, he radically elevated the mood. There was never any embarrassing hiatus in the conversation, just plenty of hilarious jokes and interesting stories. He was amusing, razor-sharp, poised and he seemed to have a limitless stream of spellbinding anecdotes. He was happy with his lot: his job, his girl-friend, his disposable women and his flat. He didn't seem to take himself or anyone else too seriously. Many would say he was the perfect twenty-first-century man. The truth was that Karl was more amusing, astounding and controversial than Tim. In short, Karl was more compelling. Tim thought it was hard to keep up.

'Do you know what, if everyone understood and *accepted* that sex is everything *and more*, the world would be a far, far happier place to dwell,' said Karl. 'There would be less war, less theft, less violence, less lying.'

Tim wondered if Neil was simply too drunk to notice that the stuff Karl was spouting was just plain old bollocks. The sort of sex that Karl was having (the sort with air hostesses and other strangers he met on business trips) inevitably led to more lying, not less. Actually, Neil was not paying that much attention to what Karl was saying now; he'd tuned out. Neil was thinking about the fact that he really had quite a good chance of getting laid tonight even though it was Wednesday. After all, it was his birthday and Natalie was not an unrea-sonable woman. When he'd called Nat this evening and discovered she was at home he had considered going straight there from work, rather than going for a beer with Karl, just in case he caught her in the mood. But then he'd reasoned that she'd probably dashed home from the office to search out some quiet privacy, to prepare for her meeting in the morning, and he didn't want to get in the way, so he hadn't suggested it.

Karl carried on. 'Sex is the ultimate secret to happiness.'

'What evidence do you have for that?' asked Tim with an irritated sigh.

'Well, mate, *I* understand and accept that sex is, you know, massive and I'm a very happy man.'

'You sound like a sex addict,' Tim said, not bothering to hide his annoyance. Mostly Tim was annoyed because Karl, with his slack morals and careless cruelty, *was* happy whereas Tim, who had always done his best to be a decent human being, was often barely content, let alone happy. Not recently. Not since he and Ali had been *trying* for a baby. Trying and failing, that was. It didn't seem fair. Tim swept his eyes around the restaurant. It was buzzing even though it was midweek. He liked it here. Despite its lofty size, the place felt intimate. If only Karl would stop going on about sex, he'd be really enjoying Neil's birthday dinner. Natalie had chosen well. The restaurant was decorated with warm chocolate browns and deep, rich reds which subliminally suggested bitter chocolate brownies and ripe raspberries. What else was on the dessert menu? Oh yes, sweet melon jelly with poached pear, walnuts and chocolate sauce. He stared up at the stunning skylight, gilded with glimmering metallic chandeliers, and wished the women would come back from the loo. Not only could he order pudding but they'd put a halt to this infantile conversation. Why did women need to go to the loo in packs anyhow?

He knew the answer and it was not a comfort. They went in gangs to gossip. Right now, Alison would be issuing the fertility update to Nat and Jen as though she worked for the BBC World Service. She'd be discussing the exact quality of his sperm, or more accurately the lack of quality. She just didn't see any reason to keep this sort of information to herself. 'It's nothing to be ashamed of,' she'd insisted when he'd asked if she could possibly be a tad more discreet. 'It's just biology.' She'd be explaining that for most men each millilitre of semen contains literally millions of spermatozoa (technical name for sperm and the one she preferred to use right now), but this was not the case for Tim, his sperm count was 'significantly below average'. That's why he wasn't allowed to get pissed tonight which was making this conversation about filthy, flirty, dirty sex all the harder to endure. Apparently, his sperm had a better chance of hitting the jackpot if it wasn't pickled in alcohol. It was astounding to Tim that Alison had insisted that they go to a doctor to have that choice piece of information suggested and confirmed. He'd have thought years of living together and seeing how getting lashed affected his ability to aim piss into the pan would have been evidence enough for her, but no, Alison needed to hear it from the men in white coats. It had been a mortifying exercise. Ali wasn't herself just now. Baby-making had become all-consuming and over a period of about eight months he'd watched his wife change from a happy and intelligent woman to an angry and irrational beast. He really hoped that if (when, he self-corrected; he always had to think positively, Ali insisted on it) *when* she got pregnant, she'd revert back to her rational and reasonable self. Otherwise any child they might have would certainly end up in therapy. Suddenly Tim felt rebellious.

'How about I get us a bottle of champagne, to go with pudding?' he asked. 'I'll get it from the bar then it won't go on the bill. My treat.' Tim stood up abruptly.

'Nice one, pal, very generous of you,' said Neil with a grin.

'My pleasure.' Anything rather than listen to Karl's bragging or at least if he had to listen to it, then he'd rather be slightly numbed. Off he strode in the direction of the bar.

'I wish Tim would just leave his car here and he could pick it up in the morning,' said Neil the moment he was out of earshot. 'I think he could do with a real drink. He's not himself tonight.' Neil was disappointed this was the case. Birthdays, by necessity, only came round once a year and he wanted all his mates to be in the right mood to celebrate. He knew Nat had put a lot of effort into arranging tonight for him. She'd been coordinating diaries all summer. Tim's jittery mood and refusal to get wasted wasn't very celebratory.

'Have you noticed that if you mention the word sex, Tim reacts as though he's just been snapped by a speed camera,' commented Karl.

'What?'

Karl leaned towards Neil conspiratorially. He actually tapped his nose which was only excusable as they were both drunk. 'The thing is, to him sex and speeding are a bit similar at the moment, a mix between occasional necessity and genuine compulsion, but if you're caught, you have to cough up big time.' Karl laughed at his own witty metaphor. Encouraged by a booze-induced belief in his own brilliance and a sneaky, somewhat pleasant, suspicion that he knew more about this subject than Neil, he continued to explain. 'Tim is drowning in domestic responsibility and being beaten by procreation issues.'

'What?' repeated Neil. He was none the wiser.

'They're doing the baby-making thing. He only gets it at certain times of the month now. He's not even allowed to shake hands with his old fella. Plus, when they do actually get down to it, it's all a bit perfunctory,' explained Karl.

'*He* told *you* this?' Neil asked in disbelief. It was generally acknowledged that friendships between boys are sustained (indeed blossom) only if all the concerned parties are careful never to talk about anything too personal which might embarrass any one of them and, besides, if Tim was ever to behave out of type, he'd confide in Neil, not Karl. Neil was pretty sure of that.

'No, you silly sod, of course *he* didn't tell me this. Alison told Jen, who told me. Alison must have discussed it with Nat. I'm surprised she hasn't filled you in. I think this conversation about me getting it up the Dutch bird is reminding Tim of what he's no longer enjoying.'

Karl and Neil both turned and watched, with some sadness, as Tim tried and failed to attract the attention of the chic barmaid. Tim used to be quite the man about town although he'd never been aware of it. In the past, he was the one they always sent to the bar because he was the undisputed looker of the gang. Since a pair of red-blooded males noticed and acknowledged he was hot, how could barmaids – mere women – resist him? They'd practically slithered in his direction if he so much as nodded. But that was then, this was now.

'He's never going to get that fucking champagne,' said Karl impatiently. 'You know what the problem is, don't you? He's fading. The receding hair, and "dad uniform" of pale chinos, pink shirt, slight paunch mean he's faded into the background and Alison's not even up the duff yet. By the time their kid is attending nursery school, he'll be invisible.' The phrase 'poor sucker' flitted in and out of Karl's mind. 'Hell. He might call me a sex addict but I'd say I'm just a normal man and he's forgotten what being a man is,' he added.

Suddenly they were swamped by an anxious, slightly despondent silence. Neil didn't like it, Karl couldn't stand it. Despondency was not their thing. Karl made an effort to claw back the former mood of irreverence, a mood more fitting for a birthday celebration. 'And as a normal man it's my given right to think about sex every thirty seconds,' he joked.

'Every thirty seconds, are you sure?' Neil looked alarmed. Instantly he felt inadequate. Hearing this statistic was a bit like finding out that your best mate understands all aspects of the quantum theory; you feel left behind.

Karl appreciated the insecurity. Even he considered every thirty seconds an unsustainable and unlikely goal. 'Don't sweat it, mate. This dubious statistic, which has seeped into modern culture as fact, originated from nothing more substantial than a women's magazine. It's ironic that it was women who gifted this particular carte blanche to us lads by publishing an article claiming pathetic single-mindedness is true of all men. The article was probably little more than an elaborate joke, initially intended to highlight men's inability to multitask, or emotionally engage, or some other bollocks. Well, that apple pie back-splattered, didn't it, mate?'

'Why's that then?' asked Neil.

'Well, if a bloke were to think of sex, say, once an hour, he is considered moderate, not deviant or imbecilic,' Karl explained.

'And do you? Do you think about it once an hour?'

'I do.'

'What are you talking about?' It was Nat who asked this question. Neil and Karl jumped guiltily as they registered that Tim had returned from the bar and was holding a chilled bottle of house champagne and six glasses and the girls had returned from the loo. As the women sat down, they rolled their eyes at one another conspiratorially. They hadn't caught the conversation but they took an educated guess as to what the blokes would be talking about.

Football. Again.

'**D**id you have a fun night?' Nat asked Neil as she picked up his arm and wrapped it round her shoulders. She rested her head on his chest, he leant his head against the cold taxi window and they both watched headlights and street lights whizz by. The very last whispers of the late summer day had disappeared behind London's skyline. Nat sighed contentedly; she loved balmy nights such as these.

Natalie felt around for Neil's hand. She found it and their fingers automatically entwined. She remembered a period in their lives, years ago, when getting into a taxi guaranteed that they would immediately pull at each other's clothes eagerly and make urgent, ham-fisted grabs at one another's flesh. Desperate for each other, they'd been unwilling to exercise any restraint. She didn't actively miss that time, not as such. It had always been embarrassing paying the cabbie after he'd seen you all but fornicate on the back seat. Yet, being conscious of the fact that that time in her life was over (for ever) was at once a comfort and a challenge for her. She saw that getting older offered all sorts of compensations but she also knew that being young was undoubtedly glittering.

'A great night, thank you,' said Neil with just a slight slur. He turned towards her and kissed her. It was a long, warm, tender kiss. He didn't try to involve his tongue which, considering his state of inebriation, was a definite act of chivalry. Yes, thought Natalie, getting older had all sorts of compensations and being settled with Neil was the biggest one.

Before Neil, Natalie had had a few long-term boyfriends and a number of flash-in-the-pan types of boyfriend. They provided an eclectic mix of amazingly passionate and rather more prosaic relationships for her to look back upon fondly. In her time, she'd dated cute but thoughtless men, frighteningly intelligent but arrogant men, kind but dull men, fabulous but didn't want her men, fun but going nowhere men, intense but too-much men. The assortment of liaisons had two things in common. One, Natalie gave each guy her best shot. She was always fair, faithful, and she tried very hard to suppress or at least disguise any weirdness she undoubtedly harboured. Two, all these men had a *but*. A big flashing *but* that signalled they weren't her One; someone else's One very probably, as none of her exes were actual monsters, but not her One.

And then there was Neil.

Natalie and Neil met one another in a pub, seven years ago. It all happened the old-fashioned way: their eyes collided across a smoky haze. It wasn't Natalie's usual sort of place, she was not a corner pub sort of girl, in fact it was her first time visiting the Goat and Gate. She'd only ended up there because her friend had a blister. Her pal had said she couldn't bear walking the distance to the wine bar that they usually went to on a Friday night, but after a long and tricky day at work they were both desperate for alcohol a.s.a.p. so agreed to take refuge in the nearest watering hole. Later, Natalie found out that whilst it was Neil's local, it wasn't his usual night to visit the pub. He normally met up with his mates on Thursdays but Karl hadn't been able to make that Thursday so they'd swapped nights to a Friday. So, neither Nat nor Neil had planned to go to the Goat and Gate that night and yet they did. Nat thought it was that sort of thing that might make a person believe in fate and such, although Neil didn't (he was resolute that fate, horoscopes, tarot cards and Karma were all bollocks; Neil was sure that life was even more random than those crutches would have you believe).

The Goat and Gate wasn't then, and still wasn't now, an especially smart place. There were no leather tub chairs, just frayed Drayloncovered benches, no potted plants, no shiny reclaimed floorboards, and there were only two wines for sale, house white or house red. But nor was it frighteningly grungy; the floors weren't sticky, the glasses weren't smeared and the loos didn't smell like cesspits.

Nat had noticed Neil, Tim and Karl almost as soon as she walked into the bar. She was single at the time and had a keen 'potential radar'. Tim was by far the most handsome of the gang and Karl looked quick, alert and fun but it was Neil who held Nat's attention. He was about five foot ten, the height where most men started to describe themselves as six foot; he had decent dress sense, the absence of a large beer belly and impressively muscled arms (which Nat had a particular fondness for). She liked his hair as it was particularly shiny, especially for a man. So far, so normal. If this had been all there was to Neil, Natalie might not have lingered. Neil would have had to live out his life with no other accolade than, 'slightly above averagely good-looking', but then he laughed. His laugh rang through the pub, turning heads and flipping hearts. If you listened carefully to his laugh you could hear echoes of the best nights out you'd ever enjoyed, you could hear your boss offering you a promotion, you could hear waves lap the shore on a hot summer day. Neil's laugh shook the cynicism out of the vicinity; those looking at life through half-empty cups suddenly saw they were overflowing. His laugh offered promise; it was full of sincerity, certainty and potential. In that instant Neil was hauled up, by the laces of his Converse trainers, out of obscurity and instantly transformed into a man of note. A man Natalie wanted to get to know.

Neil knew that he'd caught the attention of the hot chick standing by the bar. Wow, she was a stunner. She had a glow about her. She had blond, longish hair that swished around her shoulders as she animatedly chattered with her girlfriend. He'd be hard pushed now to describe exactly how long her hair had been. He'd say longer than Demi Moore's in *G.I. Jane*, shorter than Daryl Hannah's in *Splash*, sort of girl length. The thing he noticed was that as her hair swished he felt a breeze in the air, as though a tide had changed. And her smile

21

(wide and regularly bestowed) was dazzling. Neil was fascinated by Natalie's smile. It started slowly, her lips on the right side of her face rose first, almost reluctantly, and then there was a moment – no, a fraction of a moment – when she seemed to decide that she truly did want to smile and bang! It was there, broad and confident and irresistible. She had plump, plum-coloured lips. From the moment Neil saw them he knew they were blow job lips. She had blue eyes, a cracking figure – small boobs, a neat arse – and everything reasonably tight and toned but not skinny or scrawny or hard. Perfect, in Neil's book.

He'd stood in the bar, simultaneously nurturing yet battling with an image of her lips clamped round his cock (battling because which man in his late twenties was proud of an uncontrolled hard-on in a crowded pub?), wondering how he should approach her. Sending a drink over only happened in really bad movies, sidling up to her and making conversation seemed a little lacklustre; striding up to her and snogging her face off seemed a little presumptuous (even after four pints).

And then, suddenly, she was standing next to him.

'Hi. Saw you staring,' Natalie said, giving Neil the benefit of that delicious smile, which was even more compelling up close.

'Oh, yeah, I thought you were someone I knew,' Neil muttered, quite pathetically.

'No, you didn't. But I am someone you should get to know,' Natalie bounced back.

And it should have been cheesy. God knows, if Neil had been the one to come up with that line there would have been groaning in the stalls, women throwing rotting fruit, but when Natalie said it, it was funny and confident and unexpected. Neil just knew Natalie was all those things. He laughed and his laugh caused her to flash her big, beautiful beam once again.

'Are you married?' She threw out the line.

'No.'

'Engaged?' She dangled the bait.

'No.'

'Living with anyone, got a serious girlfriend?' She waited patiently like all good anglers.

'No.'

'You're not gay.' He liked the way she didn't feel the need to check, despite the fact that he was wearing cool clothes and he smelt good. 'Mine's a vodka and cranberry,' she said, reeling him in.

After an evening of, if not quite wine and song, then at least vodka and chatter, Neil asked Natalie if she was interested in going to see a movie later that weekend. He asked her because he fancied the hell out of her and definitely wanted to see her again but he also rushed to ask her as he needed to make up some macho ground. As she'd done all the initial legwork, he knew he wouldn't be able to look at himself in the mirror when shaving if she pipped him to the post on asking for a date too. He asked her what she wanted to go and see. Nonchalantly, she shrugged and assured him that her tastes were wide. She said she was comfortable sitting through films with scenes of unnecessary violence and graphic sex but she liked girly romantic chick flicks too. Neil was narrower in his taste so they went to see *Kill Bill, Vol. 1*.

He wasn't testing her, as such. It was the only thing neither of them had seen, but Neil was curious to discover whether Natalie really could handle the blood fest of a Tarantino movie or whether she was just bullshitting to impress him. After sitting through 111 minutes of pastiche kung-fu moves, punctuated (regularly) with unwarranted and unreasonable, queasy-making scenes of bloodshed (decapitations, amputations – you name it, Uma chopped it), Natalie's only comments were, 'I'd do Uma Thurman if I was a man. What am I talking about? I'd do her if she asked. Do I have popcorn stuck in my teeth?' And then Neil knew for certain that Natalie was the coolest woman he had ever had the pleasure to know. And while at that point he did not know her in the biblical sense, the image she had just tattooed on his brain made him count the seconds until perhaps that might be the case.

'Do you think things are all right between Karl and Jen?' Natalie asked, breaking the comfortable silence in the cab.

Neil was startled out of his semi-comatose state. He'd been thinking about Karl too, about his endless sexual exploits, and for a moment he was spooked into believing Natalie could read his mind (which most of the time she could). Neil was trying to decide whether Karl had been talking rubbish or was he right. Was sex everything? He wasn't sure.

'Hmmm?' mumbled Neil, not committing.

'Do you think Karl plays away?' pursued Natalie.

Nat and Neil, snug in their seven-year relationship, often gained a certain amount of pleasure by discussing other people's relationships, especially the inferior ones. Such discussions made the taxi journeys home, after countless couple dinners and parties, fly by. But Neil had always opted to keep details about Karl's infidelities from Natalie. Karl maintained that his flings (discreet and contained, usually opportunistic encounters on business trips) meant nothing. Neil knew that Nat would not see it in the same light and she'd be thrown into a complex moral dilemma, as she'd have to decide whether or not to pass the information along to Jen. Neil told himself that by keeping silent he was protecting Nat and, besides, tonight definitely wasn't the night to reveal all. Neil wanted sex with Nat when they got home and for reasons that were beyond his comprehension (but placed firmly in his gut) he knew that by revealing Karl's secrets, he would get into trouble (even though it was Karl not Neil putting it about; it was not fair but it was a fact).

Neil was pretty sure that Karl and Jen's relationship was a bullet train heading towards a signal failure. How could their story have a happy ending? Karl was a good mate. He was funny, fair about buying in his rounds, enthusiastic about all consoles (but with a slight preference for the Xbox 360) and a Man. U. supporter. As a mate Karl was exemplary, Neil couldn't ask for more. As a boyfriend, even Neil could see that Karl stank.

'He talked about his promotion a lot, didn't he? He seems really excited by it,' said Neil, neatly sidestepping the issue. Karl had some new international role. There'd be lots of travelling. Loads of shagging.

'Yes. Jen thinks he might pop the question now that he has a bit more cash. Or at least suggest that they move in together. Personally, I don't think she's got a snowball's chance in hell.' This was another thing Neil loved about Nat, she was especially clear-sighted. Romantic but realistic. It was a rare combination. 'Did he hint that he might be thinking of choosing a ring?' asked Natalie. Her tone was not hopeful. 'Because if he does ever bring it up, she wants a solitaire diamond, princess cut. That's a square to you. On a platinum band, quite thick and contemporary but she wants to be surprised by it.' Natalie sighed, torn by a desire for her friend's dreams to come true and an underlying belief that in fact being married to Karl might well be a nightmare. 'She keeps buying bridal magazines. She leaves them at his flat for him to stumble over.'

'The ones with vacant-looking women wearing tablecloths?' asked Neil, with a drunken giggle.

'Yes, that's how you'd see it,' replied Natalie with a grin.

'The ones that show societies where men have ceased to exist?'

'Well, I suppose.'

'Karl's not going to like that, he likes being centre stage.'

'I think that is the least of his long list of objections about entering into the holy state of matrimony. She leaves them in the bathroom, in the bedroom, she once left one in the fridge, right next to his beer.'

Neil burst into such a loud fit of laughter that Natalie couldn't help but join in, despite her concerns about her friend's desperate and pointless plight. If you thought about it, the magazine drop was funny.

'What is she hoping for? Does she imagine that one day he'll wake up and think, "Oh yeah, lovely. I can dress up in a kilt *and* a dicky bow, all my dreams come true?"' asked Neil, his shoulders shuddering now. 'No, no and no again.'

'I know, and Jen is normally such a rational and bright woman. Why can't she see that he regards her interest in these magazines with the equivalent horror he'd feel at discovering her secretly reading *Mein Kampf* or Jeffrey Archer?' Natalie and Neil's ribs ached. Through their helpless laughter Natalie managed to mutter, 'Poor Jen,' which she did indeed mean. 'It's such a shame that she's wasting her time trying to convert a commitment phobe.'

The couple's chuckles subsided and when Neil caught his breath he thought to ask, 'Why didn't you tell me that Tim and Ali are trying for a baby?'

'I thought he'd have told you.'

'Don't be crazy.'

'Well, if he hasn't told you, he doesn't want you to know.'

'But you tell me loads of stuff about Jen and Karl that Karl wouldn't want me to know.'

It was true. Karl certainly wouldn't be comfortable with the idea of Neil knowing that he'd cried when watching *Love Actually* (he hadn't even had a drink) or that Jen called his penis the Man.

'Yeah, interesting stuff, funny stuff,' explained Nat, fighting a yawn. 'Trying for a baby isn't that interesting. I don't know why Alison insists on going into so much detail. It's gross.' Bored of the subject, Natalie added, 'Shame Ben and Fi couldn't make it. Did you miss your big bruv on your special day?' She ruffled his hair teasingly.

Natalie often joked about how dependent Neil was on his friendship with his brother but in fact she liked their closeness. She was the eldest of four but her three siblings were all brothers. They were fun and she loved them well enough but as a child she had always secretly wished that at least one of them had been a girl and perhaps a bit closer to her in age. There was a nine-year age gap between her and her first brother, the second and third arrived in eighteen-month intervals thereafter. Her parents had clearly decided just to get on with it; obviously a nine-year age gap for each child would amount to decades of nappies, on and off – no one could want that. Fairly or unfairly, naturally the three boys being close in age and the same sex tended to be regarded by everyone as a pack, rather than individuals. It was always 'Nat and the boys', rather than 'the children'. It was hard not to feel left out occasionally. Other. Separate. There were compensations. Nat got plenty of one-on-one time with her parents, especially her mum, usually on the sidelines of rugby or football pitches while they cheered on the boys, who were bathing in mud. Having seen her brothers' closeness, Nat understood the special affiliation between Neil and Ben. She'd often witnessed the delights and darker moments of same-sex sibling relationships; one minute you love them, the next you hate them and a minute later back to love again.

Natalie sighed contentedly; she'd been lucky with her in-laws too. Neil's parents were decent working-class people who, now in their late sixties, found the world around them largely fascinating but occasionally frightening. They didn't understand what any of their children actually did for a living but they were certain that all three had 'done well for themselves' and proudly carried photos of their children and grandchildren, which they loved to flash at any willing soul. They were content. A rare commodity and as such they were not hard work at all. Largely they kept themselves to themselves, at a 130-mile distance. They only visited when invited and were always thrilled and hospitable if Neil and Nat chose to visit them, which they did approximately once every six weeks. Mr and Mrs Preston senior were uncomplicated and Ben, Neil and Ashleigh had inherited their parents' straightforward, no-nonsense approach to life.

All three were what-you-see-is-what-you-get types of people, although Ben and Ashleigh were significantly more financially ambitious than both their parents and Neil. Nat felt fortunate that Neil had inherited the gene that allowed a person to be content and undemanding; it was a great relief to her that she was enough for him. Neil had always appreciated the cosiness and continuity that his family had provided and he still preferred battered cod with chips and lashings of vinegar to the blackened variety. Ben and Ashleigh had ripped through what they saw as the limitations of a working-class childhood and firmly established themselves in the epicentre of middle-class existence, a world where Egyptian cotton sheets and ballet lessons for any offspring were seen as basic essentials. Although they were both still grounded enough that if anyone were ever to try to have a conversation with them about thread count, they would have thought that person to be clinically insane.

Neil had meandered past any limitations, real or imagined, and he had no idea what his sheets were made from. They all three went to university and none of them worked in jobs where they had to get their hands dirty or ask their bosses if they could take a toilet break. And while Neil wasn't as well paid as his siblings, he swore he loved his job more than the others. Ben was a city lawyer, he lived in Clapham (in a house that was worth an inflated fortune) with his wife (a dentist by training although no longer practising due to the arrival of Angus, Sophia and Giles). Nat loved visiting their large, noisy, warm house which was crammed with finger paintings and where the smell of organic chicken stew always lingered. Neil's kid sister lived in New York; she worked in some high-finance, grown-up, ball-breaking job and lived in an uber stylish Manhattan loft. Neil and Nat went Stateside at least once a year and then Nat and Ashleigh would hit the shops and the latest trendy bars. They'd dress up and pretend to be extras in *Sex and the City*, which made Ashleigh a fabulous sister-in-law. Nat really had been very lucky indeed.

'Yeah, I missed Ben,' admitted Neil. He was always more willing to be openly sentimental after he'd had a bit to drink.

'It's such a pity, especially for Fi. I get the feeling she was desperate for a night out.'

'When are they going to find a reliable babysitter?'

'That's exactly what I asked when Fi rang up to make her apologies this evening. She seems to think that a babysitter calling up to cancel at the last minute is situation normal. Just one of the things that goes with the territory.'

'Miserable for them,' mumbled Neil. Truthfully he thought this conversation about babysitters was a bit boring but he knew Nat liked to talk about this sort of stuff. He'd prefer to just sit quietly in the back of the cab and think about the chances of them having sex tonight. He kissed the top of her head. Her hair smelt great. Like summer fields. God, his wife was beautiful. He was a lucky man.

'They've had kids for four years now, yet in all that time they haven't found a babysitter who actually turns up when they're supposed to,' added Nat.

'I know, finding a reliable babysitter seems to be like searching for the Holy Grail.'

Natalie found this fact strangely comforting. She'd never wanted children and when she met Neil she'd made that clear from day one. Conveniently, he'd never felt the need to dispatch his genetic bank, happy to leave the breeding and passing of the family name to his brother. Hearing about the countless discomforts and inconveniences that went with being a parent cheered Natalie. It was not that she needed to hear about sleepless nights, shortage of cash, rows between partners and endless self-sacrifice to be reassured that she'd made the right decision. Not at all. Natalie was more than happy with her choice. But she found that it was helpful to remember these continual hassles faced by other people. From time to time, more regularly than was polite, Natalie (never Neil) was asked whether they were planning on starting a family any time soon. Her reply would always be a staunch, no. She tried not to be drawn into any sort of elaboration; she preferred to follow a mantra of never explain, never excuse. But often the inquirer, either through genuine concern or inexcusable insensitivity, would plunge on.

'Can't you have any?'

'We've never tried so I have no idea,' Natalie would answer frostily.

'Don't leave it too late.'

So Natalie would feel compelled to clear up the matter. 'We don't want children, actually.'

Then the imprudent inquirer might gasp, extremely shocked and not able to hide it. If Nat was lucky they'd be shocked into silence but more often than not they'd ask, 'But *why* not? Don't you like children?'

Natalie was always tempted to reply yes, she did like children enormously and add the joke, 'but I couldn't eat a whole one.' She always resisted, as she knew that very few people found this subject a laughing matter. She'd cite the importance of her career, the lack of space in their home or their dislike of the thought of endless sleepless nights as reasons she did not want to have children. She'd play back all the things she'd heard parents say. You're always broke. You lose your sense of self. You end up with a slack vagina, but rarely could she get anyone to understand. Nat was sometimes tempted to say she *did* have a medical problem, at least that way people would understand why they were childless. Childfree. But she couldn't stand the subterfuge or endure the optimistic suggestion that they could 'always adopt' which would inevitably follow.

It was impossible for Nat to explain why she didn't want to have children but she was sure, absolutely certain, one hundred per cent positive that she did not.

4

Nat and Neil stumbled through the door to their home and fell against the wall in a messy tangle of limbs that signposted drunken intentions to have a crack at passion. He urgently and continually kissed her; the kisses were sloppy but intense. He ran his hands up and down her body and she pushed the door closed behind them. As he continued to kiss her face, neck, shoulders, she considered that they could have a quickie, she could drink a pint of water and then they could still get to bed by about half past twelve. It wasn't that she didn't enjoy prolonged, lusty love sessions with Neil any more, of course she did; she adored them. She loved him. A quickie was not the perfect culmination to such a boozy, fun and loving night but it was a realistic compromise, admitted Nat with an internal mental sigh. She was very aware that she had a big meeting with her boss tomorrow at 8.30a.m. and as tempting as an all-night session might be, she just couldn't afford to be shag tired. She tried to edge her foot out of her high heels without breaking away from the kisses. The shoes were new and horribly uncomfortable but Nat considered that it had been worth the pain because both Jen and Alison had agreed with her that the patent petrol-blue shoes with the needle-thin stiletto heels were beyond beautiful. Now they could go back in the cupboard until the next special night out.

'Leave them on,' murmured Neil, once he understood that Nat was trying to cast off the sexy shoes.

'Really?' Nat did as Neil requested, even though she could feel a nasty blister bubbling on her right toe. If it made him happy, she'd put up with the discomfort for a little while longer.

Since listening to Karl brag about taking the Dutch air hostess (from behind, as she bent over the bath in the hotel room), Neil had spent the evening indulging in a sexual fantasy of his own. His fantasies were always pretty tame and tended to be anchored to the conventional (he fantasised about sex with Nat, Jennifer Aniston or Reese Witherspoon). He never fantasised about sex with colleagues or mates' girlfriends (the way Karl did), nor did he have any interest in bestiality, voyeurism or anything odd with a gas mask. He didn't even want to see Nat's buttocks pink with the signs of a gentle spanking, but he did like shoes with a mean heel. He was pretty sure that his fantasies about high heels were all very normal and acceptable, because in none of his fantasies was he the one wearing the shoes.

'My feet are sore,' muttered Nat, hoping he'd be sympathetic.

'Leave them on,' he instructed, too horny to be as considerate as he usually was. He wanted to sound forceful, vigorous and powerful. Tonight, Karl had been saying how women are really turned on if you are authoritative. But then Neil considered that he and Nat usually had an equal relationship, he didn't want to sound peculiarly bossy, so he added, 'Please.'

The timing of the delivery of the afterthought was poor. The word gushed out with a burp that hit Natalie square in the face. The smell of red wine and steak was not as good the second time round.

Nat pulled back a fraction but managed to summon a forgiving grin. Still, the moment was lost and they both knew it. They broke apart. The kisses and urgency stayed in the hallway. Without discussing it, Neil went to put the kettle on to make a sobering cup of tea and Natalie went upstairs. She carefully undressed, cleaned her teeth, put toothpaste on Neil's brush and then got into bed. Her disappointment at the lack of sex was not overwhelming; she would never have admitted it to anyone but part of her was a tiny bit relieved. Sex would have been pleasant, it always was, but really, she did have to consider that important, nerve-wracking meeting tomorrow morning. Now, they'd probably just cuddle for a bit and then drift off to sleep in each other's warmth. And Neil's disappointment, whilst intense, disappeared almost instantly as he was still too squiffy to hold on to any sort of intention; being drunk always made him mellow, not ferocious.

As Neil waited for the kettle to boil, he noticed that there was a fly buzzing around the kitchen. It repeatedly flew at the strip light even though that undoubtedly led to great pain. The buzzing became annoyingly frantic and Neil wondered if he had the energy and coordination to get the fly out of the house alive or whether he should just spray it with an aerosol can of poisonous stuff. He didn't care about the fly's life, he wasn't Buddhist, he was straightforward apathetic Church of England, but he didn't like the smell of fly spray. He stared at the fly with a death wish for a while but then got bored and his mind wandered back to the conversation he'd had with Karl that night. There was something about Karl's chat that niggled him. Not just the fact that Karl was playing away, something else.

The claim had been seductive. Sex was *everything*, Karl had said. Everything? Was it? No, it wasn't. But was it? There was something about that idea that was completely wrong and another part of it that intrigued him.

Neil thought that the best thing about having sex with Nat was that he knew every time they did, it was not the last time. Which was a relief; a comforting thought. And to follow the same argument, *not* having sex with her tonight wasn't a problem because this was not the last time he was going to not have sex with her either, marriage had guaranteed that. Neil thought about that for a long time. Was that what he meant? It was hard to know. He really shouldn't have had that last liqueur, he didn't even like liqueurs. He wasn't saying that having sex with Nat was the same as not having sex with Nat. What he was saying was that being with her, sex or not was everything. That was it!

When Neil was single and used to have sex with other women, the sex was often spectacular and always a result. But somewhere, deep down inside him, he'd always found single-man sex unsettling. He found it a problem that even in the very moment of orgasm he'd start to panic about where his next shag would come from. Being married to Nat took all that uncertainty away. He was sure he wouldn't swap his feeling of security and intimacy for a million illicit affairs, similar to those Karl had, no matter how electrifying they were. Yup, Neil Preston, thirty-five years today, was a happy man.

Sex, sex, sex, sex, sex. He said the word over and over again as he waited for the water to reach 100 degrees C. Funny little word. If you said it often enough it sort of lost its importance, its threat, its intrigue. It became more playful. What did it mean exactly? What did it all mean?

The taxi journey home and the inconvenient burp had gone some way to sobering Neil up but still he had to concentrate very hard on making the tea in order not to scald himself. He put a bag in each mug, added water, let it stew, added milk (semi-skimmed for Nat), considered and rejected the idea of opening a packet of Jaffa Cakes (after all, he had eaten three courses plus birthday cake at the restaurant). It was during those seemingly run-of-the-mill, innocuous minutes that Neil finally got to grips with the sex debate. He understood the conundrum. The answer was revealed to him.

The exact train of thought was tricky to detail as his thoughts were fuzzy around the edges due to the amount he'd drunk. Thinking about his birthday cake tonight (a rich, moist, dark chocolate cake decorated with fat marshmallows, lovingly made for him by Nina, his mother-in-law) suddenly brought to mind other birthday cakes he'd been presented with in the past. Lopsided, butter-iced, sweetie-covered affairs, often moulded into the shape of whatever craze he was into at the time. The Rubik Cube-shaped cake was legendary, the chessboard a tad embarrassing as his mother had no eye for detail and had fashioned the cake into six rows and six columns which (as all his mates had pointed out was *stupid* because everyone knows that a chessboard has sixty-four squares).

His all-time favourite birthday cake was the train-shaped cake that his mother made for his ninth birthday. He'd been going through a fervent train phase which his brother and sister teased him about, mercilessly, declaring that his early signs of geekiness were bound to lead to social failure. The teasing, of course, was in good spirit; harmless and natural. Besides, they could not spoil the day for him. Neil's mother had outdone herself as she'd embraced the train theme with gusto. Not only did Neil get to take three of his friends (including Tim) to the National Railway Museum in York (where Neil could satiate his curiosity about all things train) but they also got to have his birthday tea in the famous, long-established Betty's Teashop. Neil remembered the delight of eating a cream cake the size of his head; for once he did not have to share 'two between three', which was usually the case with treats in their home. That day his parents splashed out and bought every one of the kids their own cake, whichever one they chose. Plus, most magnificently of all, he and all his pals went home with a Flying Scotsman replica nameplate (purchased from the museum souvenir shop) and so on return to school the following Monday, Neil and his mates became an instant playground gang. Neil still owned his nameplate (Nat had generously allowed them to hang it in the loo). He wondered what Tim had done with his, he must remember to ask him.

It had been a perfect day. Well, all Neil's birthdays had been perfect. In fact, Neil's entire childhood was chipper. Of course there were times he'd fallen and hurt himself, lied, broken valuable things, worried about small things, failed exams and embarrassed himself on the sports field. These growing pains were inevitable but, as the tea brewed, Neil started to count the things he liked about his childhood, the things he loved about being a kid. Cherryade, sherbet fountains, football in the street, laughing himself sick with Ben and Ashleigh, his father hoisting him on his shoulders to see over a crowd, his mother's minty breath as she kissed him good night, holidays, summer days, Christmas Days . . . His childhood was a safe and wonderful place to live.

He would never be able to pinpoint exactly where the revelation, vision or clarity came from but suddenly he was sure, more sure than he'd been about anything before or likely ever to be again. Karl was right. Sex was *everything*. But Neil did not mean the sort of sex where several nymphomaniacs fought over your throbbing hard-on (if indeed that sort of sex genuinely existed outside Karl's imagination). The sort of sex that truly meant everything, was everything, made sense of everything was the sort that led to making a baby.

To making a life.

To starting a childhood, like his own.

The room tilted and Neil staggered slightly; it was not the effects of the booze, it was the enormity of his fresh understanding. Neil felt doused in excitement, swathed in possibility. Of course! It was the natural next step. Why hadn't he made the connection before? Why hadn't he thought of all this before? Nat was probably thinking the same thing by now. She used to say she didn't want kids, but everyone says that when they are young, don't they? Of course she must have changed her mind by now; they'd been married five years. He was thirty-five years old *today*, that was a perfect age to be a dad, and Nat was thirty-four next birthday, inevitably her clock must be ticking, you were always seeing articles about it. God, Nat was just amazing. Other women started to ladle on the pressure to start a family the minute they turned thirty, sometimes earlier, but not Nat. Maybe Nat had been waiting until he was ready to make the leap. Until he made the jump.

Neil dashed upstairs with a mug of tea in both hands and he barely noticed it slopping over the rim on to the carpet. He burst into the bedroom and was momentarily distracted from his purpose as he encountered the thirty-five helium-filled balloons bobbing around the room. He pushed through them. Nat was already in bed. She was wearing pyjamas and reading through her notes for the meeting the next morning. Admittedly she didn't look as though she wanted to make a baby right that moment but she did look just like the sort of woman who should make a baby. She looked calm and beautiful and cosy. The pyjamas were covered in tiny pink rosebuds. Neil thought Rosie might be a nice name for a girl. But first things first.

Neil put down the mugs and hurriedly tugged off all his clothes. He dropped them in a heap on the floor and dived under the covers. He started to kiss Nat's thighs through her PJs. He couldn't wait to edge those down. She had great thighs. They were often tanned (courtesy of San Tropez spray-on booths), smooth, slim and, in Neil's opinion, best when edging open. Nat was a brilliant woman to find yourself in bed with, find yourself married to, thought Neil. A brilliant woman to make a baby with! She was cute and quick and clever but not arsey and over-learned. Plus, she was generally reasonably cheerful (caveat being that at certain times of the month she turned into an unadulterated, raging psychopath). Neil considered that in his pre-Nat experience, clever and cheerful were an unusual combination to find in a woman, quite rare indeed. In his opinion clever women tended to be as bleak as the North York Moors after a thunderstorm and cheerful birds often felt the need to limit their conversation to inane twitter about Daniel Craig's arse. (OK, Daniel Craig was a dude, Neil could see that, but how long could a *bloke*'s arse be the centre of conversation?). Neil thought of Nat's tits nestled under her pyjama top. Her tits were magnificent. Not too big, not too small. A perfect B cup and Neil was a firm believer that more than a handful is a waste, unwieldy. Then he thought of her mouth. It was *the* sexiest mouth imaginable. Big, fat, red lips. Large, lush, licky lips. As ever, the thought of said lips caused an instant erection. Neil hit Nat's leg with it; she lifted the duvet just long enough to throw him a look of exasperation.

'You weren't talking about football tonight, were you?'

'Never said I was.'

'It's not like you to be so persistent. You've been talking about sex all night, haven't you?' It pleased him that she knew stuff like that. Unlike Karl, Neil had never wanted a woman who could have the wool pulled over her eyes. 'What sort of sex have you been talking about?' He didn't want to reply. He didn't want to say that every time

Nat, Ali and Jen had been out of earshot the conversation had sunk into in-depth discussions about slutty lap dancers, hot film stars and pert twenty-somethings at the office, in other words all manner of foreign, unavailable totty. Neil knew that if he confessed as much, Nat wouldn't find his raging hard-on especially flattering. Few women take a throbbing cock as the compliment men undoubtedly think it is; women prefer flowers. And even if he told Nat that he was thinking about her lips when he became hard, she'd guess exactly where those lips were clasped in his imaginings. She might not think that was especially romantic either. And he was being romantic. He wanted to make a baby, what was more romantic than that?

Nat was not responding to his under-duvet attentions. She clung to her file as though it was a chastity belt and he was some sort of foreign invader hoping to take advantage of the fact that the local men were on a crusade.

'It is my birthday,' Neil reminded her.

Natalie laughed at the honesty of the plea and finally put down her work. She inched her way down below the duvet and, showing remarkable dexterity, inched her way out of her pyjama top and bottoms at the same time. Neil gratefully and instantly clasped his lips on her nipple and Natalie let out a little yelp of unsquashable glee. Once Natalie was in the mood she was generally noted for her enthusiasm. Neil's mouth lingered over her breasts for an indulgent amount of time. He kissed them, nuzzled them, licked them and ever so gently bit them. Then he trailed kisses down her body, past her tummy button, past her hip bone and he finally buried his face between her legs. He started to kiss, lap and lick her into a state of almost painful ecstasy. He was excellent at this. Natalie had never been especially keen on this particular brand of foreplay until she met Neil, but now she possibly enjoyed it more than the main event. It was so intimate, so frank and giving.

'Let's make a baby,' he mumbled.

Natalie didn't quite hear what he said as his head was between her thighs. Did he just say, 'Let's make love, baby?' If so, it was a bit nineties of him but Neil did occasionally say strange things during sex. He'd once tried to talk dirty to her because someone (Karl probably) had told him women like it. It was not erotic. It was embarrassing and then hilarious but not erotic. Neil said it again, 'Let's mumble mumble baby.' This time he looked up and smiled at her; his was such a huge, warm grin. He had her excitement on his lips and a glint in his eye the like of which she'd never seen before. She nodded happily and pushed his head back down between her legs. Yes, she would mumble mumble. They were mumble mumbling, weren't they? Whatever he was specifically asking for she'd get to soon enough. Just after he finished what he'd started. He'd brought her to the point where she didn't want to talk; she didn't want him to stop. She just wanted more, more, again, again.

Ahggg, that was it. That got it. Nat shook uncontrollably with excitement. Tiny little darts of ecstasy fired through her body. This was their pattern, this was their routine. Nat didn't know why people were so down on routine. She loved the fact that she and Neil knew exactly where they were with one another and that they knew how to please one another, how to excite, how to hold back and when to spill forth. Nat knew how hard to suck his cock, how fast to lick it and caress it. He knew instinctively when she wanted her breasts grabbed and when she wanted them gently stroked. Now she had reached orgasm and was fully satisfied, he would reach for a condom and they'd work together to get his orgasm and, let's face it, that was not a tricky or arduous task. Nat would ride Neil tonight. She was the more sober of the two and the silent agreement always was that whoever was the least inebriated would be prepared to put in a little extra effort. Besides, it was his birthday. She waited for him to roll over and reach into the bedside drawer for a condom. They'd always used condoms. Nat had used them all her life. They were clean, safe, flexible and reliable; the perfect contraceptive. Luckily, Neil had never been one of those guys who said he couldn't feel as much with a condom. They did try the pill a few years back but it had exaggerated Nat's tendency to PMT and neither of them enjoyed that.

But Neil did not reach for a condom, instead he surprised Nat by rolling on top of her and suddenly Nat could feel his hardness inside her. The sensation was at once fabulous and shocking.

She instantly pulled away. 'Idiot, you *are* drunk.' She laughed. 'You haven't got a condom on yet.'

'You can't make a baby if you wear a condom.' Neil smiled at Nat. His sexy grin had transformed into something a little more indulgent. Never before had he seen her as some dear, sweet, Victorian innocent who needed the basic facts of life explaining. How much had *she* had to drink?

'Make a baby?' Natalie shrieked in disbelief. 'Who said we were going to make a baby?' Natalie fought briefly and ferociously to scrabble out from under Neil.

'But you just agreed.'

'I did no such thing! What are you talking about?' Natalie suddenly understood the miscommunication in all its horrifying glory but she was too shattered and shocked to explain the mix-up to her husband rationally. She'd simply misheard him. But that wasn't the point. What was he thinking? Why even in his wildest dreams would he assume that she wanted to make a baby, *ever*? She'd always made it crystal clear that the opposite was the case. And if ever she was going to re-open discussion on the matter (which she could not in a million years imagine doing), they would not act on a drunken whim, they'd give the matter due and serious thought. Natalie wanted to say all of this; instead she grabbed the duvet and pulled it high around her body, hiding herself as though she was indeed the Victorian innocent he'd been imagining only moments before and she yelled in panic, horror and frustration, 'Wanker.'

Neil's raging hard-on wilted. His strong and sexy penis looked like a tiny sausage-shaped balloon many weeks after the party. Natalie tried to steady her breathing; shouting and cursing wasn't her way and unlikely to help matters but she was panting with fear, and anger, and disbelief, and couldn't organise her thoughts in any sort of rational way. OK, OK, get a grip. This is just the drink talking. He doesn't mean it, she told herself. It's a joke. She didn't trust herself to say anything else at all. The only words that came to mind were so blue and derisive and out of character that if she uttered just a small percentage of them they'd probably end up talking to a marriage counsellor, so instead she snapped off the bedside light and said, 'Just go to sleep, Neil. Sleep it off, for God's sake.'

5

Despite the odds, the early morning, late summer sunshine gallantly forced its way through the small gap in the bedroom curtains, promising that autumn would be kept at bay for one more glorious day. Nat refused to be cheered and instead gloomily noticed that the shaft of light fell in such a way that the room seemed to be ominously divided into two.

Nat got up at 6.30a.m. She'd barely slept but instead feigned a comatose state until about 3a.m. when anxiety and exhaustion had finally got the better of her and she'd submitted to a fitful slumber. Neil, on the other hand, had fallen asleep almost the moment she'd told him to. She knew him well enough to know that he was too confused and drunk to put up a fight; besides, the idea of a 'good row' was anathema to Neil. He'd often said that in his opinion, rows were mean, low and pointless, and Nat agreed with him. Neil had often flattered Nat by favourably comparing her to his exes, many of whom had been the sort of women who seemed to like rows and, what was worse, they'd dressed it up and called it 'essential communicating' or 'clearing the air'. Nat knew Neil had always been able to see a row for what it was – painful. Therefore, he'd probably been only too pleased to do as he was told and fall straight asleep to avoid any more confrontation.

Sadly, Nat could not take any pleasure in the fact that Neil had followed her instructions to the letter. She lay awake and anxiously considered that Neil had most probably lulled himself to sleep with assurances that they'd sort it out in the morning, that he'd make her understand his point of view then, that everything would be better in the morning. It was just like Neil to think so optimistically but Nat knew that nothing would be better in the morning and that it would take more than a good night's sleep to sort this mess out. It would take a miracle or at least a very speedy retraction from Neil with regard to his desire for a baby.

Nat was envious of Neil's ability to sleep soundly whilst she tossed and turned and fretted. She often thought life was so much simpler for him than it was for her. She lay on her side and stared forlornly at him. Usually, whenever she set eyes on him she felt overwhelmed with feelings of comfort and contentment; this morning her stomach churned with anxiety and a deep, impossible-to-articulate regret. How could he sleep so soundly? She wanted him to wake up and tell her of course he'd been joking, of course he didn't want to make a baby; so when her alarm went off, instead of rushing to slam down the button that would silence Chris Moyles and guarantee Neil some more slumber as she usually did, she let Moyles's cheeky chatter float into their room. She showered, dressed, cleaned her teeth with an electric toothbrush and dried her hair on full blast but still Neil did not stir. He'd clearly drunk a lot last night. That was a good thing, wasn't it? It meant that he didn't necessarily mean that he wanted a baby; it *was* just drunken rambling. Or was it a terrible thing? Did he need the drink to give him Dutch courage so that he could articulate his latent but fervent desire? Nat didn't know. She felt so confused that she was unsure whether she was delighted that Neil had slept through her morning ablutions (thus avoiding the possibility of an inquest into his bizarre and horrifying behaviour last night) or devastated. If he'd woken up he could have reassured her that his request to make a baby was a fleeting, ill-considered whim. Neil's day in the office didn't start until 10a.m. and so all Nat could do was re-set the alarm for nine, so that he wouldn't be late for work.

As Nat dashed to the bus stop she was conscious that her mind ought to have been full of facts for the meeting but instead was crammed with worry for her husband. She shook her head violently, she couldn't think about this right now. She had a big meeting to prepare for, a busy day ahead. She had to stay focused, no matter what. After all, that was what she'd always done.

The moment Neil heard the door bang behind Nat and the familiar click-clack of her high heels on the pavement below their bedroom window, he opened his eyes. Phew, it was safe. Area cleared and locked down, enemy evacuated.

Yawning and stretching, Neil began to assess the extent of his hangover. It was a seven out of ten. The pain in his head was a pounding sensation but on balance he preferred this to the type of hangover where he felt his head was being crushed and about to implode. He could fix a pounding by popping a couple of aspirins. He was also seriously dehydrated. The way things had panned out last night meant that he never had the opportunity to drink his usual precautionary cup of hydrating tea or a glass of water before he fell asleep, but that was OK; he could fix that by drinking two or three mugs of strong tea now. But there was another pain, one that was only indirectly related to his hangover, but it was by far the most vicious pain. There was a searing disappointment sitting in his chest, in his stomach and, yes, in his heart.

Nat didn't want a baby and he did. He didn't know how to fix that.

Neil decided to walk to work; he could do with the fresh air. Besides, he was already technically late by forty-five minutes so he reasoned he might as well round it up to a full hour. He would walk along King Street, cut through Ravenscourt Park and then carry on along Goldhawk Road. It might even be quicker on foot than taking the bus.

The London streets were, as ever, overflowing. The traffic was heavy and slow. Neil stared into the cars and saw mothers returning home from school runs. The empty seats, in the back of the car, cradled discarded wrapping papers and small plastic toys rather than boys and girls. There were people in taxis dashing to business meetings or maybe the airport. Neil imagined fathers kissing their kids goodbye this morning, promising they'd return with goodies from their business trips. Neil's father only ever went on any sort of business trip twice throughout his career (once he attended an overnight conference in Saltburn and on the other occasion he went to a motivational training meeting in Milton Keynes). On both occasions he brought back Terry's chocolate oranges for Neil, Ben and Ashleigh. Neil indulged in a daydream about returning home after a business trip (destination unspecified but as it was a daydream Neil thought maybe Fiji or the Maldives). As he pushed open the front door, his kids would clatter down the stairs and dive into his arms and demand their chocolate oranges. In his daydream the hall was freshly painted and Nat was wearing a floral pinny. She greeted him with a wide smile and she didn't call him a wanker.

Although it was still August, Neil noticed that the summer sale signs were disappearing from the shop windows and already being replaced by arrangements involving pumpkins and black cats. He'd loved Halloween when he was a kid; he liked scaring himself by believing Ben's ghost stories. Suddenly Neil felt excited by the thought of taking a kid of his trick or treating, then he remembered Nat's horrorstruck face last night and his stomach sank, just as though he'd been visited by a ghoul.

Neil nodded at café owners who were slouched in the doorways of their premises, smiling their approval at the bright weather, sunshine was good for trade. Neil noticed that there were endless groups of mothers and toddlers clustered around bistro tables, chatting and giggling as they munched on croissants and sipped orange juice. The park was full of tiny pre-schoolers as well. They were chasing dogs, riding scooters, bikes and buggy boards. Whizzing past him and whirling around him. They were playing on the swings, in the sandpit and in the pool. They were everywhere.

When Neil got to the office Karl was waiting for him by his desk. He was carrying a paper bag which, from the smell, Neil deduced contained bacon butties.

'Result. You're a good mate,' said Neil with a grateful grin as he bit into the buttie. Fat dribbled down his chin but he didn't care. This was one of the reasons he loved his buddy Karl and could overlook his lax morals – Karl had the ability to plan like a woman. It was genius to anticipate the need for a bacon buttie this morning and to get the timing so absolutely spot on. How did Karl know he'd be an hour late? Well, besides the fact that he was always an hour late when he'd had a big session the night before.

Karl sat on the edge of the desk and Neil collapsed into the chair behind it. The office was open plan but the vibe was relaxed, no one clock-watched or felt chained to their desks. Indeed, Karl and Neil's respective roles meant that they had legitimate reasons to hang around gassing with one another and so were often credited with being industrious when in fact they were discussing last night's game or Karl's sex life.

'It was a good night, wasn't it?' asked Karl.

'Great,' replied Neil and he tried to sound a hundred per cent enthusiastic. He tried not to think of Nat's amazed and terrified face when he'd suggested a baby.

'What's up?' Clearly he'd failed.

Neil hesitated. Karl was not the person he wanted to confide in right now. In fact, Karl was never the person anyone ever wanted to confide anything in. And did he actually want to do any confiding anyway? The nature of the open-plan office meant that it was almost impossible to discuss anything personal without expecting to see details of your dilemma posted up on the company website within two minutes.

'Nothing,' assured Neil with a self-conscious grin.

'You've a face like a slapped arse, mate. Something's up.'

Neil glanced over his shoulder. It was KitKat break time and most people had sloped off to the canteen, so he was at least guaranteed some privacy. Was it possible to explain to Karl that he'd had an epiphany? That suddenly, resolutely, he was sure of something big and bold and serious. He'd actually half hoped that this morning his desire for a baby, a child, a family would have vanished. He'd really hoped that Nat would be right about this, as she was about most things, and that it was just the drink talking when he'd said he wanted to have a child with her. But as inconvenient as it was (and, hell, it really was) Neil found that he'd woken up more, not less, determined to have a baby.

Karl started to play with the small plastic bendy models that sat on Neil's desk. The toys had been originally purchased as a prop for a creative brainstorming session when they'd been developing their last big game. Now they sat on Neil's desk and it had become accepted that anyone going past his desk would take pleasure in rearranging the figures into one of the positions from the Kama Sutra. It passed the time of day. Karl arranged the bendy people into the plough. His apparent disinterest in Neil's issue lulled Neil into making a surprising admission as to what the matter was.

'Nat doesn't want to have a baby.'

'I know that, mate. Everyone knows that,' said Karl simply. 'She's always said as much.'

'Not *ever*,' added Neil for clarity.

'Result. You're one lucky bloke.'

'What?'

'Well, it's every bloke's dream, isn't it? You get to shag, nay marry, a hotty like Nat and you never have to share her.'

Neil rolled his eyes. Had he heard that correctly? He stared at his mate in amazement.

Karl was unrepentant. 'Oh, come on, mate, admit it. No man gets the same amount of sex after his woman's had a baby. Nor does he have the same amount of attention, sleep or money, come to think of it. Look at your brother.'

'I'm pretty sure Ben would say his children have made his life better.'

'They've made his life busier, his house smellier and his clothes shabbier,' said Karl firmly.

'God, you sound just like Nat.'

'She's a very sensible woman. Rare commodity.' Karl noted that Neil looked seriously glum but he didn't get it. Nat not wanting a baby wasn't a secret; she'd as good as taken out an ad in the *Evening Standard* when she and Neil first got together. Still, his mate looked gutted. Karl tried to be reasonable and helpful. 'Nat has always said this sort of stuff. She said it before you married.'

'I know.'

'I thought you'd agreed that you didn't want kids.'

'I did.'

'Well then, doesn't that make you two the perfect match?'

'I changed my mind.'

It wasn't a change of mind, it was a change of heart, but how could Neil say that? Karl would probably feel the need to give him a wedgie or something, the way kids in playgrounds did to one another if they felt that one of their mates was going soft. Karl shifted the bendy models. Neil subconsciously recognised that they were now performing the position Karl called the humpbacked bridge. Neil didn't believe this was a real position at all, it looked impossible, although Karl swore it existed and that it was a favourite of his.

'What brought this on?' asked Karl.

Neil could not explain to Karl that it had been his insistence that sex was *everything* that had been the catalyst. What an irony; the most deeply shallow man in history had inadvertently brought on this existential crisis. But when Neil had thought about it this morning (in the shower, as he dressed and as he walked to work), he knew, quite definitely, that he did want a baby. In fact, more than one, he wanted two at least. Not at the same time necessarily although that would be neat and probably easier on Nat's body in the long run, but whatever the details, he was sure he wanted a family. Neil thought perhaps that somewhere deep in the back of his mind he had always wanted and expected a baby. Yes, he'd heard Nat say she didn't want kids, loud and clear and frequently, especially in the early years. He'd thought it was quite sexy at the time. He'd been turned on by her independence; it had been a refreshing change from other women he'd known – the ones who had measured the circumference of his head on the first date and asked whether he carried any hereditary diseases before they'd ordered drinks. But Nat had been only twenty-six when they'd met, they had both been so young, he hadn't had much concept of for ever. At least, not in terms of being denied a baby *for ever*. He didn't believe she had either.

'A teeny, tiny part of me thought Nat would probably change her mind one day, you know, about the whole baby thing,' admitted Neil. He'd half expected it three years ago when the famous, oft talked about biological clock was supposed to kick in but apparently Nat's clock (if she had one at all) was a silent digital thing, with no alarm, not even a loud tick. 'She still might, hey?' asked Neil optimistically.

'Er, plonker,' replied Karl harshly. 'Look, Nat is the most clear-sighted and focused woman I've ever met, and you have to remember my experience with women is wide and long.' Karl chuckled at his own innuendo but then caught the look of despair on Neil's face so made an effort to stay on track. 'Nat rarely changes her mind about anything as small as what she'll eat for supper, so she's unlikely to change her mind about something as fundamental as this.'

Neil realised this was true. To date Neil had admired his wife's determination; indeed he'd found it quite a turn-on. He'd dated enough wishy-washy, dreamy types – who expected to be handed life's goodies on a plate – to rate a woman who worked relentlessly to self-improve and improve the world around her. He'd always been spectacularly proud that he was married to a woman who *never* backed down in an argument or gave up on a challenge once it was set, even a challenge she'd set herself. Now he felt daunted and defeated as he remembered that his wife, a poor sportswoman and bad swimmer, had completed the London triathlon three years ago just because someone had said she was the least likely person in the world to do so. Of course the triathlon was a good thing; she'd raised £1,800 for Sparks, a charity for sick kids, by completing it. Plus it was her grim determination that meant she'd worked her way up the greasy corporate pole at the pharmaceutical company she worked for, in order to be in a position to influence and change. It was her staunch belief in the fact that she knew what was right that made her a loyal and forgiving friend. Neil knew that it was her doggedness that had ensured that tiffs in the early days of their relationship had never rocked their boat, she'd always sailed them to calmer waters because she'd always been sure that they should be together. She'd always been sure that he was the man she wanted.

Karl interrupted Neil's thoughts. 'Look, mate, my advice to you is pull in your neck. Don't you see what a good thing you're on here? Count your blessings. You've got to remember, mate, you're a six and a half out of ten.' Neil was confused, he couldn't see the relevance of Karl's line of reasoning. Karl assumed Neil was affronted by the score he'd awarded and so added, 'OK, maybe at a push a seven. Nat is a strong nine.' Karl never gave a ten, not even to himself, no one is perfect. He paused to see if Neil had caught on yet. Neil continued to look dazed. Karl wondered if it was worth elaborating. Nat had better taste in music than Neil did, she was more active, she was widely read, she was funnier and she even earned more than him. What made Neil think this clever, beautiful, self-assured woman would ever change her mind about something as fundamental as having a baby? Neil was deluded.

Karl didn't want to say all that. He needed to move this conversation on and get back to his desk. Karl was surprisingly conscientious at work although generally he went to great pains to hide the fact. 'So what's your plan?' he asked.

'Plan?'

'Well, you have to have a plan.'

'I dunno. Haven't had time to think about it.'

'Well, mate, if you want it enough, you have to make it happen,' Karl said curtly. He wasn't clear how this could possibly be the case but he really did need to be back at his desk.

6

Tonight, Nat chose not to go straight home but instead she got off the bus a stop after her usual one and then double-backed upon herself so as she could take her favourite walk along the river path. She needed time to think and process all that had happened in the last twenty-four hours. How had all her plans for a perfect birthday party for Neil failed to insure her against such an enormous disaster? Could he really mean he wanted a baby? Her stomach froze at the thought.

Nat mooched along the thin, sandy path. She had to continually duck and dive to avoid determined joggers and cyclists; this was situation normal as it was never a quiet route, but today she found the vigilance necessary to avoid a collision was hard to muster. Somewhat defeated, Nat collapsed on to a wooden bench and stared out to the blue-green river. Sometimes it sparkled – today it was flat and solid. She looked about for the swans which often paddled near the bank. Nat adored swans, they were her favourite creatures. Yes, they were beautiful and elegant, that was a given, but she liked them for two other reasons. One, she always thought of the swan as a bird of ingenious illusion because while they appeared to glide through life, underneath the water they paddled furiously and she related to that. Secondly, she'd read somewhere that they were monogamous throughout their lifetime and while Nat realised there was probably a very rational reason relating to evolution which accounted for their mating habits, she couldn't help but think the idea was wonderfully romantic. Today she couldn't see any swans, they must have moved further up the river. Nat sighed, she felt cheated out of her diversion. There was no alternative, she had to go home.

When Natalie got home she slowly opened the door and edged into the hall; the street was full of sunlight and she wasn't sure she wanted to relinquish the evening's brightness for an awkward atmosphere indoors. How would Neil behave this evening? Would he reintroduce the subject of wanting a baby? Oh God, she hoped not. She really, really hoped not.

She was relieved to find that the house was awash with delicious smells of roast chicken and the distinct aromas of garlic, feta and tomatoes baking. She knew at once that Neil must be preparing her favourite supper, Greek chicken.

Hearing the front door click shut, Neil instantly appeared from the kitchen. He was wearing an apron. It was the one his mother had bought him as a fun novelty gift last Christmas. It had a neck down picture of a naked, curvaceous woman and even his own handsome face, emerging from the top, could do little to alter the overall effect – he looked ridiculous. Natalie was relieved that she could laugh. Neil clamped his mouth down on hers, cupping her face in his hands and spreading his fingers so they touched her neck. He knew she loved that. They kissed for a long time. The kiss was still and serious but also conveyed warmth and an apology. They both regretted that last night had ended the way it had.

'Sorry,' they chorused in unison and then they laughed. Nat was, as ever, thrilled and filled by Neil's life-affirming laugh. She felt the tension that she'd been lugging around all day (in her back, her shoulders, her heart) scuttle away. He'd cooked for her. How sweet! He was trying to make up for going wildly off track last night. What a relief. Nat had had one of the worst days of her life. She'd had no idea whether he'd been serious when he'd suggest they 'make a baby' and whether he'd renew his pleas tonight. She was terrified he would. What a disaster that would be. But it seemed she was in the clear. It had just been the drink talking last night. Well, everyone has done and said silly things because they've had more than a drop too many. She'd once thought it was a good idea to karaoke in front of her entire international division at an office evening reception and she couldn't sing a note. Nat accepted Neil's apology quickly and gracefully and decided to give one too. She scrambled into her bag and pulled out a sky-blue Diesel T-shirt.

'I bought you this at lunchtime today,' she said, revealing that she'd been thinking of him.

'Smart, cool,' Neil enthused as he gave the top full and careful attention. Perhaps more focus than he would have given it if they hadn't had a fight the night before and while that meant there was still a tension in the air, it also meant intentions were good. 'Wait, wait right there.' Neil ran into the kitchen and immediately returned with a glass of red wine. He handed it to Nat and instructed, 'Go upstairs, have a bath, dinner will be ready in forty minutes. No arguments.'

She wasn't planning on offering any.

Nat lay amongst the bubbles. Her breasts and her thighs broke the surface. Her skin glistened pleasantly. She tried to file away her omnipresent 'to do' list and instead she thought about what she should wear to eat supper. Normally Neil slobbed about in whatever he'd been wearing at work that day (one of the joys of wearing jeans to work) and Nat would change out of her suit and pull on the nearest thing to hand, jeans and a T-shirt, her misshapen tracksuit, or sometimes, if she was particularly knackered, her tatty bathrobe. But tonight, as Neil had cooked, poured Merlot and run her a bath, Nat felt inclined to dress up for him. She dismissed the idea of stockings and suspenders and a little black dress. However grateful she was for the bath and wine, she couldn't get trussed up in the full Monty just to sit in her own front room, she wasn't a footballer's wife, but she could wear a decent pair of jeans and one of her pretty, going-out tops. She'd wear La Senza silky knickers and matching bra rather than her reliable (but greying) M&S favourite pants.

'Oh, wow. This looks fabulous,' said Nat with a beam as she walked into the sitting room-cum-dining room. She didn't just mean the salad, garlic bread and Greek chicken, which were triumphantly laid out on the table, she meant the entire room. Neil had tidied around, he'd picked up magazines and gathered empty mugs and he'd lit the candles. Nat was always buying candles and cushions. Neil normally didn't give either much thought but tonight he'd plumped the numerous cushions and he'd lit all twelve candles that were scattered around the room. As there was still plenty of evening sunshine flooding through the windows, he'd drawn the curtains; he thought the effect was a bit Turkish harem but he didn't have a problem with that. He knew that Nat thought candles were enchanting and the dim light did a good job of hiding the fact that he'd scorched the garlic bread.

They sat and ate and drank, initially not bothering with conversation beyond light chatter about which dressing Neil had used on the salad and how much more they'd eaten in the last few days than was sensible. Nat commented that she'd have to cut back but they both knew she wouldn't. She hated dieting and had never stuck to one, so about four years ago she'd just given up on them altogether. Funnily enough, since then she'd stayed exactly the same weight, give or take a couple of pounds that came and went around Christmas. The fact that Nat didn't obsess about her weight and knew how to enjoy food was one of the many things that Neil found fabulous about her. They chattered about the latest reality TV programme and Neil suggested they visit Ben and Fi at the weekend. Nat agreed without having to think about it. After a while, Neil felt the need to move the conversation on. After all, he'd put a lot of effort into preparing the perfect mood tonight, he couldn't blow it by losing his nerve.

'How was work today?' he asked.

Frankly, he didn't have that much interest in Nat's work, but the most important thing was whether she liked it or not; if she liked her work, that was enough for him. He knew the names of her closest colleagues and her boss, he knew that her work involved occasional trips abroad and that to be suited to her particular field you had to be resilient, commercially minded and have strong analytical skills. He knew about the travel because when she was away he missed her warm body in bed and her chatter in the house and he knew the thing about resilience and commercial skills because he'd once heard Ben telling his father this. Ben did seem to have some idea what Nat's job involved and he was clearly impressed by it. The fact that his wife impressed his big brother pleased Neil enormously.

Natalie had joined the world's largest pharmaceutical company way before she met Neil, almost as soon as she graduated. She'd been offered places on two other graduate trainee programmes with large, respectable companies; both of those jobs had larger salaries attached than the one being offered by the pharmaceutical company. But when it came to making a decision, Nat knew that, besides wanting to be part of something big, she wanted to be part of something important. She did not want to spend her life trying to persuade more people to buy cat food X rather than cat food Y, nor was she convinced that accepting or declining mortgage applications would be enough for her. She wanted to contribute to society in a real and pertinent way.

She won a place on the competitive three-year training programme within the purchasing and procurement division of the pharmaceutical company. On countless occasions Nat had explained this meant she was responsible for managing budgets, building and running e-bid events and auctions, project management, supplier conditioning and negotiation, data analysis, market research, and stakeholder engagement. Neil always found he'd tuned out at the word project. Still, he did know that Nat was highly regarded and had been continually promoted through the ranks. She now had a team of people who reported to her, all doing stuff he didn't quite understand.

Once, when Neil had found he had three point five minutes to kill as he waited for the microwave to do its thing with his beef dinner, he'd come across Nat's company annual report that she'd left lying around. He'd used the three point five minutes (plus one minute standing time) to acquaint himself with the company mission. It was a challenging and stirring mission. The pharmaceutical company aimed to 'globally enhance the quality of human life by reaching out to facilitate people in their efforts to be notably more active, to achieve and enjoy good health and, ultimately, to live longer'. Neil wondered whether they couldn't have come up with something a little more catchy.

Nat and her colleagues endeavoured to globally enhance the quality of human life from a grey office just off the A4. The A4 is one of Britain's major arterial roads, merging into the M4 outside London and running to somewhere near Bristol. Nat's grey office was placed squarely in an area that had some of the worst air pollution in London, which was no mean feat. Local doctors were always appearing on the regional news earnestly communicating their concerns about the number of patients they saw with breathing difficulties. As far as Neil could make out, Nat spent an average of ten hours a day at a small, grey desk placed approximately one metre away from another small, grey desk, where Becky Booker, her small, although admittedly colourful, colleague sat. They shared the view of the grey A4 through a tiny window; the window was grey because the efforts of any window cleaners employed to scrape away the city's grime were obliterated within twenty minutes, thanks to the fumes from steady through traffic. Neil didn't understand why Nat bounced out of bed every morning, not really.

Natalie knew this was how Neil saw things. He had tried at the beginning of their relationship to appear interested in the work she felt so passionate about. He had listened when she chatted enthusiastically about the World Health Organisation and their rigorous regulatory processes but Nat had noticed that after a while he tended to fall silent, only murmuring the occasional word. He had a way of saying 'really' and 'interesting' that did not commit him to any sort of an opinion on whatever she had to say about her work. Nat didn't blame him. She wasn't at the coalface of medical care. If she'd been in the field, say a doctor actually vaccinating kids against river blindness, she was sure Neil would have shown more interest. But Nat had always known she didn't have the stomach and nerve to be a doctor. Still, she believed her work was valuable even though she was stuck behind a desk. On a daily basis she battled to edge people towards a cleaner, safer world. What could be more important? Generally, Nat wasn't offended by Neil's disinterest in her work. In fact, as she gave it her all throughout the long hours she was in the office, it was often quite relaxing to come home and talk about something completely different, something trivial but fun like which contestant was the forerunner in *The Apprentice*. So whenever Neil asked how her day had been she invariably replied, as she did tonight, 'Fine.'

'What did you do?'

'Oh, the usual. Meetings, conference calls. Balled at people, got balled at.'

'Didn't you have a big meeting with your boss today?'

'Yes.' Nat smiled, pleased that Neil had remembered.

'How was that?'

The meeting had begun shambolically. Natalie was not a woman easily put off her stride but Neil's talk of wanting a baby had done exactly that. She'd arrived at work half an hour earlier than the time when the meeting was due to begin but, for reasons Natalie couldn't quite explain, she'd still managed to arrive ten minutes late at her boss's office. She'd been watching the clock and somehow drifted off into memories of how the previous night's row had played out. Where had it come from? Was it going to be revisited? When she noticed the time, she'd rushed to his office in a panic and she'd dropped her file the moment she walked in. Her carefully ordered notes scattered across the floor. The notes stubbornly refused to reassemble into any sort of order, no matter how much on-the-hoof filing she attempted. She knocked over a glass and the water spread unchecked across her boss's smart glass-topped desk, brooked only by the silver photo frame which proudly showcased a snap of his beautiful wife and three healthy, smiley children. She'd mopped up the mess with tissues from her bag. The meeting definitely hadn't started well and Natalie had so wanted to impress. Nat did not want to tell Neil any of this. He would think she was blaming him (which in a way she did). Instead she said, 'Oh, it was fine.'

'Just fine?'

'Yes.'

Natalie could talk to her mum or friends on the phone for three hours solid, simply describing a dress that she nearly bought because it was perfect but didn't, in the end, so Neil found her reticence to elaborate inexplicable. He pondered for a while. Maybe she didn't want to talk about it because it had gone hideously wrong. Her idiot boss had probably dumped a whole load of extra projects on her at the last minute, projects with ridiculously short deadlines and hideously high targets. He often did this and while Nat always referred to these projects as 'exciting challenges', Neil thought that the pressure was probably getting to her. Bound to be. It was inevitable. She was only human.

Neil cleared away the plates, which were clean except for smears of tomato sauce and minuscule slices of olives (he'd been a bit heavy-handed with the olives), and then he opened a second bottle of wine. He returned from the kitchen with a tray, carrying hot chocolate fudge cake, a large bowl of raspberries and a jug of cream.

'This is not just hot chocolate fudge cake, this is—'

'Hurrah for supermarket puddings!' cried Nat, grinning appreciatively as she dived straight in with her spoon.

She looked so happy in that moment, all traces of the stresses of her work day gone. Neil felt an urge to wrap his arms around her. He wanted to protect her, for ever. To make her happy, for ever. Contrary to popular belief, men often have this thought about the women they love (fulfilling popular belief that they don't all manage to hold the thought indefinitely, sometimes something good comes on TV and they get distracted). He'd promised to do this on his wedding day, not only when he said his vows in the church but he'd promised her mum as well. Funnily enough, his promise to Nina always seemed more vibrantly real to him. Nina had collared him in the aisle before Nat had arrived and had said something along the lines of if he ever hurt her little girl she'd break both his legs. Nina looked beautifully impressive and scarily strong in her enormous purple hat. She was a slight woman, a much frailer build than Nat, Nat had inherited her father's looks, but in that moment Nina was a giant in Neil's eyes. He could almost taste the love that she emitted; he could smell it and touch it. He was desperate to prove to Nina she could trust him with her only daughter. On the spot he promised Nina he'd never hurt Nat, he said that he loved her, always had from the moment he saw her. He must have sounded convincing enough because Nina had flung her arms around him and said she believed him, she understood, she'd felt exactly the same thing. Then she'd started to weep into her handkerchief, allegedly because she was so happy. From lioness to kitten in one swoop. Women! Neil just didn't understand them. He thought he never would and he was deeply suspicious of men who claimed they did. Liars.

'You know, I've been thinking.'

Natalie stiffened. She paused for a nanosecond before she crammed another spoonful of the hot chocolate fudge cake into her mouth. If he talked about babies again she might scream. She didn't want to scream; with a mouth full of sweet stuff she minimised the risk.

'Oh yes,' she muttered cautiously through the cake.

'It was really stupid of me to bring up the baby-making thing the way I did.' Natalie thought it was really stupid of him to bring it up at all; irrespective of how he broached the subject she wouldn't be interested, she'd made that clear before they married. Yet, Nat felt sick with fear, and doubt and sadness. Part of her knew that it wasn't stupid of Neil to talk about wanting babies; people – couples – did talk about wanting babies, about having a family. Sometimes she thought it was *all* her friends ever talked about nowadays. It was, she supposed, inevitable that Neil should broach the subject. 'I shouldn't have sprung it on you,' Neil added.

'Look, Neil, love—'

'No, let me finish. I've been thinking. We need a holiday. You do especially. Your job is too stressful. Too demanding. You can't be expected to think about something as huge as having a family when you barely get a moment to yourself throughout your working day. You're always saying you often don't get the time to go to the loo let alone eat lunch. It's unhealthy. I think you should take a sabbatical.'

'I think you've lost your mind!' Natalie had wanted to remain calm, but the yummy pudding wasn't able to disguise the bitter taste of fury that rinsed her mouth. A sabbatical? She was the last person on earth who would ever want to take a sabbatical. She loved her work. It was important work. Had Neil had a blow to the head? Where was all of this coming from suddenly? 'What are you saying?' she demanded, confused and afraid.

'Just that your work doesn't have to be everything. We could manage on my salary, if we had to. You don't need to feel that you have to work.'

'But I like working. I like my job. I *love* my job.'

'But it's dull.' The words were out of Neil's mouth before he had a chance to fully calculate the consequences. Natalie threw down her spoon. Why not? He'd already thrown down a gauntlet.

'So now not only do you want to have a baby, even though we agreed before we married that we'd never have children, you also want me to stay at home and look after it! To give up my career!'

'I'm not saying that, I just—' Neil could see how she'd *heard* that but that wasn't what he was *saying*. He was always so bad at explaining himself when it came to anything big. She knew that. Normally she cut him some slack. Hadn't they long since agreed that if there were ever two ways of interpreting something he'd said, a good and a bad way, she should know he always meant the good way. He didn't want to hurt her. Not ever.

'And then you insult the job I do! It's dull, is it? Well, was it dull eating in the Bluebird restaurant last night? Was it dull going on holiday to the Seychelles last May? Because my dull job paid for both of those things and a lot more besides.'

Natalie earned more than double the amount Neil did, a fact that neither of them thought about very often. Natalie was surprised at herself for saying something so crass and explosive. She never really thought about who paid for what; now Neil would think she kept score. She'd only said that because she was feeling defensive and shocked. She didn't want to be mean. She never wanted to hurt him. Not ever. But how could he have got it so wrong? Her so wrong? Her job was not dull. It was important and she loved it. It didn't utterly define her but it was a big part of who she was. Was he saying *she* was *dull*?

Nat and Neil's friends and family often privately commented on the fact that, while the couple were clearly deeply in love and committed to one another, they were a definite case of opposites attract. Neil's parents had been rather relieved that he'd chosen such a sensible girl to settle down with, a woman who clearly valued routine and security, a determined woman not afraid of hard work, a woman who saw the importance of having a plan and sticking to it. Nat's parents had hoped that a little bit of Neil's devil-may-care attitude might rub off on their daughter. She was a worrier and it wouldn't be a bad thing if she occasionally threw caution to the wind and did something reckless, impulsive or even silly. Nat and Neil had always loved their differences. Nat was excited by Neil's thrill-seeking, daring and spontaneous nature; at least she had been, until now. In this instant, she wondered about his impetuous, madcap approach. Neil had always adored Nat's depth, her integrity and veracity. Now he was beginning to think she was just old-fashioned stubborn. Nat and Neil glared at one another from across the table and for a moment they both forgot that they'd always believed they were one's yin to the other's yang. The expression that was bubbling up in both their minds was chalk and cheese.

'Do you know what lymphatic filariasis is?' Nat demanded. Neil shook his head. He wasn't sure where this conversation was going but he knew it was off course, he could tell by the unprecedented level of sarcasm in Nat's voice. 'Oh, it's terribly *dull*. Especially if you happen to be one of the one billion people in any of the eighty-three countries that are at risk of infection of this disease, a disease that just happens to be one of the world's most disabling. It's caused by a parasite transmitted from one human to another by mosquitoes. It's as disfiguring as leprosy, and as crippling as polio, it can lead to massive swelling of the limbs, elephantiasis of the skin and hydrocele, that's watery fluid around the testicles.' Neil flinched. 'Infection is often caught in childhood, although severe forms of the disease usually appear in adults, which often forces adults to become dependant on their children, thus ruining entire communities.'

Neil was beginning to get the picture but he didn't dare interrupt her.

'However, the life cycle of the lymphatic filariasis parasite can be interrupted by treating the entire at-risk population annually with antiparasitic medicines manufactured and donated by *my* company. Do you think that's dull?'

'I understand what you're saying.' Neil took a deep breath and the plunge. 'But all of that would still go on without you. You are only a very tiny cog in that wheel. Our having a baby needs *you*. No one else can do that job,' he said.

Nat glared at him. So, now he was saying she was disposable and interchangeable. Didn't he believe she contributed something unique and important at work? Did he think Becky could do just as good a job? Well, he was wrong and her boss knew better. Today's meeting might have started off badly but once Nat had mopped up her spillage and settled down, everything had gone swimmingly. In fact, things had gone so well that she'd been offered a promotion. It was a huge role. She was a little overwhelmed by the thought of it, actually. It would involve lots of long hours and maybe more travel. Nat had wanted to discuss with Neil whether she ought to accept the offer or would it have too much impact on the quality of their life together and therefore not be worth pursuing? But now she wasn't so sure that she'd consult him. It was obvious that he'd be against her taking it. He didn't see the point of her work, he thought she was replaceable; worse still, he thought she ought to be replaced so she could concentrate on having a family. A family they'd long since agreed they were never going to have. It wasn't fair! Where had this come from?

Nat now clearly realised that she did want to take the job. The work she did was meaningful, helpful and critical. She'd go and see her boss first thing tomorrow morning and say that yes, she was ready to leave the procurement division and join the team opening a new research and development facility. She would be responsible for a large amount of the cost analysis involved in this project. Yes, she would take it. She just wouldn't tell Neil. Well, at least not straight away. What was the point of doing so? He'd only say something undermining or disheartening. He thought she was just a cog; he wanted her to take a sabbatical and talk about babies. This wasn't the time to talk about babies! The very thought sent bolts of terror jolting through Nat's body. The terror quickly morphed into aggressive indignation and suddenly Nat felt entitled to retaliate. Her bank of achievements at work were the result of extreme diligence and graft, and what should have been a celebratory moment was being spoilt. Well, maybe she was just a cog but she was a cog in a gigantic, magnificent wheel. The new facility was to focus on research and development into neurodegenerative disorders such as Parkinson's disease, multiple sclerosis and Alzheimer's.

'What did you do today, Neil?'

Neil knew that this seemingly innocuous question was some sort of a trap, although his head was too fuzzy from red wine and panic to understand entirely what the trap might be.

'You wouldn't be interested,' Neil replied cautiously.

'Explain it to me.' Nat sounded reasonable, interested and tolerant but that just heightened Neil's suspicions. Her faux sanguine attitude somehow accentuated, rather than disguised, her disdain for his work.

'I did some market research today.'

'Which means?'

'I played some of the games the competitors are currently producing and test ran one of our new ones.'

'Ah-ha.' Neil wasn't entirely sure why Nat sounded so triumphant but she did. 'Have you brought any of them home?' she asked.

Neil often brought his work home but they both knew it wasn't a hardship for him; it wasn't as though he had to paw over tricky spreadsheets or agonise over weighty documents. The biggest hardship Neil could expect to endure with his work was if he got a crick in his neck from sitting in front of the TV for too long while holding the controls of the console at a funny angle.

Neil retrieved a couple of games from his baggy leather satchel and offered them to Nat. Nat picked up one box carefully between her thumb and forefinger; she did this in a way that suggested she wished she was wearing rubber gloves.

It was a certificate 18. The packaging was boysie and bloody. It happened to be a game both Neil and Karl had worked on, not the competition; Neil was pleased that his game had caught her eye above the others. Nat read the back of the box aloud.

"'In *Damned: the sequel*, players assume the identity of a former Serial Crimes Unit investigator, Mick Grady, who has been called back to duty to track down his missing partner. The cruelly disturbing events from Mick's past have left him a desolate man – a desperate burnout drifting aimlessly through a dissolute society, in inexplicable decline.'" Nat looked up and rolled her eyes in a way that efficiently conveyed total scorn.

'Karl wrote that,' said Neil defensively.

'Yes, it has his light touch,' commented Nat sarcastically. Then she returned to the game. "'Fighting terrifying inner demons throughout his lonely investigation into a sinister conspiracy, *Damned: the sequel* players will engage in visceral combat using a variety of firearms, blunt instruments and an all-new fighting system, complete with defensive and offensive combo chains. Warning: scenes of a graphic nature include torture, rape, sodomy and decapitation.'" Lovely,' said Nat in summation. 'Your mum must be very proud.'

Neil actually couldn't see much difference between the *Damned* horror story and the one about watery testicles, but intrinsically he knew it would be adding lighter fuel to the situation if he said so.

'You have no problem with violent movies.'

'There's no role play involved.'

'I enjoy my work,' said Neil. It seemed a reasonable defence to him.

'That's fine,' replied Nat. 'I get that. I have no problem with that but you don't seem to understand that I enjoy mine and mine makes the world a *better* place.'

Neil thought Nat sounded like a Hallmark card.

Natalie thought that perhaps Neil's sudden desire to have a family was subconsciously linked to a realisation that his work was . . . well, pathetic. She'd never said so before. She'd never actually thought so before. But now she had to wonder, what was the point to Neil's work? What was he contributing? What was he going to leave behind? Maybe, if he was a bit more fulfilled at work, he wouldn't be so keen to have a baby.

As if reading her mind (which Nat considered unlikely, there was no precedent), Neil came back with an argument to counter the one she was forming in her head.

'I work as a games designer at one of the biggest video games companies in the world. I do what I've always wanted to do. I've fulfilled a lifelong ambition. Not everybody is so lucky. Ask any accountant, traffic warden or the guys who empty the bins of scooped dog crap. Working in the video games industry is evidence of my creativity and of my ability to lead, to delegate and to collaborate, at least that's what I put on my CV.' Neil offered up the weak joke like a sacrificial lamb but Nat was not appeased. She did not laugh, she didn't even smile, thus goading Neil to continue his diatribe.

'Games are an essential part of human experience and are known to every culture. I consider it an honour to be part of an industry that has a tradition dating back as far as the thirtieth century BC. Games invariably encompass cerebral and/or physical stimulation. What could be finer than designing a prepared and planned activity, mostly undertaken for delight and gratification? Although, please note, games are sometimes also used as an educational tool. I facilitate the achievement of goals and the rush of rising to and meeting a challenge whilst abiding by rules and regulations. These are life skills!'

'You play all day.'

'Video games have come an awfully long way since the naivety of Pong and Space Invaders back in the seventies. You mustn't dismiss gaming as a mere distraction for the few nerdy kids who can't make friends and stay holed up in their bedrooms when they should be gasping fresh air. The video-game industry is now worth billions. The level of sophistication, both in terms of game play and graphics, continues to grow at a phenomenal pace, and in many households they've overtaken TV as the entertainment of choice for winding down in the evening. Video-game production is now serious business. While you may think being a video-game designer is just a day-long play-about, the truth is it's a very demanding, albeit very rewarding job.'

'Great, Neil. That's all just great.'

From her tone it was clear Natalie didn't, in that moment, think anything about Neil's job (or Neil, for that matter) was great. She glanced at the video-game box between them. Her glance shouted that she thought his work was hideous, violent and pointless. Neil tried another argument. He accepted that premise and tried to make it work for him.

'Video games *are* necessary. Men and boys need a vent.'

'What?' Nat had so many objections to that statement (a vague, sexist, unsubstantiated argument) that she was at a loss to know where to begin.

'Yes,' said Neil firmly. 'Men used to be able to club one another to death over a slice of dinosaur.'

'That's not strictly accurate, you know. Mankind was not alive until about sixty-five million years after dinosaurs were extinct.' Even Nat knew she sounded like a smart-arse.

'Yeah, OK, but bear with me. After clubbing to death came hacking, stabbing, shooting, there was always some skirmish about food or land or women or something. Now there's no war.'

'Yes there is,' said Nat emphatically. Neil sighed impatiently and accepted that Nat must be more sober than he was as she was insisting on making sense and sticking to facts. He seemed to be incapable of constructing a rational argument. He panicked. God, he was pretty much turning into a woman: he wanted a baby, he couldn't stick to the point, his argument was flawed and based on nothing other than an irrational need to keep talking.

'OK,' he conceded, 'I'll put a caveat on that statement. Of course there's war. I realise that we have good men and not so good men out in the Middle East.'

'And women,' chipped in Nat. 'Good and not so good *women* too.'

'Yes, and they are being blown to bits for reasons that they believe in but I lack the courage or conviction or plain old intelligence to understand, let alone support. But for the rest of us ordinary men the only war we wage is against the weed patch in the poxy two metre square yard we euphemistically refer to as a garden. It's possible we miss it.'

'What, hacking each other to death?'

'Yes! We *need* video games.'

'Oh, I see. So you're performing a national service when you go to work every day by designing these blood fests.'

'I like to think so. A sort of Lord Kitchener in reverse. Not so much your country needs you, more your country doesn't need you but your sofa does.'

'Neil, I'm tired. I'm going to bed.'

7

Ben and Fi and their three robust and boisterous children lived in a tall, narrow, three-storey Victorian terrace in Clapham. Neil and Nat each felt a surge of excitement whenever they rapped on the shiny red door, behind which happy domestic chaos was guaranteed. Nat might not want children of her own but she adored Angus, Sophia and Giles and was an exemplary aunt; it was Natalie, not Neil, who remembered birthdays and painstakingly selected gifts for all the big and small occasions. Today she was armed with a packet of small plastic monsters called Go Go Crazy Bones – these were for Angus, as she had been reliably informed by her PA that they were the latest playground must-have; an Angelina Ballerina glitter pen (in pink) for Sophia, and a bean-filled soft toy frog for Giles.

Fi flung open the door and her beam flooded out at about the same speed as the kids, who launched themselves at Neil and Natalie's groins. Fi was in her late thirties and was a woman who had grown into her looks – she'd always looked as though she was in her late thirties and no doubt always would. This had been a curse when she was sixteen but she knew it would be an advantage when she was sixty. She kept her hair short because it was practical and, above all else, Fi was practical. She had it cut at an expensive hairdresser because paying a lot for something gave it gravitas and otherwise there was a serious danger that hairstyling might simply be frivolous or vain, which wouldn't do at all. She had sparkling green eyes and rosy cheeks. She never wore make-up beyond lip gloss (not even on her wedding day) and so always looked as wholesome as a land girl. She welcomed Neil and Natalie with a quick jovial smile that was instantly wiped off her face as she sharply told Giles to, 'get that worm out of your mouth!' Then turning back to her in-laws, she shrugged apologetically and said, 'Goodness, I don't know where he finds the constant supply of wildlife to eat. We live in London! This is why we could never move to the country.'

Neil swooped down and picked up Giles. Using his forefinger to have a quick swab around the mouth, he was able to retrieve the masticated wiggler. Natalie grabbed Sophia's hand and Angus chased behind as they all trailed into the kitchen. Natalie was looking forward to a natter, a huge pot of tea and some home-baked cakes as this was what she was usually furnished with on arrival at Ben and Fi's home. The women and smallest infants usually sat in the kitchen and nattered while Neil and Ben kicked a football about in the long, thin garden, ostensibly to amuse Angus but in fact to challenge one another competitively. Natalie found this cosy familial ritual a pleasant antidote to her busy days and boozy nights. But today, rather than filling the kettle, Fi reached for her smart Chloe bag, ignoring the large, sloppy, scruffy shopping bag that usually accompanied her everywhere. It was clear from a glance that the Chloe bag had never been desecrated by a single baby wipe or sticky, malfunctioning plastic toy. The Chloe bag only ever held lip gloss and credit cards.

'It is so good of you to do this,' gushed Fi with a huge grin. 'I can't think when Ben and I last had a day out together sans children. Shops, lunch, theatre, here I come!'

Before Natalie could fully compute what Fi was on about, Ben burst into the kitchen and bestowed big hugs all round. 'Bloody good of you. Bye now.'

In a flash, Ben and Fi had gathered their jackets, phones and keys and were making towards the door; clearly they had no time to lose as they made their bid for freedom.

'You have our numbers. All instructions are pinned on the notice-board. There are bottles already made up in the fridge for Giles, you just have to take the chill off. Don't forget Angus is allergic to fish.'

'Bye,' added Ben, who was by now in the street.

The door slammed behind them. Natalie gawped at Neil. 'What the . . .?'

'Language,' said Neil in a tinkly, very high voice. He sounded annoyingly like a pantomime dame. 'Not in front of the children.'

Nat and Neil occasionally babysat for Fi and Ben but mostly they did this in the evening when the kids were safely in bed or, if they did help out during the daytime, they were usually only left with one or two of the kids at a time (so there were enough adults and pairs of hands to go round) and then they only did an hour or so at most. 'Are we babysitting today?' asked Nat.

'Yes.'

'All day?'

'Yes.'

'All three?'

'Yes.'

'Sh—' Nat stopped herself. She stared at the three children, who were now in various states of undress and distress, although she could have sworn that only a minute ago all three were suitably attired for a shoot for a Boden catalogue, including the obligatory smile. Now Giles was sockless, his romper suit had a suspicious stain spreading on it and an odious smell was coming from it; there was only one conclusion to be drawn, his nappy was leaking. Sophia was drawing on the floor with felt tips, including the new glittery Angelina Ballerina one. How had she got that out of Nat's bag? In a flash, she had also changed out of her normal clothes and was now wearing a Snow White costume with a Batman mask. The effect was disconcerting, at least Giles thought so because the moment he looked at her he threw out a loud, hysterical howl.

Angus had spotted an opportunity. Aware that the adults in charge were temporarily paralysed with shock, he had dragged the ironing basket out of the corner up to the kitchen counter, climbed up on it and was flailing around in search of drinks that would stain, sharp knives, or sweets stuffed with additives; in fact anything off limits would do.

Neil and Nat shared a terrified glance.

'This is not a time to panic,' said Neil. Or yell at me, he thought.

'Quite. You get Angus and Sophia, I'll cover the baby.'

Like a swat team they leapt into action, snatching up crayons, removing masks and knives and soiled nappies. Nat scooped up the smelly baby and dashed him up to the nursery. She'd changed his nappy before. It wasn't her favourite job but providing she remembered to breathe through her mouth and look at his *eyes* throughout, she could manage it. Then she scrabbled around the drawers and tried to locate a clean romper suit that wasn't pink (why had Fi kept those!), had no sleeves, was big enough, but not too big. She then wriggled the fidgeting bundle of baby into said romper. When she returned to the sitting room, Nat found Neil on all fours with the two older children clambering on his back. Neil was slightly flushed with the exertion but he was smiling good-naturedly and Nat couldn't help but grin back at him. They shared a smug moment; they had the situation under control. See, this wasn't so hard.

'Gee-up, ass,' said Angus, slapping Neil on the bottom.

Nat considered that Angus was aware that he was being borderline rude but she couldn't be sure; maybe he did mean donkey. She decided not to pursue the issue. No doubt there would be enough battles to fight today.

For about ten minutes the children were thoroughly amused and Neil and Nat were feeling superior and self-satisfied. Then the children announced they were bored. Not wanting to fall at this early hurdle, Nat dragged out the enormous trunk of toys that Fi kept under the dining-room table but before she could interest any one of them in the tambourines, jigsaws, cuddly toys, finger puppets, balls, bells or whistles, the smallest two children had taken up residence under the table and Giles, who was just able to sit up, was repeatedly slamming his teething ring into the table legs. In seconds he had scratched it so badly that it looked as though Fi and Ben bred Labrador puppies for a living. Nat didn't have the energy in her to wonder if she could hide or fix the damage because even though she knew the table was from Conran, she was pretty sure Fi would have seen worse. Besides, as Sophia took it upon herself to discipline her small brother by smacking him in the face with a toy car, creating a renewed bout of bawling, Nat's immediate concern became to locate the arnica cream. She briefly wondered whether she'd be able to disguise the bruise with Clinique super-fit foundation but decided against it. Again, chances were Fi would have seen worse. It amazed Nat how quickly things had deteriorated. The feelings of control and self-satisfaction began to flood away.

Neil saw dread flash in Nat's eyes and knew he had to act quickly. He crawled under the table (banging his head as he did so) and retrieved both children. Natalie soothed (the kids, no time to waste on Neil's injury) while Neil went to hunt for Angus, who had been suspiciously quiet for eight minutes which transpired to be long enough to have found his way into the en-suite and to have opened (and emptied) all of Fi's expensive toiletries. Neil fought his way through the clouds of talcum powder, almost slipping on an enormous pool of Molton Brown bubble bath which sloshed over the bathroom tiles. Neil did his best to clean up the gunky mess while Natalie read a story. The children found the story amusing for ten minutes and then once again they announced they were bored. Neil and Nat played tea parties, for ten minutes. Bored. Then football, for ten minutes. Bored. Then they found drawing books; the activity lasted ten minutes. Bored. By now, there were no traces of the initial complacency; both Nat and Neil felt exposed, overwhelmed and fraught.

'Shall we go out?' asked Neil desperately.

'Yes,' agreed Nat firmly.

It took the pair three-quarters of an hour to get the children and their associated paraphernalia into a fit state to leave the house. The pushchair was stacked with a nappy bag (containing a stack of nappies – Nat had wondered how many Giles could reasonably get through in an afternoon and then trebled the amount – nappy sacks, baby wipes and soothing cream), a change of clothes for all three, wellington boots for the oldest two (Neil had an image of them all visiting the small pond at the centre of the common and paddling there, he'd wanted them to be bare-footed but Nat pointed out that there was a risk of stepping on syringes. Besides, the kids were non-compliant: Sophia wanted to wear her ballet pumps and Angus wanted to wear his Crocs to leave the house). They also packed healthy snacks (to please Fi), unhealthy snacks (to gain favour from the kids), bottles of milk, bottles of water, cartons of tooth-rotting juice, books, toys, sun hats, woolly hats (unreliable British weather!) and security blankets. Nat commented that there was barely any room for Giles but somehow they managed to squeeze him in. Sophia jumped on the boogie board and Angus grabbed his scooter. But no sooner were they three steps outside the door than the baby started to cry. Nat and Neil looked at each other for inspiration.

'Clean not fed,' guessed Nat, as she rolled her eyes.

They returned to the house and the eldest two sat in front of the TV while Neil fed Giles a bottle of tepid formula milk. The children were sweating but Nat was strict and wouldn't allow them to take off their jackets, knowing full well that if they did so it would take another eternity to ready them all once again.

An hour later, back outside on the pavement, Nat asked, 'Where shall we take them?'

Neil wasn't sure. Right now, a trip to the common seemed ambitious enough, even though it was only two hundred yards away. If ever Neil travelled into central London he took the tube, which involved a short overground section of travel. Neil had often watched mothers amuse their kids on a particular scrap of uninspiring tarmac just near the track and he'd always wondered why, with all the glorious parks and gardens in London, anyone would choose to do that? Now he had some idea. He'd bet his bottom dollar that those mothers lived a stone's throw from the scruffy tarmac that was split with nettles and decorated with discarded drink cans. He was finding it exhausting trying to get kids anywhere just this once; obviously if you had to do it day in, day out, you'd be tempted to take the line of least resistance, and if getting 'fresh air' involved practically playing on the District line, then so be it. But Neil couldn't admit defeat after only three and a quarter hours of sole care. That wouldn't give Nat the right impression at all. The reason he'd volunteered their services today was because he'd wanted to show Nat just how much fun it was being around kids. How great he was with kids. How great she was with kids. He'd had visions of him galloping around the garden with a giggling Angus riding on his shoulders, Nat might have strung dried pasta on string with Sophia the way he'd once seen Fi do or, he'd thought, perhaps they could have baked or done some finger painting. Neil now realised that his initial thoughts were horribly unrealistic, considering the house looked as though a hurricane had raged through and they hadn't even tried to introduce anything as ambitious as flour or paint.

'The Aquarium?' he suggested.

'Did that last week,' said Angus with a yawn.

'The Science Museum?'

'Hate it,' pronounced Sophia. Neil had always liked the Science Museum as a child and was rather disgruntled but chose not to push the point.

'Cinema?' suggested Nat. She could do with a sit-down.

'Giles is too young,' pointed out Angus in a tone that clearly communicated he felt the adults who had been left in charge were idiots. Nat and Neil took it in turns to suggest possible places of amusement. Neil's suggestions were initially of the worthy variety. He'd secretly searched the internet this morning before Nat had even got out of bed and he wanted the green light on an amusement that would reflect well on him, something thoughtful, educational and edifying. Something that said 'excellent dad material' in neon pink. Nat wanted to go where they'd sell cake.

'We could do some brass rubbing in the St Martin-in-the-Fields crypt,' Neil suggested.

'No.'

'Take a look around HMS *Belfast*?'

'No.'

'St Paul's Cathedral?'

'Are there any buttons to press?'

'Erm, no.'

'No, then.'

'We could do the Winston Churchill wartime experience,' suggested Neil enthusiastically.

Sophia promptly burst into tears. 'Scary!'

'The London Eye?'

'Done that with Grandma and Grandpa.'

'Buckingham Palace?'

'Seen it a trillion times,' said a weary Angus.

Nat thought the best idea was that they all went home and came back in about four years when Neil's suggestions might be a little more appropriate but instead she offered London Zoo.

'Giles is allergic to fur and feathers,' said Sophia seriously.

'I thought it was Angus who was allergic to fish, eating them,' challenged Nat suspiciously.

'Also true,' said Angus with confidence. Nat realised, too late, that they had made a fatal error as novices in charge of children; they had given the minors too much choice. She realised they could not win. Inevitably everything and anything they now suggested would be rejected. Her head was beginning to ache and they were still standing outside Fi and Ben's home. The neighbours had twitched their curtains four times in the last ten minutes. Nat gave in.

'OK then. What do *you* want to do today?' she asked.

'Hamleys,' chorused Angus and Sophia. Giles gurgled as though in agreement.

Nat wondered, could they have rehearsed that?

8

They took the bus to Regent Street. Neither Natalie nor Neil could quite face getting all three children and related baggage down the stairs to the underground. It seemed an overwhelming, impossible task. At least they only had to manage the one step up on to the bus. Nat wondered how the disabled ever got around London. She adored London and saw it as a genuine melting pot of excitement and eccentricity. She loved the bars, the clubs, the restaurants, the galleries and museums. She admired the variety, potential and enthusiasm that London, doubtless, embodied but she saw now that it could be a merciless city.

The bus journey was relatively successful. No one threw up or got lost and so the adults felt a sense of achievement. Neil had adopted a rather irritating faux joviality that didn't convince anyone that he was truly enjoying himself. Nat knew what he was doing, she wasn't a fool. She grudgingly admired his determination. He must really want her to see his point of view if he was prepared to give up a Saturday morning playing football and a Saturday afternoon watching football just to prove that he could be a good dad.

On the other hand, she hated him.

Seriously. How was this going to help? How could he think spending a day with these leaky children would make her change her mind? Any rational human being would surmise that a day playing clown, nurse, umpire, teacher, cleaner, disciplinarian and librarian was overkill and likely to unearth new reasons to object to motherhood. Neil would have been wiser to limit their visit to an hour, tops. What was he thinking? Did he imagine she had stage fright about being a mother and needed a dress rehearsal? Did he hope they'd charm her? It wasn't as though she was oblivious to the allure that children could, no doubt, display. She'd felt her heart flutter when Sophia planted the smallest 'phut' of a kiss on her cheeks and breathily declared, 'You're beautiful, Auntie Nattie, like a princess.' She was not made of stone. None of this was the point. Neil's blatant strategy was naive and patronising. Nat sighed and admitted it was also understandable. No doubt she was a puzzle to Neil.

Hamleys was hell. Hell in reverse, actually; the higher you traveled, the hotter and more agonising the experience became. One of the cheery staff told Nat that Hamleys welcomed five million guests per year; Nat thought they were probably all here today. On entering, she was confronted with an overwhelming glut of soft toys. The remarkably diverse array of stuffed animals included everything from regular teddy bears to more exotic plushes, such as turtles and dolphins and enormous life-sized giraffes and elephants. The stuffed menagerie had spooky glass eyes that gave Nat the willies. She'd never been the sort of girl that boys gave soft toys to, not even ones they might have won at a fair.

'Look at this, Nat!' yelled Neil, who was pitching his tone somewhere between that of Father Christmas and Willy Wonka. 'Isn't it cute?' he asked, waving a purple bear in the air.

'No, it's not cute, it's weird.'

Unperturbed, Neil insisted, 'Isn't this adorable?'

'No, because I'm not three years old.'

'This is a must-have.'

'It's a duck in a hat with a rainbow splattered across its backside, how can that be described as a must-have?' snapped Nat who was clearly alone in thinking that the cuddly toys looked menacing, Neil and the three kids spent an eternity oh-ing and ah-ing.

There were games on the first floor, the traditional type that Nat remembered from her own childhood, Monopoly and Cluedo etc., but she was disgruntled that many of the games had received a commercial makeover. Monopoly now came in a million versions: Spongebob Monopoly, Chelsea Monopoly, Tottenham Hotspur Monopoly, I Love Lucy Monolopy, an electronic one, a Spiderman version, even a Make Your Own Monopoly. Nat hated it. Why couldn't things stay as they were? Why so much change and choice? And Cluedo was no better. In her day the only vaguely sexy character had been Miss Scarlet who, while depicted as a coiffured blonde lollipop head stuck on the end of a plastic blob, had still managed to ooze mystique and allure. Now, *all* the female characters (even Mrs White) were depicted with plunging necklines and scarlet lips, there was no mystery or innocence. Nat felt old.

The second floor was full of whirling, flashing, squeaking plastic stuff and small children who were crawling on the floor, on shelves, down stairs and swinging from light fittings. This must have been where Matt Groening got the inspiration for the fearless, intrepid Maggie in *The Simpsons*, as the place was full of dummy-sucking plucky types. The third floor was pink. Entirely so. Rosy, cherry, cerise, crimson, fluffy, feathery, sparkly, shiny and shimmering pink. The fourth floor was the boy equivalent and was full of monsters, gore, blood, guts, war, aliens, spears, swords, gun-wielding plastic figures and the odd train. There was something else on a fifth floor but Nat failed to notice exactly what as she scrabbled to install herself in the café. She forgave it for having yellow tables and purple and red seats and gulped down sweet, scalding tea and crammed large gobfuls of chocolate cake into her mouth. She was in shock. Neil tried to pretend the whole experience was something approaching fun but she was not convinced. Maybe for him a toy shop was interesting; he was a boy and he'd never grow up.

Just a few minutes' walk from the hell that is Hamleys, there is Liberty's, which was one of Nat's favourite stores. It's a serene haven of splendid adulthood. Liberty's had an air of unadulterated sophistication and security which Nat wished could stretch to every part of her life, big or small. The polished wooden floors had been worn and bruised by endless generations of elegant, well-heeled women, all of whom would have 'oohed' and 'aahed' over exquisite fabrics, funky furniture and sparkling jewellery. The store offered a wonderful and unique blend of appreciation of the past and a promise of a dazzling future. Nat wasn't sure what it was about the rows of cosmetics, the charming tea room and the glossy handbags that made that promise exactly, but she was sure that she wanted to go there right now. She wanted to snoop around the amazing stationery and drift through the clouds of perfume, but she knew it was an impossible desire. While there wasn't actually a sign pinned to the wooden doors that said 'No Children', it was somehow implicit in the very plasterwork of the sumptuous Tudor revival, Grade II listed building that suggested driving Giles's buggy through the elegant merchandise was tantamount to a criminal offence.

Instead, when they finally left Hamleys (several pounds lighter and several bags heavier), they pushed their way through Carnaby Street. Soon exhausted by the feeling that they were salmon swimming upstream, they headed towards the quieter, smaller side streets, without a particular plan in mind (other than the one of avoiding being trampled to death). Nat couldn't bring herself to look at Neil. His desperation was upsetting, but then her frustration was throbbing.

Giles had fallen asleep in his buggy which Natalie pushed. It was insufferably heavy because besides the weight of the baby and the bags, a sleepy Sophia who stood on the buggy board had collapsed across the hood of the stroller. Neil carried exhausted Angus on his shoulders. They needed to find somewhere to slump, even if that meant buying their second round of drinks and cakes in less than an hour. They collapsed into seats outside a coffee bar and spent a trust fund on lemonade and ginger tea. With the children dozing, Natalie thought she could risk talking to Neil.

'Why are we here, Neil?'

Neil stared at Natalie. 'That's a silly question. We're here because

the kids wanted to come to Hamleys and then you wanted to get out
of Hamleys and we all needed a sit-down and—'

'No, Neil. You know what I mean. What did you hope to achieve
by arranging this day trip?'

Neil could have said that his only motivation for arranging this trip
was to give Ben and Fi some free time, Natalie herself had said how
disappointed Fi was that they hadn't managed a night out on
Wednesday, but he decided not to hide.

'Isn't it obvious?'

'Yes.' Natalie sighed. It was scarily obvious.

Neil looked as though he was in pain. His breath was shallow and
laboured and his smile was awkward and artificial. He wanted this so
much. He mustn't fuck up this negotiation. It wasn't like trying to
persuade your other half to visit your parents for Christmas or to head
for the mountains rather than the beach for a holiday. This was vital.
Imperative. Crucial. He glanced up and down the pretty street. The
late summer sunlight was fading and the street looked blue. Sharp. The
dozing children looked pink and rosy cosy by comparison, their sweet
button noses and bud mouths peeking out from under sun hats; his
chest hurt. 'I don't get it, Natalie. You're so good at dealing with kids.'

'I have quite a way with dealing with dust mites too but it doesn't
mean I want to nurture them,' replied Nat steadily.

'How can you make jokes?'

'How can I do anything else?' Natalie reached out and put her hand
on top of Neil's, she patted him. It didn't create the effect she wanted;
the gesture seemed like one that should pass between an aged aunt
and petulant nephew. She wanted to connect but she couldn't find
the words he needed. Or rather, wouldn't say the words he wanted
to hear, not ever.

'What shall we do when we are old?' Neil asked with a sad sigh.

'Lawn bowls probably,' she offered. No response. 'Look, we can
travel the world, visit galleries, read all the books we don't have time
to read now.' Natalie wanted to sound excited, she feared she sounded
desperate.

'I don't like reading much.'

'Well, I do.' Neil shot her a cold look. She knew she sounded strident and harsh, fear did that to her voice. Natalie was frustrated. He was so unfair. He had no right to change his mind. They'd agreed. They'd discussed it. She took a deep breath and tried a deliberately softer approach. 'Look, we can be good to our nieces and nephews and godchildren. We can offer them a bolt hole when they decide they loathe their parents. There are a million things we can do.'

'I feel incomplete.'

'Well, I don't,' she said firmly, without giving the idea a chance to germinate. 'Conversation over.'

'No, it's not, Nat. You can't decide that.' Neil banged his hand down on the small, rickety table and the glasses and cups shuddered. Nat wasn't sure whether the drama was to emphasise his resolve or as a vent for his frustration. Either way, it was distressing; this sort of tension between them was unprecedented. She threw a wary glance at the snoozing children but they hadn't been disturbed by Neil's sudden and unusual display of temper. She then threw an accusatory look at Neil, the type of look she'd often seen slide between parents when children were in the vicinity. A look that challenged something that one or the other had said or done, without having to turn up the volume. She'd always thought it was a low and depressing expression, so sanctimonious, and she immediately wished she hadn't used it.

'I see that it's really inconvenient to you that I've changed my mind about this,' muttered Neil. Nat didn't like his choice of the word 'inconvenient', it somehow belittled her position, but she let it go without comment as she was all too aware that they were heading for a big row anyway; there was no sense in pouring fuel on the fire at this early stage. 'It was daft of me to suggest you give up work. That's not necessary at all,' Neil pointed out. He was using a more conciliatory tone but Nat could tell it was strained. 'We can get a nanny or the baby can go to nursery. There are loads near where we live.'

Nat played with the idea of saying she didn't think it was right to have a baby only to allow someone else to bring it up, but this wasn't really her point of view, just something she'd heard a friend of hers (who was a stay-at-home mum) spit out when she'd had a particularly trying day with her kids. It seemed dishonest to use the argument when she didn't even believe it.

So instead she said, 'Haven't you been listening to our friends who are parents? Every single one of them started to panic about which nursery they could squeeze their kid into pretty much the moment after conception. There might be loads of nurseries in Chiswick but they are all full until about twenty thirty. Getting a nursery place is not straightforward and nannies are prohibitively expensive.'

'Well, I could look after it, at least part-time,' offered Neil.

'You couldn't give birth to it. That can't be done on a part-time basis,' snapped Nat.

Neil couldn't believe his desire for a baby, a family, was going to be thwarted because Nat was worried about getting a spare roll around her midriff. No, that couldn't be right, could it? She wasn't at all superficial, was she? He'd never thought of her as such but then he'd never thought of her as unreasonable, until now. Did he know her as well as he thought? Just in case his greatest need, his most fearsome longing was hinged around something as trivial as Nat's dress size, he chose to be reassuring.

'You'd get your figure back in no time.'

Nat shook her head sadly but didn't comment. She wondered whether she ought to take refuge in the usual excuses. Babies cramp your style, steal your sleep, your time and even your identity. They're expensive. Your home becomes a mausoleum to all things plastic and ugly. For at least five years, you never again have the opportunity to finish a sentence, after which time you have little of interest to say anyhow. Going unaccompanied to the supermarket, or even the loo, becomes the ultimate in 'Me time'. And the birth . . . Before Nat decided whether she wanted to articulate any of this, Neil chose to change tack.

'OK, if you won't tell me why you don't want a baby, will you at least hear me out while I tell you the reasons I do?'

Nat gave a stilted nod, although truthfully she'd rather have stuck sharp pencils in her eyes.

Neil took a deep breath. He started resolutely upbeat. 'We've got a good life, Nat. A beautiful home, wonderful family and fun friends, plus we've jobs that we love.' He confidently counted off their blessings in a way that Nat knew was definitely going to culminate in a 'but'. 'We're so lucky. *But* I want to share our good life. More than that, I *need* to share it to make sense of it. To . . . to . . . justify it. To . . . *honour* it.' Neil blanched a fraction. No one, other than Nat, would ever have perceived his paling. But she understood; it was difficult to discuss honour in a busy London street in broad daylight. It demanded a special sort of courage. Or desperation. 'If we had a family, we'd pass on all that good fortune and happiness. Without a baby I'm not sure if it makes that much sense to me.' The upbeat tone had completely disappeared and a more earnest anguished one had replaced it.

'Nat, I've sky-dived and bungee-jumped. I love waterskiing and riding really fast motorcycles. You know I love extreme sports – the scarier the better. And do you know why?' No, Nat didn't know why. Her husband's thrill-seeking was complete anathema to her; she sought safety. It was complicated. While she found it sexy and exciting that he accomplished these daredevil antics with such style and gusto, a part of her was eternally terrified by his endeavours. 'Because I want to feel *alive* while I am alive. I want it to matter. I want every damn moment to count. *I* want to matter. I want to count.'

Neil paused and picked up a Giles teething ring which had fallen on the ground. He appeared to be carefully scrutinising the chewed piece of plastic but Nat knew he was struggling to find the right words in order to continue. If she interrupted him now – cut him off – he'd lose his thread for ever and she'd be protected from the pain of hearing the full extent of his longing. But she could not do that. However sickening it was for her to listen to him ask for something she just couldn't agree to, she owed him the audience.

'You see, I think,' he corrected himself, 'I *know* that becoming a dad would blow all those other experiences out of the water. I realise now that the scary stuff I've done in the past, they were time-fillers, rehearsals for the real deal. Having a child would be the one thing that would show I counted. I'm certain that becoming a dad would be the most overwhelming experience I've ever had.' Neil dragged his eyes away from the gaudy teething ring and stared at Nat. She wanted to look away because his gaze was torture but she was frozen and her body seemed incapable of following her brain's instructions. 'A baby is the future.' Neil looked as though he wanted to swallow back the words. They were perhaps not accurate enough for what he wanted to say, not big enough or special enough. The words had become hackneyed and traumatised by a naff pop song but still he bravely pushed on. 'Aren't they? Children? And I'd be so proud to have a baby with you.'

His words scalded her ears and tore at her heart. Nat ached. Every fibre of her body revolted as pain bounced from her All Star trainers up to the tips of her Aveda salon trimmed hair.

'Do you understand what I'm saying?' Neil asked.

'Yes.'

'And does any of that matter to you?'

'Of course,' replied Nat hastily. She realised there was a danger that Neil would interpret her stunned silence as indifference. What a bloody, bloody catastrophe. She had ferociously hoped her husband's change of viewpoint was just a whim. That hope was now stone dead. It was clear Neil was resolute. Nat felt panic surge through her body; dread pounded through her veins and poisoned her blood-stream, horror tightened around her heart. This was not fair! She had been so careful in her choice. She'd been upfront about her position on children long before she married Neil. She'd never wanted to inflict her point of view on anyone who didn't agree with it. She'd been so sure that Neil was her soul mate because of countless big and small, fun and grave reasons, but most importantly they'd agreed on this fundamental issue.

'So then why, why, *why* don't you want a baby? Can you at least explain that?' asked Neil.

'No, Neil. No, I can't,' replied Nat, distraught. She wished she could.

Summer disappeared and autumn took hold. The season's bony, clasping fingers grabbed hold of fleshy green leaves and turned them darker and more brittle. The long, careless, boozy outdoor evenings vanished as Londoners scuttled off the streets and took up camp in front of their TVs. There was a distinct chill in the air and the constant threat of rain. Natalie felt the season reflected her mood.

She knew that she needed some space and perspective. Last night Neil had sung 'Twinkle twinkle, little star' in his sleep while she lay awake and worried about how the hell this stalemate was going to be resolved. For nearly a month now he'd mooned over every stroller and toddler in west London. Mothers had started to look nervous when they saw him walk into Starbucks; Natalie feared it might only be a matter of time before the police were involved. Last week he'd bought a small knitted monkey and sat it on the kitchen window sill. When Nat had asked what it was for, Neil had replied, 'A gift.'

'For who?'

'Whoever,' he said, with a huge sloppy grin.

'For Giles?'

'Not really. I just saw it in the toy shop and I thought it was sort of cute. Irresistible.'

This wasn't going away.

Natalie wasn't sure if Neil was waging a sly war of attrition. As she hadn't been able to articulate her objections to having a baby beyond constantly reiterating, 'I just don't want one!' maybe he held the vain hope that he could break her. Or maybe he simply could not help himself and was genuinely all-consumed by baby thoughts. Either way, the situation was dire.

Natalie, an independent, autonomous, resolute thirty-three year old did what she always did in times of stress or uncertainty, she ran home to visit her parents. They still lived in Guildford, in the house where she'd lived when she was a little girl. She liked visiting Guildford, which is only thirty miles from London and a quick drive down the A3 from Chiswick. Guildford is a pretty place with a sturdy history (there were an inordinate number of hanging baskets and a Saxon castle). It is exactly the sort of place parents are supposed to live, safe, orderly and known. The high street is cobbled with granite setts and as a market town there are distinct occasions of bustle as the fabulous shops attract yummy mummies and affluent teenagers, yet Natalie also found that there was often a strange almost magical hush throughout the town, suggesting the sort of calm that other places only ever achieved when it snowed. As a child Natalie had believed that maybe the people of Guildford invested in rubber-soled shoes and they certainly seemed to talk in whispers, as though permanently in a library. Loud talking on mobile phones was very much frowned upon in Guildford. Residents would, if they could, put the offender in the stocks and throw rotten eggs (although quietly).

Natalie's parents lived in an ugly 1950s semi, which even back in the seventies had been sold as a 'fixer upper'. Natalie's parents were blissfully ignorant of the suggestion that interior design was the new sex and had never put much effort into fixing up anything much, other than the garden, which was a riot of colour and delicious smells. The house was boxy, with small windows, brown carpets and tatty, fraying wallpaper but the bringing up of four children meant that Brian and Nina Morgan had never had the money or energy to move. The only thing to recommend the house, and indeed the reason her parents had bought it in the first place, was that it backed directly on to the Pewley Downs, giving Natalie and her brothers a playground, complete with grasslands, that provided all manner of mini beasts and woodlands, that afforded countless dens and natural climbing frames. Despite the unreliable central heating and dated décor, the Morgans' house always felt like a home.

Natalie had rung ahead to tell her parents that she was visiting. This way she was more likely to cadge lunch or, at the very least, half an hour of their devoted attention. Her younger brothers had all ostensibly moved out of the family home but whenever Natalie visited she was, as likely as not, to find one or another of them (and an enormous bag of laundry) spread across the front room or blocking up the hallway. The boys sucked up time like black holes, they always had. They seemed to have a genetic need to be at the centre of everyone's attention (a Y chromosome thing, perhaps) and so Natalie secretly had been a little relieved when Nina said that none of them was expected this weekend. Nat had a better chance of finding a quiet moment for a chat with her parents if there wasn't a constant commentary from her brothers about their drinking, sexual, athletic and (occasional) career prowess.

Besides the fact that their children seemed to live on a piece of elastic that sprang them home regularly, her parents had other calls on their time. They were busy sorts and if they were not given notice of her arrival, they would almost certainly have been engaged elsewhere. Nina taught piano to local schoolchildren. Brian liked to take long walks on the Downs; he carried a pointed stick and a hessian bag for litter collecting. Because Natalie had called ahead, Brian had got up two hours earlier than usual to do his Womble impersonation and Nina had cancelled three piano lessons. Neither parent thought to mention to Natalie that they'd adjusted their schedules to suit her. It put far too much pressure on the visit. They couldn't quite explain why that would be the case but like so many truisms about family life, it was just the way it was. Natalie ostensibly hated it if they made a fuss of her but equally often she complained that she was largely ignored. They weren't always sure what to do for the best. The compromise of making an effort but not admitting to it was in fact unlikely to please anyone but it was the policy they'd adopted. Brian and Nina wished Natalie visited more often, the way the boys did, and they didn't quite understand why she didn't.

They sat in the garden, clasping mugs of steaming tea. The Morgans were outdoorsy types and only ever retreated indoors if rain fell like slivers of glass. On this September day the air was cold and damp, drizzle threatened, but it wasn't actually pouring. Besides, the garden was aesthetically superior to anywhere in the house, even in autumn when the rose bushes were becoming thorny twigs once again and the borders needed tending to.

'The greenhouse needs a good wash,' commented Nina. She wasn't telling her husband that he had to wash away the grime and algae accumulated on the glazing, but since the dirt reduced the amount of light that could get through to the plants inside, she thought her observation made it perfectly clear that the task needed to be done by someone.

Brian recognised the directional hint for what it was, it had taken years but he now had the knack of knowing when Nina was managing him gently.

'I'll get to that this afternoon,' he replied mildly, 'with a hose and a stiff brush.' He didn't mind. Part of him looked forward to slowly spraying and brushing every panel in turn. If a job was worth doing, it was worth doing well.

'So, any news?' asked Nina, turning to Natalie. Natalie wondered if the question meant, 'So skipped your period yet? Grandchild on the way, is it?' But then she realised that was ridiculous, Nina had never asked her such a thing. Why would baby-making be top of Nina's mind? Neil's weird behaviour was making Nat paranoid.

'I got a promotion.'

'Oh, well done! That's fabulous news. Tell us all about it.'

Natalie was happy to describe the exact nature of her new job and to recount the humorous circumstances that had surrounded the appointment. She told of the scattering files, fluttering like butterflies across her boss's office, and the water spilling like a tidal wave across his desk. Her parents laughed at her self-deprecating humour but inwardly shone with pride that their daughter was doing something so interesting and important.

'I bet Neil is proud,' said Brian.

'Hmmm,' replied Natalie, not actually committing or commenting. Nina, with a woman's intuition for recognising intrigue or a secret, pushed a little harder.

'Did he take you out for a meal? How did you celebrate?'

Natalie didn't have the energy to enter into a deception. Wasn't that why she was here in their garden so she could confide in them, explain her problem, get their perspective?

'I haven't told Neil about my promotion,' she confessed. Brian and Nina became rigid. Brian had been slouching against the wall, nursing his tea mug in one hand; now he was stiff and upright like a flagpole. Nina's smile and gentle curves seemed to vanish as her jaw and shoulders squared. With finely tuned animalistic instincts they sensed an *issue*. Natalie saw the concern flood into their eyes and felt guilty. They were too old to hear this. They were too weary to still be listening to her problems. Yes, for years they had oozed sympathy when she had fallen over at school, in front of a crowd or, worse, fallen out with her crowd, both regular states of emergency for a child. They'd sat through the door-slamming stage and the agonising over spots, boys and the 'what to wear for a party?' stages. They had been as wise as their limited experience had allowed when she'd applied for universities and they'd sympathised when she didn't get her first or second choice, then celebrated when she got decent results. She'd run home to them when her flat had been infested with mice and when her bag had been snatched, she'd called them when her suitcase had got lost en route to a hot holiday destination. But this. The baby thing. This wasn't something that could be fixed by opening a packet of digestives or even calling the insurance company.

They looked tired. Not at all how she imagined them in her head when she brought them to mind. Her father was absolutely white-haired now, he often tripped up over his own feet when he was walking anywhere. He wouldn't ever discuss it but he found it a nuisance that he needed two pairs of glasses, one for long distance and one for short. It was irritating always having to swap between the two, even worse in the summer when sunglasses were required. Nina was baffled by all things modern. She had been quite an 'it' girl in her day and in her small town. She'd been regarded as fashionable, fun and funky. But her youth, squandered in the seventies, sometimes seemed so irrelevant she might as well have been born in Tudor times. What the hell was a laptop, or an iPhone? One of the boys had been so excited about a notebook; another, his blueberry or something. Neither item turned out to be what she expected. She wasn't even comfortable sending a text and if she did she would insist on spelling everything properly and using the correct grammar. All these gadgets made her feel so old. As did the fact that O levels were extinct and even their replacements were under threat. Internet dating was practically de rigueur. Women went to bars without underwear to guarantee free drinks from the landlords. In her day they'd burnt bras, discarding undergarments for political reasons, not to get drunk. What was the world coming to?

Natalie had only arrived half an hour ago but in that time Brian and Nina had told her that her eldest brother had split up from his long-term girlfriend, which was a shame, everyone had liked her and Nina had been hoping that there might be a wedding to look forward to at some point. The middle brother still hadn't settled on a career or, rather, he did not have a settled career. He was in a band and so earned his money by working at a biscuit factory. The shifts were convenient for his night-owl lifestyle but his parents couldn't help but wonder if he would ever put his impressive academic qualifications to use. The youngest son was travelling somewhere in Asia, he hadn't called for three weeks so no one knew his exact whereabouts. He'd sent one email but it hadn't been specific about location. Apparently he was outside a 'mind-blowingly beautiful shrine'. It irritated Natalie that he was so lazy and such a poor correspondent. It was selfish.

As it would be selfish of her to bring more worry to her parents' door. They needed her to be the successful one, the sorted one, the one who was happily married, with a good job and a clear vision of exactly where her life was going. All of which was true. Natalie did know where her life was going. It was just that Neil seemed to want to go in a completely different direction. To have a baby or not to have a baby was not an issue one could compromise on. It's not as though you could have half a baby or a baby for some of the time. Natalie sighed. What would be the point in bringing up this issue with her parents? They couldn't offer a solution. They wouldn't understand. No one did. All they would do was ask themselves what they'd done wrong to make her think this way. It seemed to be a default setting for a parent to blame themselves for their child's irregularities and they would see it as irregular. They might be tempted to dig deep, look for explanations. Digging wouldn't help. Not at all.

'Why haven't you told Neil?'

Natalie didn't say she was terrified an announcement of this sort (of any sort) might lead to another row as Neil would insist on re-exploring their status quo. Undoubtedly, Neil would view the promotion as either a stumbling block to her having a baby or a great way for them to save before the event and perhaps secure better maternity leave conditions when his imaginary baby was born. He would not be able to see the promotion for what it was: something quite apart from his fantasies. She knew this because he'd made sure that just about every conversation they'd had in the last month had found a way back to discussing starting a family. Last night Natalie asked him what he wanted for supper, fishcakes or toad in the hole. He replied by telling her about the importance of fish in a child's diet, especially in the early years. When she mooted the idea of them buying a new car, something fun and sporty, he said a two-seater was ridiculous if you were planning a family. But she wasn't planning a family. Nat felt she couldn't admit to her parents that she'd decided it was better to just get on with the new job without mentioning it to Neil. While she was based in the same office, Neil wouldn't notice she'd been promoted. He wasn't noticing anything about *her* now. None of this would comfort her ageing parents. Instead she lied.

'I'm going to surprise him when I get my first big pay cheque through. I might buy something nice for the house. He's been after a flat screen TV.'

'Oh, I'm sure he'd want to be involved in choosing his own TV,' said her father, his concern now instantly switching to Neil.

Although Natalie was the one who regularly checked the household drains for blockages (she made sure outside grids were clear of leaves and moss, and was sensible about disposing of cooking fats), and although she took the car to be serviced (where she was able to check confidently that terminals had been cleaned and protected from corrosion with a layer of petroleum jelly or grease), and although she could succinctly explain the offside rule, Brian was old-fashioned enough to believe that there were certain things that were (and always would be) Man's Work. Reading *Which?* magazine to select any sort of gadget was just that, even if the gadget was a set of hair straighteners.

Natalie didn't say that she'd be delighted if Neil's attention reverted back to a normal pastime like making endless cost and performance comparisons between various flat screen TVs but to do so she'd have to persuade him to put down the baby naming book. Instead, she nodded and said, 'Maybe you're right.'

Nina changed the subject. 'Sweetheart, your father and I have been having a big clearout. A spring clean if you like.'

'It's just turned autumn.'

Nina chuckled and shrugged at her own inefficiency. 'Yes, so we'll be in time for Christmas or ahead of the game next year. We have a couple of boxes of your junk that we need you to sort through.'

'You mean the items that I hold dear and have unlimited sentimental value.'

'Yes, if you say so,' smiled Nina indulgently.

Natalie had lived in a series of tatty bedsits and flat shares throughout her twenties. She'd once been victim of a break-in and, more times than she could remember, she'd been a victim of damp so she'd developed a habit of bringing home all her prized possessions for safe keeping. Brian often drily remarked that long after she'd flown the nest she returned to feather it. Her 'prize possessions' included a handful of old CDs that she had now uploaded on to her iPod (but she still couldn't bring herself to let go of the original discs), a number of books she'd read in the mid-nineties (an eclectic mix ranging from Thomas Hardy to Patricia Cornwall with Armistead Maupin in between), a clutch of certificates for swimming lengths and perhaps even her degree certificate (she never could find that) and numerous photo albums, negatives, postcards, letters and other relics of the past.

Natalie and Neil had lived in their grown-up home for over five years now and she was vaguely aware that she owed it to her parents to retrieve the boxes and store the stuff in her own home. But she'd never done as much for two reasons. One, the Chiswick terrace was tight on space and, two, the memorabilia belonged to a different era. A different Natalie. The memories showcased Natalie the teen and twenty-something girl around town. Natalie before she became a wife. Natalie didn't want to obliterate the Athena postcards and yellowing books but she didn't think they fitted in to her stylish home which was full of carefully selected, thoughtful pieces from Habitat and Heals. They were too much about where she came from, not enough about where she was now or where she was going. She'd been happy not to have to deal with the messy boxes but it appeared Nina had decided it was crunch time.

'We're going to take in a lodger. A Chinese student. We responded to an advert that the university placed in the *Surrey Advertiser*.'

'The cash will come in handy,' clarified her father.

'And we miss having young people around the house,' added Nina. 'So you see, we're going to need the cupboard space.'

Natalie nodded. 'OK, OK, I'll go and take a look at the stuff now.'

Natalie pushed open the door to the smallest bedroom of the house which had always been hers. The boys had shared two rooms between the three of them. Their consoles and stinky sports kits had taken up more space than her range of Boots 17 make-up. Natalie's room, while the smallest, was the prettiest. It caught the morning sunlight and was closest to the bathroom and she'd always liked it. When she was a girl the room had been decorated with flowery wallpaper, flowery curtains and flowery bedspread, none of which matched, thus creating the not unpleasant effect of a wild, overgrown country garden. As it was odd for her parents to make any effort with décor, Natalie was surprised to find that they had stripped the wallpaper and painted the walls a neutral magnolia and that the faded, embroidered bedspread had been replaced by a plain green duvet. The room was ready for the new lodger to stamp his or her personality on to it. Natalie didn't mind at all. Generally, she was a very practical woman. She could never understand her friends who insisted their parents keep their childhood rooms as shrines to what once had been. Natalie wasn't interested in that. She looked forward. She took what she needed from her past and kept it with her as she moved forward. This wasn't her room now and it hadn't been for a long time. She knew that in the unlikely event of ever needing to return to this house, the decorative state of the walls would not define home for her. She had a home with Neil. This room belonged to her parents and it was theirs to do with as they pleased. Plus, she supported the idea of an overseas lodger. A lodger would provide them with a new interest.

There were three cardboard boxes set in the middle of the bed. Natalie instantly remembered that one box contained old photos and negatives from a pre-digital age, another was full of her books and the third was marked 'miscellaneous'. She could take the photos out of the albums and reduce the space by seventy-five per cent. In fact, if she scanned the pics on to her Mac she wouldn't have to hold on to many of them at all. The books could all go to a charity shop as in all honesty she rarely reread old books, it had been an indulgence to hang on to them as long as she had. It would be much better if someone else got the benefit. The third box demanded a little more attention.

Natalie sat on the bed and sifted through bundles of letters and birthday cards from friends and relatives, some of whom were still vibrant and a part of her life now, others long gone, not forgotten but not remembered as often as she perhaps should. There was a small box full of cheap fashion earrings. Natalie giggled as she pawed the shocking pink loops and the gaudy gold hoops. Nowadays she only ever wore the diamond studs that Neil had given her for her thirtieth birthday. She unearthed old business cards detailing her more junior positions and she found a hoard of invites to friends' weddings and their children's baptisms. There were loose keys but she had no idea what or where they unlocked any more. She found a small music box that played 'Hey, Jude' that had been given to her by an Italian she had once had a holiday romance with. Then, at the very bottom of the cardboard box, wedged between a tin of prehistoric make-up and some ancient copies of *Just 17* magazine (the reasons she'd kept those were beyond her), Natalie spotted her Little Black Book. She let out an involuntary gasp of excitement.

Natalie had never kept a diary. Too busy living to bother recording or analysing but her Little Black Book had all the potency, secrecy and illicit pleasure that any diary could hold. Nina and Brian had given Nat the small black leather address book as a gift after she'd sat her A levels, just before she'd travelled to Sheffield to start her BA in Geography. Nina had already carefully copied down telephone numbers and addresses of the extended family and close family friends, just in case Nat ever needed to reach any one of them. Nina and Brian told

Nat to fill the address book with the names and addresses of numerous new friends; they teased her, saying that no doubt soon the pages would be full of the names of new boyfriends as well. Nat followed their instructions with gusto for nearly a decade after the original purchase – until she'd met Neil, actually, when fidelity and technology had made the book obsolete.

Natalie couldn't imagine writing down anyone's address in a book now but nor could she imagine her BlackBerry ever creating such an overwhelming sense of sentimentality and joy. Natalie sniffed the book's cover. It smelt of something more than leather. It evoked a feeling of possibility and youth. Suddenly Natalie was awash with memories of intense friendships, silly antics and heated debates with bright and intense women, beautiful and unsuitable men. The leather address book reminded her of occasions when she drank red wine in dingy bedsits and champagne on cold beaches. The book provoked unlimited recollections of sweaty nightclubs, blustery town centres and endless boxes of tissues.

She opened the Little Black Book. The pages were alive with names of friends, dear and distant, fleeting and steadfast, deeply missed, barely recalled. When they'd married, some of her friends had changed their names from the ones that were written in her neat hand and they'd almost all changed their addresses; a few had done so with such frequency she no longer knew where to send Christmas cards. Where was Debbie Hill nowadays? How had they ever lost touch? She had been such a sensational friend. What must she be up to now? Didn't Nikki Davis emigrate to Canada? Not far enough, thought Nat ruefully as she remembered how gossipy the girl had been. Nikki Davis attracted trouble like a magnet attracts iron filings. Nat had hastily made friends with her in her first week at university, when everyone was simply desperate to talk to anyone; then Nat had spent approximately eight years trying to shake the woman off. Nat recalled some of Nikki's catty comments about her dress sense and figure; she had a tongue that could slice paper! Nat quickly turned the page. Ohhh, Chloe Kemp, now she was a sweeter face to recall; what a giggle she used to be! Nat was pretty sure she'd moved to Singapore. Nat had got a postcard from her a few years ago but Chloe hadn't given her address and Nat could never track her down. Perhaps Chloe had unearthed an old address book and acted on a whim by reaching out to Nat, a long lost pal.

Besides the names of her female friends, there were the details of the men friends who once had caused Nat's heart and stomach to sink and flip by turn. Nat had had seven lovers before Neil. She was never quite sure if this was a shockingly huge amount or an embarrassingly meagre total; she'd never compared her score with anyone else, it was simply not the sort of thing she'd ever do. Nat knew that the details of each and every one of her ex-lovers were nestled in these pages; their addresses – email and postal – their telephone numbers and birth dates. She had always been quite scrupulous about recording this sort of thing. So many relationships never limped passed infancy because someone or other lost the scrap of paper where the all-important telephone number had been jotted. Nat was not prepared to take that sort of risk in her emotional life and used to carry her address book with her wherever she went. That's why her friends had fondly christened it her Little Black Book. They'd tease her that it was crammed with hordes of names of men she'd got naked with. Nat had not minded the teasing and happily adopted the saucy rebranding of her address book. Although it wasn't strictly accurate, it was fun. She had smiled enigmatically, rather enjoying the illusion that she might be capable of being casual with her heart like some sort of female Casanova. Of course, there had been other boyfriends, men she'd shared evenings with but not chemistry and men she never even bothered to upgrade from the title 'acquaintance'.

In her own handwriting she saw the names Michael Young, Alan Jones, Richard Clark, Daniel McEwan, Matthew Jackson, the Hunk, aka Gary something or other – had she ever known? Lee Mahony. They all had a place. A point. Michael was her first love. Alan was her starter 'marriage' (not that they were married but they practically lived together at uni and when they left uni they shared a scabby rented flat). Richard was the one that got away. Daniel, the one she ran away from. Matthew, the one she never understood. Gary, her mindless fling. And, finally, Lee, her most passionate encounter.

Natalie read the names. Dusty angels and horny devils fluttered out of the pages. It was amazing. She'd all but forgotten that there was a time in her life when relationships were fleeting, unsettled, scary, exciting and finite. When sex was filthy, fun, flirty, unforgiving and urgent. As she read the names of long lost loves something flickered between her legs. Something that was at once thoughtful and lusty. Private and commonplace.

Natalie was surprised that her reaction to the names in her Little Black Book was so physical. It wasn't as if she was lacking in that department. The sex she had with Neil was great. She always had an orgasm or, at least, she usually did. If she didn't, she'd expediently and politely fake it and Neil would gratefully and politely pretend to believe that she'd had the real thing. Neither of them would ever want to hurt the other's feelings. Their sex was consistent and caring. It was a mature response to, and manifestation of, their deep and devoted love. And sometimes it was just a quickie to get him to stop pestering her and go to sleep. Yes, admittedly, the sex they had was predictable, in the sense that it could be relied upon, but not in the sense that it was staid or dull. They sometimes went away for a weekend and made love three times. Not that such a score was likely if they stayed at home. But even if they stayed at home they varied positions and had sex in different rooms of the house. Actually, thinking about it now, it had been a while since they'd had sex anywhere other than in their bed; they'd done it on the sofa last Valentine's Day. Hmmm. The memory was a good but distant one.

Maybe they had become a little too settled, prematurely middle-aged. It wasn't as though they were exhausted with the demands of childcare like so many of their friends. Natalie made a mental note that they ought to take advantage of their childfree state a little more. Not that they could still expect to be swinging from the chandeliers after so many years but maybe they ought to be shaking it up a little bit. It would be fun to feel some of the old magic again. At the very least if she sent some cheeky photos to his phone he might be temporarily distracted from his campaign to procreate. Or maybe not. Natalie tossed the address book back into the cardboard box and went downstairs. She was starving and she wondered what was for lunch.

10

Natalie stayed with her parents until mid-afternoon and then she returned to Chiswick and squandered the rest of the day mooching around shops that sold unnecessary but pretty things such as photo albums covered in diamanté love hearts, retro ceramic milk jugs and glossy coffee table books about designer shoes. Nat could never justify buying this sort of stuff for herself but she loved to endlessly finger the goodies on offer and would often purchase something as a gift for someone else. Today Nat bought an over-the-top floral shower cap for Neil's sister, Ashleigh. They had developed a habit of sending one another daft gifts through the post for no other reason than the fun of writing a note that read, 'I saw this and thought of you.' Then she bought Neil a pair of Paul Smith cufflinks which had cartoon pictures of buxom women on them. He rarely wore shirts, a fact that Nat was aware of even as she handed over her debit card. She had been buying him a lot of tiny gifts recently. Bars of expensive organic chocolate, decent bottles of wine; she bought him a new sports bag last week and a pair of trainers the week before. Part of her – a deeply buried, difficult-to-examine part of her – felt disgustingly guilty that she wouldn't give him what she knew he wanted most and so she'd got into the habit of buying little gifts instead. She knew it was hopeless. How could a chocolate bar compensate?

When she arrived home, Nat was surprised to find Neil surrounded by bags of groceries and bending over a cookbook. Her heart sank as she remembered the last time he cooked for her. Was he about to relaunch the 'can we have a baby' convo? She really couldn't face it. It had been a busy week and what she'd been hoping for tonight was the two of them cuddling up in front of *The X Factor*, guzzling wine and eating crisps, hardly bothering with conversation beyond a grunted, half-hearted preference for one act above the other. The sort of warm, effortless night they'd enjoyed together forever – or had up until this last month at least. Recently, the time they spent together was spiked with a sense of mutual criticism and confusion. Nat longed for a rest from the unvoiced but palatable hostilities. In fact, she longed for them to stop altogether. But she was at a loss as to how to make things better.

Besides, frankly, since she'd discovered the Little Black Book she'd been feeling a tiny bit horny so she'd upgraded her perfect Saturday night in from grunting at the TV to grunting over something a little more physical. It would be amazing to reconnect on at least that level but the chances of them making love would be drastically reduced if he started on again about having a baby.

'What's all this?' asked Natalie, as she put down the cardboard box full of photos on the table and pecked Neil on the cheek.

He pulled her into a huge hug. 'We're having a dinner party.'

'What? When?' Nat tried to keep the disappointment out of her voice.

'Now. Well, in an hour and a half, to be exact,' he said as he checked his watch and then turned back to the cookery book.

'But why?' asked Nat, stunned.

'Why not?' Neil replied with a beam. Natalie and Neil never threw dinner parties. They were occasionally invited to them but whenever they had to return the hospitality they preferred to take their friends to a restaurant and foot the bill. 'I thought it would be fun,' added Neil.

Natalie wondered if he'd been body-snatched. Couldn't he remember that while neither of them were particularly diabolical cooks nor were they spectacular? They had both often agreed that devoting a whole day and evening to shopping, chopping, cooking, serving and clearing dinner was not a good use of time. Especially since the actual amount of conversation you could have at your own dinner party was inversely proportional to how successful the prepared dish was likely to be. She didn't think it was fair that he kept changing his mind about things they'd decided on.

Neil continued, 'Don't worry, I have everything under control. I thought we'd kick off with a meze-style, no-cooking-required starter. Cured meats and salami, with pickled artichoke hearts and black olives served with some top-notch bread and unsalted butter. I picked it all up at the deli.'

'Right.' Maybe not body-snatched per se, maybe he'd undergone a Stepford Wife transformation.

'And then I've opted for fish pie. It's already prepared. I'm going to serve it with pink fir apple potatoes and crimson chard. I picked up the spuds and herbs from the farmers' market after footie. What do you think?'

Natalie didn't know what she thought. She wasn't sure what crimson chard was. He'd been food shopping rather than sitting in the pub with Karl and Tim, that couldn't be right.

'Aren't you full of surprises,' she muttered. She knew sugar was good for shock so she reached for the bitter chocolate that was already broken into squares and sat in a small bowl. In fact Neil was surrounded by small bowls full of oil, sugar, chopped fruit and herbs. Men thought that these bowls were obligatory to the cooking process, it was clear he wasn't planning on doing the washing up. Neil swiped at her hand.

'Get off. That's for the fondue we're having for pudding. You'll have to wait,' he instructed cheerfully. Neil had mistaken Natalie's shock for pleasant surprise and was clearly relishing the effect of his industry. He thought he'd impressed her; actually she was terrified by this changeling. Where was the Neil she knew and could predict?

'Who's coming?' she asked.

'Tim and Ali and Mick and Karen.'

'Not Karl and Jen?'

'No.'

'Were they busy?'

'Don't know, I didn't ask them. I asked Mick and Karen instead. Eight won't fit round the table and we owe Mick and Karen.'

'Do we?'

'Yes, we went round there twice before the twins were born. Had you forgotten?'

Natalie had not forgotten but since the twins had been born she'd found Mick and Karen's company less enticing than she used to. For three years the two couples had lived as nextdoor neighbours but Karen and Mick had moved out of the street once they'd decided to start a family. They'd moved to the suburbs as they'd argued that the Chiswick terrace was too cramped to accommodate more than a couple. Now they had four bedrooms and a garden but Nat couldn't help thinking that what they'd gained in space, they'd sacrificed in soul. There were no shops, or cafés, or parks or galleries anywhere near Karen and Mick's new home. Karen frequently pointed out that the commute to central London was only forty-five minutes on the overground, but in her more mischievous moments Nat couldn't help but imagine there were a fair few delays on the journey home as people flung themselves on to the tracks at the thought of where they were heading. Besides, Nat didn't agree that the terrace was too small for a family, there were two bedrooms. Karen and Mick could have managed in the short term and still had the comfort and support of living near their many friends in the tricky, early months of parenthood.

Nat was pretty sure the new parents did need support. Having twins, no matter how adorable they were to dress up, couldn't be easy to handle. But it was hard to give support when Karen was weepy and nervous one moment, condescending and brash the next. Mick was no better; he now limited his conversation to a rather patronising patter which ran along a single theme, his unique brilliance as a dad. He'd opted to be a stay-at-home dad, 'allowing' Karen the 'freedom' to return to her career as a solicitor. Undoubtedly, he did know a thing or two about child rearing but Natalie found it wearing that not only did he insist on turning every second of Lily and Milo's young lives into 'a meaningful moment of discovery' but he also insisted on detailing those moments in real time to his friends. The twins were stunners, Nat could see that and it was natural that the parents' pride was off the scale, so she'd been reasonably patient when the twins were tiny and Mick had called her at work to say that Milo had taken a swipe at a dangling toy or that Lily could push down on her legs when her feet were placed on a firm surface. But the babies were over a year old now and while it was lovely that they could both gurgle nonsensically and walk around the furniture, Natalie didn't think this news necessitated an email. Frankly, she'd lost any crumb of interest when they'd hit the stage of being able to extend arms or legs to help when being dressed.

Neil and Natalie had agreed that as regrettable as it was to see yet more mates go over to the dark side, Karen and Mick were now officially very, very boring. They'd promised to look them up again in eight or nine years' time, not before. What could Neil be thinking of?

Babies. That's what.

Natalie doubted that the guests for this evening's get-together were a random selection. She recognised them for what they were – part of Neil's campaign. Tim and Ali were desperately trying for babies and Mick and Karen never spoke about anything other than the twins; Neil might as well have invited the local branch of the National Childbirth Trust. Too angry to speak, she returned to the car, fetched the other boxes full of memorabilia and went upstairs to run a bath, pausing just long enough to pour and drink a large G&T. She was going to need it.

11

Natalie felt as though she was sitting an A level without having done any revision. She fought the feeling of dread and tried to enter into the spirit of the dinner party. If she could keep everyone off the subject of babies she was sure to have a great time. After all, these were their friends and she clearly remembered the heavenly days when they still talked about films, books, gigs and even politics. She wanted to believe they still all had interests in common but sometimes it felt as though everyone else was speaking a different language, perhaps while swimming underwater and wearing a mouth guard; certainly she struggled with communicating with them right now. She prayed the evening would be relaxing. Neil had made such an effort; despite having no practice, he'd cooked what looked like a delicious dinner, he'd splashed out on the vino and he'd bought flowers for the table. What was not to love?

Tim and Ali arrived first. Tim practically knocked Natalie over as he shoved past her in the hall.

'I've brought a bottle. Ali says I can have a drink tonight,' he yelled from the kitchen, where he was already rattling around a drawer looking for a bottle opener.

'Come in, can I take your coat?' joked Natalie. Tim had perhaps been a little lacking in common courtesy but she was relieved to hear he was drinking, maybe that meant they were being less regimented about their approach to impregnation and there would be altogether less talk about babies. Nat hoped so.

Alison leant into Natalie and gave her a hug in greeting. She grinned and gushed, 'We've already done it today, so the pressure is off. That's four times in three days in total. He's done his duty. He's off the hook for another month now. Maybe for longer if we get lucky. I have a really good feeling about this month.'

Or maybe not.

Tim was drinking but Ali wasn't because of her 'good feeling'. She said that she thought that last night's session, 'although efficient rather than leg-shaking', had been successful. On hearing this, Natalie accepted the very large glass of wine Tim was proffering and, like him, she quickly knocked it back in an effort to subdue the feeling Ali's shared intimacy had created in her, which was one of nausea. Ali and Tim were good friends but Natalie really didn't want to think about them at it. It was just one step away from being reminded that your parents had a sex life. Neil emerged from the kitchen and started enthusiastically quizzing Ali as to exactly what she was eating to increase her chances of conceiving. Was there anything she should avoid in case her *feeling* proved founded? He'd already taken the precaution of taking the prawns out from the fish pie, he added solicitously and somewhat smugly.

'She's not even pregnant yet,' muttered Tim. He looked pale and drawn. You could almost see the thumbprint on his forehead; it was where his hair used to be. Natalie shuddered.

'I might be,' said Ali in a sing-song voice. 'Tim's been a slave to the natural food diet that focuses on fresh vegetables, fruits, whole grains, fish, poultry, legumes, nuts, and seeds. He's utterly eliminated processed and refined foods, junk food and sugars.'

This was indeed true, except on Friday lunchtime when Tim nipped out of the office and bought a double Mac cheeseburger and fries.

'He's hardly touched a drop of alcohol or caffeine for weeks now and he's been snacking on pumpkin seeds, as they are naturally high in zinc and essential fatty acids which are vital to healthy functioning of the male reproductive system. All of this is likely to shake up his sluggish spermatozoa,' added Ali with a grin.

Nat put down the bowl of crisps she was about to proffer. She didn't know what to say. Ali was clearly ensconced in her own little selfish world and she was oblivious to the fact that she was making Natalie feel uncomfortable and Tim feel exposed. Nat was pretty sure that if ever Ali and Tim were successful in trying for a baby, Tim was the sort of man who would prefer to wait in the hospital corridor or, better yet, the pub until the messy bit was over and the cigars were passed around. Natalie tried to catch Tim's eye. She wanted to share a conspiratorial grimace as Ali started to detail, once again, the issues behind a slow or low sperm count. He kept his head down.

'If the cold showers and healthy diet don't work then it's IVF for us.' Ali was trying to sound cheerful but she sounded terrifying and terrified.

The doorbell rang and Nat ran to it, surprised at her own enthusiasm at seeing Karen and Mick. At least they would not want to talk about conception. Natalie flung open the door and then tried very hard to keep her smile pinned to her face, there was a serious danger of it sliding to the ground for her to slip on. Karen was carrying a baby in a car seat and so was Mick.

'We couldn't get a sitter at such short notice. Neil said it was no problem bringing them.'

'Erm, no, no, none at all,' Nat managed to mutter, before ushering them into the hall and closing the door on the cool night.

'Where shall we put them?'

'Erm, upstairs.' Nat managed not to add, 'Out of the way.'

She glanced at Milo and Lily as they were whisked past. She had to admit they were cute-looking, especially when asleep, but their presence was unlikely to restrict the baby conversation. The opposite. Ali had already nearly torn a ligament in her haste to follow the twins upstairs, 'just for a peek.'

'Don't worry,' said Neil who had sneaked up behind Natalie. He rubbed his hands up and down her bare arms and she felt her body erupt into goosebumps. How was it possible that she could fancy him while being livid with him?

'The babies won't be an inconvenience tonight. I remember I once got a text from Mick saying that they were both sleeping through nights.'

Neil kissed her neck and she could feel his smile. Despite the fact that he was cooking a three-course meal for six people, was in charge of wine and the music selection, *and* his team had lost three nil this morning, he looked remarkably serene. At peace. They pulled apart and he beamed at her. The crinkles around his eyes were speaking to her. 'Isn't this cosy?' they seemed to ask. 'Look, babies don't have to cramp your social life! Even with twins you can still see your friends and go out for dinner.'

Bastard, her glare replied.

It took a while for everyone to sit down. Mick wasn't happy with putting the kids in Natalie and Neil's room because their cat was asleep on the bed and cats were notorious baby murderers. Natalie reluctantly offered to kick the cat out for the night. She wasn't keen to do so, she always worried when Kitty roamed the busy London streets. Luckily she didn't have to follow through on her offer as Mick said that he thought Lily had a slight allergy to cat hair and so it would probably be best to find the room that the cat visited least often.

'That would be the bathroom,' Natalie deadpanned.

Neil led Mick into the spare bedroom which didn't actually have a bed in it. It had a desk (so Natalie could work from home whenever the need arose), a basket with a pile of ironing that looked scarily like the leaning tower of Pisa, and now the three boxes that Natalie had brought back from her parents. After Mick erected a makeshift black-out curtain, Natalie moved the boxes again and Neil cranked up the heating. At last the room was considered baby appropriate. They squeezed in the travel cot (scraping it down a wall) and then laid the babies side by side. Natalie was just beginning to enjoy a feeling of satisfaction and relief when Milo rolled over in his sleep, bashing into Lily who let out a blood-curdling scream.

Karen managed to get to the table by 8.45p.m. She came down the stairs waving two little parcels of crap which she put in the kitchen bin. Natalie leapt up from the table and hauled the black bin bag to the outside bin. She made a mental note to carry the contents of the cat's litter tray to Karen's house next time she visited; she could put it in their wastepaper basket perhaps.

Mick and Karen acted like jack-in-the-boxes all night, constantly running up and down stairs to check on the babies. Natalie didn't get it. It was unlikely either child would light a spliff or shimmy down the drainpipe to dash over to King's Cross for an all-night rave in a warehouse, no matter how above average their cognitive development was.

Natalie valiantly tried to stay on plan. If she could steer the conversation away from babies, she was sure she could have a decent evening.

'What did you get up to today?' she asked the table.

'Baby massage class,' replied Mick promptly.

'Really, how fascinating. What does that involve? Tell me all about it,' gushed Ali, instantly dropping her hand to her uber flat stomach. She wasn't even taking the piss.

Natalie couldn't allow that line of chat to develop. She cut in. 'Neil played football, then mooched around the farmers' market.' She was trying subtly to point out the benefits of a childfree day to Neil.

'The farmers' market at Belmont Primary School?' asked Karen.

Oh crap, Natalie hadn't seen that coming. There was only one way this conversation could lead now.

Predictably, Neil asked, 'Have you put the twins' names down for any schools yet? I understand it's always a struggle.'

'I visited my parents,' added Natalie, determined to stay on track.

'Do any of your siblings have kids?' asked Mick.

'They're still kids themselves.'

'Does your mum ever hint she wants to be a granny?' asked Ali.

'Never!'

'Mine is knitting.'

'They made me clear out a whole load of junk. Boxes full of old books and letters. Gosh, just picking through that sort of stuff brings back so many memories,' Natalie persisted.

'I had exactly the same experience when I was nesting. I had to throw out box after box of tat,' said Karen. Bloody hell! Was there any subject that didn't somehow circle back to babies? Then, when Nat thought there was no hope, Karen looked momentarily dreamy and added, 'I'd kept cinema stubs and boxes of matches from various bars.'

'Where you had hot, meaningless encounters,' laughed Mick, winking at her.

'Exactly,' beamed Karen. And for an instant Natalie saw what she'd been looking for all night. She saw Karen. Karen, tall and triumphant, giggly and carefree, wearing fashion brands not baby spit.

'The Met Bar?'

'On Brewers. I remember!'

'Do you remember the Globe Club?'

'God, yes!'

'And the Atlantic.'

'The nights we had there.'

For a moment the table erupted into wide beams and dizzy laughter. They all remembered sweaty, often drunken encounters. Different ones, separate ones but all the same in a way, all bursting with possibility and challenge, all confirming their youth and invincibility. But then, in an instant, the bonhomie was sloshed away as quickly as it arrived and Mick said, 'Still, I wouldn't go back.'

'No, never swap that for what we have now,' agreed Karen vehemently.

'Done all that,' added Ali.

'Finished with,' muttered Tim.

'You have to move on,' threw in Neil. He turned to Natalie and looked right at her, almost boring a hole through her. Natalie glared back and reached for the wine. Who were they trying to convince? Themselves? Her? Well, she wasn't convinced. Ali turned to Karen and asked where she bought her maternity clothes from. Mick was explaining to Tim the importance of introducing babies to music while they were still in the womb. Why, were the twins going to take grade 4 violin next week? wondered Natalie. Or perhaps the harp? Natalie felt she had only one option. She was going to get wasted and hope that tomorrow, when she woke up, she'd discover this entire evening had been a bad dream.

She grabbed bits of salami with her fingers and crammed them into her mouth, swallowing without chewing or tasting. She slugged down the best part of a bottle of wine before the fish pie was placed in front of her and by then had lost all interest in the food, preferring to stick to liquids that didn't require any digestion. The drunker she got, the harder she warred with the urge to tell them all that they were boring, blinkered and desperate. That she thought it was pathetic that they were abandoning their own lives and living through their kids, kids that in Ali and Tim's case weren't even conceived yet! In Neil's case, never would be.

It was a good thing the doorbell rang at 10.30p.m.

'I'll go,' said Natalie carefully, over-pronouncing the words in an effort not to slur. She opened the door and was whipped by a surprisingly chilly blast of autumn night air; summer seemed well and truly behind them.

'Jen?' Natalie knew it was her friend but her unexpected presence and her obviously distraught state meant her greeting was more of a question than a welcome.

'God, sorry, Natalie, I didn't think you'd have company,' said Jen as she heard gentle laughter and supportive murmurs coming from the front room. Nat imagined someone must have made an incredibly original comment such as they loved the smell of newborns' heads.

'It's not company. It's Ali and Tim and Mick and Karen. Come in, what's wrong?'

'I think Karl is seeing someone else.' With this, Jen burst into a tsunami of tears and so Natalie ushered her into the hallway.

'Come and have a drink.'

On seeing Jen's distress, Karen and Mick immediately made their excuses and said it was late, they had to head home; after all, they would be woken at 6a.m. the next day by the twins. Natalie wanted to believe that they were being tactful and solicitous but she couldn't help but surmise that they just didn't give a toss. True, they didn't know either Jen or Karl as well as Ali and Tim did, but Natalie couldn't imagine ever getting to the point where a tale about break-up or infidelity (whatever it might turn out to be in Jen's case) was no longer compelling enough to justify a late night. How dreary.

As soon as Jen repeated her suspicions to the gang, Neil and Tim said that they would do the washing up and vanished like rabbits up a hole. If Jen had been a more distrustful type, or even a more alert type, she might have interpreted their actions for what they were – proof positive that Karl was playing away and that Neil and Tim were privy to the fact. Instead she wailed, 'Seeeeee. There are some nice, thoughtful, decent men out there! Men who marry you and do the washing up too. Why can't Karl be more like that?'

Nat and Alison didn't reply but quickly established the facts of the night's drama. Jen had been at Karl's house that evening, doing his ironing, when the phone rang. Because she didn't officially live with Karl she didn't pick up, but let it go through to the answer machine. The caller was a woman, who was clearly in a bar and a bit tipsy. The woman had said, 'Where are you, baby? You're late. Oh, there you are! I can see you. You are sooooo handsome. Bye. I mean hi.' And then she laughed a lot, there were kissing sounds and she hung up.

'Oh. My. God,' said Ali.

'You do his ironing but you daren't answer his telephone,' commented Natalie.

'Do you think he's having an affair?' asked Jen.

Nat and Ali both thought that Karl probably had numerous affairs, or flings or dalliances. Call them what you will, they amounted to the same thing. Betrayal. They'd thought this before Jen had told them about the tipsy woman's telephone call. The issue was, could they tell their friend the truth? Would she want to hear it? *Really* hear it? Was it their place or even their responsibility? It was difficult to know for sure. It might be that Jen had come to them hoping that they'd offer a reasonable explanation to the phone call, other than the obvious one. It might be that she knew he was having an affair, knew it better than they did, but didn't want to believe it or have it confirmed.

'Did you call 1471 and make a note of the number?' Ali asked. Clearly she was buying time, making up her mind about what a judicious response might be.

'Withheld.'

'Oh.'

'Have you called Karl?' asked Nat.

'His phone's switched off.'

'Where is he supposed to be tonight?'

'Out having drinks with a big gang of uni friends.'

'She might be a university friend,' offered Ali half-heartedly.

'Maybe. But why would she call him handsome?'

'A term of endearment between friends?'

'It sounded more than that.'

It sounded like treachery, duplicity, disloyalty. The girls all reached for their glasses and gulped back the wine which slipped too easily down their throats. Nat poured refills. Jen began to cry again. Big, fat, silent tears slipped down her face and splashed on to her lap. Ali and Nat shared desperate glances above her head.

'Why didn't you go with him to meet his uni friends?' asked Natalie gently.

'He said I'd be bored.' Yes, she'd definitely have much more fun staying in doing his ironing, not. 'I want him so much, you see. All I think about is our wedding day. I know I shouldn't, since we're not even engaged or anything, but I can't help myself.' Jen started to sob again. 'It's all I want. He's the one I want. He's my One.'

'Really? You're sure?' Natalie doubted it. How could feckless, hopeless, faithless Karl genuinely be lovely, sweet, trusting Jen's *One*? Besides, she was pretty sure she remembered Jen saying exactly the same thing about Christopher Shaw, her ex. Nat didn't really understand Jen's obsession with getting married. It wasn't like marriage magically solved everything. Did she think that being married to Karl would defini-tively pin him down? Nat doubted it. She feared that Karl would continue to go to 'reunions' with his 'uni friends' even after he'd said his vows.

Bloody hell, Natalie wished she'd never introduced Jen to Karl. She hadn't been actively matchmaking, she'd just happened to have a spare ticket for the Scottie Taylor comeback gig at Wembley Stadium and she'd offered it to Karl on the off chance. Now she wished she'd just taken a hit on the fifty quid. But how could she have guessed that Jen would be taken in by Karl's obvious charm? Yes, of course she'd seen countless other women fall for his wily ways, but she'd thought her own pal would be as impervious as she herself was. She thought they'd all have a laugh and that Jen would roll her eyes in exaspera-tion when Karl recounted tales of his womanising days or tried to hit on someone else in the crowd. But Jen had found him unutterably sexy. Compelling. Compulsive. It had been quite embarrassing, actu-ally. Jen and Karl had practically had sex in the car on the journey home and probably would have done if Neil hadn't kept coughing so hard that he gave the impression he was coming down with bubonic plague.

'You are so lovely, Jen. You have choices,' Nat gently reminded her friend.

'Well, of course. I know that. There's always a choice. But I don't want any other man. Karl's the one for me.' Nat wondered whether Jen was simply terrified about starting over once again. She often talked about how she'd invested years in Christopher to no avail (by which she meant he hadn't offered up an engagement ring) and she wasn't going to make the same mistake again. 'You know when you know,' she said with blind determination.

'Do you?'

'Yes. Like you knew with Neil.'

'Right.'

Jen froze and stared at Natalie. 'And you did know, didn't you?'

'Yes.' Nat wasn't sure how this conversation was helping. She should try to get back to the point. The tipsy floozy calling Karl's home was the point. Of course Nat knew Neil was her One.

'How? How did you know?' pursued Jen, who seemed to think this was the point.

'He was kind and decent.' And of course there's his fantastic, never-before-heard-the-like laugh, thought Nat but she didn't say so; that was private, hers alone to enjoy.

'What else?' demanded Jen.

'And . . . well . . . it's difficult to explain.' Nat wondered how she could articulate falling in love with Neil. Loving Neil. Where to start? It was so intense and certain and yet so easy and ephemeral. She took a deep breath and gave it a go. 'I was attracted to the things about him that were so different from me. You know, his careless, fearless approach to life but, at the same time, I was reassured by the fact that when it came to the big things, like loyalty and values and our goals, we had so much in common.'

'Had?'

'Have,' Natalie said firmly, although she felt a little woolly on this point, right now. No doubt because she'd drunk too much red wine and was fed up with the incessant baby talk, but at this exact moment in time she was aware that their goals were no longer in line. Neil wanted a baby.

'For me it was timing,' said Alison. She spoke quietly, glancing across to the kitchen door because she didn't want Tim to hear her. 'I love Tim, I really do, but I believe you can be happy with a number of people. One just happens to come along when you're in the settling-down frame of mind, and if they're in the settling-down frame of mind too then it happens. All the other near misses and lost opportunities aren't great tragedies, they're simply about poor timing.'

Jen and Natalie stared at Ali, dumbfounded. Nat was unable to process whether she was shocked by her friend's cool, calm and collected revelation, or impressed. She had never considered her relationship with Neil in this composed and detached way that Ali was suggesting. She had always been passionately certain that she was with Neil because he was her One. They matched. They fitted. They were in love. But what if Ali was right? Was it possible that she could have ended up with any number of men, providing she'd had enough in common with them to convince her they fitted in some sort of mystical, important way? Oh God. A more traumatic thought punched Nat with such force that she was sure she was actually spinning; she gripped the arm of the chair as though she might steady herself. What if Neil could have ended up with someone else? What if he *should* have? Should Neil be living in another postal address, with a pretty brunette and a dozen bouncy babies? Was she Neil's One? Was he hers? The question was so overwhelming that Nat fought a physical reaction. Her nose felt scratchy with threatened tears, the hairs on the back of her neck bristled in protest and her stomach defied gravity and leapt into her mouth. Luckily, Jen started to sob again and Nat was grateful to be yanked out of her stunned and appalled state. She pushed the devastating thought to the very back of her mind, a trick that she specialised in, and forced herself to once again listen to the conversation.

'Why doesn't he love me? Aren't I lovable? What's wrong with me?' Jen's entire body heaved so Nat pulled her into a hug. Jen's desperation was pitiful and Nat wished she could come up with a plausible explanation for the phone call. Jen was not a girl who wanted to hear the truth tonight; that much was clear.

'Did this woman actually say his name?' asked Alison.

Jen stopped howling for a moment and considered. 'No,' she replied cautiously.

'There you go! It might be a wrong number!' said Ali enthusiastically.

Nat thought Ali was a genius. Nat was saved from the nightmare of gently but firmly suggesting to Jen that she needed to see Karl for the worthless, two-timing git he really was and that she needed to see the blood on the wall and move on, but now the issue was averted. At least for tonight. Natalie and Alison were relieved. Jen was delighted.

'I never considered that!'

Why would you? wondered Natalie wearily. Still, it was late. Everyone was feeling emotionally battered, she wasn't making much sense to herself about her own relationship, how could she possibly comment on anyone else's? This wasn't the moment to point out that the reason Jen hadn't thought of that excuse was because it was clearly spurious, bordering on stupid. Of course this mystery woman hadn't called a wrong number. Of course she wasn't a university friend. Of course Karl wasn't meeting 'a big gang of people'. Right this moment he was probably being sucked off in an alleyway or something equally grubby.

'Is it safe to come back in?' asked Neil, as he popped his head around the doorway. 'We have chocolate.'

'In that case, yes,' replied the women.

12

Neil undressed and carefully put his clothes in the wash basket. He wanted sex tonight and he thought that being tidy might increase his chances and so he was disappointed when he noticed that Natalie had left her clothes in a heap on the floor. This was not a good sign; she only ever did that if she was extremely tired. If she was extremely tired there was little chance of them having sex tonight, even if it was Saturday *and* he had cooked *and* washed up. Neil followed Nat through to the bathroom. She was wearing a pair of pyjamas. Definitely far too weary to have sex tonight then. That was the code. Pyjamas equalled 'not a chance'.

It was true Nat was quite drunk and her stomach full, which was not compatible with shagging, but also her head was full too which made things worse.

'How did you know I was the one for you?' Nat asked as she brushed her teeth.

Neil found this question difficult to understand, not only because they both used noisy electric toothbrushes but also because Neil had no idea why she would ask this question or where it might be going, although he had a terrible feeling it was definitely 'going' somewhere.

'You told me,' he replied.

'Ha, ha,' she said without mirth. 'Was it timing? Did I just come along at the right time when you were in the settling-down mood?'

'No.' Neil spat and rinsed then turned to his wife. 'Totally honestly, when I first set eyes on you, settling down was the last thing on my mind.' He'd been thinking about getting it up, actually.

Neil went back into the bedroom and dived under the covers. Brrrr, it was cold. He lay flat on his back and spread out his limbs, he opened and closed his legs, moved his arms up and down, making the same action that created an angel print in fresh snow. He always warmed the bed for Nat if he could because she was one of those people who really felt the cold; her feet were usually like two massive ice blocks.

'Alison thinks it's all about timing. That you could love any number of partners and you just settle down with whoever comes along at the right moment,' said Nat when she finally emerged from the bathroom.

She always spent much longer in there than Neil did, as she had more lotions and potions to wade through. Neil wondered whether it was possible that Nat had discovered plastic bottles with the ability to procreate; every time he looked, they'd multiplied. He'd once had a sneaky count up of the number of bottles which had found a home on the bathroom window sill. He counted forty-seven including anti-age concentrates for the eyes, antioxidant serums for the bust, antibacterial facial cleansers, a skin strengthening complex for the jaw and a skin tightening complex for the stomach. There was also an assortment of other pots that promised to rejuvenate, retexture and revitalise generally. He had three bottles in the bathroom cabinet: shampoo, shaving cream and deodorant. He found that covered his needs. Natalie seemed to be fighting a war with all her strengthening and recovering and complexes and anti-thingies. It was terrifying. Besides, Neil worried that Nat was so well moisturised that if he grabbed her too quickly or forcefully she'd slip through his fingers. *Pop*, straight up in the air she'd go, the way it sometimes happened when you were holding a bar of soap in the shower.

'Ali's not very romantic,' muttered Neil as he buried his face into Nat's neck. He loved the feel of her ear and cheek pushed against his nose and mouth (he never made the connection between that silky soft feeling and the numerous bottles in the bathroom, although Nat did).

'True, but look at Jen, she's uber romantic and things aren't turning out that brilliantly for her, are they?'

'Has she tumbled Karl?'

Natalie stiffened and turned to her husband. 'She has her suspicions. What do you know? *Is* he shagging someone else? Do you know that for definite? Does he confide in you?'

'Oh, you know blokes,' Neil said vaguely. He hoped that this answer would be interpreted as, 'Oh, you know blokes, we don't talk about stuff the way you girls do.' In fact Neil meant, 'Oh, you know blokes, they will get it where they can, at least Karl's sort will.'

Luckily for Neil, Nat was far too distracted with her own concerns to really want to pursue Jen's issue with any tenacity.

'I thought you were my One because we matched. We fitted. Right?'

'Yup, that's love,' murmured Neil, without giving it too much thought. Why did women need to talk about this stuff? His love for Nat was a given. Her love for him was a given. What more was there to say?

'But Ali's point is that love alone isn't what a marriage is about. We've all been in love more than once. What distinguishes the ones that didn't work from the One that did?' Nat began to feel panic swell in her stomach once again. She didn't want to pursue this line of thought but couldn't ignore it. Now the idea had been mooted, it crawled around her head like an insidious infection. 'It has to be something extra. Like agreeing about shared goals and values, don't you think?' Nat asked anxiously.

'Dunno,' muttered Neil, as he gently resumed kissing Nat's neck. She had a small mole just under her chin, not much bigger than a freckle really. He adored it.

'Remember, we agreed on the small stuff to start with, like which movies to watch, how often we should go out, where we should go, and then we found we agreed on the big stuff too. Hey?' Nat turned to Neil for reassurance. Neil was now repeatedly kissing her shoulder.

He'd managed to edge the neck of her pyjamas to one side so her flesh was exposed.

'Absolutely,' he mumbled. He wasn't listening. The kisses were soft and gentle and had his entire focus but they were beginning to irritate Nat as she wanted to talk.

The problem was they no longer agreed on the biggest issue of all. What did that mean? Nat wanted to hear Neil say that they had other things that glued them together – enough other things – so she pushed on.

'*Do* you think we have a lot in common?' she demanded, pulling away from him and yanking her PJs back over her shoulder.

'The things we have in common are not insubstantial,' replied Neil carefully. 'We both believe in global warming and are conscientious about recycling.'

He wasn't sure why this thought had popped into his head first. Probably because he'd just taken out the empty bottles and put them in the green bins at the end of the street. God, they'd knocked some back tonight. Ali hadn't even been drinking and Karen only had one glass but they'd thrown out six empty wine bottles, and that wasn't taking into account the vodkas they kicked off with and the whisky they finished off with. Tim had drunk like a condemned man. Neil glanced at Nat, who was staring at him, emitting anxious vibes. She was often tetchy and unpredictable after she'd drunk red wine, although it was more than his life was worth to say as much.

Perhaps he'd have been better telling Nat that he thought they'd ended up married to one another because they loved one another a fucking huge amount. They were soul mates. He could have said that she was his right to his left, he sometimes ached he missed her so much when she went away on work trips, and that occasionally (and this one really was soft) he even thought that perhaps he'd known her before they'd met, in another life or something, maybe. Crap and ditsy as that sounded. It was just that she fitted. Absolutely one hundred per cent. Perhaps he should have said that he didn't believe you could quantify exactly why you chose to be with someone for the rest of your life but that you knew when you knew and that was that. And maybe he should have said that he also thought that once you'd made that commitment you had to stand by it. Thick and thin, good and bad, sickness and health. That was the deal.

Instead he said, 'Mind you, it's always me who goes to the recycle banks to place the cardboard, glass and plastics diligently in the proper place, while you're the one that's most likely to put on an extra jumper rather than turn up the heating. You're a tight bugger.'

'And that's it for you, is it?' asked Nat, exasperated. 'That's why we're married because we more or less agree on environmental issues?'

'No, of course not. I'm just saying—'

'What else?'

'What do you mean?'

'What else do we have in common?'

'We both still dream of being obscenely rich. We both doubt this will ever happen. We both adore smelly cheese. We both love watching reality TV, even if it does glamorise the scourge of society, and we both hate Marmite.' Neil paused but Nat was still staring at him expectantly. 'Neither of us has ever been to an opera. Neither of us wants to. Our favourite city is New York. We'd both like to visit Tokyo one day.'

'And?'

'And sex. We both like sex, especially in the missionary position, if we're honest.'

'Neil, be serious.'

'I *am* being.' After a moment he added, 'OK then.' With a sigh, Neil sat up in bed and on his fingers he counted off the things that bound them together. 'We like each other's friends and families. We both vote the same way. We would never cheat on an insurance claim or avoid paying our taxes which, I think, makes us fundamentally honest people. We always honour the first invite we've accepted, even if something better comes along. We both hate litter, lateness and lying. We both want to grow old together. We love each other.'

But people could fall out of love. People could stop loving each other. 'And what about the stuff we don't have in common?' asked Nat, turning to Neil. She had a lump in her throat; it was the mass of inconvenient questions which she couldn't swallow, as much as she might like to after that wonderful speech.

'I don't fancy James McAvoy and you do and I will never understand why you use so many cosmetics. You don't need that crap. You're beautiful,' he added.

Nat smiled at Neil. It was her best smile. The slow starting type that became wide and dazzling. Neil lay back down again and she tucked her head under his arm. He pulled her close to him.

'You think that's OK, do you? Enough for us?' she asked. Nat wanted him to say yes it was OK, everything was OK. They could carry on just as they were, happy in their Marmite- and child-free existence.

'For now,' answered Neil truthfully. Had she forgotten? Neither of them liked lies.

'For now?'

There was a silence and then Neil said, 'You're nearly thirty-four, Nat.'

'I know.' It was a fact that recently Neil had repeatedly reminded her of. She wished that meant he was planning a big birthday bash but she didn't think so. 'So what?'

'Have you any idea what that means to a woman?'

Natalie knew exactly what that meant to a woman. That's why she had forty-seven bottles of hope on her bathroom window sill.

'I'm going to get bat wings?' she said jokily. Now, irrationally, she was trying to avoid the topic that she had pursued since they came to bed. She knew this was what they needed to talk about but she wished the issue had never raised its ugly head.

'There's a time limit on these things, Nat.'

'No, you're not up against a timeline,' Natalie spat like fat in a pan. She scrambled around her mind for the facts she'd Googled just yesterday. 'Rupert Murdoch became a father at seventy-two. Charlie Chaplin was seventy-three.' Even as Nat relayed these statistics she knew this wasn't the heart of the matter and she wasn't surprised that Neil stared at her as though she was insane.

'I get it, Natalie, and I'm dead chuffed for Daniel Quinn who sired a kid at eighty-one, was it? But frankly I'm not sure exactly how that relates to me because I want a baby with *you* and so there *is* a time limit on it – yours.'

Nat sighed and sat up, pulling away from him. The sorrow and distress sat stalemate between them. Neil could feel it, taste it and hear it in the silence. It climbed into his head, mouth and ears.

'I'm not saying we have to have a baby right now but I don't want us to leave it too late.'

'We can't leave it too late because I don't want one, *ever*. Late is only applicable if you are assuming the event is ever going to happen.'

Neil still hoped that she might change her mind. She was bound to, wasn't she? You read it all the time in the *Mail*. There were armies of women who never wanted babies, wanted big careers instead and then when they hit their forties, *whack*, out of the blue it struck them. But it wasn't so easy then. Sometimes it didn't happen at all. They were left nursing yearnings and nothing more. He didn't want that to happen to Natalie.

'Look, honey, why don't we agree to give it, say, three months' serious thought and then we can pick up the discussion after a clear appraisal,' he suggested.

'I've given this a lot more than three months' serious thought,' said Nat, wounded and fraught. How could he not know that about her? 'I'm sorry but I'm not going to change my mind.'

'Natalie, I want to be a father. I want a child.'

'I don't'

'That's it, is it? End of discussion?'

'As far as I'm concerned, yes.'

'I need a family.'

'No, you *want* a family. You *need* food and shelter.'

'Don't be an arse, Natalie. You know exactly what I mean.'

'I'm not being an arse. I'm just saying you can't pressurise me in this way, by confusing your desires with genuine needs.'

'Being a dad *is* a genuine need.'

'On a par with needing clean water?'

'Yes.'

Nat felt sick. If he believed that, then they were in trouble, deep, deep trouble. So far, throughout the exchange, she'd talked to the wallpaper. Now she glanced his way. Her heart broke. Neil's face, body, entire being, was scrunched into a tight ball of profound disappointment and dissatisfaction. Part of her wanted to put her arms around him, soothe him, reason with him and reassure him.

Another part of her wanted to punch him.

'You knew how I felt about having kids before we got married. We talked about it,' insisted Nat. She was screeching now, panic, frustration and terror ambushed her ability to be reasonable.

'I know,' Neil shouted back.

'You agreed!' Nat took her anger and volume up a notch.

'But now I've changed my mind.' He met her tone.

Silence. A bitter, spiky tension seeped through the house. Nat felt a cold, clammy sweat gathering in the crook of her elbow and the back of her knees. Neil felt his heart thundering against his chest. The only sound was a gang of drunks in the street who were singing and swearing by turn.

'Well, I haven't,' said Natalie hoarsely.

'Where does that leave us?' Neil asked.

Nat had been asking herself the same thing for weeks now but still her honest reply was, 'I don't know.'

13

He was not her One. He couldn't be. Not if they disagreed on something so enormous. So fundamental. And yet she loved him. She loved him, still. That hadn't changed. Had she married the wrong one? How the hell had she married the wrong one? It wasn't like she'd skimped on her research; she'd dated enough guys before Neil. She'd always thought he was exactly, entirely, irrefutably, absolutely the perfect guy for her. It wasn't fair. She'd been upfront, honest. He knew her feelings on babies before they walked up the aisle.

Natalie found it hard to concentrate on Sunday while she cleared out the boxes from her parents' house. She managed to sort out the junk into three piles: charity, bin, keep. She handled dropping off the stuff at the charity shop in the high street but if quizzed she'd have been unsure as to exactly what had gone into each pile as she was having such difficulty keeping her mind on the task in hand. She and Neil hardly said a word to one another all day. They'd avoided each other's accusing and disgruntled stares, which was quite a feat in their tiny home and went to show what you could do if you put your mind to it.

That night they lay stiff and silent side by side. Sleep eluded Nat who was used to Neil spooning into her; her bottom tucked into his groin, his arm heavily thrown over her body, cupping her breast, her cold feet on his shins. They always fell asleep in that position and they always woke facing one another; his morning breath, warm, not unpleasant, starting her day. Not on Sunday night. Nat stayed plank-like, flat on her back, staring at the ceiling. When she woke up she had a crick in her neck.

Now she was finding it difficult to put her mind to anything at work. The words on her Mac flittered about like skittish insects on a picnic blanket on a hot day. *A series of clinical studies . . . the efficacy and safety of paroxetine . . . children and adolescents . . . obsessive compulsive . . . results available . . . second technology appraisal . . . consultation document . . . Tyverb, in combination with capecitabine . . . treated . . . metastatic breast cancer.* She reread the reports four times each but still the dot dot dots appeared in her head at regular intervals. She couldn't make sense of anything today.

The tea lady with the trolley dawdled into the open-plan office, carrying hot drinks, a wide selection of chocolate snacks and a small selection of suspiciously uniform and shiny fruit. Her arrival was greeted with unilateral enthusiasm. Chocolate! That was the answer. Nat reached into her bag and felt around for her purse. Her bag was like Dr Who's TARDIS. She found an umbrella, a notebook, business cards, Tampax, make-up but where was her damn purse? Then her fingers met the soft, warm leather of her Little Black Book. How did that get in there? She thought she'd chucked it. A smile hopped on to her face for the first time since Saturday night. Why did the address book make her smile? Even just the thought of it. Some sort of magic? Suddenly Nat didn't feel like chocolate any more.

'Do you know what this is, Becky?' Nat asked, waving the small address book at her colleague.

Becky looked up from her desk, pleased to have an excuse to take a break from reading her screen. Becky had (as usual) partied hard all weekend and was struggling to stay awake on this dull Monday morning. 'No idea,' she said through a stifled yawn.

'It's my old address book.'

'And?'

Nat knew it would probably be wisest to just put the book back in her bag or in the bin like she'd originally intended; it certainly wasn't sensible to start flashing it around the office. The names in it belonged in the past and Nat had enough confusion in her present not to waste time thinking about the past and yet, talking about the book was somehow irresistible.

'Fondly referred to as my Little Black Book,' added Nat with a self-conscious grin.

'I see!' laughed Becky, and of course Becky did see, probably more than Nat intended her to. Still single, Becky counted her BlackBerry amongst her greatest and most treasured possessions, far more important to her than a pretty clutch bag or even designer shoes could be, probably on a par with her driving licence. Becky's BlackBerry was a more or less comprehensive list of the contact details of half of London, the male half. Often, if Becky was bored, she trawled through names she stored in her BlackBerry and amused herself by thinking about a series of near misses, grand passions and wet squids. She found it a marvellous way to pass the time. The shy smile on Nat's face made Becky wonder whether Nat had been indulging in a similar harmless and delightful trip down memory lane. 'Hence the grin,' she said, pleased to see Nat more cheerful. She hadn't done much smiling in the past month and this morning she hadn't said a word. Becky had been on the verge of asking Nat if everything was OK. She hadn't, because her experience of working with Nat was that Nat wasn't one for shared confidences, she certainly wouldn't be pushed into saying anything she didn't want to. She always played her cards close to her chest. Becky thought it best to pursue the line of conversation that actually had brought a smile to Nat's face. 'So, this book is full of the details of men you once had salacious love affairs with, is it?' teased Becky.

'No,' Nat replied, quickly enough for Becky to be certain she'd hit the nail on the head. 'Well, there are a few ex-boyfriends' numbers in there, I suppose,' Nat admitted. 'But there're also names of friends, a proportion of which I've now completely lost touch with. It's strange to think these people could have once meant so much to me, and now I don't even know which continent some of them live on.' She hoped she'd managed to hit the correct tone, one of someone making a general passing comment. She didn't want to admit to Becky, or anyone else, how exciting she found the old address book. Or, more specifically, how exciting she found the names in it. Or, if she was being absolutely accurate, how exciting she found the names of the men she'd loved before she had fallen in love with Neil.

'Well, it's impossible to stay in touch with everyone we've ever met,' pointed out Becky.

'Quite,' agreed Nat. She held the book in her right hand and was caressing it with her left, as though she was trying to absorb some of the vibrancy and warmth it once represented; she hadn't noticed that she was doing so, although Becky did. It wasn't like Nat to be at all dreamy or distracted. 'I found the address book amongst a load of junk at my parents'. I can't think what it's doing in my bag. I thought I'd binned it.'

'Why would you bin it?' asked Becky.

'Well, what's the point of keeping it? It's not as though I'm ever going to look up any of these guys – these people – again, is it?' said Nat with a shrug. She prayed Becky hadn't noticed her telling slip of the tongue. It became apparent Becky had noticed when she replied.

'I don't see why not. I keep in touch with all my exes. Well, most of them. Not the axe-wielding psycho types.'

'Yes, but you're single.' Nat thought that Becky was probably single precisely because she kept in touch with all her exes; when would she have time to meet anyone new?

'It's fun to see what they're up to. Meeting up with a sexy dork from your past is healthy. It stops you romanticising the old days as it reminds you why you split up. Plus, it's a harmless ego boost. They always tell you that you were the one who got away. They never mean it of course, but if everyone is aware of that then what's the harm?'

'No, I can't see the point,' said Nat, shaking her head. 'Besides, it's been years since I talked to any of them. I don't imagine these contact details are still current.'

'I wouldn't bet on it. If your exes are anything like my exes they will still be living in the same place, doing the same job, probably still have the same haircuts. It's scary how little the majority of us move on.'

Nat laughed and put down the address book. Becky was funny, but no. No. She had enough problems right now. The last thing she needed to do was go and search out more complications. The people who had made the leap from her address book to her BlackBerry were the important people in her life; Neil, first and foremost, and her friends who had grown with her were enough to fill up her life. She had no need to dig about in the past. And no desire. No, none. She turned back to her screen.

Now, about tyverb combined with capecitabine.

Michael Young. The name drifted into her mind from nowhere. Nat wondered what was he was up to now. Married? Odds were against it as he was a bit of a loner and a bit prone to dark thoughts. Glass half empty, definitely. She couldn't see him settled down, bouncing a plump baby on his knee. But then again, they were still teenagers when they split up. It was years and years ago. He might be completely different now. All that angst might have vanished with his acne.

She wondered.

No, no, it was a daft thought. The number she had in her address book for Michael definitely wouldn't work, even if she did want to call it, which she didn't. The number she had was his mother's telephone number. They'd dated throughout sixth form and then for a couple of weeks at uni. But when she went north to Sheffield he went to London to see if the streets were paved with gold. Of course, they'd both met other people within weeks. She couldn't even remember who'd done the chucking now. The end had sailed down a telephone line, that much she did know. The break-up with Michael Young had put her off long-distance relationships for ever.

OK, right. The safety of paroxetine. That's what she had to think about just now.

Alan Jones. Now he was the sort of bloke parents liked. He was sensible, prudent and serious. He'd picked up where Michael left off. Four years she'd spent with him, but now they didn't even swap Christmas cards. That was a bit odd, if you thought about it. Their relationship safely saw her through university and into her first London job. The official reason they broke up was because they wanted different things out of life. Although looking in from the outside it might have been hard to see exactly what they each wanted that was so irreconcilable. Alan currently lived about a mile from where Nat lived, also in a two-bedroom terrace (almost identical to her own), with his wife (of five years). Nat had heard that much from a mutual friend from uni. From time to time Cathy casually dripped through information about Alan but Nat never pressed for any details. Her curiosity about him had remained cursory. She was able to look back on this relationship and understand it but not miss or regret it, which generally speaking was an achievement when it came to exes.

Richard Clark. He was more of a Dick really, in every sense of the word. She couldn't remember him with any fondness. Why would she want to look him up? She wouldn't. Hunt him down, perhaps with a gun. Natalie realised that she was holding the small leather book once again. The book fell open on Gary's contact details. Gary, aka the Hunk. He had been a six-month long moment of madness. They'd met at the gym when she was twenty-four. On occasions when Natalie came across an old photo of herself with the Hunk she would always feel an urge to examine the girl in the snap closely with a wonderment that bordered on bewilderment. Natalie believed the girl in the photo must be her doppelgänger because the Hunk just didn't make sense on any level. They had nothing in common. Not education, values, interests or even cuisine preferences. For the first month of their relationship they had enjoyed great sex. *Great* sex. The thought of that initial month could still bring a smile to Nat's face, even now, even if it was pouring down or she was squashed in a commuter carriage. But the following five months were an elaborate exercise in trying to recapture that initial rush. An exercise that had been doomed to failure as the Hunk loved his own body far, far more than he loved Nat's. He'd regarded the initial month as an intensive workout and not much more. There wasn't a single reason on earth that would make Nat want to call him. What would they talk about?

14

Natalie pushed open the pub door and was slapped by the usual smell of beer-sloshed carpets, hot bodies and chips. She'd suggested this pub because it was near her office but not one that either she or Neil normally visited. It was busy and noisy and as such perfect for her current needs. She spotted a couple just leaving a table and headed directly to it. She took off her scarf and put down her bag and as she started to unbutton her coat it struck her, what in God's name was she doing here? This was a stupid idea. She should just leave now. *Right* now. Walk out of the pub before he even got here. She quickly started to gather together her bag and scarf.

'Hi, babe, barely recognised you.' Too late. Gary the Hunk was standing right in front of her. A little too close to her in fact, he never did have any idea about personal space, she'd forgotten that but now she remembered it all too clearly. What did he mean, he hardly recognised her? Had she changed so much? 'You weren't running out on me, were you, babe? Not after going to all that trouble to look me up.'

'Erm, it wasn't any trouble, actually. More of a spur-of-the-moment thing. I just called the number I had for you. You still worked at the same gym so—'

Gary waved away her comment and smiled – it was more of a leer, really. He seemed to want to believe that she'd hunted high and low for him. 'I *manage* the gym now.'

'That's nice.'

Nat had been surprised at herself when she made the call this morning and stunned that Gary had suggested they meet *today*. She'd vaguely thought that they'd have a chat, maybe put a date in to meet up in a week or so, which would mean she would have had opportunity to cancel. An opportunity she fully expected to take up even before the arrangement was made. But then Gary had said he was free that very evening and she hadn't been quick-witted enough to think of a reason not to do so. After all, that's why she'd called him, wasn't it? Besides, she had nothing better to do. Neil was going over to Karl's. Normally on a Monday night they had a quiet night in together, in front of the TV, but Karl was still avoiding Jen and so had invited Neil over. Neil had readily accepted and Nat prayed it wasn't because Neil was avoiding her. She feared it might be. Truthfully, neither of them wanted to sit on the sofa with a resentful silence that screamed unresolved issues sitting between them.

Nat quickly appraised the Hunk. Had his arms got larger since she saw him last? They were enormous or maybe they just seemed that way because Neil had ordinary-sized arms. Slightly bigger than average probably, but Gary's were gigantic. He looked like Popeye, a little comical. Odd that she used to find those arms irresistible, she'd loved the fact that he was so big and strong as she used to feel petite and dainty in comparison. But now Nat measured strength by a totally different scale. For instance, Neil had been very firm with the estate agents when they'd bought their house; turned out that he was a demon negotiator.

Gary's hair was blonder than she remembered. That was a bit of a shock. A few of her friends were getting greyer and she wasn't overly fond of grey and all it stood for. In fact, she'd tried to persuade Neil to start colouring his dark hair now that it was sprinkled with white. He'd refused, citing George Clooney as his role model for greying with dignity. She'd laughed herself sick at the time, but now she was glad he'd ignored her. There was something disconcerting talking to a guy with glossier, blonder hair than her own.

'Hate the paperwork that comes with the job, babe. It's a bore. Mostly I stuff it in the bottom drawer of my desk and ignore it. You know?' He'd hovered over the word desk, checking that she was suitably impressed. What? Did he think if he confirmed that he owned a laptop she'd shag him? 'But the staff *love* me. Especially the ladies, if you know what I mean.' Gary winked at her. She thought there was a real danger that he might kiss his own bicep, the way weightlifters did just before they picked up something exceptionally heavy. If he did, she'd laugh. She wouldn't be able to stop herself. 'Drink?' he asked.

One drink. One drink and then she was going. This was idiotic. How could she have believed this was a good idea? What was she thinking? She'd go home, wait for Neil to get back from Karl's and then tell him all about this episode. He'd split his sides laughing. But she couldn't leave now, that would be more embarrassing than staying. Reluctantly she said, 'Yes, OK. I'll have a vodka tonic, please.'

'Ohhhh.' Gary looked in pain. He pursed his lips (but Nat noticed his forehead stayed smooth, he couldn't have had Botox, could he?) 'You cannot be serious, babe. That's one hundred and eighty calories.' Gary's eyes dropped from Nat's face to her waist.

Oh God, she'd forgotten how he always did that. She'd ended up getting so skinny when she dated Gary. Skinny and miserable. It was hard to enjoy food if it was always accompanied by a breakdown of calorie and fat content.

'No, really, that's what I'd like,' she said resolutely, proud of herself for holding firm. When she used to go out with him, she always ended up sipping Diet Coke and sucking the lemon slice for fun.

'OK, babe, it's your temple. I'll get you a slim-line tonic, though, hey? That will save you eighty-nine calories.' He winked at her, convinced he was doing her a favour.

Natalie had never spent such a boring hour in her life. It amazed her that she'd used up six months of her life seeing this man at least three times a week. Tonight, it was all she could do to stay in her seat long enough to wait for him to finish his smoothie. What kind of bloke ordered a smoothie in a pub anyway? Yes, he had big hands and she remembered that they were in proportion to his other big member but she now also remembered that the muscles were inversely proportional to his grey matter. Why hadn't she cared back then?

'Are you seeing anyone serious at the moment?' Hunk asked, after a while.

'I'm married,' said Nat, waving her left hand in the air. How come he hadn't checked out the ring? Was he that slow? She was certain that if she'd been wearing her wedding ring on either one of her nipples he'd have noticed.

'Oh, I see.' Gary smiled a broad all-too-knowing smile and winked at her. 'So what *exactly* made you look me up? Trust all is OK with hubby.'

'Yes . . . great, thanks,' mumbled Nat. She turned scarlet. What a question to ask. Didn't this man have any social graces? He really was Neanderthal. The way he said hubby made her skin crawl. The problem was that somehow, despite him being as dense as Campbell's soup, he'd nailed her. What an idiot she was to have called this man. Of course he'd jump to the obvious conclusion. What could she expect from him, or anyone, for that matter? He'd assumed that she was a bored housewife looking for a little extra-curricular. She had made herself look like such a ridiculous cliché. Desperately, Natalie searched her mind for a plausible reason or even a tenuous excuse for calling Gary. She couldn't mention the Little Black Book. She couldn't say that in some vague ill-thought-through plan she was just confirming that she had married her One. It would be too horrible to admit that currently her confidence was dented because she now found that she and Neil disagreed on the fundamental issue of whether they should or should not have a baby. She could not admit that she'd wanted to have a quick look round at all the also-rans just to reinforce her original choice. She was an idiot! She sounded insane even to herself.

'I was thinking of getting a personal trainer and I thought you might be able to recommend one,' Nat mumbled. Hoping her excuse sounded plausible.

'I do a lot of personal training myself, actually. Some women like two or three sessions a week. It pays really well, it's very lucrative,' he said with a practised smile.

Oh. My. God. Was he talking about personal training or had she just made matters far worse because she'd inadvertently stumbled on to some sort of code for an altogether different type of workout? Either way, there was only one response. 'Oh no, I wasn't thinking of *you*.'

'You weren't?' Gary looked confused.

'No. Wouldn't seem very professional, would it? Not with us having a history. There's probably some code that prohibits it, the way there is with doctors and psychotherapists and other professionals.' It was like talking to a child. She was flattering him to get off the hook. How could a personal trainer ever be equated with a doctor?

'None that I'm aware of.' He looked puzzled and concerned.

'Yeah, I'm sure there is. The Hippocratic oath or something. But if you think of anyone else who could do the job, do let me know. In the meantime, I'll just have to cut back on the vodkas.' In fact Natalie was already imagining her next vodka, a large one, in the comfort of her own home. She stood up and started to gather her belongings.

'Er, OK.' Gary looked surprised that the evening had ground to a sudden halt. Had he been having a good time? Natalie wondered how that was possible, but then she thought of the last few times they'd had sex together. He'd always seemed to be having great fun, irrespective of her participation, and this conversation had been just the same. 'I'll call you then, if I think of anyone.'

'You do that,' said Nat, not bothering to tell him that her number had changed.

15

Becky howled with laughter when, the following day, Natalie up-chucked the details of the encounter with the Hunk.

'So, I take it you don't want his phone number?' deadpanned Nat.

'Erm, no.' And then pretending to hesitate, Becky added, 'How well hung did you say?' Then shaking her head, 'No, no, not worth it. Thanks anyway.' She laughed.

'Without a doubt, it was the most boring evening of my life. He spoke about muscle-building techniques for forty minutes without pausing for breath!' squealed Natalie.

'He's built like a Greek god, though, yeah?'

'Yes. In fairness, whatever he's doing, works. If I saw him in a magazine I'd pause and ogle but that man has no place in the real world.'

'You didn't fancy him?'

'Not an insy winsy bit.'

'That's because you and Neil are so happy,' said Becky confidently.

'Mmmm,' said Natalie.

'What did Neil make of it all? Bet when you told him he was all jealous at first, then grateful and then you had hot sex, right? Men love to hear how pathetic you think your exes are. It's a big turn-on.'

'You live in a dream world,' said Nat with a strained grin. It was unlikely they'd make love on a Monday night, and besides . . . Becky instantly saw exactly what Natalie hoped to disguise.

'You didn't tell him?'

'There was nothing to tell,' replied Nat defensively.

'You met up with an ex of yours.' Caution had sneaked into Becky's voice.

Nat didn't want to give the encounter any gravitas. 'No biggy,' she said, hoping to sound airily dismissive.

'That's not what you told me.'

Both women burst into infantile giggles over Becky's pun and Nat hoped the conversation would be dropped. She *had* intended to tell Neil all about Hunk. Well, maybe not *all* about him. She'd never planned to confess that she'd called Gary, Neil wouldn't understand why she'd done that, *she* barely understood why she'd done that. She'd planned to say she'd bumped into him on the street and had agreed to have a drink with him. She'd wanted to laugh about the encounter with Neil, and yes, she'd hoped that they'd then make love. Not as a response to him feeling jealous or threatened but as a celebration of their relationship. But Neil had come back from Karl's later than he'd done before and drunker than ever before. He'd said he was just going round to play some Xbox games and have a takeaway pizza, nothing more adventurous than a quiet boys' night in. He didn't get home until after two in the morning and stank of booze. Nat had opted to feign sleep, much easier than bickering or bringing up the subject of her having a drink with her ex. Then this morning, the only thing Neil said to her was, 'I bumped into Jack Hope last night, remember him?'

'Vaguely.'

'You met him at a couple of work parties. He designed the website for *Mad Metal II*.'

'Oh yes, it's ringing a bell.'

'He married a woman with two kids of her own and now they're expecting another at Christmas.'

'Lovely,' said Nat. She threw her toast in the bin, as she'd suddenly and completely lost her appetite. 'Where'd you bump into him?'

'We went to a club in town. Poseidon or Poison or something. I can't remember. We were lashed before we made the decision to go there. Karl's a regular.'

'I thought you were having a quiet night in.'

'I changed my mind.'

'You appear to be doing a lot of that recently.'

With that Nat had banged closed the front door and rushed for her bus. There seemed to be an enormous space between them all the time at the moment and it was easier to bear if they weren't in the same room.

'Are you going to call any of the others?' Becky asked, bringing Nat back to the here and now.

'Others?'

'Old flames.'

'Definitely not!'

'Why not?'

'Well, it was hardly a successful evening with the Hunk, was it?'

'On the contrary, it was a total success,' said Becky assertively. 'You said your motivation for going was to clarify that everyone else you ever dated was a loser.'

'I don't think I said exactly that.'

'No, but something on those lines. Look, Nat, it's been clear to me these last few weeks that you haven't been quite as happy as you normally are.' Becky looked at her hands. Nat's glance followed involuntarily. Becky always had great nails, they were long and white-tipped, it was one of the first things Natalie had noticed about her. That, and the fact she liked to wear hats. 'It's none of my business but I sort of hazarded a guess that perhaps all was not well between you and Neil.'

'Why do you say that?'

'He doesn't ring the office any more, you don't rush home at six o'clock, you don't text him so much during the day like you used to.' Becky risked looking up at Natalie. She was making a leap. They were friendly colleagues but not yet friends. They shared a filing cabinet, ideas for initiatives, tea breaks and a table in the cafeteria most lunchtimes. Plus, when the team went for drinks together after work, they always found that they gravitated towards one another. Becky was sure that if she'd been married or Nat had been single they would have socialised a lot. As it was, they had very separate ideas of what constituted a good time on a Saturday night. Still, they liked and respected one another and Becky didn't like to see Natalie so unusually down in the mouth, but a discussion of this kind was altering the balance. They hadn't talked before about anything quite so personal and once they did there would be no going back; they would be friends, not just friendly colleagues. Becky was unsure how Natalie would react. Nat was fun and gregarious but deeply private at the same time. Becky tentatively edged on.

'Your Neil seems like a nice bloke. I chatted to him for ages at the Christmas party last year. Until I got off with Don in PR. You've always been really happy, until recently. I just thought it might be good for you to see how crap being "out there" is.'

'I'm not planning on being "out there", if that's what you're worried about,' said Nat tetchily. She was agitated by Becky's insight and her suggestion that she might need to know what was 'out there'.

'I know that, but sometimes it's easy to forget how good something is, or *someone* is, and I just thought if you reminded yourself why you chose him and how few decent blokes there are . . .'

Nat looked irritated. Becky clamped her mouth closed, she'd gone too far. But in fact Nat wasn't irritated by what Becky was saying, she was horrified. Horrified that her problems with Neil had caught other people's attention. Terrified that she might just find herself 'out there' again. Petrified that this baby issue wasn't going to go away and that she and Neil wouldn't be able to sort things out. It wasn't that Nat totally accepted Becky's rather bleak view on the male population in the twenty-first century, it was more the fact that she didn't want anyone else. Neil was her One. Wasn't he?

Nat turned back to her screen, signalling to Becky that she considered the conversation over.

'I'll go and get us both a cup of tea, should I?' offered Becky, keen to make amends. She didn't want to scupper their amicable working relationship and now she wished she'd kept her mouth shut.

'Yeah, thanks, that would be nice,' said Nat with a nod.

Nat didn't understand why she did what she did next but the moment Becky moved away from her desk, she reached into her bag and pulled out the ancient leather address book. It was as though she was hypnotised or functioning on autopilot, performing actions she neither authorised nor anticipated. She firmly pressed the numbers on the phone with her pencil end; in some dark crevasse of her mind she was dimly aware that she was pressing her self-destruct button but she battened down any feelings of misapprehension.

'Hi, hi, Matthew. Matt Jackson? It's Natalie. Natalie Morgan. Yeah, it *has* been a long time.'

16

Neil called Karl and asked him if he wanted to meet for a quick pint, even though it was a Friday and normally Neil went straight home from work to curl up on the sofa with Nat. It was their habit to watch a DVD and eat a takeaway. But tonight Nat was going out with Becky. They were going to some gig at the Royal Festival Hall. Not to see a band or anything remotely hip like that, Nat and Becky were going to listen to readings of 'experimental' poetry. Nat had invited Neil along but she had to be taking the piss, she knew that there wasn't a hope that he'd choose to spend his Friday evening listening to a group of pretentious, self-indulgent hippies drone their nonsensical, amateur philosophies, *and* manage to pretend he thought it was art. No thank you. It didn't seem much like Nat's cup of tea either, actually. It must have been Becky's suggestion. She seemed the type to enjoy poetry recitals, thought Neil, as he remembered that she always wore hats, even indoors.

Clearly, Nat was bonding with Becky. After years of being cautious about befriending work colleagues, it appeared that suddenly Nat and Becky were best buddies. On Monday Nat had gone for a drink with Becky, straight from work on the spur of the moment, not that he could complain about that, after all he'd been with Karl, and Nat probably didn't want to be at home alone. Monday had been an unexpectedly heavy night. It had taken Neil until Wednesday afternoon to shake off the hangover. The plan had been a quiet pizza but then they'd ended up going to a club. Karl had said he needed to find a distraction because Jen was being sulky and his new bit on the side was being clingy. Neil had found he needed a distraction too, although he didn't say so. But now, tonight, a *Friday* night, Nat and Becky were off out again. Two nights in one week. Neil didn't mind, as such. Not exactly.

It would be ludicrously outdated and unreasonable of him to insist that there were only *certain* nights that he should meet up with his mates and she could meet up with hers (boys' nights out and girls' nights out, so to speak). Hoping everything could coincide neatly was daft. But . . . it was just that . . . well, that's what they'd *always* done. Thursday nights were independent nights. Friday nights were for curries and watching the box. Saturdays were for dinner parties and restaurants with friends, Sundays, a trip to the movies. Mondays and Tuesdays were quiet nights in (often Nat would stay late at work or bring stuff home, Neil would play video games). Was she getting back at him for his excesses on Monday? It was true that he'd been the one who broke the unwritten rule first; he admitted that. Neil wished he hadn't gone out on Monday. Knowing where you stand was one of the perks of being a couple. On Wednesdays the pair of them always went to the local Italian and then it was back to Thursdays. That's what they'd always done. That was their routine. But now Nat wanted to go and listen to poetry readings on a *Friday*. The next thing would be she'd be suggesting they visit Bellisimo's on a Monday!

It was uncomfortable. Something wasn't as it should be. He somehow instinctively knew that Nat's visit to the Royal Festival Hall tonight was linked to his request for them to start a family. He couldn't formally tie up the two events but it was something he felt in his gut. It was as though Nat was saying, 'Ha, look, it's not just you who can throw a curve ball! You want a baby, well, I want poetry!'

Neil shook his head in an effort to clear it. Saying such a thing, even to himself, made him sound ridiculous. How could the two things be related? Nat wasn't petty or reactive. If she had a problem with his request for a family, she'd discuss it with him.

Neil shook his head again. Honestly, that was even more ridiculous. There was no *if* involved. *Obviously* Nat had a problem with his wish for a baby; he knew that, he just didn't understand why. And she hadn't discussed it. In fact she'd stonewalled his attempts to do so, over and over again. She tenaciously hung on to her point that she'd always said she didn't want a baby, that it shouldn't be a surprise to him. OK. He got that, but why? He had once said he didn't want one either but now he'd changed his mind. Surely his repositioning at least re-opened the debate.

Nat had behaved strangely skittishly this morning as she dressed for work. There had been something excitable and unpredictable, almost rebellious, about her. She'd changed her top three times and worn high heels. It wasn't that Neil disapproved (he loved to see her in heels), it was just unsettling. He'd turned his desk calendar to October yesterday; shouldn't she be comfortably slipping into her Uggs now? Bloody ugly things but comfortable and practical when dashing for a bus in the rain-splattered streets, that's what she always claimed. Weren't Uggs good enough for a poetry recital? Fuck it, Neil couldn't put his finger on exactly what was bothering him, so he did the thing he always did in situations where he felt confused, he chose to ignore the feeling. Better to go out with Karl and get blathered. Nat was simply going to listen to poetry with her pal from work, on a Friday, end of story. It was nothing to do with him wanting a baby. She'd probably be furious if she knew he'd imagined a connection. She'd call him a self-obsessed wanker (playfully, he hoped).

Karl was always free for a swift one (woman, fag or pint) and so he instantly agreed to meet up. Neil noticed that Karl did not check with Jen to see whether she had plans or she minded him making independent arrangements on a Friday night. Neil also called Tim. He wasn't hopeful that Tim would join them but he knew Tim was easily offended and hated to feel left out. Surprisingly, Tim agreed to join them too (although he did clear it with Ali first).

Neil was the first to arrive. He ordered three pints and sat on a bench in the corner, waiting for his mates. Everything about the Goat and Gate was reassuringly recognisable. Neil felt comforted by the fact that he was familiar with every inch of the smelly, tatty, beer-doused floor and with every single brass hanging and insipid water painting that poxed the walls. He knew all the available brands of beers, stouts and lagers, on tap and bottle. He knew all the tracks on the juke box. He even knew the exact order in which the crisps boxes were lined up under the bar (ready salted, cheese and onion, salt and vinegar, smoky bacon). The Goat and Gate was one of the few pubs in Chiswick that had avoided being sucked into the horrible, soulless vortex of a bar franchise. It remained shoddy cruddie, not even shabby chic, and Neil, Tim and Karl loved it all the more for that fact.

The three of them had been going out for pints together for years. Between them they'd probably drunk a lake. Sometimes they met up to watch a match on the pub's big screen when they would be either jubilant or angry depending on whether their team had been victorious or thwarted. Either way, they'd scream themselves hoarse. Sometimes they bickered or blathered inanely, they told jokes, climbed on their soap boxes or (just to fulfil female expectation) lapsed into lengthy silences. Slow, still, deep, comfortable silences.

Tim and Karl arrived within minutes of one another. They sat down, sank their waiting pints and then Karl swiftly went to the bar and ordered another round.

'I'm on a mission,' he said as he slammed the fresh pints on to the table with such force that beer splashed on to his hand. 'Thank fuck you called.'

'Why?'

'Jen is being a nightmare.'

'Yeah, well, it's to be expected now she's got an inkling that last Saturday, when you said you were with your big gang of friends from uni, you were with some girl you hooked up with through Facebook,' commented Tim, not bothering to try to sound anything other than judgemental. Tim thought Jen was a decent girlfriend and didn't like the way Karl chose to treat her; he wished he wasn't privy to it. 'I suppose she wants to split up now,' he added.

'Well, that goes to show what you know about women,' said Karl shortly. 'Her response to her suspicions of my infidelity has been to intensify her campaign for us to get married.'

'Why?' asked Tim, bewildered.

Karl did not bother to explain, he thought Tim was a dope when it came to women but since Tim was already married, Karl didn't think it was worth wasting his time educating his friend. When Karl looked at Tim he saw a man who had already committed the crime of ignorance and he saw a condemned man serving out his punishment.

'Being around her is like picking through a field scattered with undetonated landmines. Everything I say leads to a row,' grumbled Karl.

'Are you going to finish it?' asked Neil.

'No.'

'Are you going to finish it with the other woman?' asked Tim.

'No.'

'Have you ever considered the benefits of being faithful?' inquired Neil.

'No.'

'What are you going to do then?' probed Tim.

'Told you. Get drunk.'

'That's not very helpful,' pointed out Tim.

'But very predictable,' added Neil.

'It's Jen that's being chronically predictable in this,' said Karl, outraged. 'All she wants is her big day and a big bump to follow. It's not even that she wants to marry *me*, especially. She just feels entitled. I blame Christopher Shaw.'

'Who is Christopher Shaw?' asked Tim, confused.

'Her ex. She did four years' hard labour with him but he dumped her because he didn't feel ready to commit. Then, to add insult to her injury, he got engaged to the very next girl he dated within a year. She feels competitive.'

Neil was impressed that Karl had given the issue so much thought, although this new insight only confirmed Neil's belief that Karl and Jen's relationship was a debacle. Jen only wanted Karl because her ex had ditched her and was going to marry someone else and Karl didn't want Jen at all, at least not exclusively and not consistently. What a mess. The guys finished their pints and it was Tim's turn to go to the bar.

When he returned, he sighed deeply and said, 'I don't get the way women think.' He was in fact considering his own situation when he made this comment, not Karl's. Ali had recently spent £400 on baby equipment and clothes, even though they had yet to see the necessary life-confirming blue line on the pee stick. But she'd hyperventilated when he'd suggested their car would look cool with new hubcaps.

'I am deeply suspicious of any man who says he understands the way women think,' agreed Neil. Why wouldn't Nat want the traditional bump? Jen wanted one. Ali did too. Most women did, didn't they? It was part of their *being*, wasn't it? Why not his wife?

'Why would Jen imagine I'd want to spend all my savings on the aforementioned atrocity, aka a wedding day? I'd rather fly club class to Barbados or Australia and, I don't know, swim with dolphins, dive amongst the coral or something. She could come too,' added Karl, smiling at his own generosity. 'Or, we could go to Vegas and blow it at the tables. She could even wear a spangled dress out there and get pissed on champagne. That would be a lot like a wedding.'

The three men stared at their pints and shook their heads. The pints they'd already drunk in quick succession sloshed to their senses and drowned grey matter.

'There's only one reasonable response to tonight,' said Karl emphatically.

'What's that?' asked his friends, relieved that Karl, as always, had a solution or at least a distraction to take them away from their problems.

'Hush Hush.'

'You mean Hush Hush as in the lap-dancing venue?' asked Tim, showing more shock at the suggestion than he knew to be cool.

'Well, I don't bloody mean hush hush as in I'm not going to tell you. What would be the point in me having a solution to our problems but not bloody telling you?' laughed Karl. Neil shot Karl a look of warning. He wished his mate was kinder to Tim. Tim could be a bit square but he was sound and it always made Neil uncomfortable that Karl felt compelled to bully Tim like some sort of bulky schoolboy picking on the tiny kid with glasses. Neil just wanted a quiet pint with his mates, was that too much to ask for? Karl clocked Neil's warning glance and pulled his neck in. 'Sorry, mate. I'm being an arse. I'm tetchy. Nagging women. I can't handle it. What do you say? Bit of tabletop?'

Tim was grateful for the apology and didn't want to look like the wet weekend he often felt himself to be. Of course he'd been to strip clubs before. Twice, actually. Both occasions had been stag weekends and of course he could see the attraction. He had eyes and a pulse, didn't he? But he wasn't in the habit of frequenting such clubs. They were expensive, for a start, and he and Ali only had a joint bank account, that's how he knew about the £400 she'd spent in Mothercare. Ali would definitely ask questions if she saw a big transaction at a nightclub.

'I'd need to get some cash out,' Tim said.

Neil was stunned by Tim agreeing to Karl's proposal. He'd been sure Tim would say no, thus saving him the bother and shame of having to say no himself. Neil didn't want to go to a strip club, not really. He hadn't been to one for years. He was through that stage, at least he thought he was, but he didn't want to look like a jerk in front of his mates.

'Get your coats on,' he said, feigning considerably more enthusiasm than he felt.

17

Nat had suggested meeting Matthew Jackson at the Royal Festival Hall because ordinarily she never went there any more and she didn't know anyone who did. It was a place she used to visit a lot, with Matthew, actually. They'd dated for about eight or nine months, some time not long after she'd split from the Hunk.

During those months she had sat through countless concertos and watched as a fair few prodigious conductors led numerous renowned symphony orchestras. She'd never once mentioned that she was tone deaf, there never seemed to be the right moment. That sort of thing ought to be discussed on the first date, after that it was distinctly too late. When Nat had commented on the 'insight and sensitivity' of the dynamic partnership between the Chamber Orchestra of Europe and the exquisitely talented pianist Mitsuko Uchida, Matt had assumed she possessed a knowledge and understanding that was profoundly beyond her level of expertise. In fact she'd read the 'insight and sensitivity' thing in the programme. Men had often assumed things about Nat before, the way men did about all women, and not many of them had been this flattering so it seemed easier to just accept his delight at this pronouncement rather than admit that she would struggle to identify a piece of music beyond which advert it appeared in.

That's why she'd finished it in the end.

It wasn't just music. It had been impossible to pretend that she cared about the works of ancient Celtic bards (especially when their mini break to Scotland had been spent in a dusty research hall in a damp library; she'd wanted to take a brisk walk on the beach or drink malt whisky by an open fire). Nor did she care about modern abstract expressionism (which more often than not culminated in an installation that looked like something a *Blue Peter* presenter had prepared), and she thought street art was graffiti (she was old-fashioned like that). But Matthew did care. He really did. He was so achingly arty and enormously informed that it was impossible to feel anything other than inferior when you were with him. He read the *Guardian* before breakfast and often dismissed it as 'light' and he had an encyclopaedic knowledge of investigational short films directed by emerging Lithuanian talent.

Natalie had forgotten the cold fear she regularly used to experience whenever she was on a date with Matthew, but now as she was sitting in the Royal Festival Hall, with her double espresso before her, she began to remember all too well. It was nonsense that she'd ordered a double espresso. What was she trying to say by picking such a dark and brooding drink? Normally she opted for a latte with extra cream and chocolate sprinkles but she couldn't bring herself to be herself with Matthew. She never had been able to. She'd always wanted to be more sophisticated, more erudite, more urbane. More.

Matthew was late. He always used to be. Nat had resented it then and she resented it now. She always believed that someone being late was a not-too-discreet way of saying 'my time is more valuable than yours is'. Nat had already killed ten minutes by examining the glittering colourful stuff in the Festival Hall shop but close inspection uncovered the fact that everything for sale was disappointingly worthy and expensive. What was she doing here? Wouldn't it make more sense to hop on to the tube and scurry back to Neil?

She glanced around the enormous hall. Nat didn't want to notice them but she couldn't help but see a number of tired and earnest couples with small babies. Was this the new and fashionable place to hold post-natal classes? The mothers flopped against the leather sofas in order to breast feed in comfort and then, after the babies had gnawed at their tender knockers, the mothers handed the babies to the fathers, who wore them strapped to their chests like medals. That would be the sort of father Neil would want to be, an actively involved one. The thought made Nat sigh. The truth was, while the men wore the babies as though they were the veterans, it was the women who did the hand-to-hand combat. The women who stood up along the front line. The women who fell.

She looked at the other visitors to the hall and noticed that there were more people wearing glasses than average, few of the women were wearing make-up, although many of the men were, there were lots of hairy types and cyclists and there was a group of twenty-something girls knitting. Broadly speaking, she was a live and let live type. She'd never understood why everyone had got their knickers in a twist when Julia Roberts allowed her underarm hair to grow, but then nor did she criticise if some soap C-lister opted to have the fat sucked out of her arse and plugged into her boobs. Nat's job had brought her into contact with all sorts of people and she'd learnt to make only one judgement in life. Is this person a well-intentioned human being? Charity and funding came from hairy lefties as well as the pearl and twinset-wearing brigade. But what did slightly depress Nat about the twenty-something girls knitting in the middle of the RFH was that she couldn't help but think there were better ways to squander one's youth. They could be getting drunk in a club, or learning to salsa or sitting outside the Houses of Parliament waving a big banner objecting to war and poverty. Had their mothers endured the pains of labour for them to behave like grannies before they'd even lived? Nat fought the urge to dash across to the junior WI meeting and insist that they all rush outside into the dark London night to show the world their youth and vitality. She wanted to tell them that they were mortal and their youth and vitality would insidiously, imperceptibly seep away before they knew it. Wasting it knitting, even in public, was a sin. But she knew there was no point in her trying to tell them this. They wouldn't believe her. No doubt they believed themselves to be eternal and perpetual.

'Good to see you. Isn't this marvellous, just like old times,' said Matthew.

Nat jumped. She hadn't noticed him approach but now suddenly he was sitting down opposite her, just the small metal bar table between them. She'd waited thirty minutes for him to arrive but now didn't feel ready to see him. She didn't want to see him. He leant across the table and kissed her cheek, left and right. Their noses banged, which was embarrassing, not erotic or intimate. He did not comment whether she had changed or not, as Gary had. It was never his way to notice her external qualities. He believed that even commenting on a pretty coat was beneath him, somehow sexual and inappropriate. She'd have liked to receive a compliment occasionally.

Matthew flashed a broad grin but Nat remembered him well enough to know that he was nervous. His Adam's apple was quivering rapidly and his fingertips trembled as he unbuttoned his coat and loosened his tie. He must have come straight from work. Matthew looked well. He was tall and athletic, well groomed (as always). He still wore his hair short and there was only the slightest smidge of grey around the temples. He had deep crevasses around his mouth and across his fore-head. Nat would have liked to imagine that the lines were laugh lines but she thought it was more likely that they were the result of a constantly furrowed brow, catching endless anxiety and worthiness.

'So here we are!' Matthew had his elbows on the table but expanded his arms wide.

'Yes,' agreed Nat.

'After all these years.'

'Yes.'

'Why?' Matthew was a journalist. He'd written for an arts industry paper when Nat dated him but since then he'd written seriously as a critic in the broadsheets. Occasionally, Nat's father would point out an article with Matthew's by-line and comment that it was 'very inter-esting'. Of course Matt was going to ask why she had called him and as he was infinitely brighter than Gary, he had not flattered himself that the call was a precursor to a clandestine sexual liaison. Or if he had presumed this was the case, he clearly had a need to have that pertinent discussion upfront.

'I'm not sure, exactly,' admitted Nat.

'Are you dying?'

'No.'

'Good. And it's not your big Three O, we've passed that.'

'Right.'

'You're wearing a ring, so not husband hunting.'

'No.'

'Are you after my sperm?'

Nat laughed, even though she was pretty sure Matthew wasn't joking. With his direct line of questioning he'd taken a pickaxe to the icy small talk that might have surrounded this occasion.

'You're laughing but you can't imagine how many women friends of mine have asked me to make a little donation to that particular fund,' said Matthew, rolling his eyes dramatically.

'Really?'

'Really. It's very *London*. Now should I get us a drink? Then you can tell me what sort of internal crisis you are having, exactly. A Burgundy, a Bordeaux? I can't allow you to drink a Chilean Sauvignon, even if they are terrific wines. One has to consider the air miles. Should we go dutch? I'm happy to pay but if it offends your sense of political achievement as a woman, just say so.'

'Erm.'

'Fine, you can buy the second bottle,' said Matthew, already halfway to the bar.

Natalie had not remembered him being so jittery, or funny, come to that – although she would have put money on the fact that he'd be the sort of guy who cared about the carbon footprint of his vino. She racked her brains for something impressive to say when he came back to the table. She wanted to talk about books, or art or music or something similar. Now, the idea of having to explain why she'd called him was the truly terrifying one. Her stomach gurgled with stress. Oh God, he'd think she was a dreary, 'trip down memory lane' type.

Someone stuck in the past, incapable of moving on. It was not a picture she wanted to draw of herself.

The moment Matthew put down the glasses and wine, Nat excitedly said, 'Hey, isn't that Disney's *Fantasia* playing? You know, the part where there are volcanoes erupting, lots of boiling lava and earthquakes, and a large carnivorous dinosaur attacking another dinosaur.' She started to nod her head to the tune bursting through the sound system. She'd recognised the music from an afternoon when she and Neil had visited the niece and nephews last month. Angus had played the DVD on repeat for about three hours, mostly to scare his younger sister. Nat had thought the DVD should come with a certificate classification, she thought *she* might get nightmares, let alone Sophia. But now she was thrilled that she'd heard the music and made the link. She thought it was an impressive conversation opener.

'I think it's more commonly recognised as Stravinsky's *Rite of Spring*, a condensed version of the natural history of the earth from the formation of the planet, to the first living creatures, to the age, reign and extinction of the dinosaurs,' said Matthew. 'I'm gay.'

For a moment Natalie was too struck by the depth of his general knowledge to fully take in what Matthew had said, and when she did, it took all her self-restraint not to laugh out loud. She wasn't able to entirely suppress her amusement, though. A grin started to seep across her face.

'Always have been,' he added.

'That's usually the case,' she said, now chortling slightly.

'What's funny?' he asked, nervous and offended.

'I am funny,' said Nat. She poured the wine and clinked glasses. At least now she was sure she'd enjoy herself.

18

The pink brick building stood on the outskirts of the town centre, nestled next to respectable residential streets. Neil wondered what the neighbours thought about living cheek by jowl with a strip joint. He decided they probably didn't care; it was part of London's rich tapestry. The residents were only likely to complain if the girls were irresponsible about their recycling or if they did not scoop poop deposited by small pets. Besides, it was quite a discreet strip joint. The windows were blackened and there were no neon flashing lights advertising the activities that took place within. The thin blue canvas canopy that poked into the street and the roped-off doorway, complete with a substantial-sized geezer checking the suitability of punters, could have signalled a private casino or even a smart restaurant. As Neil squeezed past the greasy, hefty guy, he wondered what the bouncers were looking for. Who wasn't suitable to pay fifty quid to take a look at a stranger's snatch? Who was?

The friends stood in the small reception for a moment, waiting for access into the inner sanctum. Karl looked relaxed and confident. Tim looked wasted. Neil tried to hide behind a yucca plant, a plastic one.

'Look, Tim. They say, "Fully nude table dancing", no half measures,' Karl said, pointing to a notice Blu-tacked to the wall.

'Is it possible to be partially nude?' slurred Tim.

Neil thought that it probably wasn't. Nude, by definition, meant naked, didn't it? Bare. Undressed. Exposed.

'Look, here in this leaflet, they claim to have a "worldwide reputation",' Karl added.

'Right up there with the Eiffel Tower and the Pyramids,' mumbled Neil.

Karl ignored him and continued talking to Tim. 'You'll like it in here. There's an incredibly friendly personal service.'

'Yup. That's guaranteed, providing you have a wad of cash,' added Neil.

'Why can't you just be cool?' snapped Karl, exasperated. 'Just relax. Try and get in the mood.'

Suddenly, a woman in her twenties appeared from behind a crimson curtain like a genie in a panto. A genie with bleached hair and two fantastical orbs. She looked as if she had a couple of goldfish bowls surgically attached to her rib cage. Despite his best intentions, Neil couldn't take his eyes off them. E cups, at a guess. The woman caught him looking and winked lasciviously. He wanted to explain he wasn't admiring them so much as staring in genuine amazement but he stopped himself. It was hardly a compliment. She was wearing a clingy, glittery red dress which plunged to her waist at both the back and the front and split to her upper thigh, both left and right. Neil wasn't sure it would be absolutely necessary for her to take the dress off later as very little was being left to the imagination anyway. The dress put Neil in mind of making Christmas decorations with little Angus and Sophia last year. They'd taken a circle of white paper, folded it into eight and then hacked away chunks of the paper. When they unfolded the circle, they'd been left with tremulous, dainty snowflakes which were more space than substance. This woman's dress was the same.

She smiled at them. It was a cursory, efficient smile but Neil couldn't blame her for not putting her heart and soul into the smile. When Neil had first visited a strip joint with Karl, many years ago, he'd imagined the strippers would all be pitiful eastern Europeans with endless degrees but no legal right to work in the UK. He had expected that they would all be the sort of girls who sent their earnings home to poor, sick mothers. Unfortunates. In fact, the strippers were mostly hardened London girls who knew they could make more money taking off their clothes than either serving coffee in a greasy spoon or laundering hotel sheets. Most of them pitied the punters, not the other way round, and few managed to entirely hide the fact.

The hostess waved her arm in the direction of the club and wished the guys a pleasant evening.

'Will do, babe,' said Karl with a leer.

'Absolutely,' enthused Tim.

Neil wondered which one of them sounded most embarrassing. They scooted through numerous red lace sheets and curtains of dangling beads which glimmered and shone like tears. They passed purple walls and plastic plants in pots and headed towards the bar, where Neil walked directly into the arms (or more accurately, the tits) of another hostess. This one was also wearing a snowflake dress, a couple of goldfish bowls and a professional smile, but she had dark hair, not blond. Her face was very shiny as she had glistening eye shadow, diamanté stones on her eyelashes and her plump red lips were wet with gloss. In fact everything about her glimmered: her earrings, dress, shoes and nails all sparkled and glinted so that it was almost painful to look at her. She was holding a glass of champagne. She dipped her finger into the bubbles and then placed her finger in her mouth. She sucked on it, hard, while trying to establish eye contact with Neil. He thought he might giggle. He thought of Nat. It was the sort of thing she did when licking out baking bowls on the rare occasions she made a cake. Nat swore nothing else tasted as delicious as uncooked cake mix.

Neil shook his head. Hell, that thought wasn't going to help him get a hard-on. Nat baking! Could things be any more domesticated, any less erotic? Although, thinking about it, they usually did make love after she'd baked, there was something about the smell of baking in their home that made both of them feel like it. He was aware of a twitch in his groin.

He looked round and noticed three things. One, Karl was already surrounded by a group of four girls, a couple of whom were topless. They were brushing up against Karl's arm, although Neil was pretty sure that actual physical contact with nude parts was prohibited. Two, Tim was sitting at a table and there was a stunning redhead on his knee. He looked like a rabbit caught in the headlights but a rabbit that was excited, rather than terrified, by the thought of the inevitable collision. And three, less than a metre to his right, there was a woman gyrating against a pole. She was wearing little other than nail and hair extensions.

'Should we have a drink?' he asked 'his' hostess. It seemed only polite as she was making such an effort, still earnestly sucking her forefinger and all.

'Mine's champagne. I'm a girl who likes it fizzy.' She shimmied a little when she said the word fizzy, lest either of them were in any doubt about the meaning of her innuendo. Neil was aware that the 'champagne' that they were given was probably cava and yet cost ten times over the odds. Still, he had to push on. They'd sunk about six pints before they'd left the pub but he wasn't floating, he had yet to hit that exquisite feeling of carelessness. He quaffed a glass of bubbly and then another, which finally supplied him with the confidence to take a more leisurely look around.

Despite the gruelling aerobic workouts the girls performed on stage, he noticed that the dancers were all pleasantly curvy. Besides the surgical enhancements, they had large bottoms and strong thighs, perhaps as a result of the idea that most men like something to hold on to. Fair enough. It was a busy night. There were three large groups that looked like stag parties or gangs of colleagues. They sat in the corners and competitively tried to out-spend, out-drink and out-cuss one another. Plus, there were at least half a dozen smaller groups of mates, similar to their own, and a large number of loners. The loners unnerved Neil. They seemed to take it all too seriously. Because it was so busy, there were not many girls floating around the club looking for someone to dance for, most had attached themselves to a punter and stayed close by.

Neil knew the routine. These women had to chat to the customers, make them feel really special, get them to buy lots of overpriced drinks and then, ideally, take them to the private rooms for private dances. They had to do it in such a way as to create the illusion that they found beery, leery, often fat, balding and old men simply *fascinating* and that they were just *dying* to take off their clothes for them. Indeed they'd do it even if they weren't being paid hard cash! It was a chimera that was eluding Neil tonight. It was a blatant fact that the event was all about a transaction and the balance of power. Who had the most money? Who had the most sex? How much sex could be bought for how much money?

Neil swallowed down another glass of bubbles and willed himself into the mood. He just wanted to lie back and sink into sex. Not think about anything much at all. Another glass was sunk. Another bottle bought. Finally, sex started to close in on him. Overwhelm and overawe him. Sex was in the air. In his head. In his fingertips. The hostess watched him pass the point of no return as she played with her hair, her throat, as she brushed her hands across her nipples and thighs.

Neil was nervous and hard at once and somewhat relieved to suddenly notice that Karl and Tim were back by his side. Their hostesses stood by while the guys propped themselves up against the stage. Their eyes were level with the calves of a dancer. She crouched down, so that for a fleeting, exciting moment her sparkly gusset flashed just in front of their faces.

'Good legs,' slurred Tim.

'You're looking at her legs?' asked Karl in bewilderment.

'It's because she wears heels all day,' Tim added.

Neil couldn't speak properly. He was hypnotised by red talons, bleached hair, year-round tans and slinky dresses that threatened to slip at any moment. How much had he drank with his hostess? More than was sensible. More than normal. More than ever before? Enough, at least, to stop him thinking about babies.

'Many of the girls are trained dancers, Cherry was just telling me so,' commented Tim.

'Maybe these strippers do refer to themselves as dancers and they very well might have a talent that way, it hardly matters,' said Karl dismissively. 'None of the punters care if the girls can do-si-do or demi plié, the important moves are thrusting and flicking. Now, who's up for a private dance?'

Tim shook his head emphatically. 'No, enough is enough. Ali would kill me as it is.'

'But you are not planning on telling her.'

'No, but if she found out.'

'You might as well be hung for a sheep as a lamb,' pointed out Karl.

'No,' said Tim. But he couldn't take his eyes off Cherry, the redhead he'd been drinking with. Was she a genuine redhead, he wondered. Would she be freckled? Would her nipples be pink? Would her pubes be that same erotic, charged colour? Neil was staring at his brunette in the same curious and intense way.

'OK, I will,' slurred Neil.

'What?' Karl and Tim chorused, turning on Neil. In the past Neil and Karl had, on occasion, visited a strip joint together – corporate entertainment if they had their big boss over from Japan or maybe a stag do – but never before had Neil agreed to a private dance. He would watch the girls on the poles on the centre stage and he'd buy drinks but he'd never entered the VIP lounge. Karl often had and he returned from the concealed rooms with stories of girls sitting on his lap, feeling his erection through his thin trousers, stories of blow jobs and hand jobs which were legally prohibited if money changed hands but Karl always insisted that the girls simply found him irresistible and did it for free. Indeed, he had once dated a stripper that he met here, for a month or so. Neil wasn't sure he believed Karl's stories but suddenly he felt a need to be up close and personal, even if he had to pay for it. He couldn't remember when he and Nat had last had sex. Weeks ago. Before he mentioned wanting a baby. Even then, it wasn't the raunchy sort of sex where Nat thrust her breasts in his face and threw her head back and moaned. It had been quiet and pleasant. Neil didn't want sex with his hostess, just a dance, just a bit of sexiness. What was the harm?

Neil straightened up, raised his chin and, in the manner of someone going off to war, he marched (or rather swayed) in the direction of the VIP lounge.

19

'Don't, don't. Seriously, I'm going to be sick,' Nat said as she battled to sit straight. She was literally laughing so much that her stomach hurt. She'd forgotten just how hilarious Matthew could be, or maybe she'd never known, or maybe she just wasn't used to laughing much at the moment; she and Neil hadn't shared as much as a grin for days now. She reached for her water glass and took calming sips.

'Don't gulp because, knowing you, it will come back out through your nose,' warned Matthew.

He was referring to an incident where once Nat had 'snorted' Fanta out through her nose and on to his best friend, just before said best friend had to attend an important job interview. The memory no longer caused Nat to shrivel in shame, and she chuckled. 'God, Yes, I was accident-prone, wasn't I? Do you remember when I met your mother and father for the first time?

'Yes, you decided to dye your hair before the lunch date.'

'It turned a sort of mucus green colour.'

'Lovely picture you paint.'

'That's how your dad described it!'

'Rude bugger. Sorry. I apologise sincerely on his behalf,' said Matthew formally.

'I was mortified at the time but when I look back now I think he was trying to make a joke, you know, lighten the atmosphere.'

'You mean because you'd knocked my mother's plate of spaghetti on to her lap and ruined her Jacques Vert dress.' Matthew couldn't help but grin at the memory, it was so utterly slapstick it was impossible not to.

'I didn't do it on purpose,' giggled Nat.

'Really?' He raised an eyebrow in mock suspicion.

'No!' Nat paused. 'Although if I had, no one could have blamed me. Your mum hated me.'

'She did, didn't she?' agreed Matthew honestly.

'And she never hid the fact.' Even through the laughter, and after all this time, Nat was still a little hurt and indignant. She glanced at Matt and he seemed to understand her old insecurity. Gracefully, he opted to put the ancient history to bed.

'No. But she doesn't like anyone, least of all herself,' he explained simply.

Nat felt an enormous wave of liberation swoosh through her body. It wasn't her fault; it was Mrs Jackson's problem. Oh, what a relief.

'I'm sorry,' Nat mumbled.

'It's OK. I know you really didn't drop the spaghetti on purpose.'

Nat considered explicitly explaining that she was saying sorry that Matthew had an unhappy mother, rather than sorry about the dry-cleaning bill, but when she glanced at him, she knew he understood. He was retreating into humour and who could blame him? Parents were so complicated.

'*And* I'm sorry I broke that weird, antique boot rack at your boss's house. Do you remember? I thought it was a stool and sat down on it to take my shoes off.'

'Ah, you did him a favour. It was as ugly as hell,' grinned Matthew.

'Quite. But you didn't see it like that at the time.'

'No, sorry, I was quite stroppy about it then, wasn't I?'

'I think the final straw was when we got home that evening and we realised I'd locked us out of the house. I'm sorry about that too.'

It was clear, without either of them having to say so overtly, that they were both sorry about anything big, or small, that had ever caused the other upset, discomfort or disappointment. The bottle of wine and time had helped them reach this affable amnesty.

'Are you still a disaster zone?'

'No. I'm not,' said Nat, thinking about it.

'What changed?'

'I suppose I'm simply not as nervous as I used to be.'

'I'm sorry but *I* get the monopoly on nervousness. I spent the eight months of our romance wondering when I could admit to being gay.'

'I spent the eight months wondering when I could admit to being tone deaf.'

'Oh, yes, that's much more of an obstacle to the happily ever after, I agree,' Matthew joked.

Nat could barely remember the accident-prone, nervous, miserable being she once was, but talking to Matthew was bringing back memories of her more gauche and glum self. When she'd first picked up the Little Black Book, all she'd thought about was the numerous beginnings the small leather book represented but Nat knew there was more to the past than beginnings. There were endings too and disappointments, mistakes and insecurities. She hadn't considered that before she'd picked up the phone.

It was true to say that as a child and very young woman Nat used to feel constantly inept. It wasn't that she felt there was an impending disaster, it was worse than that – she thought the disaster had already happened. *She* had already happened. She *was* the disaster.

Nat was aware that she suffered from a classic and hefty dose of low self-esteem. She was one of those people who when offered a choice of two drinks would *always* reply, 'Whatever is easiest, I really don't mind, whatever you're having.' She would say this even if she detested one of the choices, and by responding in this way she had spent a good proportion of her life eating and drinking things she wasn't too fond of, going places she had no interest in and, frankly, frustrating countless hosts who were never absolutely sure Nat was having the good time they were trying to provide.

As Nat got older she realised that, gallingly, her policy of trying to disappear often had the opposite effect. She never wanted to cause a fuss, or put anyone to any extra trouble on her behalf as she believed there had already been far too much trouble on her behalf, but well-intentioned friends and acquaintances would lavish even more attention on her as they tried increasingly hard to draw her out of her shell. Nat was finally forced to change strategy when she was thirteen and her form tutor had demanded (in a tone of barely disguised irritation), 'But you *must* have a preference as to which subjects you want to pursue as GCSEs, Natalie!'

Nat had replied, 'I don't mind. You can pick them for me.'

The teacher was unprepared to take on such a responsibility, it was unreasonable to expect it. 'I'll have to call your parents in, they can make the decision,' she'd snapped.

In a split second Nat listed the subjects she would study. Her biggest nightmare was inconveniencing her parents. Nat's dose of low self-esteem was so extreme and sincere that she was not prepared to brandish it about the way *Big Brother* contestants felt compelled to.

It had taken years but Nat had forced herself to be witty, bright and assertive. When she had felt wretched and worthless she had gone for a walk or called a friend. When she had wondered what was the point of herself, she'd switched on her laptop and worked. It had been the only way to get through; being shy and reclusive seemed so damned indulgent and Nat wasn't sure whether self-indulgence and low self-esteem genuinely sat comfortably together. Eventually, years of pretending to trust herself had paid off and Nat started to believe her own performance. She hadn't felt desolate or dejected for a long time. She was now an entirely different woman to the one she had been when she was with Matthew. She had her own lovely home, an exhilarating job and, of course, she had Neil.

'So why are you less nervous now than you were then?' asked Matthew as if following her thought pattern.

'Age, I suppose. I guess that's one of the advantages of getting older. You become more confident in yourself or at least resigned to what you are. There's not the same amount of constant striving to impress or improve,' she replied, scratching the surface of her reasoning and not prepared to do any more.

'For me, coming out of the closet was, well, you can imagine, so liberating. Such a relief. I hated skulking around gay clubs, not being able to introduce my love interests to my friends and family. Constantly living with skeletons is truly hell.'

'Yes.' Nat looked at her hands. She knew that. She didn't want to comment.

There was a hiatus in the conversation and then the inevitable.

'So why the call?'

Matthew and Nat had eaten a large plate of delicious tapas, finished a bottle of Burgundy and they were sipping their water and coffees now. They'd caught up on one another's careers. They knew that they each owned a property. He knew she had a cat, she knew he had a dog. They'd swapped names of people they'd once held in common, both those they still saw and those they'd lost touch with. There was only one topic of conversation left. The obvious one. The big one. Why the call?

'I'm checking out whether I married the right one. You know out of my, well, choices, I suppose,' confessed Nat with a big, deep breath.

'Sounds serious. Well, at least I can put your mind at rest that I wasn't really in the contest,' joked Matthew. He was male and therefore unable to resist bringing the conversation back round to him, even if just for a moment. Then, more thoughtfully, he added, 'Why do you doubt Neil?'

She had to tell him, so she said it carefully, in a whisper that imbued importance. 'I don't want babies. Neil does.'

'Ah,' he replied and comfortingly he didn't rush to fill the silence that ensued. He didn't demand to know why she did not want babies or what was wrong with her. He simply digested the enormous fact.

'Do you want them?' Nat asked Matthew curiously.

'Never been an option for me. I'm glad gay people have rights to adopt, or incubate or whatever they want to do to become a parent, but fundamentally I think being a parent is about putting the child first and I'm not sure I could do that. More, I'm not sure adopting a baby to be brought up by me and another guy would demonstrate that.'

'Are you seeing anyone special?'

'No. I was but we broke up because he wanted cats and as I mentioned I'm a—'

'Dog sort of guy.' Nat smiled.

'There was more to it than that, of course.'

'Of course. Maybe you understand me then,' she said hopefully.

'Maybe.'

'Neil doesn't.'

'Right.'

Neither of them could think of what else to say on the subject so they finished their coffees and then wandered back to Waterloo. They kissed on the cheek and Matthew got on the Northern line while Nat navigated her way westwards. He was renewed and relieved, glad to have told one more person the truth about who he was but Nat felt nothing of the sort. She was as churned up as a berry smoothie and did not feel a clear sense of anything. She was glad to have seen Matthew again, it had been a fun evening, but she was disturbed to recognise that her feelings of insecurity had been reawakened. It wasn't meeting Matthew that had caused her to feel frail again, it was just that being with him helped her remember that she used to always carry around with her an unreasonable notion of impending doom. This sense of fear and disaster used to cling to her like a foul and deadly stench but had long since been banished from her life. Until recently. Until Neil had started to talk about a baby. Now that awful feeling had started to insidiously creep back into Nat's heart and head.

20

It was obvious what Nat needed to do. She needed to reconnect with Neil. These secret wild-goose chases were damaging her peace of mind. They were pointless and silly. It was Neil she loved. Neil she had chosen and who had chosen her. This time, she would tell Neil all about her night out with her ex, her innocent, hilarious night out with her *gay* ex. It was pretty clear to her that these trips down memory lane led to dead ends. Large, solid brick walls, covered with graffiti and moss, walls she had *no* desire to scramble over. While Matthew was good-looking, funny, charming and successful, he was notably, inarguably, out-loud and proud gay. This fact indisputably negated any possibility of him being suitable as a lifelong partner. Gary, on the other hand, was a walking bag of testosterone, but he glazed over whenever she used words with more than two syllables. When she talked about her ineptitude in the gym he thought she was discussing some state-of-the-art equipment and he became anxious that he didn't know what an ineptitude machine was exactly. He'd demanded, was it to work biceps or pecs? Meeting up with these two old exes confirmed she hadn't taken a wrong turning; how could she have possibly doubted it, even for a moment? Being with Neil was as life should be. Even when they were wobbly, even when they were frustrated or angry with one another, they were still meant to be. She saw that now.

She wouldn't continue to make her way through her address book.

She'd probably discover that her other near-miss Mr Rights were serial killers or bigamists, which isn't good for a girl's ego! No, it was a waste of time and energy. What she needed to be doing was spending those resources on reconnecting with Neil. How had she allowed this gulf to open up between them? She must not let this baby business ruin them.

Nat practically ran from the tube station to their street, as fast as her heels would allow her. The drizzle had temporarily eased off, which was a relief, although the wind lashed the trees and the branches danced in an agitated, uncoordinated jig. Nat suddenly thought of Neil dancing and she giggled to herself at the subconscious link. It was fair to say that they were both noted for their enthusiasm, rather than their skill, on the dance floor. They were the sort of couple who had too much fun to bother whether they looked cool when they danced. With Neil, Nat was prepared to be bold, rather than skulk around the edge of a party room, tapping her toe. Suddenly, Nat had a fantastic idea. They should go to a club and go dancing again! It had been ages since they'd done that. As their friends had started to pair off and procreate, wild nights of hilarity and abandon had been replaced by sophisticated dinners at elegant restaurants which were reviewed in the Sunday newspapers. They should do something crazy together.

Better than her doing anything crazy alone.

Nat arrived home buoyed up with red wine and good intentions; she expected to fall straight into bed with Neil. But once again, for the second time in just a week, he was not at home.

Neil staggered in at 5a.m. By this point, all Nat's positive intent had perished. For five hours she had spun through the emotional mill that every wife tumbles through when her husband is late home. Initially she had been excited and expectant, then she became weary and frustrated, and then panicked and despairing. She rang his mobile several times but it was out of power or switched off. When Neil finally fell through the door, a mighty tidal wave of relief soused her soul, but in an instant the relief morphed into fury. This time she didn't want to feign sleep, this time she was ready to have an enormous row.

'Who is she?' she demanded, the moment her eyes became accustomed to the bright bedroom light that Neil had inconsiderately flicked on.

'Who is who?' slurred Neil.

Nat had not planned this to be her first question. She'd expected to ask, 'What time do you call this?' or even, 'Where the hell have you been?' but as Neil had walked in with lipstick smeared on his cheek, Nat had a new imperative.

'Who is she?' she screamed again. It was surprising to her how she'd reached this aggressive, take-no-prisoners pitch in just seconds. She sounded terrifying to herself, but Neil was protected by the huge quantities of alcohol he'd consumed and couldn't respond to her fury.

'Who is who?' he slurred for the second time, trying, and failing, to look innocent. Neil attempted to pull his face into a suitable expression. But he couldn't decide what suitable might be. Rakish but charming? Or lovable and puppy dog? The result was an inappropriate smirk that served to enrage Nat further.

'You've been with another woman!'

'No.'

'You liar. I can see lipstick on your face.' Nat leapt out of bed and quickly examined Neil. 'And fake tan on your crotch! Who the hell is she?'

'Barbie, or Bella, or Cindy or something,' giggled Neil. Clearly too pissed to grasp the seriousness of the situation.

'I don't want to hear made-up names inspired by bloody Disney videos. What is the name of your other woman?' demanded Nat. Hot tears sprang into her eyes. She wanted to hit him. Punch him and wound him as brutally as she was wounded. How had this happened? How could Neil be seeing someone else?

'I'm not making it up,' insisted Neil. 'Strippers have funny names like that. Cherry and Jaz and things.'

'Strippers?'

'Yes. We went to Hush Hush. You don't mind, do you?'

Nat knew that in the past Neil had on occasion visited a strip joint. Usually he cited the tenuous excuse of corporate entertainment if they had their big boss over from Japan, or maybe a stag do. And while she didn't love the idea of him paying to watch women take their clothes off, she didn't hate it any more than the fact that he snowboarded off piste, which she considered seriously dangerous, or that he was saving up to buy a Ducati Monster motorbike, come to that. She thought he had a lot of dumb hobbies. But why had he gone to a strip joint tonight? It wasn't anyone's birthday.

'Why did you go to Hush Hush?'

'Felt like it.' Neil considered saying it was Karl's idea but he knew she'd think it was a cop-out. She might even respond, 'If Karl suggested jumping into a lake, would you say yes?' He *would* actually, because if Karl suggested jumping into a lake, it would probably be a damn fine idea, but he knew it would be stupid to say as much, inflammatory. He felt sick. He really had drunk far, far too much. He hoped that in the morning he'd clearly remember the magnificent orbs that belonged to Cherry, or Barbie or whatever she was called, but he doubted it. He'd probably only know he'd visited the strip joint because of the banging in his head and the hole in his finances. He tried hard to commit to memory the exact colour and texture of her nipple, the mesmerising, tantalising bumps that were so familiar and yet completely strange.

'You're not bothered, are you? You've never been bothered before and I know you're not one to change your mind,' said Neil. He hadn't intended to place such heavy emphasis on this point but it was beyond his control. He actually believed (in that deluded way drunks have) that he was being subtle.

So there it was. The *reason*. The great fucking elephant in the room. She didn't want a baby. She wouldn't change her mind about wanting a baby. Nat's fury dissolved and was replaced by fear and a hideous sense of loss. She was nauseous with that sense of doom again. Why couldn't this issue just go away? Poof, be gone! Vanish! Disappear!

She closed her eyes tightly and wished as though she was a child. But after some moments she had to open them again and everything was the same. The same warm and creased duvet had slipped off the bed and lay in a pile on the floor. There were the same pictures on the wall although one wasn't hanging straight as Neil had knocked it when he staggered into the room. There he was, the same drunken husband swaying in the door frame and he was wearing the same expression he always wore nowadays, one of confusion and sadness. She realised he'd backed her into a corner. There was nothing she could say to his comment. She would not change her mind on the pertinent issue, so anything she said now would be used against her, even though she was pretty sure he was the one in the wrong. He was the one who'd visited a strip joint.

And she was the one looking up exes in her Little Black Book.

Her ex was gay.

The stripper didn't have any interest in Neil beyond how much cash he was going to spend that night.

And yet . . .

It was a mess.

'I'm going to be sick,' said Neil, dashing from the room.

Nat heard the vomit splash into the loo. She slammed shut their bedroom door, picked the duvet up from the floor and pulled it over her head.

21

Neil didn't think of himself as the secretive type. Keeping secrets demanded energy and a zeal for complications which he simply didn't possess and yet now he found himself, for the third time in twelve days, withdrawing cash from the hole in the wall and heading towards the pink building with blackened windows. He'd visited the night before last, without Karl. He'd told himself that he was just popping in for a pint on the way home from work but even before the excuse had fully formed in his own mind, he knew he was a liar. They didn't sell pints at Hush Hush and the bottled beer cost four times the amount it should. But Nat was out with Becky again, so why not? There was nothing and no one to stop him.

He'd learnt from the ponytailed barman that 'his girl' *was* called Cindy. He'd been worried that he wouldn't be able to describe her, not exactly. He couldn't remember the colour of her eyes. Many of the women at the venue had viciously bleached hair so he could rule out those ones, as his girl had dark hair, but that still left a fair few. None of them wore clothes and inconveniently, but understandably, they didn't have any distinguishing birthmarks. It was unlikely you'd choose to strip for a living if you had a raspberry mark the size of a football on your arse, however convenient that might be for drunken clients who were hoping to track down a particular girl. But, right away, the barman knew which girl Neil was tracking. Neil wondered if on his previous visit he'd been conspicuous in some way and he hoped not.

'Cindy's not in tonight. Her night off,' said the barman. He held a bottle of something pretending to be champagne in his hand and moved it an inch in a tiny gesture which meant he was offering Neil a drink. Neil hadn't wanted to stay if Cindy wasn't around but before he could shake his head the barman had already poured him a glass. 'Do you want to open a tab?' he asked, holding out a hand to take Neil's credit card. The barman's hand was pale and podgy, too many late nights in dark rooms. Black hairs scampered from under his shirt sleeve, across the back of his hand and down to his knuckles. His appearance, with werewolf undertones, was vaguely threatening.

'No. Cash.' Neil passed over a note and wasn't offered any change.

Neil took a sip of the fizzy drink, and before the vivacious bubbles could hurtle towards his tonsils, two dancers were at his side. They both had deep tans and shallow smiles. Their thighs and arms glistened, their lips were moist and their faces glimmered with sparkly make-up. In fact they were so heavily made up Neil thought they were wearing masks, and maybe they were. He knew then how the night would pan out. They would ask if they could join him for a drink. He'd buy a bottle, then another and then he'd follow one of these flicky-haired women behind the dangling beads, so he could get a close look at what a fabulous job her beautician had done on her Brazilian. He felt numb. He didn't particularly want to see these women naked. He had come here tonight to see Cindy. And even then, not to see her naked.

The odd thing was, the day after his visit to Hush Hush, when his hangover had been raging with such an intensity that he'd started to believe he was being subjected to some medieval torture and his wife was silently sulking in a way that screamed her discontent and disappointment with him, Neil did not feel one hundred per cent awful. Ninety-nine per cent, certainly, but there had been a small glimmer of hope. There was something that was not quite ugly, wrong or painful in his life. There was Cindy. OK, he couldn't remember her name at first and he called her 'his dancer' but now he knew. There was Cindy.

As he'd expected, it was not her nipples he remembered the next day, but it was a surprise to him to discover he remembered the exact nature of her smile. Not the unconvincing smile that she bestowed as a professional courtesy, no. The smile that he remembered was the one she'd launched his way when she'd asked if he had a wife and kids and he'd replied yes to the former and that he 'longed for the latter'. At the time her smile had warmed something deep in the pit of his stomach and for a moment he believed that he wasn't unreasonable for changing his mind about wanting a child (as Nat maintained) or out of his senses (as Karl insisted). He thought his decision might be OK. Might be quite sound. If only Nat could see it.

It wasn't standard stripper talk, he was pretty sure of that. Karl could mock and say that these women were just trained to spot your Achilles heel but Neil saw sincerity in her smile, and so what if the smile had been paid for? He was almost certain she would have bestowed it for free. They had a connection. Definitely. Outside of this place, with its plush cushions and sparkly beads, he was sure they could be friends. Not that he was saying he wanted to take their friendship outside these four walls. No way. Neil wasn't a fool, he could see that would lead to trouble. He was just making the point that he believed there was something real about the way Cindy had listened to him when, after the first private dance, he'd asked her to sit down, put her dress back on and just answer him, was he so unreasonable? She'd been happy to do it. At least, she had been once they'd agreed a price for the next forty minutes. On the way home Karl had pointed out that minute for minute Cindy was more expensive than a trip to the Bahamas, and while Karl had spent approximately the same money on Gina, Lottie and Ava as Neil had on Cindy, Karl thought it was pissing cash down the drain to pay for *talk*. He'd pay a woman to shut up maybe but to talk? It was inconceivable. But Karl was always sarky, that was his thing. Neil did his best to ignore him.

'When is Cindy in next?' Neil asked the barman hesitantly. He wasn't sure of the etiquette. Were the punters allowed to request particular girls or was it a bit creepy? It felt vaguely disturbing. He stood back from the bar so that the guy could see he was wearing head-to-toe Diesel, not a dirty mackintosh. He wanted to say that he had never owned an inflatable doll.

'Wednesday lunchtime.'

Lunchtime? These girls took their clothes off during the day? It didn't seem right. Who came to this sort of place during the daytime? Only the seriously sad and desperate, thought Neil

Which is why he was surprised when, today, he found himself shuffling past the chunky bouncer in broad daylight. The werewolf bar guy nodded in recognition. He passed a bottle of beer across the counter which Neil gratefully picked up and gulped back even though he wasn't usually a lunchtime drinker.

'On the house,' said the werewolf.

'Thanks,' muttered Neil, not sure if he was secretly thrilled or disgusted that he'd turned into the sort of man who was awarded free drinks in a strip joint.

'You should get a membership,' suggested the werewolf.

'Oh no,' objected Neil.

'Why not? You'd save lots of dough in the long run.'

Neil felt uncomfortable as he didn't see himself as someone who needed a membership to this sort of place. Was he planning on a long run?

'I'll think about it,' he said pathetically.

'Come on. I'll take you to her. She's waiting in the VIP lounge.'

Before Neil had a chance to thoroughly contemplate what the barman said, he was led towards the VIP lounges. There Cindy was waiting for him as promised, or at least she was waiting for someone and it suited everyone's purposes to pretend that the someone was Neil. She patted the velvet seat next to her. Obediently, Neil sat down; he could feel the warmth of her thigh next to his. She offered him a drink.

'No thanks. I've already had a beer and to be honest it's a bit early for me,' he said demurely.

'You'll have to order something, love. Or else I won't be able to sit here with you. I'll have to go and see the other punters,' said Cindy flatly.

Neil had noted that the place was all but empty, there weren't any unattended punters but he wasn't in the mood for a row, those he could get at home, in abundance. Instead he nodded at the werewolf barman who was hovering close by precisely because he was expecting to take an order. The werewolf didn't wait for explicit instructions but once given the nod, he quickly disappeared and then returned almost immediately with a bottle of fizz in a bucket. The efficiency suggested another rehearsed routine, the thought of which vaguely irritated Neil. He wished he'd specified that he just wanted another bottle of beer. This chat he wanted with Cindy was becoming scarily expensive. He could buy an updated iPod touch for about the same as that bottle of pop (which he had no intention of consuming) had cost him. Cindy sensed his resentment and treated him to a broad smile.

'So, Nile, lovely to see you again,' she said crossing her legs, causing her dress to fall open, exposing the toned, tanned flesh of her upper thigh.

'Neil,' he corrected.

'Sorry, angel. Neil, right.' She shrugged, too shrewd to bother being abjectly apologetic. They both knew where and how they met. They knew the score. 'I didn't have you down as a lunchtime visitor,' she added.

'No. I'm not, really.'

'Would you like a dance now?' She stood up and started to fiddle with the clasp on her halter neck of her sparkly dress.

'No, not really,' replied Neil awkwardly. Cindy looked colder than he remembered and her heavy make-up was gathered around the creases of her eyes in a way that drew his attention. She was still an attractive woman, or at least she was still an attractive caricature of a woman which was the best he could hope for in a strip joint. It wasn't that Neil had gone off the idea of seeing her naked, he just wasn't sure he was ever *on* the idea of seeing her naked. That wasn't why he was here.

'I can't sit here for free,' she pointed out.

'Of course.' Neil reached into his pocket and pulled out a bundle of twenties. He threw them on to the table. Cindy reached for them, snaffling the cash with a feral determination that put Neil in mind of an urban fox rummaging through bin bags late at night. He shifted uncomfortably on the plush sofa. She hadn't appeared so mercenary the other night. Was he a fool? A prize twat? Of course she was mercenary. She was a stripper, everything was for sale. Neil felt hideously sad. What was he doing here? Was he some sort of desperate, friendless wanker that he needed to pay a stripper for a chat? A moment's thought revealed the answer: yeah, he was. Mortified, he considered that what he should do right now was stand up and walk out immediately. But Neil had kept his eye firmly on the werewolf's shoes as he'd followed him into this lair and now he wasn't sure of his bearings. Nervously, he cast his eyes around, looking for the exit. It was surreal to be in an erotic bar in the middle of the day. From the VIP lounge (a raised area) he had a unique view of the stage where, currently, a woman was performing breathtaking aerobic feats with a pole. Neil wondered at the strength in her thighs.

'In the evening some of the girls are suspended from the ceiling over the stage,' said Cindy, pointing above where they were sitting. 'I don't do the circus bit because the blokes that sit here can see right up when they do the mid-air splits. That's a bit much for me. Just the midwife who delivered my girl has had that pleasure in the past two years.'

Neil stopped looking for an exit. 'You have a child?'

Cindy eyed him warily and wearily. She didn't usually talk about her daughter to the punters. The two things were entirely separate, they had to be. Cindy remembered something about this Neil. Oh yeah, he wanted kids and his wife wasn't interested, that was what he'd been going on about the other night. On and on and on about, actually. His wife must be some sort of career bitch, Cindy concluded. Well, he looked trustworthy enough for her to continue.

'Yeah, a daughter. She's twenty months old. Heidi. You know, like in the book.'

'I never imagined.' Neil stuttered to a halt. Anything he had to say could only be misconstrued as insulting. What? He never imagined strippers could be mums? He never saw strippers as women? At least not that sort of woman?

'Want to see a picture?' Cindy, unable to suppress her maternal pride, reached for her glittering clutch bag and pulled out a picture of a smiley, pretty kid sitting in a pool of colourful plastic balls. Neil had seen hundreds of similar pictures but every one moved him to smile.

'Must be tough, bringing her up on your own,' said Neil.

'I don't. Her dad is really hands on,' said Cindy with a shrug. She wasn't bothered by his assumption that she was a stereotypical struggling, single mum sort of stripper. She was too used to the assumption to waste energy being offended by it. She glanced at the photo, blew her daughter a kiss and then carefully replaced the snap back in her bag. 'I wouldn't have married him if he was like the useless bastards you see in here. My Dave understands his family responsibilities.'

'Right.' Neil didn't know what else to say.

'God, sorry.' Cindy put her hand to her mouth and clearly wished she could grab back her words and swallow them. 'I'm not saying *you* are a useless bastard. You seem very useful. Erm, I mean, nice. You seem nice.' All the coldness had melted from her and been replaced by embarrassment. 'Look, forget it. I shouldn't have started to get on about me. It's against the rules, actually. You won't say anything, will you?' Cindy looked concerned so Neil shook his head in an effort to reassure her. 'Thanks. Ruins things if the punters know we're married. Does their heads in.' Neil understood that. 'I wish we were allowed to smoke in here,' said Cindy desperately. Neil understood that too. Many an awkward social occasion could be eased by simply lighting a fag. 'Not deathbeds of lung cancer patients, though,' Nat would say. He could hear her now, loud and clear in his head.

Neil and Nat had both been smokers when they met. Natalie had given up smoking four years ago, the very day she hit thirty, just as she'd declared she would on her twenty-ninth birthday. Neil hadn't thought she'd manage it. It had seemed unlikely that if she were ever to give up, that she would do so actually on her birthday as birthdays are a time when it's accepted you will eat until you're gross, drink until you're sick and smoke until you're hoarse. But she'd stopped. Just like that, as though she was turning off a tap. She didn't arse around with cutting back, with patches or with hypnotherapy, she just went cold turkey. Neil had used all the above methods and more to try to quit but still sneaked the odd fag whenever he thought he could get away with it. Neil considered Nat's strength of mind. It was scary really, the extent of Nat's willpower. Terrifying.

Neil dropped into a deeper, darker silence as he thought about Natalie's determination and how fixed and focused she could be. History showed that once she decided a thing, she wouldn't budge. Oh hell. Fucking hell.

Cindy poured them both a drink.

'Shall I do a dance, since you're here?' she offered half-heartedly.

'Yeah, go on then,' said Neil because it would seem rude if he said no again.

'I bet if your missus saw my Heidi, she'd want a baby,' said Cindy as her dress fell to the floor.

22

'Hello, darling,'

'Hi, Mum, what's up?' asked Nat.

'The sky,' Nina deadpanned in reply, as she was a stickler for grammar and all things proper. 'Nothing is "up", darling, if you intend me to interpret that question to mean what is wrong? Did you?'

'No,' said Nat with a patient sigh. 'I meant what news?'

'You tell me, dear. What's your news?'

If Natalie had been listening carefully, she might have noted that her mother's tone was not quite as relaxed as usual. Nina was in fact using exactly the same, slightly suspicious tone of voice that she had used when she had asked a fifteen-year-old Nat whether she was bunking off school (having found daytime cinema ticket stubs in her blazer pocket). The same tone of voice that she had used when she asked Nat if she was having sex (having spotted condoms in her purse when Nat was paying for a coffee). A tone of voice she used practically all the time when talking to her sons. But Nat wasn't listening carefully.

'Oh, you know. Same old, same old. I'm working really hard on a big project on lymphatic filariasis. It's fascinating,' Nat replied, having switched to automatic pilot. Her head was full of concerns, very few of which were connected with lymphatic filariasis, despite what she wanted her mother to believe.

'And Neil?' probed Nina.

'Oh, you know, he's fine.'

'Working hard too?'

Frankly, Nat didn't know for sure. He wasn't at home much, she assumed he was in the office or hanging out at Karl's but honestly she hadn't really delved too deeply as to his exact whereabouts and he hadn't been especially forthcoming with any information. Not that there was anything unusual there, he never had been. It wasn't that he was a secretive sort. It was more that they trusted one another enough so as not to have to account for every single moment of their days. Or at least that's how it had been until recently and Nat found it comforting to pretend that this was how things still stood between them. Although late at night, when she lay awake staring at the shadows thrown at the wall by the light of the street lamp outside their home, she faced the fact that she no longer deserved Neil's absolute, unquestioning trust. Her guilt stupefied her reasoning and she never went on to wonder whether he still deserved hers.

'Hmmm,' she replied not lying but not committing or denying either.

'Michael Young called here.'

The name, so long ago put away and so recently and feverishly retrieved, sounded odd on her mother's lips. Nat's stomach lunged nervously as she felt something a lot like guilt churn inside her gut.

'Really?' Nat didn't want to say any more.

Nina waited, giving her daughter enough rope with which to hang herself, but Natalie saw the importance of remaining silent and so Nina was forced to push on.

'I thought it was rather strange hearing from him, out of the blue, after all these years. Lovely boy, of course, well, man now, I suppose. Wonderful to hear from him but a surprise.'

'Yes,' said Nat carefully.

'Not to you, though, dear. Not a surprise to you,' said Nina. 'Michael said he'd called us because he was returning *your* call but for some reason you hadn't left your home number when you left a message with his mother and Mrs Young took down your mobile incorrectly.'

'Oh.'

'So he called ours. He was wondering why you'd got in touch. He asked me if I knew.'

'Oh.'

'And I was stumped, darling. I couldn't imagine why you'd be calling a boy you dated in sixth form.'

'No.'

'Are you feeling sentimental?' Nina's question was ostensibly polite but was designed to poke. It hit the crux. Natalie panicked. How could she explain to her mother why she'd started calling her exes in her old address book?

'No, no, nothing like that,' Nat replied. 'Do you remember that junk I cleared out of my old room? Well, I found some old CDs in there that belonged to Michael and I thought I ought to return them.'

'Really? Do you imagine he's been missing those old tunes?' asked Nina, aware that she wasn't being given the truth, the whole truth and nothing but the truth; nowhere near.

'Some of them are collector pieces now.' Nat was rather pleased with her own quick thinking, her excuse sounded plausible. Indeed it sounded more reasonable than the real reason she had decided to call Mike. She squirrelled away the excuse and decided to use it when she did finally talk to him.

'I gave him the telephone number to your and Neil's home,' said Nina. Nat thought Nina's choice of words was a bit odd. Wouldn't it have been more natural to have said, 'I gave him your home telephone number'? Nat thought she'd heard some heavy emphasis on Neil's name but she might be being paranoid. 'I asked him to remember me to Mrs Young senior. There's a Mrs Young junior too, now, you know.'

'Erm, no. I didn't know.'

'Yes, he says he's been married for nine years.'

'Gosh, he never seemed to be the marrying sort.'

'Why do you say that?' asked Nina.

'Well, he was a bit moody and always thinking about the end of

the world. You know, nuclear explosions and the disintegrating ozone.'
Nat hoped she sounded casual and convincing.

'Darling, you were teenagers! Of course he was moody. It was essential.' Yes, Nat had to agree, she'd briefly considered that herself. 'He's grown up now. People change. He has two children. A boy and girl. The salt and pepper set,' said Nina with a bright giggle. The very thought of such a happy family was enough to lift her day.

'Two children,' mused Nat. She wasn't exactly sure why but she had rather liked the idea of Michael not having children, not conforming to the standard 2.4 and a dog that seemed to be expected. She liked the idea of them staying as they were.

'Well, darling, it's no surprise. I mean you're *all* grown up now.' Then, somewhat abruptly, Nina changed the subject and started talking about her plans to buy a new second-hand piano.

23

Nat idly flicked through the well-thumbed wedding magazine that lay on the sofa, while Jen made tea in the kitchen. Jen's flat was extremely neat and feminine. There was a heavy emphasis on the colours cream and lilac and all the furniture was delicate and fragile, so however often she visited, Nat could never shake the feeling that she'd been invited into a playhouse. Privately she thought the place would benefit from some neutral browns. Nat stared at the immaculate cream carpet with feelings somewhere between envy and mystification. What determination and effort it must take to maintain that pristine, show-home perfection. Nat's carpet was beige and splattered with numerous war wounds from party spillages.

'Do you make Karl take off his muddy trainers at the door when he visits?' Nat asked, as Jen emerged from the kitchen. She was carrying a tray which held a teapot, milk jug, two cups and saucers and a cake stand that was heaving with chocolate biscuits. She'd been reading a lifestyle magazine that said tea served the way grandma used to serve it was vogue. Last month they'd drunk cappuccino in tall glasses, and the month before that they'd had fresh mint tea in earthenware beakers. Nat was beginning to think Jen really did need a wedding to organise but the bridal magazines were still wishful thinking. Karl had not proposed and Nat seriously doubted he had the intention to ever do so. Besides, she was still unsure whether she wanted her friend's dreams to come true. She wondered whether Karl was the right man for Jen to hope for a genuine commitment from. Come to that, was Karl the right man for anyone to hope for genuine commitment from, anyone other than the barman at the Goat and Gate?

'He doesn't come here that often. He's not keen on my flatmate, Chloe. They were quite pally when she first moved in but I think they must have had a fall-out. So I tend to go to his, rather than him come here.'

Nat wondered if Karl preferred Jen visiting his place because that led to the efficient dispatching of his ironing pile or whether he'd slept with Chloe and that was the source of the unease between the two of them. She couldn't face pursuing the thought. It was a bleak conclusion to draw but Nat was finding it hard to trust anyone fully at the moment. Even herself.

She was riddled with anxiety and excitement. She'd had no idea both could sit side by side in her life. She had been determined not to revisit the Little Black Book, but days after Neil's trousers had been through the wash and the fake tan stains had sloshed away, Nat found she was still irritated with him for visiting the strip joint. Why had he done that? His thoughtless behaviour had provoked her to more reckless actions; she called more numbers in the address book. Why had she done that?

She was surprised but Becky had it nailed, few of her exes had moved on and even if they had, it was easy enough to track them down through Facebook or simply by Googling their names. It seemed extraordinary to her but each of her exes readily agreed to meet up. Nat didn't know what motivated them to accept her invite. Was it curiosity about her life, boredom with their own lives, or simply old-fashioned good manners? The result was always the same, her exes willingly agreed to meet for a drink. She hadn't told anyone about these recent meetings. Not even Becky, who had more or less instigated the whole thing in the first place. Nat tried to convince herself that there was nothing to tell but in fact she knew that what she was doing was slightly below the belt because she paid an inordinate amount of attention to her clothes when she picked out an outfit for the dates.

Well, it was natural to want to look your best if you were meeting up with an ex, no one could blame a girl for that. Dates? What was she talking about? They weren't dates, they were meetings. At coffee shops, pubs and bars, that was all.

Weren't they?

Whatever, it wasn't something she felt she could talk about with her friends. Nat repeatedly and defiantly asked herself, what was there to tell? Really? So, she'd had a coffee with Daniel McEwan. That had been a total disaster anyway; unquestionably one of the most uncomfortable experiences of her life. Nat hadn't been that into Daniel the first time she went out with him and things weren't any better now, several years on. He had been a friend of a friend's boyfriend and they had started dating because Nat's friend had insisted they were well suited. Daniel was a pleasant enough looking guy, he had big brown eyes that he used to his advantage, he was a bit thin on top, he said it was a hereditary thing and indeed his dad and big brother were both bald as coots. He had nice manners; he had always opened the car door for her and walked on the side of the pavement that was nearest to the traffic. But he could be sulky and he had no hobbies nor many friends. Nat had always felt responsible for entertaining him, which was a little draining. Nat remembered very few specifics about their relationship. She knew they must have visited interesting places, got pleasantly pissed together and sometimes talked late into the night; she just couldn't remember the actual occasions. She did remember that he was a dog-lover and that they had taken his Great Dane along on all their dates. While this limited the sort of dates they had (mostly walks in the park culminating in a pub garden), Nat had never had a problem with this as truthfully she'd felt more affection for the dog than she did for Daniel. She'd allowed the relationship to go on far longer than it should have done. They dated for about a year and then, finally, she found the courage to tell him that she didn't think they had a future. Nat had thought she'd never forget the icy hurt and disbelief in Daniel's big brown eyes as she delivered her exit speech. His eyes had screwed up to shrunken disappointed raisins right in front of her. But she had forgotten his hurt and disbelief, or else she would not have called him.

Within minutes it became clear that Daniel McEwan had only agreed to meet up with Nat to show her how he was well and truly, completely and utterly over her. He'd insisted on showing her photos of his wedding day, his kids, his car and his cottage. Natalie genuinely wished him well but he didn't believe her. She didn't much care because the fact that he was so besotted with his kids showed that she'd made the right decision in ditching him all those years ago. Daniel McEwan was not her One.

And she'd had a meal with Michael Young, so what? Oh yes, and a cocktail with Richard Clark (yes, she'd even met up with the Dick and she'd managed to resist clubbing him with a blunt instrument). It wasn't as if she was whipping off her knickers and waving them above her head. A girl had to eat and drink, didn't she? That was all she was doing. Nat stole a glance at Jen and weighed up whether she could tell her about Richard Clark. Jen would be quite interested in the outcome of Nat's drink with him. It was the sort of episode they used to laugh and chat about.

Richard represented so many lost hours to Nat; he was all about unanswered questions, regrets and longings for replays. Nat hadn't expected that she'd ever have the nerve to call him but secretly she'd wanted to from almost the moment she saw his name whizz past her eyes when she first flicked through the worn address book. Nat knew she'd never retrieve the endless hours she'd spent examining how and why he had slipped through her grasp (had she held him too tightly? Had she allowed him to roam too free? Had she been too furtive? Had she talked too much? In short, what was wrong with her?). Still, she longed for the opportunity to put some of the questions to him, rather than those questions forever being confined to her bathroom mirror.

Nat had always considered Dick Clark, a male model, out of her league, but truthfully nobody minds punching above their weight. When Nat had been in her early twenties, she'd met Dick in a nightclub. He was captivating to look at. Everyone agreed, male and female alike. Wherever Dick walked, a tidal wave of heads would swivel in his direction. People stared, open-mouthed in astonishment or anticipation. Nat had stared too but with the eye of someone appreciating a piece of art in a gallery, not because she had any expectation of tenure. Nat was used to a certain amount of male attention, enough to inform her presumptions about who she was attracted to and who she would attract. There were better looking women in the bar the night they met and in Nat's experience people as beautiful as Dick only ever left bars with other people as beautiful as Dick. It had therefore been astonishing to Nat that Dick had singled her out. He'd made an obvious beeline for her, bought her drinks, danced with her and talked to her all night. Then he took her home and made love to her between his black satin sheets. It had been flattering. Extremely, breath-stealingly so.

In truth, Nat had been so flattered by the attention of this cruelly beautiful man that for the duration of their short romance (and long after it was over) she'd managed to ignore the fact that he always borrowed cash from her in order to buy drinks (and clothes and CDs too). She'd pretended to enjoy the fact that they always attracted a whooping crowd as Dick confidently strutted his funky stuff on the dance floor, while she stared at her feet and tried to ignore the irritation flash in his eyes if she stepped on his toes. She had been so flattered to be the woman he outshone that she ignored the fact that his conversation often made her feel uncomfortable. He was undoubtedly witty but he was often mean-spirited or downright nasty (unless of course he was talking about his favourite topic – Dick Clark; then he had nothing but praise). Nat had also managed to ignore the reality that when they made love, Dick never put any effort into satiating her needs or desires. She'd even managed to ignore the fact that she had once found scanty, frilly pants, which definitely weren't hers, in his wash basket. Yes, she used to do his washing! His attention had been so utterly and completely flattering that when he ditched her (nastily and unceremoniously, by introducing her to his new squeeze),

Nat believed her heart to be broken and thought she'd never, ever recover.

At first, Nat had found it difficult to flick through magazines or catch a bus because she'd spot his face, in all its terrifying beauty, staring out at her from the pages or posters. She'd stroke his glossy image, longing to feel his real cheek beneath her fingers. Nat had feared that she'd never have such an amazing boyfriend again and that she'd already peaked; she'd believed that it would all be downhill from then on. But Nat was ultimately a sensible woman and after a few months away from Dick's realm of charm, she'd had to admit, at least to herself, that stroking his image on a glossy magazine was not a bad substitute for actually dating Dick. Indeed, it was an almost identical experience. As his girlfriend, all that had been required was to remain adoring. Their relationship had been a one-way street and nothing had changed now that they had split up, except she wasn't lending him hard cash. It was true she never did have such a beautiful boyfriend again, but it was comforting to know she'd dated many more amazing and amusing men.

Over the years Nat had taken a certain amount of pleasure following Dick Clark's career. It had been fun to point at the beautiful man in the adverts and say, 'I dated him.' She hardly ever added that she'd only dated him for six weeks until Neil had called her on it one day. By then the sting had long since died and when Neil had narkily pointed out that advertising agencies constantly touched up models' photos to hide imperfections, Nat had been able to agree enthusiastically, admitting that Dick did suffer from open pores. Dick's career had gone very well for a period of time. He became 'the face' of a designer perfume, securing TV ads as well as print. Nat had read somewhere that he was going to be an actor although she hadn't ever seen him on TV. She'd assumed he'd gone to LA to make his fortune there.

Dick had his own website. It was covered with black and white pictures of him moodily staring at the sky or the ground or the camera, it didn't matter where he was staring, he always looked moody and sensational. There was no doubt about it, Dick was delicious. The more Nat stared at the website, the more she thought that maybe Dick was what girlfriends might playfully describe as the one who got away. He certainly looked just like someone who eternally got away. She had said she never wanted to see him again but Nat found herself hovering over the 'contact me' button on his site. Did she dare? Would he even remember her?

Nat hadn't thought it likely that Dick would agree to meet up with her. No doubt he'd be too busy going to film premieres or being interviewed for *Vogue* and so she'd been surprised when he'd replied within minutes of her sending her tentative blast from the past message. Dick had said he'd love to meet up 'and talk about old times'. He'd suggested they meet at Soho House, adding that he was a member and so Nat mustn't worry about gaining access.

Face to face with Dick, Nat had found herself assessing him as she'd always done, as everyone had always done. Throughout his life Dick had got used to the fact that when people looked at him they did not think, 'Oh, he's looking happy/worried/tired', or even, 'That's a nice tie, I wonder where he got it from', which is the sort of thing most people think about one another when they first set eyes on each other. No, when people looked at Dick they thought about how beautiful he was. At least, they used to. Now, people thought about how beautiful he had once been.

He wasn't fat, exactly. Well, yes, he was fat but not gross. But where precisely had his cheekbones gone? Were they slumbering somewhere beneath the squidgy flesh? Nat wondered. His jacket no longer fitted properly, it strained at the shoulders and he'd tugged constantly at the sleeves all evening. His fingers were like unwieldy sausages. His eyes were still as blue as ever, of course, *they* couldn't go to seed, and they still darted questioningly around the room. Nat used to think he had an inquisitive mind, now she suspected that he'd been checking over her shoulder for someone more interesting to talk to or someone hotter to screw. His eyes were sharp and cold – had they always been that way? Why hadn't she noticed?

She'd sat opposite him in a big leather armchair. He'd sat comfortably far back on his so she'd been forced to hover uncomfortably on the edge of hers, leaning towards him in order to catch what he had to say. It was tricky as the place was full of loquacious people who all seemed to be talking at once – Nat was unsure who was doing the listening.

'Are you married?' he'd asked. Nat nodded but before she could add any detail about how long she'd been married or who she was married to, Dick jumped in, 'I'm divorced.'

'Oh, I'm sorry.'

'Her loss. Fucking bitch. She was screwing some photographer,' he'd snapped bitterly. 'Fucking models, you can't trust them.'

Nat didn't have the nerve to point out that Dick was a model too. Besides, she wasn't sure that he could still be modelling; she noticed that the zip on his trousers was gapping open. She pitied him, not for his fatness, that didn't matter one way or another to her, but for his anger – that was truly ruining. Dick's conversation betrayed the fact he found life disappointing. His laugh was forced and unnaturally high-pitched. Throughout their drink, he'd grumbled that there were no jobs, grumbled that those who did have them were incompetent, he'd dismissed good fortune as good luck, upgraded bad luck to conspiracy theories or a confirmation of the apocalypse. He'd frequently muttered, 'I haven't got a clue,' and Nat thought it was the truest comment he articulated all night.

When Nat had thought about meeting up with Richard Clark she'd privately hoped that she might discover why he'd picked her out just to drop her unceremoniously again after only a few weeks, but as the clock slowly ticked (and, oh Lord, that minute hand did drag!) she'd discovered she didn't really care. It didn't really matter, not any more. She wondered if it ever had. Nat realised she'd had a lucky escape. If Dick's attention span hadn't been quite so limited, then she might have wasted more than six weeks with him. After just one round, she'd made an excuse to leave. She didn't need to discover whether Dick wanted kids or not. She left in a hurry, letting out a huge sigh of relief; she was quite sure Richard Clark was not the One that got away.

Nat had initially secretly nursed a niggling worry that when she met up with her old flames she wouldn't be able to stop herself using an unacceptable familiar, flirty tone. She'd worried that it would be all too easy to slip back into old ways because once you'd had sex with someone it could be difficult to limit the conversation to the weather, but meeting up with Gary and Richard (men who had always created pleasant sensations between her legs, although notably not between her ears) proved that in fact she had no difficulty in steering away from anything remotely disreputable or risqué. She found that she didn't reminisce about where they used to put their tongues, how she and these guys used to get hot and sweaty together, or even about which movies they'd watched way back when. In fact, she talked about Neil most of the time. Usually, although she never intended it to be this way, she ended up talking about Neil wanting babies and her not wanting them. How weird was that? The one subject she was hoping to escape from by arranging these meetings was the one subject she returned to again and again and again. It didn't make sense. Michael Young, her boyfriend in sixth form, had said that it was understandable that she wanted to talk about this problem.

'Is it? I thought that by meeting up with you and my other Little Black Book guys I'd be leaving all this domestic dross behind.'

'You're not that callous, Nat. You never were.' He'd smiled fondly. 'Although, for the record, I'm not too thrilled to be ganged in with a whole host of other "Little Black Book" names.'

'Sorry.' Nat had blushed. The redness bloomed from her neck, up her chin and into her cheeks. Michael thought how Nat's propensity to blush had been so much a part of who she'd been when she was a teenager. He would've been surprised to learn that she rarely blushed nowadays.

Nat had considered that perhaps she was being naive. She'd ended up telling Michael the truth about why she'd suggested meeting because it was easier than making up a lie. Easier for her, no doubt, but maybe she should have been a bit more considerate of his feelings, just a little more tactful. She could have said that she'd found the Little

Black Book and desperately wanted to catch up with him *alone*, instead of confiding that she'd met up with many of the others too. The problem was there were too many lies floating around her head right now and she didn't have the energy to invent another; she was losing her grasp on what she'd said to whom as it was. For instance, the other day Becky had asked her what she was doing that evening and Nat had replied, 'I'm going to the movies with you.' She was not in fact, she'd been planning to meet Daniel McEwan, but she'd told Neil she was going to the movies with Becky (a girlie weepie with lots of changes of clothes and at least one dying boyfriend, not his thing, she'd assured him). So then she found herself saying to Becky, 'Sorry, did I say with you? I meant with Neil, obviously.' The next day she reported back to Becky, 'Blood fest, horror film. Neil loved it.'

With each lie she told, Nat imagined she was filling a balloon with hot air. She held tightly to the strings of the lies but soon she worried there would be so many that she'd be lifted into the air and carried far, too far, away.

'So, why am I talking about babies when it's the one topic I try to avoid at home?' Nat had asked Michael.

Michael had smiled, he'd marvelled at how little Nat had changed. She was still asking other people for answers when there was no great mystery, at least no mystery that couldn't be solved if only she'd be prepared for some honest and deep self-investigation. It'd always been her way to gloss over and hurry on, to leave things behind, rather than fix them. It was that attitude that had finally killed off their relationship. When they'd headed off to university, she'd declared that they were bound to meet other people and split up. Her certainty that it would be so had made it so. Perhaps they could have managed a long-distance relationship, if only she'd been certain that it would work.

'Well, have you talked about this baby business with your parents?' Michael had asked.

'No!'

'Or your friends?'

'A bit. Well, a lot actually. I think they're fed up of the conversation so, no, not for awhile.'

'And you've made it clear to Neil that the subject is off limits.'

'There's nothing more to say to *him*. Besides, he's rarely at home nowadays.'

'Where is he?'

Nat felt the hairs on her arms shudder, as though her body was registering something that her conscious mind refused to acknowledge. What was Neil doing with all his time nowadays? She wasn't sure she really wanted to know. It wouldn't surprise her if he'd been test driving family cars and conducting extensive research into strollers of choice. 'I've no idea,' she replied abruptly. 'Work, I guess. I don't ask because—'

'You don't want him asking too many questions either.'

'I suppose.' It was a bleak thought.

'So you've never actually sat down with any of your nearest and dearest and talked them through why you've made the decision that you don't want a family?'

The question had stung, as though he'd pushed her into a patch of nettles.

'Just once. I tried to explain once,' she replied finally and with a deep sigh. 'He didn't understand.'

'Well, it's clear you need *someone* to talk to. These meetings with people you once cared about afford only a temporary intimacy.'

Nat had looked at Michael with surprise. Could that be right? 'When did you get so wise?'

'Leisurely, over the last decade or so.' He'd grinned.

Nat had beamed back at Michael. In that instant she'd forgotten that his beautiful, previously coal-black hair was now scattered with white dots, it wasn't such a bad look, he looked like a groom with confetti permanently lodged in his hair. She'd forgotten that he was at least twenty pounds heavier than he had been the last time she'd seen him (in her bedroom, Take That smiling down from their superior position as poster idols and Nat had been sure that there was something in their smiles that suggested her teenage romance was inadequate). Suddenly, Michael seemed deeply profound and attractive. For the first time since Nat had started revisiting her ex-boyfriends, she felt a flicker of lustful excitement. She briefly wondered, could Michael have been her One? He was so calm, considerate and gentle, not something she could accuse Neil of at the moment.

'I have something to show you.' Michael reached for his wallet and Nat knew what to expect – a photo of his children, the son and a daughter her mother had told her of. The faint glimmer of lust was instantly snuffed dead. She plastered a polite smile on to her face and searched her mind for the appropriate compliment that would now be required.

Before handing the photo to Nat, Michael gazed at it for a moment and Nat saw love ooze from his every pore. He must have been familiar with the snapshot and yet he looked at it as though it was for the first time. The lust that had flickered and died in Nat's stomach was replaced by something else. Envy? Envy that he found the parenting thing so simple and fulfilling? Maybe a bit. Plus, something better than that – cheer? Cheer, that a decent guy like Michael was so clearly happy with his lot. Yes, cheer had flared up in her belly.

'I just want to say, Nat, I know the baby thing isn't for everyone. And tonight, you've given some good reasons as to why it's not for you.' Had she? Nat had expunged her usual set text. She'd said she was into her career, she wasn't sure whether she was able or ready to love in the required self-sacrificing fashion and she'd said that kids were expensive. All of which she partly believed, none of which she totally believed. 'All I want to say is that I used to say some similar things and then one day Lisa announced that she was up the duff, so all the theory went out the window.' He shrugged. 'And I'm glad. I'm glad there wasn't a choice for me because my kids, well, they are my world, Nat. They're everything.'

Michael had passed the photo to Nat. The kids were seated on a floral sofa; they waved sticky fingers and flashed fat grins. It was the same photo many parents carried around but different for Michael, because these were *his* babies.

'Harry and Ellie,' he said as he pointed unnecessarily to each child. Nat wasn't an expert on kids but even she could have deduced their genders, as one was wearing a Barbie nightdress, the other Thomas the Tank PJs, so it wasn't tricky.

From the photo it was clear Ellie was a Downs baby. Nat didn't mention it. What was the right thing to say? Anything she could think of struck her as completely wrong. She wished she wasn't so tongue-tied at the moment, so miserably confused about her own lot, and then she might have managed to say the thing that struck her, she might have commented on the kids' beautiful smiles. They looked like really happy kids.

Michael didn't seem to notice her silence. He continued, 'I love them both so much. Equally, differently, ferociously. Ellie's challenges haven't been a picnic, but then nor have Harry's and he's a kid with a normal, straightforward health history.'

The way Michael said 'normal' somehow implied that he knew no one else ever saw Ellie as normal and the fact wearied him. To Michael, Ellie was and always would be a princess. The cheer in Nat's stomach blazed into a powerful sense of admiration.

'Being a parent is not a picnic, Nat. It's messy and difficult a lot of the time but for me it's *always* been worth it. You should give your decision a lot of thought. You see, Nat, these meetings with old loves can only offer a temporary, inadequate, leaky intimacy. You can't cling to that.'

His words had slapped her hard across her face and throbbed deep inside, as they had done every time she had recalled them this past week. She'd left pretty swiftly after that and although they'd made promises to meet each other's spouses, perhaps have the kids over too one Sunday, Nat knew this would never happen. How could she explain such a visit to Neil?

Nat had caught the number 94 bus home. Bus travel was a mood magnifier. If, when you touched in with your Oyster card, you were feeling giddy and light-hearted, then by the end of your bus journey you would be left with the certain sense that you were king of the crop, top of the world, Mr Big. But if you were feeling at all negative or depressed when you boarded, then you were pretty much guaranteed travel sickness and rainy windowpanes. Nat had leant her hot head against the cold glass of the bus window and had tried to ignore a group of teenagers dressed as ghouls and ghosts on their way to an early Halloween party. They had been laughing and shouting, taking turns to shove each other aside and then flirtatiously grab at one another again. They were so obviously high on the fact that they all looked vaguely ludicrous and yet quite impressively realistic and were definitely catching the attention of every passenger, Nat had felt unreasonably disconcerted by the noisy gang. It wasn't just the fact that they were celebrating Halloween a week early and she thought that was a bit daft, it was something more profound.

Nat had never been very keen on dressing up. She had always been far too self-conscious to find the necessary mood of abandonment and she especially hated Halloween. Where was the fun in celebrating death and horror? There was enough in the world to be scared about without plastering bed sheets with red paint and shouting boo at passers-by. It was ridiculous. Nat had noticed that one of the crowd, a painfully skinny girl who was dressed as a witch, seemed self-conscious and ill at ease. The girl had reminded Nat of her young self. The skinny witch had repeatedly tried to hush her friends; she nervously insisted that they would all get thrown off the bus if they didn't quieten down and that it was too wet to make the short walk to the party. The torn sheets, tall black pointy hats and faces painted green were supposed to be a bit of fun but Nat felt unnerved. The boisterous gang struck her as vaguely threatening and she had been relieved when they stood up to alight. It was as they leapt off the bus that Nat had caught the eye of the skinny, nervous witch, just as she put her fingers to her lips in a renewed effort to shush her rowdy companions. Had Nat imagined it or was the girl gesturing that she could keep a secret? Was she gesturing to Nat? Did she know Nat's secrets?

No, that was ridiculous. Nuts! Nat had definitely drunk too much. Yet there had been something knowing in that girl's expression or her demeanour that had convinced Nat that the girl knew a thing or two about secrets. Maybe that was what had reminded Nat of her young self.

She had stared out through the grimy rain-splashed window, on to the grubby rain-spattered streets, aware that by keeping the dates a secret from those she normally spent her days chatting to and gossiping with, she was certainly casting herself adrift. She was left feeling vaguely ashamed and disconnected.

Nat now considered whether she could tell Jen what she'd been up to. It would be a relief, actually. She sipped the scalding tea and wondered how to approach the topic. She couldn't just dive in. It was impossible to explain that in the last five weeks she'd met up with five of her exes because she was suddenly terrified that Neil's new position on wanting a baby and her staunch position on not wanting one meant that she was unsure whether they should be together, that they'd stay together, that she'd married the right man in the first place. Such reasoning sounded so extreme and desperate, even to her; could anyone else possibly follow it? Jen would not understand her reluctance to have a family, it was all Jen wanted. Would Jen understand how lonely she had felt of late, since she and Neil rarely talked to one another nowadays and never about anything more meaningful than whose turn it was to clean out the cat's litter box? She needed to think of a way of highlighting Neil's other recently exposed shortfalls. Jen would surely be empathetic to those; after all, she was going out with Karl, she had lots of experience when it came to men with shortfalls.

'What do you think about our guys visiting a strip joint the other week?' Nat asked.

'Boys will be boys,' said Jen with a shrug. Jen's sanguine attitude surprised Nat. Normally she was the rational one and Jen was the one with a tendency to be emotional and overly demanding.

'Neil spent a fortune,' Nat added grumpily.

'Think of it as the equivalent to you visiting a day spa.'

As Nat never visited day spas, although she often said one day she might, Jen's words were not soothing.

'But is it responsible behaviour from a man who claims he wants to be a father?' Nat added. 'No, it is not.'

'But Neil is not going to be a father, is he? You've decided on that,' replied Jen.

'I didn't decide. We both agreed,' fumed Nat.

'And now he's changed his mind.' Jen sighed, she was more than a little bored with this conversation. Why wouldn't Nat have a baby? Everyone else did. Everyone else wanted to! Why did she think she was so special? Jen privately thought Nat was being irrational and unreasonable. Jen's sympathies were with Neil but her loyalties were with Nat, all she could do was remain tight-lipped.

'So you are saying because we're not having kids that maybe he is entitled, or at least likely, to go to strip joints, possibly even on a regular basis.'

'I didn't say that,' said Jen defensively.

In truth, this was something Nat had deduced on her own, she was just playing out the theory. By refusing to have a family, was she suspending them both in a time that was free of responsibilities? If so, what would the consequences of that be? She shook her head. She didn't know the answer. Everything about her future with Neil appeared blurred and agitated, everything about her past before Neil seemed murky and disappointing. Oh, how she'd enjoyed just being! Why had things changed? Why had Neil introduced this chaos by suddenly deciding he wanted babies? Nat didn't know the answers. The only thing she was sure of was that none of her exes was her One; not dog-loving Daniel, or dishy Dick or even matured Michael. How had she thought otherwise, even for a fleeting second? They were all ancient love affairs and she had no right to resurrect them. The past belonged in the past; that's what she'd always believed. No good came from poking about there. What had she been thinking? What if she had discovered an intense sexual, emotional and mental compatibility with one of those blokes (an element or other that had been notably lacking when they had dated), what was she proposing? She wouldn't want to take any of them away from their families and real lives. Would she really want to give up on her own real life? What was the point of her goose chase? Did she imagine she could turn back time? Her old, dearest fantasy. Of course not.

Nat couldn't think about this any longer; she forced herself to concentrate on Jen who had made an effort to diffuse the tension by talking about something else.

'If Karl doesn't propose by Christmas we won't have even the slightest chance of marrying before next September at the *very* earliest, as all the best venues are booked up months and months in advance. Do you think I should start looking at hotels anyway, just to get ahead of the game, so to speak? Or at least go and have a look at some dresses. I saw a really lovely one when I was going out with Christopher. It was a beautiful oyster colour. But do you think cream is making a comeback? Perhaps I ought to try a couple on. What do you think?' Jen paused. She clearly expected Nat to respond but Nat didn't know what to say.

Oh God, so this is where we are after two billion years of evolution, she thought. One thing was decided, she was not going to confide in Jen about her Little Black Book.

24

Neil would swear that he never had any conscious intention of taking his relationship with Cindy out of Hush Hush. Inside the sparkly, exotic red rooms he could convince himself that their relationship was nothing to do with his real world and it was, in fact, strictly business. He'd visited her about half a dozen times now, in total. Or put another way, six times in four weeks. The tally made him uncomfortable. It struck him as overly keen, maybe even a tad desperate. He had no idea why he repeat offended with Cindy. Yes, he fancied her but no more or less than he fancied a hundred women that he saw walking down the street in one day. Nice arse here, eye-catching pert tits there. Great cheekbones, good shoulders. Yes, he did objectify women. What were you going to do, shoot him? It was normal. Besides, he didn't objectify women that he knew, he had relationships with those women. When he thought of the women he worked with, he was more likely to think of time sheets or marketing ideas than he was to think of their bodies. He didn't objectify his mates' wives and girlfriends, they were off limits. Once he knew a woman, she became a person, obviously. But if he didn't know her and she was walking down the street, she was just a treat to look at (a treat or a horror). Was it a hanging offence? And of course he didn't objectify Natalie. He loved Natalie. Appreciated her and loved her. So where did Cindy fit?

The first time he met her at Hush Hush she had just been

something to look at, lust after and fantasise over. Pure and simple. Well, maybe not so pure. But straightforward and understandable. Even Nat had understood. That first time, when he'd come home with make-up on his clothes and explained he'd been in a strip club, he could see that while not overjoyed she accepted that he was male and boys would be boys. She probably thought he'd done something a bit disgusting but instinctive, like eating snot or a worm. But after that? Why had he returned? Why did he keep going back? Yes, it was sexy. Her nipples were larger and darker than Nat's. Her muff was considerably neater. Nat would never agree to a Brazilian. She said a straightforward bikini wax and a half-leg hair removal was penance enough for having a better eye for colour; there was no way she'd be persuaded into smooth, erotic baldness. But that wasn't it. Over and over again Neil told himself that his relationship with Cindy was simply a business transaction. She had a lovely pair of tits and he paid a vast amount to see them, end of. But the more he told himself this was the case, the less he believed it. He was kidding himself. He wasn't actually paying a vast amount of cash to look at her tits or even her minge, no, it was sadder than that. He was paying for her company.

And now there was the attraction of having Heidi's company too. Over the past ten weeks, since Neil had decided he wanted to be a father, he'd naturally become incredibly curious about other people's children. Well, it wasn't as if he had any of his own to be interested in. He made small talk with mothers in the queue at the supermarket checkout. He now knew that if the baby was crying, the standard comment was, 'Hungry?' or 'Tired?' and if the baby was gurgling, the thing to say was, 'How old?' All three of these questions had to be delivered with a knowing nod that was at once reassuring and open, somewhat informed and very sympathetic. He knew it was crucial to avoid gender. It was all too easy to ask, 'How old is this little chap?' and a cross mum would snap, 'She's eight months, her hair is still growing in.' He smiled at toddlers and sometimes even asked them questions, like what were they going to have for tea or whether their mummies were going to cut out a cat's face in a pumpkin?

Neil asked these questions in an odd, overly jocular voice. Nat said if he carried on like this he was going to be arrested. She maintained it wasn't normal to take so much interest in other people's kids but he found that parents quite liked it.

There was a woman at work who had twin boys. Every day he asked how their football was coming along. He'd started to call his brother regularly and ask about his niece and nephews' progress at nursery. He'd become expert at showing concern over parental moaning about broken sleep and the speed at which kids grow out of their shoes. He found himself staring at kids in the street and wondering what these kids chatted about with their parents when they got home, what toys they played with and what they liked to watch on TV. He wondered if his own childhood experiences were at all relevant to the way kids rumbled through childhood now. He wondered if he'd ever get to tell a son or daughter of his own that Snickers were once called Marathons and that they used to be bigger. He wondered what gave kids nightmares nowadays. Not *Chitty Chitty Bang Bang*'s child-catcher, surely. More likely some character he'd helped create for a video game. He desperately wanted the chance to soothe nightmares into distant, impotent memories.

Cindy believed that the three of them were together in Ravenscourt Park by coincidence. This was reasonable as the park was sandwiched between Chiswick and Hammersmith; Neil lived and worked somewhere in Chiswick, didn't he, and Cindy lived and worked in Hammersmith. She accepted that Neil was taking a short cut through the park and just happened to spot her. She'd been quite chuffed that he'd come over to say hello.

'Most of my clients pretend not to recognise me. Or maybe they really don't recognise me,' said Cindy, as she glanced apologetically at her tracksuit bottoms.

Bizarrely, Neil thought Cindy looked more, not less, sexy now her body was covered up. The tracksuit was not shapeless and bobbly, (like Nat's comfy one, which she tended to wear to watch TV as often as to go to the gym), it was a clingy, apple-green velour number, that subliminally suggested fun and freshness. She certainly stood out against the grey day as she wore a short, sleeveless, hot pink padded jacket and yellow trainers. She looked like a yummy dessert. But she must be freezing. Nat had pulled her winter coat out of the wardrobe last weekend; it was almost floor-length and black. If you looked carefully at Cindy (and Neil found that he was looking carefully), it was possible to see the muscles in Cindy's peach-like bum flex ever so slightly when she pushed her daughter on the swing.

The daughter.

Heidi was a beautiful child. Neil had spent an awful lot of time adoringly staring into prams and pushchairs but even he was not blind to the fact that a huge number of kids and babies were really quite odd to look at. They were often sticky or had two tracks of luminous snot running from nose to lip, which was never a great look, and besides that he had to admit that many of them had thin, wispy hair, weird, gummy smiles or overwhelming foreheads. This observation did not make him want children any less, he found the gummy smiles cute and simply thought that it was a sin the snotty, sticky kids weren't being attended to more efficiently. Neil was certain that any baby he had with Natalie would be a beauty and he'd definitely always carry a tissue. Still, it was a bonus to catch sight of the sort of child that took your breath away and Heidi was such a child. She looked as though the angels had made her to celebrate a special occasion, the first day of summer perhaps. She had blond curls that bounced around her cherubic face, a tiny button nose, fat, pink, pouty lips and enormous blue eyes, framed with lashes that caused draughts when she blinked. She looked pretty much how Neil imagined a child belonging to him and Nat might look (if Brad Pitt was willing to donate).

'What are you doing in a park at this time of the day?' asked Cindy.

'I got stuck on a project at work, thought I'd stretch my legs, get a bit of fresh air and maybe find some inspiration,' lied Neil. The truth made Neil uncomfortable, it would probably terrify Cindy. He sure as hell couldn't risk admitting to Cindy that since she'd mentioned that she sometimes spent her mornings off here in the park with

Heidi, he had taken to mooching around, hoping to catch a glimpse of them. He wasn't sure why he was so curious about Cindy's life, it didn't make sense, but he had an increasing, overwhelming urge to be with her. Being with her was straightforward and relaxing. She didn't trade sarcastic comments with him nor did she sulk, seethe or swear at him, unlike his wife.

'Fancy a coffee?' he asked tentatively.

Cindy glanced at Heidi and for one awful minute Neil thought she was going to say no. He fought the disappointment that was surprisingly bitter and potent. 'I can throw in an ice cream,' he added, hoping he didn't sound quite as pathetic and desperate as he felt. Neil was banking on the fact that even on a chilly autumn day children were always keen for an ice-cream cone.

'Scream!' cried Heidi with excitement. She pushed at the iron bars that harnessed her into the swing, straining to get free, clearly keen to accept the invitation. Cindy and Neil laughed at her enthusiasm and Cindy nodded.

The café was cramped with noisy kids and mothers whose attitudes towards those kids tended to be equally divided between harassed and indifferent. The windows were steamed with the effect of the hot drinks being made and the hot gossip that passed between the women. Cindy scanned the room and then told Neil she'd prefer to sit outside, she liked the fresh air, even at this nippy time of year when their breath could be seen on the air. She already spent more than enough hours in hot, sticky rooms.

'OK, you grab a bench and I'll bring the stuff out. What do you want?' asked Neil.

'A skinny latte for me and a vanilla ice cream for Heidi, just a small one. Thanks.'

Neil ordered the coffees and as it was nearly midday he added a ham sandwich and an egg sandwich on white bread (no cress, he thought cress stalks were the devil's pubes; no child could want to eat them). He also bought a couple of slices of carrot cake, two packets of crisps (ready-salted and cheese and onion as he couldn't decide which flavour Cindy might prefer). He considered the soup but wasn't tempted by carrot and coriander and wasn't sure Cindy would be either. He thought she'd be a chicken soup sort of girl. When he was in front of the ice-cream cabinet, he found himself asking for a triple scoop ice cream (vanilla, chocolate and strawberry). The server smiled. 'Good, that will finish it off.' She piled the ice cream high upon the cone and then threw away the tub. It was time to defrost the freezer and push it to the side of the café, out of the way until next spring. There would be more room for indoor tables that way. 'We'll be selling mince pies before you know it,' she commented. With difficulty, Neil carried the tray and the cone out to Cindy where the goodies were greeted with muted appreciation.

'She won't eat lunch if she has that,' Cindy grumbled, glaring at the extremely large ice, embellished with a chocolate flake and coloured sweet sprinkles.

'I bought egg sandwiches for lunch, maybe she could have the crisps and sandwich first and then the ice cream,' offered Neil. 'Or there's ham.'

'We have to get home for lunch,' Cindy said. She swiftly scooped off half the ice cream with her coffee spoon. It landed with a splat on the ground. Neil and Heidi looked at the gloopy mess; it was unclear which of them might cry first. 'Thanks, though,' added Cindy more kindly, perhaps seeing that she'd upset one of her best clients, perhaps seeing she'd upset a decent bloke. She grabbed the plastic boxes of sandwiches and the packets of crisps and shoved them into her rucksack. She forked a small piece of cake into her wide mouth and said appreciatively, 'Great cake.'

Neil watched Heidi lick the ice cream. She was surprisingly methodical and neat for one so young. She took tiny laps, putting Neil in mind of a small kitten. 'Her photo couldn't do her justice. She's dead cute,' he mumbled.

'Isn't she?' agreed Cindy, not managing to suppress her maternal pride. She rummaged in her bag, retrieved a woollen hat and then plonked it on Heidi's head, pulling it down firmly about her ears. 'Can be a little bugger though, obviously. When she wants to be.'

'Will you have more?'

'One more. Two kids is plenty. Don't want three. Three does terrible things to your stomach muscles, not a good idea in my line of work. But I'd like her to have a brother or sister. It's just finding the right time. I mean, you can't dance and give birth.'

'No, of course not. Did you, erm, dance while you were pregnant with Heidi?'

'Yeah.' Cindy did not offer any explanation or excuse, or explore the moral connotations of this fact. Neil felt uncomfortable. This beautiful child should never have been inside Hush Hush, even if at the time she had been inside her mum's womb. Especially then. Cindy correctly interpreted his silence and commented sardonically, 'Not all mothers get the chance to spend their pregnancies at pre-natal yoga classes.'

'No.' Neil blushed that his condemnation had been so transparent.

'I wouldn't have kept on dancing if they'd still allowed smoking in there but it was banned by then and exercising during pregnancy is a good thing.'

'Right.' He didn't want to ask the next question but found he couldn't help himself. 'And how long did you go on with—'

'Eight months. I was very neat. Such a small bump. We did a special show, early teatime slot. A lot of men find pregnant women very sexy.'

'But—'

'You, for instance.' Cindy stared at Neil, silencing him.

Neil blushed again and searched around for a change of subject. If he couldn't come up with something fast, he was pretty sure that Cindy would swiftly drink her coffee and then shoot off. He didn't want that. After a pause, he offered, 'Do you watch much TV?'

Cindy and Neil chatted about reality TV, soaps and game shows. They both admitted to loving *The X Factor* and *Strictly Come Dancing*, although Cindy said, 'The ice skating one bores the tits off me,' and

Neil said he stopped watching *Big Brother* (celebrity or otherwise) a few years back. 'Bloody freak show.'

They discovered they both liked cooking and they competitively compared recipes for lasagne. Cindy's husband had bought her a Wii last Christmas but she said she didn't get much time to play on it; she was shocked at how many hours Neil owned up to playing games.

'When do you get time to shop?' she asked, aghast that anyone might compromise how much time they spent on that national sport.

'Not much of a shopper,' mumbled Neil. 'Although I do like Westfield shopping centre.'

'I go there all the time. It's my idea of heaven.'

Neil wondered if they'd ever passed one another, slipped by, shoulder to shoulder, unnoticed, shrouded in an anonymous crowd.

Cindy talked about Heidi and revealed she was a good sleeper and that the birth had been easy. 'Six hours from water breaking to weigh-in,' Cindy said proudly. 'She's perfect.'

Neil couldn't help but agree. Heidi seemed remarkably calm and easy to amuse. Cindy was right, she was just the sort of child that could seduce anyone, even Nat, into wanting to become a parent, surely. When she'd finished her ice cream, she climbed into her stroller and curled up for a nap.

Cindy confessed to having a 'desperate sweet tooth' that she constantly had to keep in check. 'I eat a lot of wine gums, there's no fat in them.'

Neil told her about a scruffy newsagent in Chiswick that still sold sweets from enormous jars. 'Sadly, not glass jars, just plastic ones. I'm sure I remember there being glass jars when I was a kid.'

'Bollocks. What are you, Victorian? They were plastic jars. You idealise things too much, Neil.'

Despite her gentle mocking, Neil confessed to buying a quarter of strawberry bonbons whenever he passed.

'If they sell sherbet fountains, will you pick one up for me? I haven't had a sherbet fountain for years.'

It was Cindy's stomach growling raucously that finally brought their chatter to a halt.

'Shit, it's ten to two,' said Cindy, glancing at her watch. She quickly began to snatch up baby wipes, small toys, bibs and the other child paraphernalia that littered the table. 'I'm meant to be in work by two thirty and I haven't given Heidi any lunch yet.' Heidi was still asleep in her pushchair. Plump and rosy-cheeked, she looked, if possible, even more delectable than she had when she was awake. The adults gazed on adoringly and even though they were both conscious that they ought to be elsewhere, they allowed themselves a silent, still moment to revel in her perfection.

'I'd better be getting back too.' Neil knew he had a meeting at two. He'd be late. Plus he'd taken a two and a half hour lunch break, how was he going to explain that? He had been a bit rubbish about time-keeping recently although he was pretty sure no one had noticed his morning strolls or early evening departures. But his manager had had a winge about his late start last Wednesday; he'd been at Hush Hush until late the night before and he just hadn't been able to drag his carcass in by ten, no matter how much Nat nagged. 'It's been lovely bumping into you, Cindy.'

'Yes, and you.' Cindy didn't look at Neil but continued to pack up the stroller efficiently. Heidi, disturbed by the activity, woke up and looked around placidly. As Cindy set off along the path, she threw out a cheerful wave and called, 'Till next time.'

'Yes.' Neil felt his body become weightless as a reaction to the delight that he might anticipate a next time.

'Wave goodbye to Neil, Heidi,' Cindy instructed.

'Beb bye,' gurgled Heidi as she waved enthusiastically from her buggy. She craned her neck around the side of the buggy so that she could keep her eyes on Neil as Cindy pushed her in the opposite direction. When she was about ten metres away, she very carefully enunciated, 'Beb bye, Neeeeeil.'

Neil took a mental snapshot of the image of the beaming, waving child and the obviously attractive mother marching away from him.

He stored the memory in his head but allowed its prettiness to filter down into his stomach, creating a feeling similar to the one he got when on rare occasions he drank malt whisky. A lovely comforting, intimate feeling.

25

Natalie had not been planning on calling Alan Jones. Her recent meetings had shown her that there was no mileage to be gained in poking about in the past. She was wasting her time, indeed she was wasting everyone's time. Besides, out of all her exes, he was the one she had absolutely no desire to catch up with. There was no mystery there. No ifs or buts. She knew he was not her One. They were unsuited. They wanted different things, they had agreed as much twelve years ago. But fate was a cruel and bossy minx and she intervened.

Nat was queuing in Mortimer & Bennett, a charming, rustic deli just off Chiswick High Street. The deli had been brought to the attention of the foodies in W4 as it was often listed by the likes of Nigella Lawson and other celebrity chefs as a great place to buy difficult-to-find products like marron glacé, La Maison du Miel honey or tasty legs of Jabugo ham. The result was that the place was always jam-packed. Passionate foodies stood elbow to elbow alongside under-confident housewives who wanted to impress their dinner guests by buying locally and organically. Nat was visiting Mortimer & Bennett because she was buying a present for Ben and Fi. She hadn't seen much of her in-laws recently and felt bad about it. In truth, she'd been avoiding them. Neil had made their previously precious visits to Ben and Fi uncomfortable as he endlessly and obviously extolled the joys of parenthood. The last time they'd visited, he kept picking up one or other of the children and then dropping them in Nat's lap, much to the embarrassment and distress of all involved. Angus was happier playing Lego than being forcibly made to give Nat a cuddle, and Nat appeared reluctant to deliver said cuddle because when Neil demanded it of her she happened to be holding a cup of hot tea and she had nowhere to put it down. She was sure her apparent reluctance was noted by everyone and of course Fi would have taken offence, any mother would do so. It wasn't fair. Left to her own devices Nat was a fantastic aunt, she was lively, loving and interested, but in the hothouse atmosphere that Neil had generated recently she appeared reluctant and gauche.

Nat had decided to buy some handmade chocolates for Fi and a selection of rare, smelly cheeses for Ben. She'd drop round at the weekend and deliver her peace offerings. She had no idea what Neil's plans for the weekend might be but she assumed he'd be happy to visit his brother and family. She could take some sparklers; she wondered if the kids had gone to a firework display last night. She and Neil usually went to the display in Ravenscourt Park which always took place on the Saturday nearest to the fifth; that would be this Saturday, but neither of them had mooted the idea as yet. Nat decided she would suggest it tonight. She'd call up Ali and Tim and Karl and Jen and ask if they wanted to come along too. They could all eat hot dogs and toffee apples and have some fun, it had been a while since they'd got together, too long. Of course it would be icy cold and probably wet as well, that was traditional, but it would be worth it to see the fireworks whoosh, flash and bloom against the black sky.

Nat stood in the jostling queue for twenty minutes, finally secured her purchases and was just wiggling and winding her way out of the shop when she bumped into Alan Jones. At first she did not recognise him, she simply apologised for standing on the man's foot and planned to keep pushing through, head down.

'Natalie? Natalie Morgan.'

Nat lifted up her head as she heard her old name. 'Alan?'

Nat was surprised the encounter hadn't happened before, considering they lived in such close proximity; but the inevitability did little to alleviate the shock of being face to face with Alan Jones, the only naked friend Nat did not want to see again. Once upon a time she had loved him and they had been together longer than she had been with any of her other exes but that was not a problem. Theirs had not been an earth-shattering sort of love that might inconveniently re-ignite and threaten her relationship with Neil. Nor had it been an intensely or especially sexual affair, it had been rather more ordinary than that. But, at a particular moment in history, theirs had been a comfortable, confiding sort of relationship and *that* was what terrified Natalie.

Alan was the only one who knew. He alone. He was the one she had divulged her big secret to, just weeks before they'd called time on their relationship. Of course the two things were related, Alan had never pretended anything other. They wanted different things, that's what he'd said. She thought the point was that they *had* very different things. Very different experiences.

'Oh my goodness, how are you?' Alan asked the question with exactly the correct mix of enthusiasm and delighted surprise that is acceptable when old friends bump into one another.

'I'm fine, thank you, very well. And you?' It hardly covered it, but what else could they say to one another after twelve years? Nat was plainly more practised than most at catching up with old flames but even she was thrown by the unexpected nature of the meeting; with the others she'd had time to prepare. Alan followed her out on to the pavement, squeezing between the other customers and giving up his place in the queue. Nat wished he hadn't.

'How extraordinary bumping into you like this, especially as I don't normally have a chance to visit the high street on a week day. I just happen to have a day's holiday today,' said Alan.

'Yes, quite a coincidence, because I don't normally shop in my lunch hour, I just popped out. I work nearby.'

'Still work in pharmaceuticals?'

'Yes.'

'Marvellous.' Nat could not remember for sure what Alan did for a living; something in the city, a lawyer, or maybe he worked in insurance. She decided not to hazard a guess. 'It's a lovely store, isn't it?' Alan pointed his thumb towards Mortimer & Bennett. 'An Aladdin's cave for an olive lover.'

Nat wondered what sort of person categorised themselves as an olive lover? She was as happy as the next person to eat an olive, she liked them more than anchovies but less than tomatoes; did that make her an olive lover?

'I'm so sorry, Alan, but I'm in a rush. I have to get back to the office. It would be lovely to chat but—'

'Yes, it would, wouldn't it,' smiled Alan. His beam was wide and rather more enthusiastic than her own. 'What's your number? I'll give you a bell, we'll fix something up so that we can have a longer chat.'

Alan Jones had not been a particularly prepossessing youth and he was not an especially striking man either. He had very bad teeth, below even the standard 1970s NHS issue, but as Nat was not American she didn't have particularly high standards where teeth were concerned. Besides, the slight greyness and crookedness of teeth were not something someone ought to be judged by. But then what should a man be judged by? Natalie didn't know any more. His conversation? His morals? His actions?

His desire for a family?

Alan was average in every way, almost to the point of being nondescript. He wasn't notably short or tall. He had mid-brown, wavy hair that dared not be dramatic enough to be straight or curly. He preferred grey T-shirts worn with jeans or blue shirts worn with chinos, depending on the formality of the occasion. His personality avoided extremes too. He was not especially passionate about anything but then again (and Natalie often used to remind herself of this when they dated), he was never mean, rude or unreasonable. No, not at all, he was always mild-mannered and polite. Nat thought it was probably his habit of being polite that had led to him asking for her phone number. Alan was the sort of man who was often asked to be an usher at his friends' weddings but never asked to be the best man. Nat had dated him at university because he kept asking her out and she couldn't think of a really good reason not to. Alan had not been put off by her shyness or gauche ways, which many other men had not managed to see past. The truth was, Alan actively took comfort from Nat's insecurities as he believed that were Nat to overcome her shyness and recognise her own worth, she would have been out of his league. About this, at least, he was absolutely correct.

Old habits died hard and so Nat found herself muttering her telephone number, all the time wondering if she ought to give a wrong digit. Even as Alan Jones stored it in his mobile, Nat wished she hadn't popped out to the shops in her lunch hour and she prayed he'd never call her. Suddenly, Nat didn't think she would bother rousing a party to go to the firework display, all she felt like doing now was hiding. Hiding from everyone and everything.

26

Alan called early the following week and suggested they meet that coming Thursday. Nat accepted Alan's invitation, certain that she'd cancel on the day. She planned to make up an excuse that was at once believable enough to be irrefutable and weak enough to drop the hint that she did not want to rekindle their association. Alan suggested that they should meet at All Bar One in Leicester Square. It was a bar that was famous for brief and drunken encounters, nothing more than a watering hole for tourists who knew no better. There was a perfectly wonderful All Bar One on Chiswick High Road, just minutes from their homes. That All Bar One had high ceilings and friendly staff, but Alan had suggested the Leicester Square branch to provide anonymity, and Nat felt the slight. She didn't think the crowded, noisy bar with its paucity of seats was befitting a four-year relationship, however long ago they'd given up on that liaison. Nat's plan to blow out Alan was foiled when on Thursday morning she was called into an emergency day-long meeting about budget cuts; by the time she got to a phone she knew it was too late to break the arrangement. No doubt Alan would have set off in plenty of time to reach central London. She had no alternative other than to brush her hair, re-apply her lipstick and hop on the tube. She wouldn't stay long.

Nat was right that Alan, a well-mannered man, had at least made the effort to ensure he arrived first. She glanced around the dim bar and before her eyes even became accustomed to the gloom she spotted

Alan who waved enthusiastically to guide Nat to his spot. He'd thought-fully bought Nat a white wine spritzer; she didn't say that she preferred red wine nowadays as it might have appeared unnecessarily rude. They efficiently exchanged the bare facts about their lives, most of which they were both already aware of (because their mutual friend, Cathy, had drip-fed titbits to both parties for years) but they pretended not to know much about one another, just for conversation's sake. Once they'd asked about one another's spouses, jobs and families, Alan spun off in a completely different direction.

'I'm pleased to see you haven't dyed your hair,' he said suddenly.

Nat was startled. Truthfully, she was not as naturally blonde as she liked to appear. She was fair, yes, but not quite what she seemed. Who was? Nat had her hair highlighted on a regular basis. Neil didn't care if her blondeness was chemical or not and yet about once every six weeks they entered into a charade whereby Nat went to the hair-dressers with an enormous shadow over her head and returned sunny. Neil always asked, 'Have you done something with your hair?'

Nat would reply, 'Yes, a trim.'

Then Neil would confirm, 'Lovely.' No more was ever said on the matter. It wasn't that Nat felt the need to be deceptive about her hair-dying to Neil, she was certain he knew what really went on at her hairdressers, it was just a rather charming little play act between a tactful and happy couple.

'All women seem to torture their hair nowadays,' added Alan. 'There must have been a time in the world when women had curly hair or mousy hair. Both are now all but extinct. Every woman I meet nowa-days is either extremely dark, stunningly blonde or a fiery red, there's no room for mediocrity in this world.' He sighed elaborately.

Natalie thought that Alan's comments sounded somewhat rehearsed, perhaps something he said at dinner parties to cover the gap between starter and main when the hostess was busy in the kitchen. Nat could have forgiven him for relying on a practised conversational fill-in; after all, their situation was unusual and a little embarrassing, but what was he saying about her hair? Did he think it was mousy? Wasn't she stunningly blonde? And anyway, what was wrong with improving your looks? Suddenly, Nat remembered that Alan had never encouraged her to wear fashionable clothes, he had been dismissive of her experiments with her hair or make-up and he'd always preferred flat shoes. They had been so young when they dated, it was a time in her life when she should have been crazy and audacious but Alan had preferred her to be conservative and staid. He had always worried that if she changed too dramatically he'd be left behind. Neil never worried about being left behind. He encouraged Nat to try new things and constantly challenge herself and all that was around her. Neil alone believed she would bungee jump three hundred feet off a crane in Windsor; everyone else she knew had insisted that she'd chicken out at the last moment. Neil had taken bets on her daring and he'd made a killing. Neil always thought she looked amazing in the fashionable clothes sold in the high street; he also thought she was exceptionally fanciable when she wore a cagoule and walking boots. He did not believe she had a particular style she ought to be tied to. Neil's confidence in her allowed her to find a robust self-assurance. What was she doing here?

'Close up most women's hair looks like a stretched Brillo pad,' said Alan, reminding Nat of someone's grandmother.

'I do have it highlighted, actually,' said Nat defiantly.

Alan looked startled, tutted, and then mumbled, 'Is there a single woman who hasn't dyed or straightened her hair, *ever*? Just one?'

Nat thought that she might as well gather up her handbag and head home.

'Is it a vanity thing? All the hair-dying stuff? No one can stop ageing, that's a given. It's a fact that in the end everyone wears slippers,' added Alan. Suddenly, Nat's mind was washed with a vision of Neil in slippers and she started to laugh. Alan didn't know what he'd said to amuse her but grinned back, clearly relieved. Thinking of Neil had doused Nat in a warm feeling of general compassion; it helped her to be kinder to Alan than she might otherwise have been. She knew that if she left Alan abruptly, he'd be offended and confused; after all, she had agreed to meet up. They were ex-lovers trying to be old friends, it wasn't an easy situation. He was probably edgy and he was wittering on in this slightly miserable and churlish way to cover his nervousness.

'Would you like another drink?' offered Nat.

'Yes, that would be nice. I'll have what you're drinking.'

'A white wine spritzer?' Nat asked in disbelief. This guy definitely didn't get out enough.

'If that's easiest.'

'Tell you what, I'll buy a bottle of red and we'll drink it straight. Hard-core style,' she teased gently.

After a glass or two, Alan began to relax and became more like the Alan she'd remembered. Inoffensive, affable, unchallenging. He spoke frequently and proudly of his children and wife and laboriously about his job as a computer programmer. Neither subject bored Nat quite as much as she expected. It might have been the wine numbing the tedium or it might have been the fact that she was genuinely heartened to see Alan so thoroughly content. She was lost and discontented at the moment but she was not so low as to resent his achievement.

'So, you never did have kids?' he said inevitably.

'No,' confirmed Nat, although she'd already answered the question once that evening.

'You always said you didn't want them.'

'That's right.' She took a gulp of wine.

'Everyone said you'd change your mind.'

'Yes, they did. They still say that.' She took another, bigger gulp of wine.

'But I knew you wouldn't. What with your mum dying and everything. I knew you'd never get over that fear.'

Nat had never heard those words said aloud before. She knew the truth of them, of course. She's said them first to Alan, twelve years ago as they were lying spooned together on their lumpy couch in their grotty rented flat. She said the same words, or more or less that arrangement, to herself every single day of her life, but hearing them said aloud was a shock. Annihilating.

'Each time my wife was pregnant, I thought of your mum,' said Alan. 'It's a husband's worst fear, his wife dying in childbirth, being left alone to bring up the baby.' Alan pinched his nose at the point between his eyes. The thought of such anguish had momentarily made him insensitive to the fact that Nat knew this more than most. He caught a glimpse of her face and realised he'd punched her emotionally. 'I'm sorry. I didn't mean to be—'

'No, no, that's OK.' The last thing Nat wanted now was his sympathy. That was the last thing she'd ever wanted from him or anyone.

'But then your dad married Nina and she's been a good mum to you, hasn't she?' said Alan in a jovial voice that sounded a little forced. He was trying to cheer her up but Nat couldn't understand why people might want to convince her that the death of her mother was nothing more than a cloud that came with a silver lining. Yes, it was true Nina had been a fantastic mother but even that was a source of pain for Nat.

She didn't want to get into this. Not now. Not ever.

'Absolutely,' she said wholeheartedly. She hoped her tone would be stout enough to convince him that it was OK to change the subject. It shouldn't be that hard to do; not many people liked to talk about death.

Christina. Her mother's name had been Christina. And Christina had died so that Nat could live. Of course no one had ever said this to Natalie. Not explicitly, but Nat had worked it out for herself. Even if there hadn't been a dramatic situation where the doctors had asked her mother who they should save, the facts were that her mother died giving her life.

Oh, the guilt.

The guilt and the fear. And the loneliness. It sat in her throat like a ball of vomit waiting to explode on to her life at any given moment. A life that she'd carefully, laboriously pulled together. By controlling her grief, all but denying it, Nat had created a life that was damned near normal. Spewing up her guilt, fear and loneliness would ruin everything. It would stain and spoil everything.

Her father had done his best. He'd never blamed her. He had not punished her or shut her out of his life like a cruel Victorian father in a TV costume drama. No, he'd carefully, quietly and tenderly nurtured her. He'd made an effort. He'd made sacrifices. Brian Morgan had trained as an architect but if he'd ever held any ambitions to design influential, prestigious and powerful spaces that would have a lasting influence on how people viewed buildings, thus creating for himself an unrivalled worldwide reputation, he'd put them on the back burner when he accepted a job at the local council. Dealing with building compliance documents within the health sector (which largely boiled down to ensuring there was wheelchair access to public conveniences and sufficient nearby car parking spaces) may not have been especially inspiring work but it was valuable and the nine-to-five hours allowed him to be a better dad and maybe (he hoped) even a partial mum to Natalie. Brian had played tea parties with his daughter and her dolls, he'd built Lego towers and carefully iced pink birthday cakes and he'd managed to perform these tasks with conscientious concern. If he'd ever wanted to smash the tiny china cups, throw the Lego towers at the wall or slam the gooey cake mix across the kitchen floor because he felt the injustice of losing his spouse and his child's mother, then he managed never to betray the fact.

Natalie's grandparents had helped out as much as they could, until Christina's mum had had a fatal stroke when Nat was just two. At the wake, over strong cups of tea, neighbours and distant relatives had whispered that the woman had never recovered from losing her daughter, no parent ever quite deals with outliving their child and perhaps the responsibility of looking after such a young grandchild had been a little too much ... The sentence was rarely expanded upon, knowing looks and nods were shared. It was enough. Everyone agreed it was a tragedy. Another tragedy. Brian wouldn't allow his parents to do as much as they would have liked to fill the care gap that Christina's mother had left. They had both been in their seventies; he'd delivered too many eulogies for a man not yet thirty-five years old and while he didn't believe that caring for Nat had contributed to her grandma's death, he really couldn't take a risk. So Nat had been cared for by a series of nannies.

The nannies had all liked Nat. She had been a quiet and obedient little girl. A little needy, perhaps, but no one resents delivering cuddles demanded by a cute infant, however constant and insistent those demands might be. The nannies had prepared homemade food, bathed her, cleaned her teeth and brushed her hair. They'd played with her, painted with her and regularly took her on outings to the park or local bird sanctuary. They did all this for her with conscientious concern but they did not mother her, as that was not possible. If asked, each nanny would have sworn they loved her. They did, they loved her in exactly the same way that Natalie now loved her job at the pharmaceutical company and this had been proven when the nannies had handed in their notice to accept a better paid job, or in order to go travelling or (the hardest resignation Brian and Nat ever had to take) in order to have their own children. With each resignation and rehire Nat understood that no matter how kind, or pretty, or wise, or funny these nannies were, they were not her mother. They did not stay.

But then, nor had her mother.

Nat began to expect departures. She did not allow herself to become too accustomed or attached to any of the pretty or not-so-pretty nannies as she knew they were finite. With a child's logic, Nat reasoned that perhaps she deserved the constant departures, that she wasn't someone who was worthy of an eternal commitment or constancy. Nina went some way to repairing that viewpoint.

Nina had come into Brian and Nat's lives when Nat was four and a half. Nina had been Nat's reception class teacher. She was already half in love with the child before she'd even met Brian at the October parents' evening. Brian instantly noticed Nina's cheerful smile and kind eyes but he was used to well-meaning women smiling at him with compassion and tenderness and that alone would not have encouraged him to move the relationship outside the classroom and away from the mini chairs and chalk boards. It was only when Nina crossed her legs and her wrap-round skirt split open, providing Brian with a flash of her thigh, that he thought to offer to take her out for a coffee. Had she shown him her thigh on purpose? Had he really felt a flicker of desire? It had been so, so long since he thought about anyone in *that* way, since he'd noticed anyone think of him in *that* way, that he wasn't sure.

Nina had burst into Nat and Brian's lives with spectacular energy. While Nat and Nina might now scream with laughter if they ever looked back at old photos of the eighties, at the time Nat had regarded Nina as some sort of modern-day fairytale princess. Nina had been fashionable, informed and energetic. It seemed that she knew everything there was to know about the New Romantic movement, which she talked about with great animation. Nat had no idea what or who the New Romantics were but she was sure that somehow Nina embodied it, whatever *it* was. After all, Nina was new and romantic, reasoned Nat. In the classroom, Nina chose to wear frilly blouses and tartan skirts, with her hair scraped into a tight knot, but at the weekend she wore her hair wild, wide and teased. She liked ripped jeans and neon fingerless gloves, she accessorised with large hooped earrings. Impressively, Nina could complete every side of Rubik's cube and she could moonwalk; plus she was prepared to demonstrate both skills whenever Nat asked her to. No matter where they were or how often Nat asked, Nina didn't tire of her.

Nina liked the fact that the Prime Minister of Britain was a woman but she loathed the woman herself and would often shout heatedly at the TV. On one occasion she'd thrown an open packet of tomato-flavoured crisps in frustration. Nat had thought this a waste, as tomato was a difficult flavour to come by and the newsreader had no idea of the protest. Nat liked it that Nina would try to explain the images that flashed across the screen and that she talked to Nat about the things she read in the newspaper, even though most of it remained complex and inaccessible. Somehow, Nat understood that it was a compliment that Nina wanted her to be part of the world and that Nina had a commitment to bringing the world to her. Mostly, Nat liked it when they played with her cabbage patch doll and Care Bears.

Nina had views and plans and politics, she had fashion sense, a record collection and a make-up bag, but most of all she had love. So, so much love. She had wanted to wash Nat and Brian in her love, she wanted it to flood around their bodies and flow through their veins, and very soon they admitted they wanted that too.

Until Nina, Nat had always carried, somewhere deep in the pit in her stomach, the hard, bleak feeling of loneliness. Even when she was in company, even when she was sitting on her father's knee, she felt alone. It was as though she had swallowed a filthy, huge rock that she could not digest. Initially, it had sat in her belly, causing a cramping, disabling pain, but in time, as Nat had become accustomed to the loneliness, she no longer felt pain, she felt something more akin to a throbbing discomfort or the occasional flare-up of irritation. It took some time but eventually Nat stopped feeling quite so lonely. Nina's constant, unwavering commitment to Nat's welfare and happiness and Nina's frequently and eloquently expressed assurances of love salved the loneliness.

There was a period when Nat felt guilty for loving Nina back with such ferocity and a few years later she also wondered whether it was OK to be quite so delighted with her bridesmaid dress and slippers and the fact that Brian and Nina were marrying. After all, these things were only happening because her mother was dead and she, Nat, had been the cause of that death. The guilt and grief caused her to stuff her bridesmaid dress down the loo and try to flush it away, as she would flush the shame and guilt if only she could. Nina had understood. She'd held the weeping child until her fury and fear had subsided. She rightly saw terror where others might only have seen a tantrum or anarchy. They secretly bought a new dress without even mentioning the incident to Brian. Both females agreed that even dry-cleaning would not make the original bridesmaid's dress OK.

It was such a little secret. Quite understandable. But then there were bigger secrets, equally well-intended but undeniably bigger. Nina became Nat's mother and everyone wanted it to be so. Nat wanted it so badly that she called Nina 'Mummy' from the moment the confetti was launched into the air. And so when, a few years later, Nina discovered she was pregnant, Brian and Nina made the decision that they would not tell this new baby that Nat was a half-sister. They did not see a reason to mention the dead mother to any of the small boys that followed. Nina and Brian reasoned it might potentially lead to Nat feeling left out again. No one wanted that. She was doing so well. She was overcoming her shyness, she rarely stuttered and even her clumsiness was abating somewhat. Children could tease horribly. It terrified Nina that one day the boys (mid sibling squabble) might taunt Nat with the fact that Nina wasn't her real mother, so they decided not to mention the fact. They took this decision and then moved to Guildford where none of the neighbours knew their history. Nat had seen the best intentions and accepted her parents' plan as she accepted anything her wonderful parents suggested (other than early bedtimes and extra recorder practice, those things she would argue about!). Indeed, Nina's keenness to pass Nat off as a blood daughter made her feel especially wanted, just as Nina had hoped.

Years of normal family life, including rows about homework, TV watching and curfew times went a long way to healing Nat and Brian. Their grief, quite different but equally real, was stored away somewhere deep and private. From time to time Brian deliberately accessed his grief in order to commemorate or in order to celebrate. Nat kept hers securely buried and the only lasting tribute she bestowed on her mother's memory was to swear that she would never, *ever* give birth. She would never, ever risk bringing a baby into this world and then leaving it all alone. No matter that she now had a loving stepmother. No matter that the odds of the same thing happening to her were minuscule. No matter that her husband wanted a baby. No matter what.

'Lucky that you met a man who understood that you didn't want babies and why you don't,' said Alan, interrupting Nat's private thoughts. 'I said you would, didn't I?'

Yes, he had said that, as he'd hastily picked up his things and packed his bags. He'd said that Nat was a super girl and that she'd definitely meet a man who didn't want babies just as she didn't. Probably many, many men, he'd reassured. After all, they were only twenty-two years old. At that time in their lives Alan had been slightly unusual in his certainty that he *did* want kids, just as Nat was unusual for her certainty that she didn't. But, despite his consolations and his predictions about her finding a future soul-mate, there had been something about the look in Alan's eyes that condemned her. It had been there from the exact moment she'd told him *why* she didn't want babies. That look sickened and haunted her. He regarded her as a crazy woman; that much was crystal clear. Not necessarily crazy because she didn't want babies but crazy because she believed that she, too, might die in childbirth. He'd thought her unreasonable and hysterical. He'd spent a few days reciting statistics to her about how very few women suffered this tragic thing. He'd asked about her mother's health so that he could ascertain whether she'd suffered from a condition that Nat might have inherited. He'd tried to reason with her, but she was not reasonable. Nat could not shift her fear that she might leave a tiny baby girl alone in this world, a baby burdened with the knowledge that she had killed her mother. She couldn't do that. She wouldn't risk that. Not for anyone. Alan, who had encouraged Nat's timidity in terms of hemlines and social interaction, was now demanding that she be brave and fearless about the one thing that scared her most. He did not understand how she could be such a coward. That was the word he had used, just once, in their final row. He'd regretted it immediately and rushed to retract it but the word had been branded on to her consciousness. Of course Alan would think she was a coward. That was what most people would think. Crazy or a coward. Unreasonable or gutless.

Nat decided she would never again risk telling anyone the truth; it was better that they thought she was a career bitch or just plain selfish as she was not willing to bring up kids. She reasoned that it didn't matter why she didn't want kids, what mattered was that she didn't want them.

'I've never told Neil why I don't want kids,' confessed Nat bluntly.

She wasn't sure why she felt compelled to tell Alan as much. Wine consumption possibly. Desperation probably.

'Oh.' Alan looked surprised.

'And now he wants kids.'

'Oh.' Now, Alan looked uncomfortable.

'Should I get another bottle?' offered Nat. Getting drunk seemed like the only answer.

'No, I'll get it. My round.'

27

'So I take it you had a good time with Becky last night?' Neil asked this question while lying prone in their bed. He stared at the ceiling, rather than meet his wife's eye. This wasn't the question he wanted to ask but it was a start.

'Uh huh,' said Nat.

'Where did you go?'

'I thought I told you.' Nat was pretty sure she had made up a lie about where she'd supposedly been last night but was now uncertain as to exactly what it was she'd said. She didn't want to say anything more, in case her second lie contradicted her first one and Neil noticed.

'Oh, yes, the pair of you were going into Leicester Square to see a movie and grab a bite to eat, right?'

'Right,' said Nat carefully. She thought Neil was behaving a little strangely. As they'd operated like ships that pass in the night of late, she was no longer used to him taking so much notice of what she'd been up to. She checked the date on her watch. It was the thirteenth. A Friday. Friday the thirteenth was not a date to get sloppy about alibis, thought Nat superstitiously.

'Did that pan out?' he asked, trying to sound casual.

'Well, we missed the start of the film, so we skipped that and then we drank more than we ate,' said Nat. She realised she had to account for her drunken state last night. Her heart beat at treble speed. Despite popular wisdom, Nat had found that lying didn't become easier with

increased frequency. In fact, the more lies she embedded in their relationship, the worse she felt.

Neil's stomach plummeted. He'd hoped to hear that there'd been
a change of plan.

'Why aren't you getting ready for work?' asked Nat. She hoped for
a change of subject.

'I'm taking it easy this morning. I'm planning on having a lie-in
and then going to work after the rush hour is over.'

Neil wanted to say that he was hanging around the house because
he thought there was a dire need for them to talk. The opportunities
to do so in the evenings were increasingly infrequent, whereas the
need to do so was patently increasingly urgent.

The room smelt stale, full of sour breath, sweat and yesterday's
alcohol. Neil wanted to fling open a window and let in some fresh
life, even if that meant an icy, November blast of wind, but opening
a window would require moving and he didn't feel ready to give up
his duvet yet. Where had she been last night? Really been? Neil didn't
believe his wife's account as he'd spotted Becky, quite by chance, at
Hammersmith tube station last night and she'd been alone, Nat was
nowhere in sight.

Or at least he thought it was Becky, he was *almost* certain the girl
in the blue hat, recharging her Oyster card, was Becky but he supposed
there was a possibility he had been mistaken. A possibility he both
embraced and doubted, like he would an errant lover. The problem
was he couldn't mention the sighting to Nat outright. How would he
explain why he was in Hammersmith at 5.45p.m.? It wasn't his usual
route home from work. He'd said he was having a quiet night in and
it was true, in part. He'd left Hush Hush early, even Cindy couldn't
distract him. He had been home by 9p.m. Then he'd spent the rest
of the night quietly stewing.

Neil was not normally the sort of man to wrap himself up in livid
tangles of desolate nasty imaginings. Stupid suspicions and distasteful
deductions were a sure route to a sort of hell he never wanted to
visit. That said, if a wife (who was refusing to even *discuss* having a

baby) had recently taken to frequently going out alone (offering up only the most cobweb-thin alibis and excuses as to her whereabouts) then most blokes would leap to the conclusion that said wife was having an affair. They might then try to get hold of her phone to get a look at her call log or they might hack into her email account to see if they could find evidence to back up their torrid, sordid, horrid conclusion. But not Neil, he was above that and Nat was better than that. Wasn't she? He told himself that there'd be some uncomplicated reason to explain why Nat hadn't been with Becky last night and yet had said she was.

He just couldn't think what that simple explanation might be.

Maybe Becky had just popped to the station to refill her Oyster card and then returned to work to meet Nat. Or maybe Nat had followed Becky into central London once she'd finished up at work. Nat was very conscientious, that was possible.

Possible but not probable.

Neil looked at his wife. Could she be having an affair? She looked just the same as she had the morning before. Same blond hair swishing around her toned shoulders, her lips were still as plump as ever (although the smile seemed to have gone AWOL). Her eyes were the same vibrant, stunning blue and her arse was just as tidy. Yes, she looked the same as she always had. She didn't look like someone who was lying and deceiving him. He caught a glimpse of himself in the dressing-table mirror. But then nor did he look like someone who was lying and deceiving, he looked unchanged too. What a shambles.

'You'll be late,' she warned.

'Yes, technically.' He couldn't bring himself to care about that.

'Won't you get into bother?' Nat was conducting this conversation while rushing around the room pulling together the things she needed for work. Last night, she'd carelessly dropped her handbag in the corner of the room, the contents of which were now scattered nearby. She hurriedly picked up her mobile phone, her lipstick, her purse and the Little Black Book; slyly, she slipped it out of sight. She couldn't imagine Neil asking her about the book, let alone him associating the book with her ever more frequent independent nights out, but it was a risk she didn't want to take. A flame of guilt roared in her gut, which manifested as exasperation with Neil. 'Well, won't you get into bother?' she snapped.

Neil was becoming immune to Nat's irritated tone; it was white noise to him nowadays. 'It's not as though I'm scrambling up the corporate ladder, desperate for my next promotion. I leave that to the family men in the office,' he snapped back.

Nat bit down hard on her enragement. So, he was making another point. Or rather, he was making the same point in yet another way. He didn't have a family, so why bother with work? Was that it? 'That's so responsible,' she said sarcastically. 'Do I have to remind you we might not have kids but we do have a mortgage?'

'Oh, relax. I'm going to be forty minutes late, I'm not handing in my notice. You're overreacting because you're hung-over.'

'I'm not hung-over.'

'I'd say you are.'

'Oh, well, if *you* say I am, I *must* be,' Natalie muttered. He was right, actually. She felt terrible.

Meeting up with Alan had been a mistake on a number of levels. For a start, the second Friday in the month was a bad day to have a hangover as that was when the monthly heads of department status meetings took place at work. Nat usually tried to be especially perky and responsive for those meetings and that was particularly important now, considering yesterday they'd been told budgets had to be cut and head count too, possibly. This was not the time to become slovenly; she needed to be at the top of her game. She looked at Neil and considered explaining all of this to him, but what would be the point, she asked herself with a defeated internal shrug. He didn't even know about her last promotion, he wasn't aware that she was head of a department.

Besides hampering her chances to shine at the office today, Nat also deeply regretted meeting Alan Jones because the evening was categorically the worst of all her get-togethers with her ex-boyfriends.

Talking to Alan had reawakened all her old feelings of grief and guilt and sadness, a lethal cocktail when mixed with vulnerability, insecurity and paranoia; feelings she had worked for years to put aside.

Bugger.

Nat was ashamed that she'd got so drunk last night, that she was lying to her husband and that she couldn't explain her refusal to give him his heart's desire. It was irritating that her hangover didn't numb her stinging conscience. Her head felt fluffy and her tongue was furry, her fingers were cold and her legs were slow. She wanted to admit this and much more to Neil. Part of her desperately wanted to tell him all about Alan, and her other exes, and the Little Black Book come to that. She wanted him to put his arms around her, to soothe her, then perhaps draw her back into bed. She knew the cosy, warm comfort that being under the duvet would guarantee; she still remembered that. If only they could talk and make love, she'd feel better, so much better. She was sure of it. If there was one thing that meeting her exes was teaching her, it was that no one ever healed her with such a tender touch as Neil did. A word from him, a hug, a joke and she could practically feel her self-esteem repairing like skin cells in the sunshine.

Of course it was impossible. She couldn't tell him about the meetings with her old boyfriends. At the moment they couldn't talk to one another about setting the Sky Plus box without rowing. How could they possibly navigate a conversation about exes? For a start, she'd have to confess that she hadn't been out with Becky at all last night. Then she'd have to explain that recently she'd become ill with the thought that she and Neil were not suited to one another and that would mean they'd have to talk about his desire for babies and her reasons for not wanting one. No. No way. It was impossible.

Nat glanced around the bedroom; she was looking for her left shoe. It wasn't under the bed or near the bedside table. Where was it? It had to be somewhere. Last night she'd taken off her shoes in this room, here was the right shoe to prove it. She couldn't have got home wearing just one shoe, so where the hell was it now? And why wasn't

Neil helping look for it? Was he punishing her for coming home drunk? Or was it bigger than that? She feared that, nowadays, on some level he was constantly punishing her for not agreeing to have a baby. His entire attitude of late had been remote and irritable. During the first month of Neil's campaign for a baby, he had been as sweet as it was possible for any man to be. He'd repeatedly tried to demonstrate his paternity potential by being thoughtful, helpful and reliable. Nat had been inundated with bunches of flowers and impulse purchased bars of Dairy Milk chocolate. She'd benefited from numerous home-cooked meals and Neil making an effort to put the loo seat down. But then something changed around the beginning of October, he had become sulky and grumpy and too often he was drunk. Nat didn't think he was helping his case for being seen as ideal father material, but as she didn't intend him ever to be a father, she thought she'd resist saying so and simply ride out his moods.

Neil was at a loss. The problem was that despite putting hours of thought into the matter he could not imagine why Nat might refuse to have children. He was terrified that the only explanation was the least welcome, the most cruel. She was having an affair. She was in love with someone else. The oft repeated chant that she'd 'always said as much' simply didn't seem explanation enough for not having a baby. She liked kids, she was good with them, she would make a wonderful mother; he didn't doubt that for a moment. Neil had wondered if his wife doubted *his* ability to be a decent, responsible parent. When Neil saw that his consideration was having no effect on Nat's decision to remain childfree, he became withdrawn, absent and awkward. He channelled all his thoughtfulness, charm and joy into Cindy and Heidi. If questioned (although no one ever did question him, not even Cindy, certainly not Nat) Neil might have admitted that, yes, perhaps he was meeting Nat's uncooperative behaviour with his own, but then it was hard for a man to find the enthusiasm to hunt for a court shoe when his wife was refusing to have so much as a cursory glance around for her maternal instincts.

Like a couple of kids they resentfully pointed a metaphorical finger at one another and cried, 'You started it.' They lacked a third party who cared enough to insist someone must 'finish it', the way exasperated parents did with argumentative children.

'We need to talk,' said Neil flatly. He rolled on to his side and finally looked directly at her. Nat was on her knees next to the bed, taking her fourth look under, just in case her black patent court shoe happened to suddenly, magically appear. Their eyes were level, although nothing else between them was. Inwardly, she froze but she was careful not to slow up her movements, even for a moment. She was pretty sure this comment translated to, 'I need to reiterate my case for you giving up your job to incubate my sperm.' She didn't want to hear it all again, certainly not this morning.

'Isn't that supposed to be my line?' Natalie mumbled flippantly. Then she reached under the bedside chest of drawers where there was nothing other than fluff and hair, yuk, she must remember to hoover under there.

'I'm serious, Nat, we have to talk.'

Sometimes Nat resented the fact that Neil was able to communicate. Her friends all told her how lucky she was that Neil was able to discuss, debate and theorise on subjects other than football fixtures but Natalie wasn't sure. On days like today, days when she was guilty and hung-over, confused, when she had a meeting with her boss, she was late and she couldn't find her shoe, Natalie wished Neil was a typical bloke, who limited communication to the occasional grunt and then only when he'd lost the TV remote. A typical bloke who didn't yearn for babies.

Instead of responding to Neil's comment, Natalie stared despairingly at the jumble of books, magazines, coffee cups and discarded clothes that littered their room.

'We need to sort this place out. It's a tip. Ah-ha! There it is.' Natalie pounced on her shoe like some sort of ninja. 'Look, I'm sorry, Neil. I can't talk right now. I'm late. I'm sorry.'

Neil thought that in fact he was the sorry one. He knew what Natalie meant when she said sorry. She wanted to say, 'I'm not sorry at all but I need to get out of the door and this is what you want to hear.' And she meant, 'You'll be sorry.' She was right; they did work against their gender stereotypes. He realised he wasn't going to get anywhere this morning. Maybe he'd try for answers again tonight.

'By the way, Ali called last night,' he said.

'Oh yes?'

'She's asked us round for dinner tonight.'

'Tonight?'

'Yes. That's not a problem, is it?' Neil asked suspiciously.

'Well, I had plans tonight,' said Nat haltingly.

'Who with?'

'Becky.'

'Again? You saw her last night.'

'No, I— Well, yes. I meant that tonight we have plans to work late. We have to run a critical cost analysis on a new project. It's big. Very big.'

Neil wasn't convinced but nor was he prepared to believe that all was lost. 'Don't be a lunatic. You can't work tonight, it's Friday night. Besides, Ali was pretty insistent so you'll have to cancel Becky. I said we'd go. We can't let her down,' he said firmly.

'OK, I'll cancel my plans,' Nat replied simply.

Neil let out an enormous sigh. See, no affair, he reassured himself. Otherwise she wouldn't have changed her plans for Ali. He was being insane even imagining Nat could have an affair. Nuts. Relief and gratitude washed over him. He didn't want her to go, leaving an atmosphere between them. Showing sudden agility and determination, Neil jumped out of bed and just as she was almost out of the room he caught her by the arm. He pulled her close to him and wrapped his arms around her. He wanted her to feel cocooned but she felt trapped. Her body was rigid beneath his touch. He tried to kiss her on the lips but she was still looking round the room trying to locate something, perhaps an earring or a file, not his gaze, that much was for sure. His kiss scratched up against her cheek.

She put her hand to her face and said, 'You need a shave, you're all prickly.'

She wasn't wiping the kiss away, more trying to catch it and hold it tight as they hadn't been doing much kissing recently but Neil misunderstood the gesture and felt rejected. There had been a time, really not so long ago, when if he ever leant in to kiss her she would clasp his face in both her hands and hold on tightly. Her fingers were always cold, his cheeks were always warm. She loved to feel the bristles of his shaving shadow tingle under her fingertips. Now, she treated him as though he had an infectious disease.

'I'm thinking of growing a beard,' he joked, as he let his grip on her slip.

'Haven't we got enough problems?' Her retort was supposed to be funny but the comment fell heavily into their history; too close to the truth to raise a laugh.

'You'll definitely come tonight, won't you?'

'Yes,' said Natalie, although he could hear that her agreement was reluctant.

Neil didn't want to think of Cindy but suddenly an image of her twenty-three-inch waist and thirty-six-inch bust erupted into his brain. The thing about Cindy was that she was never, ever reluctant.

28

Neil watched as clusters of parents dashed along the street, presumably heading home, or to the supermarket or a coffee shop, having completed the school drop-off. They were identifiable as parents, not only because some pushed empty strollers, having deposited their toddlers at pre-school, but because they seemed to walk with a sense of confidence and purpose. At least, that's how it appeared to Neil. These people had a reason. These people knew why they were on the planet, why they shopped and cooked, why they cleaned their houses, why they did or did not go to work. Every decision, immense or minute, made sense to parents.

There were mostly mums but there was the occasional stay-at-home dad. The dads who'd opted (or been pushed) into the role as main care provider always looked overly earnest or exhaustingly enthusiastic. As two such dads walked past him, Neil heard snatches of a conversation about a robot that used sensors to navigate itself around the floor and so the robot could wash, scrub and dry tile, linoleum and sealed hardwood floors. Neil was unsure whether the invention was real or just a figment of the dad's imagination but it was clear that even in this field boy-toys were of paramount importance. This thought was confirmed when he spotted one dad riding a skateboard that was ingeniously attached to the back of a pushchair, allowing him to skate along and push the buggy at the same time. Neil stared in admiration and only just resisted asking if he could have a go. He had already noticed that the dads he watched in coffee shops were often to be found reading the latest parental manual, which they liberally referred to and quoted from throughout their conversations. Neil wouldn't mind taking on the lion's share of the childcare, if he was ever given the chance. The parents walked in chatty groups. He heard one or two huddles debate Costa over Starbucks and then watched them wander in the appropriate direction. They wore a uniform, these parents, and Neil did not mean the uniform of beige shapeless slacks and blue and white striped tops (although those were spotted in abundance), they all wore a similar expression. They all looked contented and fulfilled. They all looked happy. Happy enough.

He'd once (or twice or maybe more often than that) pointed out as much to Nat. She'd argued that parents were always happy and content just after they'd dropped their kids at school; it was because they relished the time to themselves. She'd rolled her eyes in exasperation as she'd delivered her retort. But Neil wasn't a jerk. He could see that they weren't all doing a full song and tap routine, he realised being a parent was hard graft but, on the whole, the parents he saw looked happy, some looked ecstatic and he didn't believe it was all due to the fact that they had a few uninterrupted hours to buy groceries and drop off dry-cleaning. He believed it was because these people, these parents, *were* happy. Why couldn't Nat see that? Why wouldn't she even look in that direction and acknowledge that having a family might be the best thing ever? She had argued that they were happy as they were but in the last couple of weeks she hadn't bothered saying that any more. Probably because she knew it wasn't an argument that would hold up.

The parents drifted away and then the streets were awash with gangs of hooded teenagers (presumably bunking school, having been to registration) as well as determined, lone pensioners bundled up beneath layers of hats, scarves and gloves who were heading towards Hammersmith with the intention of pulling the shopping trollies around Primark and Marks and Spencer. Neil watched a cat cross the road and then settle on the boot of a car that had just been parked.

He waited outside Hush Hush for forty minutes until he heard voices inside and the sound of keys as someone unlocked the door. He realised hanging about a strip joint early in the morning was a new all-time low but he didn't care. He had to see Cindy.

Three cleaners greeted him. Two of them looked like a female Laurel and Hardy and clearly thought they were funnier still. 'Mrs Hardy' (who was undoubtedly in charge) shook her head disapprovingly, her disgust registered all over her body as her hips, thighs and upper arms seemed to shake in protest too.

'What you doing here at this time of the morning?' she demanded crossly. 'Haven't you got a job to go to? Or a home?'

Neil wasn't sure how to answer that. In theory at least he had both and yet, here he was, outside Hush Hush waiting for Cindy.

'Mrs Laurel' lingered in the background and sniggered. She was more amused than disgusted. The third cleaner (the only one actually doing any work) tutted as she threw mops and buckets into a cupboard behind the reception. She took off her apron and thrust it into her shopping bag and then shoved past Neil and her gossipy colleagues. She at least was keen to go home; she did not want to have to spend a moment longer than necessary in the place.

'See you tomorrow,' she muttered at her co-workers and then vanished up the street.

Mrs Laurel and Hardy were not in such a hurry to leave. Neil got the sense they didn't hurry anywhere or anything.

'You're a good-looking lad. What you doing hanging around a place like this? You don't manage any of the girls, do you? I'd know your face if you did. I know all the managers.'

Neil felt uncomfortable that he'd been mistaken for what amounted to a pimp but accepted that it was a reasonable assumption to make under the circumstances. He rushed to explain he was a regular client, not a position he ever imagined he'd be keen to admit to. He explained that he desperately wanted to see Cindy as he had something important to talk to her about. The two women exchanged a look which explicitly declared him to be a saddo.

Neil would have been surprised to learn that 'Mrs Hardy' had once been a dancer, back in the sixties. Ruby, she'd been known as then. She'd reduced men to weeping, trembling lumps of desire in her time. Ruby liked to declare that there was nothing she hadn't seen, nothing she didn't know when it came to lust. So she was intrigued to see this man at the door of the strip joint so early in the morning because he didn't look like your usual desperado. By the look of him you'd have thought he had more compassion than that, more sense at least. Ruby scrutinised Neil again. He did have a funny look in his eye, mind. A look she'd come to be wary of, the one that said obsessive. And why else would a man be here at this time unless he was a complete loser? Ruby saw it as her unofficial job to look after the girls, especially when the bouncers weren't around. She knew for a certain fact that Cindy was inside having a coffee and putting her make-up on, killing some time before she took that lovely girl of hers off to nursery. Cindy was working the day shift today which began at 11a.m., but Ruby was not going to let on as much to this strange man.

'Well, love, none of the girls get here until about lunchtime. Sorry, you'll have to come back then.'

'Is there anywhere I can wait?'

'Out here on the pavement, if you must.'

'Please, it's important.' Neil reached out towards Ruby. His intention was to rest his hand on her arm in a winning way but she was used to rougher treatment and thought he might be about to grab her so she used her best weapon – her large gob.

'GET YOUR HANDS OFF ME!'

Startled, Neil jumped away but Ruby's protest had been heard inside. Within seconds the beefy bouncer and the werewolf barman were at the door.

'What's up, Ruby?'

'This man was going to hit me,' Ruby declared. She lived a drab life but was rather fond of a drama, so she never missed an opportunity to orchestrate one. The other cleaner was a more peaceful woman and felt compelled to defuse the situation.

'Now, Ruby, he wasn't. He just wants to see one of the girls. We were telling him to come back later.'

Neil's heart beat at a hundred miles an hour. Oh crap, the enormous bouncer was going to kill him. He was going to be murdered outside a strip joint on a Friday morning. It occurred to him that his mother would never survive the shame. He wanted to protest his innocence but things were happening too quickly. The bouncer looked as though he was squaring up, both the women were talking at once, they were saying opposing things but it didn't matter because no one could hear them as they were both high-pitched and hysterical. With relief Neil realised that the werewolf barman was saying that he recognised Neil and that he was a *very* regular customer but Neil didn't know if the emphasis on very was going to help him at that moment. Did being a regular customer work for him or make him sound like a jerk or, worse, a stalker? Suddenly he heard Cindy through the din.

'What the hell is going on? Can't a girl do her eyeliner in peace? Oh, hi, Neil. You're early today.'

'Sorry,' muttered Neil. It was the first word he'd managed to chuck up.

'So what's going on?' Cindy asked.

'He was going to hit me,' said Ruby but this time she made her accusation with a lot less confidence and everyone knew that her statement was questionable.

'Neil? He wouldn't hurt a fly,' said Cindy. Neil was surprised to discover that he was relieved and vaguely offended at the same time. He felt that Cindy's assertion, and the bouncer's easy acceptance that she was probably right, was somehow an assault on his manhood. Still, at least no one was going to break his nose or legs.

The cleaners, sensing the drama was over, instantly disappeared and the werewolf went back to the cellar. It was delivery day, he had to stock up for the weekend, and he didn't have time for this. The bouncer eyed Neil suspiciously for a moment longer and muttered, 'I'm watching you, son.' But his manner of speaking now caused Neil to feel amused rather than threatened as he sounded exactly like some tough, old-time copper off *The Bill*; a parody rather than the real thing. Besides, Cindy's presence somehow made him feel safer and braver.

'Sorry,' said Neil once again, the moment he and Cindy were alone. 'I just really needed to see you.'

'It's too early for dancing,' she pointed out. She stifled a yawn which somehow underlined the point.

'I know.' He paused, embarrassed and unsure where to take the conversation next. 'I thought I could buy you a coffee.'

'Oh, right.' Cindy looked at her watch. She had three-quarters of an hour to kill before Heidi had to be at nursery. 'You can buy me and Heidi breakfast. We had our first one at six thirty. I'm starving again.'

'Heidi's with you?' Neil couldn't keep the surprise out of his voice. He was thrilled at the thought of seeing Heidi again but irritated with the thought of her hanging around in a strip joint.

'Wait here, I'll just get her and the buggy.'

Neil and Cindy opted to visit a nearby greasy spoon rather than one of the chain coffee shops. Neil thought that Cindy in her canary-yellow clingy T-shirt and skin-tight cherry-pink tracksuit might draw more attention than they wanted in Starbucks or similar. In the greasy spoon, of course, the builders (arses spread over the rickety chairs and their stomachs popping out under their T-shirts) noticed Cindy's plastic talons and her false eyelashes but, after one appreciative glance, they quickly returned their focus to their fry-ups and tabloids. Neil had a feeling that the curiosity of the mums living in the W4 postcode would have been harder to shake.

Cindy ordered egg and soldiers for Heidi and coffee and fry-ups for her and Neil. Neil was unsure he wanted to eat but went along with Cindy's suggestion as it was easier than thinking for himself. How could he waste head space on deciding whether or not he wanted breakfast when his wife was having an affair? Or at least she might be having an affair. She probably was. She possibly was. Oh, he didn't know and he quickly grew impatient with himself just thinking about it.

They chose the table in the window. Heidi sat patiently in an immaculate but old-fashioned high chair that the café owner dragged from a back room, surprising both Neil and Cindy. For a moment neither said anything but just looked out on to the high street. It was a bright winter morning. The sky was a solid blue and the cold sun sloshed on to the frosty road, throwing off a gleam that was annoying for drivers and delightful for children who saw joy in a road that sparkled. The light bounced in through the window and danced on the cutlery. It was actually a beautiful day but that only made things harder for Neil.

'So where's the fire?' Cindy asked.

'I think Nat's having an affair,' announced Neil solemnly.

'Oh.'

'Do you?' he demanded, somewhat affronted that his huge announcement had induced such a clearly underwhelmed response.

'I don't know her.'

'But do you think it's likely? From what I've told you,' he persisted.

'Maybe.' Cindy sliced into her fried egg. She anticipated the yolk running across her plate and into her toast. She loved soggy, eggy toast but she was disappointed, the egg had been in the pan a fraction too long and the yolk had solidified. Still, other than that it was a good breakfast and an unexpected treat. She'd been on a diet all week and she hated diets. That yogurt she'd eaten this morning simply wasn't enough for a girl to manage on. Least, not a dancer. It was tricky, she knew she had to keep her figure but she didn't want to go collapsing with hunger, did she?

'Maybe yes or maybe no?' pursued Neil.

What was he on about? Oh yes, he wanted to know if she thought his missus was having it away with some other bugger. Well, probably. Who wasn't? Cindy glanced at Neil and saw that this was not the answer he wanted.

'The point is, why do you think she might be?' Cindy asked, nicely deflecting the issue. She leant over to Heidi and tried to encourage her to eat a bit more toast or egg. Was it the white bit that was good for you or the yolk? Cindy couldn't remember. She'd ask Cherry later on. Cherry knew everything there was to know about food nutrition and stuff; it came off the back of an eating disorder.

Neil told Cindy that Nat's account of her night out last night didn't seem likely as he'd spotted Becky at the tube station and Nat hadn't been with her. He told her that Nat had come home drunk and distressed, and that this morning she'd been elusive and argumentative.

'Doesn't that seem to add up to a rotten conscience to you?' he asked.

'Yes, maybe.' Cindy didn't usually get into this sort of stuff with her clients. She wondered what to say. Her job was to take her clients well away from their reality. She was supposed to brighten their days and nights, she wasn't supposed to collaborate with their paranoia and confirm their misgivings. Yet her experience was that everyone was capable of infidelity and that many, many people actually actively pursued it, but Neil was the last client she'd want to say that to. He was not like her other clients. He was a little more earnest and sincere. She'd called him soft to the other dancers but she hadn't meant that in a mean way. He seemed to take an interest in her too, beyond her arse and tits. When they met in the park they'd behaved like friends. A lot like friends. She liked the idea of having a male friend. It was a novelty. She had lots of girlfriends, of course. Loads and loads of them as she was definitely a girl's girl, it wasn't easy to like men in her chosen profession. And then there was her Dave. But he wasn't her friend, he was her husband. Friends were the people you talked to about your husband and so by that line of reasoning her Dave couldn't be a friend, as lovely as he was. Cindy racked her brains as she thought what to say to Neil that he might like to hear. After all, that's the line she took with most of her girlfriends, she always told them what they wanted to hear. 'Yes, of course he loves you!' 'Yes, he'll phone.' 'No, your bum definitely does not look big in that! Have you lost weight?'

'It's not total proof, though, is it?' offered Cindy. It was the best she could come up with. 'Come on, you pay the bill and you can walk with me and Heidi to her nursery school.'

Neil was so excited about the prospect of dropping Heidi off at nursery he didn't hesitate to pay the bill in full; after all, he'd said he'd take them to breakfast, he couldn't expect her to pay half. In fact, Neil never expected Cindy to pay for anything when they were together, which was just as well because Cindy didn't expect to pay for anything when they were together either. Her pleasure in their friendship didn't stretch that far.

He wanted to push the buggy but he didn't dare ask so he settled for walking along next to Cindy and Heidi; sometimes on narrow pavements he had to drop behind them. He wondered if onlookers would assume they were a family. He found that he hoped so.

Heidi liked her nursery school and rushed in, making her way directly towards the playhouse. Cindy almost had to drag Neil back out of the premises. He craned his neck in an effort to see the tiniest kids plod around the play dough table and the slightly older kids tear around the playground. Even in his wretched and confused state he felt a sense of joy snaking up inside his stomach. Look at them, he thought to himself, every one of them is a bloody fabulous miracle. OK, so that boy in the red top was nipping the girl in the green skirt and that wasn't nice, Neil admitted, but all the same they were miracles. Why couldn't Nat see how wonderful kids were? If looking at strangers' kids made him feel this much better about life, he could only imagine how wonderful it would be to have one of his own. How would it feel to stare into the eyes of his son or daughter? To feel the weight of them as he carried them from the car to their bunk beds, as his dad had carried him when he was a small kid who'd fallen asleep in the back seat during a long journey home. Why didn't Nat want it?

'But if there isn't another man then why is she being so bloody obstinate about having a baby?' Neil asked Cindy as they walked through Ravenscourt Park on their way back towards Hush Hush. Neil knew he should probably be heading off to work but he had started to think of Ravenscourt Park as 'their park', his, Cindy's and Heidi's, and he didn't want to miss the opportunity of strolling through it with Cindy again. He realised this was a bit presumptuous. Really, he had no right to imagine that the three of them had anything that was 'theirs'; besides, this was only the second time they'd visited together. Well, third if you counted the trip to the nursery, to drop off Heidi, as a separate trip to this one, coming back from the nursery. It was no good; no matter how he massaged the figures, he realised that it wasn't 'theirs'. Nothing was 'theirs'. They didn't share a name, or a home or even a TV. What was he thinking, trying to pretend they had something more solid? The truth was they had an embryonic and slightly unexpected friendship at best, and a complicated commercial arrangement at worst. Neil didn't want to think about that right now. He strode along the path, pushing the empty buggy as he'd seen real fathers do, just about an hour ago.

'You know, Nat not wanting kids is not normal. It's not natural.' There, Neil had said it aloud. The thoughts he'd so often played with of late had finally been voiced. His wife was not behaving rationally in refusing to have a child. She was being unreasonable to the point of unnatural.

'I know what you mean,' said Cindy. 'My Dave didn't want babies. Nor did my best mate Di's partner. Nor did my dad, come to that. It's usually men who are not as keen. Not the women.' Cindy shrugged, clearly stumped by Nat's attitude and then added, 'I just took matters into my own hands.'

'In what way?'

'I stopped taking the pill, you idiot. What did you think I meant?' Cindy laughed as she delivered this piece of information. She didn't see it as the terrible abuse of trust that it no doubt was, she saw it as an age-old trick used by the desperate and determined. 'I just said it was a slip-up. I was taking pills for a kidney infection at the time so I blamed the tablets that the doctor had given me. I said they must have worked against the pill or something and so my Dave wasn't suspicious. And then it was a done deal and he quickly got used to the idea. I've told you before that there isn't a better dad than him, now. Once he got used to the idea.'

'It's not quite the same for me, though, is it?' pointed out Neil.

Cindy stared at him for a moment and then grasped his meaning. 'Oh no, I suppose not.' She laughed. 'Oh well, it doesn't always work out so well as it did for me, anyway. My friend Di's boyfriend buggered off and in the end she couldn't face it on her own so she had a late abortion.' Neil winced. He felt powerless and distraught. Cindy noticed and tried to cheer him up, she didn't like to think about Di's abortion either; it had been painful, shocking and heartbreaking. None of the girls ever talked about it to Di. Cindy squeezed his arm. Her touch was strange. In many ways they were intimate, for example Neil could recognise her deodorant, as many times she'd stood in front of him naked, raising her arms above her head, but they rarely touched. 'Don't worry, Neil, I'm sure if we put our heads together, we'll come up with something.'

Neil seriously doubted this was the case. He'd spent hours and hours considering his problem over the last few months and hadn't managed to find a solution, so it seemed unlikely that Cindy could crack it before her shift started.

'Oh, look! Heidi didn't take Mrs Flippy into nursery.' Cindy crouched down beside the buggy and pulled out a raggedy stuffed toy rabbit from the shopping basket.

'Mrs Flippy?' asked Neil.

'Mix between Floppy and Lippy. When Heidi was a tiny baby I used to hold the rabbit in front of my face and say to Dave, "She's crying, it's your turn to change her nappy," or whatever, you know in a funny voice. And so he renamed the rabbit Lippy instead of Floppy but that seemed a bit wrong for a baby's toy so we settled on something in the middle.' Cindy grinned as she relayed the memory.

This small insight into Cindy's domestic life bit into Neil's consciousness and embedded itself there. He was beginning to see it was a bit fucked up that he knew what this woman's minge looked like and what her kid's toys were called and yet he had never touched her with any sort of affection. His relationship with her was a bit like a relationship someone might have with their favourite soap star while following a particularly compelling plot. Neil knew he should sit down and think about all this. He and Nat were both chasing about, getting drunk and avoiding stuff, they had to sort themselves out. But right now he had Mrs Flippy to think about.

'Will she miss her rabbit?'

Cindy looked concerned again. 'Yes, she probably won't settle at nap time.' Cindy checked her watch. She didn't have time to take the rabbit back to nursery. She glanced at Neil, wondering how far his good nature could be stretched. He understood her unvoiced request.

'I'll take it to her. I'll drop it off on the way to work,' he offered.

'You don't mind?'

'I'd be delighted.' That statement was almost too true. Neil wondered what was wrong with his life that his biggest kick could come from pretending to be someone's father, or at least acting as a useful family friend. Cindy held out the rabbit towards him and as she did so he noticed her wrist. It was, quite usually, patterned with her thin blue veins. Funny, he'd seen every fragment of her body: her smooth and strong inner thighs, her neat, nipped-in waist, her out-y belly button and of course her scarcely there pubic hair and her surgically enhanced tits, but he was sure her wrist was the most erotic part of her body. He felt slithers of appreciation and excitement scamper around his body. He stared and stared at her wrist as she impatiently waved the toy rabbit at him. She was wondering why he hadn't reached out and taken it. She was going to be late if he didn't get a move on.

Her wrist was definitely the prettiest and most startling thing he could imagine. It was a tiny, feminine wrist, a mother's wrist. It carried her lifeblood and she had given life, too, actual life. To Heidi. She'd reproduced. Cindy had reproduced. Of course he'd known that for weeks but now the importance of that information hit him. This woman was a miracle. These veins were miracles. They were important. Important to him. Suddenly, Neil grabbed Cindy's hand and he brought her wrist to his mouth. He kissed it long and hard, not caring that they were standing exposed in the middle of Ravenscourt Park. Anyone could have walked past them. A colleague of his, a client of hers, but Neil didn't care. Cindy stared at him, unsure what to do. His kiss was charged and erotic and kind. She recognised all three incarnations and was flattered by the third. So he'd kissed her wrist, where was the harm in that?

Suddenly he let go of her wrist and with his right hand he grabbed the back of her head and pulled her face close towards his. He landed his lips square on to hers and before either of them gave the scenario much thought, his tongue entered her mouth. The unfamiliar territory set off numerous sparks. He felt bolts of excitement in his mouth, his chest and, inevitably, his cock. His left hand moved a fraction towards her breasts. He didn't actively decide to grope her in the middle of the park; it was more spontaneous than that, his hand just moved towards them without permission from his brain. Her tits were closer than he anticipated. He banged into her hard nipple before he expected to. So there they were, in the park, kissing and fondling. Perhaps it was a natural extension to all that had gone before. He knew the colour and texture of the nipples that he could now feel through her T-shirt. They'd been inches from his face on many occasions. He'd often had the opportunity to just stick out his tongue and he'd have known them before now anyway, unless of course some huge bouncer had punched his lights out for touching one of the performers. He'd have known their roughness, their texture, their hardness, their sweetness. He knew their colour. They were a dark burgundy colour. He knew their shape. They were large ovals, bigger than Nat's.

'Get your fucking hands off my wife!' Neil heard the words just a second before he felt the air being thrown out of him as he was shoved away from Cindy and the incredible crack across his jaw.

Neil had never been hit before. Least not since the playground and that stuff was nothing in comparison to this intense agony. He didn't fall to the ground, like he'd seen on TV and in movies, he stumbled backwards in an ungainly way and found himself clinging on to Heidi's buggy. Cindy was screeching something and trying to stand between him and her husband. Neil couldn't take it all in. Jesus, that hurt! His jaw throbbed and his neck ached. Did he have some sort of whiplash? Was he bleeding, were his teeth loose? He could taste blood. The man was small and spitting. He had yellow teeth and acne. He had disproportionately large hands, or at least it seemed that way as he unleashed a flurry of blows on to Neil's crouched and quivering body.

29

Alison and Tim took dinner parties very seriously. They were quite old school in their approach as they prided themselves on showering their guests with every attention and courtesy; casual entertaining was anathema to them both. They worked as a team, with clearly defined roles. Alison invited the guests, bought the ingredients and flowers, set the table, put nibbles into bowls and placed the bowls in accessible places around the sitting room. Tim did the cooking and was good at it. His lamb and minted potatoes were legendary; their guests were always only too pleased to pepper the conversation with a shameless number of compliments, in the hope of a repeat invitation.

Alison always paid attention to detail. From time to time, she cut out helpful articles from magazines, ones that explained how to entertain in style. She always ensured that her napkins matched the flower arrangement and candles. Nat was often struck by the fact that not only did Ali *have* napkins but she had sets in at least *three* different colours. Nat usually put a roll of Bounty on the table and her idea of going posh was to buy paper serviettes from Ikea. Every time she ate at Tim and Ali's she flirted with the idea of visiting John Lewis and buying some proper table linen; the problem was, whenever she got to John Lewis she invariably stumbled across a lovely lipstick that she preferred to spend her money on.

Tonight Ali had put extra effort into her preparations; she wanted her friends to remember tonight. She had bought a new damask tablecloth in a deep purple (with matching napkins, of course), she'd pulled out all her best glassware and china, the stuff that she had been given as wedding gifts but had used only five times since. This was because she didn't like putting the best things in the dishwasher (in case it got chipped) and yet she hated washing up by hand, so the best things tended to stay in the cupboard. Ali realised this wasn't too sensible but just couldn't think her way round it. Her mother had been chairwoman of the local WI branch for as long as Ali could remember, and was the sort of housewife who absolutely abhorred chipped china (or indeed mismatched table linen); she thought either of these was evidence that the woman of the home was one step away from moral bankruptcy. Her mother's standards of cleanliness and neatness now appeared as natural to Ali as the blood that ran through her body; there were just some things from your childhood you simply couldn't shake off, no matter how much you wanted to or knew you should. Anyway, if there was ever a night for the best glass and chinaware, tonight was it. Alison wanted everything to look amazing. Beyond amazing! She'd spent a huge amount on fresh cut flowers. She'd bought long-stemmed white roses and arranged them with bits of twig, in three purple glass vases, which were dramatically lined up along the centre of the table, and she had put tea lights and candles on every available surface. She gazed round her home, assessing the effect. She smiled contentedly. Yes, everything looked wonderful. Everything was as it should be.

Natalie and Neil arrived first. They were prompt because Neil had rung Nat three times during the day to remind her about the commitment. She obliged by leaving work on time but she couldn't bring herself to be cheerful, especially when she saw the state of his face.

'What happened to you?' she asked, concerned and ready to pour on the sympathy.

'Oh, Karl and I were messing about with these prototype guns and targets that might be marketed in one of our games. They're sort of modelled on paintball guns but with small plastic balls. They're in early development. You're not meant to use them at close range,' Neil blathered.

'So what happened?' demanded Nat. Her concern was already draining away and quickly being replaced by exasperation.

'Well, Karl pointed it in my face.'

Nat glared and huffed and puffed her irritation as though she was the big bad wolf trying to blow down the third piglet's brick home. 'What an idiot.'

'Obviously it was an accident,' reassured Neil.

'Well, I didn't imagine he was deliberately trying to shoot you at point-blank range but, for goodness' sake, Neil, when will you two grow up? Plastic balls, you say?' Nat examined the cut and bruise on Neil's face more closely. It looked really nasty.

'He was closer than the manufacturer recommended,' said Neil nervously. 'I think I have one or two bruises on my ribs as well.' It had taken him and Karl most of the afternoon to come up with this excuse, he hoped Nat was going to accept it.

'Well, I hope to God you see that you can't market this game. It's potentially lethal. Can you imagine it in the hands of teenagers?'

'Yes, you're right, we won't be going ahead with that game, I don't imagine,' said Neil. Of course he wouldn't; it didn't exist. He touched his jaw tentatively. Bugger, it still stung like hell. Although he considered himself lucky. He was pretty sure Cindy's husband had been set to kick seven shades of excretion out of him, and would have if those policemen hadn't come along. He was really *very* lucky. It went to show, there *were* sometimes policemen on the beat when you needed one. Not that Cindy's husband Dave was likely to agree. No doubt he felt very hard done by. To Neil's relief the policemen didn't accept Dave's story that he was just defending his wife's honour. One of the coppers recognised Cindy and knew what she did for a profession and apparently Dave had a reputation for getting arsey with her clients, plus Neil was holding a cuddly toy rabbit in one hand and he was laid out across a kid's buggy; he looked innocent. Well, actually, he looked like a sap. He was middle-class and living in the twenty-first century, he had no idea how to defend himself in a fist fight. It was an enormous relief to Neil when the cops pulled Dave away. It had taken two of them, though, because even though Dave was a slight man he had been fired up with furious indignation and therefore lethal. Neil had made as hasty an exit as humanly possible. He'd scurried back to his office without so much as glancing behind him. He didn't want a further clobbering and he didn't want to hang around long enough for the policemen to discover that their assumptions about Dave were off course.

Neil wondered whether he should call Cindy. The entire incident had been over in moments and so he hadn't had a chance to take in her expression. He had no idea what she was thinking or feeling about any of it. Was she pissed off that he'd kissed her or just relieved that while making a hasty exit he'd shouted that he didn't want to press charges? Was she glad Dave had come along at that moment or had she been enjoying the kiss? Did any of it matter anyway? The worst of it was he'd run away clutching Mrs Flippy. He'd agonised all day. Was it possible for him to go to Heidi's nursery and return the toy or was it too risky? He might run into Dave, who probably had now been released without charge. But Heidi wouldn't be able to get to sleep tonight, not without Mrs Flippy. The thought niggled Neil.

When Alison opened the door, Nat thrust a box of Lindt chocolates into her hands, threw out a brief smile that she regretted wasn't as warm as her host deserved and then marched straight through to the kitchen, where she knew she'd find a bottle opener and be safe from Neil's constant questions about her recent nights out. She supposed he was trying to take an interest, make conversation and perhaps even reconnect. She understood that he was trying to be ingratiating but she was exhausted, frayed around the edges; she didn't like keeping secrets but she no longer knew how to be honest.

How could she start to tell him about her recent nights out? She wished she could respond more positively to Neil. She, too, longed to reconnect but she didn't know whether it was even possible any more and that thought terrified her, brutalised her. Irritatingly and irrationally she found herself snapping at Neil as though she was emotionally backing away from him. She heard Ali gasp, 'Goodness, Neil, what happened to you?' and she heard Neil start to recount his idiocy with the toy gun. Another flame of frustration shot through her body.

The kitchen was hot and steamy, a welcome contrast to the bitter night outside. Nat feared a long winter and she wished she could hibernate. Tim was bent over a recipe book, his forehead furrowed in concentration. Nat wasn't sure whether he'd noticed her come into the kitchen, even though she was huffing and puffing quite theatrically. Despite her glum mood, a huge wave of affection swept through her body. She liked her husband's best friend a great deal. There was something sweet and earnest about the way he carefully measured white wine vinegar on to a tablespoon and then dropped it into the dish he was making. Nat flung her hat, coat and scarf on to the back of a kitchen chair and started to open the bottle of wine she'd brought with her. Startled, Tim turned. His strong and long friendship with Neil meant that he thought of Natalie as something akin to a sister and he could read her moods almost as well as he could read his own wife's. He saw at once that it wasn't just his casserole that was simmering.

'Fill me up too, will you?' he said, throwing her a quick grin. 'Would kiss you but I'm at a tricky bit. I have to sear these scallops and every second is crucial.'

'It's OK, I know you think kissing your mate in greeting is soft southern bollocks,' said Nat, taking her first sip of the wine. She realised that she must have been scowling when Tim cut to the chase.

'What's up? Find out how much he's spent on strippers in the last six weeks?'

Tim asked the question flippantly, irreverently. Neil had confessed to Tim that he'd returned to Hush Hush, although he only admitted to one return visit. Tim had thought that Neil was being a bit foolish. What was the point in spending a fortune to watch some stranger strip when you had someone as gorgeous as Nat at home?

Nat turned to face Tim and he couldn't help but notice that she was wearing a really flattering wrap-round dress that clung to her body, gratifyingly showcasing her small but perfect boobs and neat bum. She was wearing knee-high boots with a tall heel. All that and she understood and accepted Neil's new hobby of watching naked women dance. What a find.

Nat glared at Tim.

Ah. Maybe she wasn't so understanding of Neil's new hobby, after all. There was something about Nat's face that told Tim that she hadn't known Neil had revisited Hush Hush. Damn. Tim was flustered. He'd put his foot in it. Why the hell didn't she know? Nat and Neil never kept secrets from each other. Not usually. That was one of the many things that Tim loved about their relationship and something he had searched for when he was looking for his own life mate. He'd failed actually. He and Alison kept all sorts of secrets from one another and from other people. Details such as how often Ali went to the gym (her figure was not achieved effortlessly, although she publicly professed that was the case), how much Tim earned (not as much as people might assume), how huge their mortgage was (bigger than sensible). Ali said they were all little, inconsequential secrets and, besides, she maintained that these things were no one else's business anyway. Tim couldn't help but wonder, if these secrets were so inconsequential, why did they have to be secrets in the first place? Tim thought keeping secrets from his friends made conversations stilted. He never knew when he was inadvertently going to say something he wasn't supposed to, like he had by mentioning the business with the strip joint. Bloody hell, Neil should have warned him. Whenever they had guests coming round Ali always gave him a list of subjects that were off limits, just to avoid this type of situation. Of course,

Ali didn't know about the strip joint, otherwise it probably would have been on the list.

'How much?' Nat demanded.

'Erm, not sure. Not much. Just joking,' said Tim apologetically but he was a lousy liar and Nat smelt a rat.

'It couldn't have been that much. It was just the one night,' asserted Nat.

'Right,' lied Tim.

'And he never goes in for those private dancers. Those are what racks up the cost.'

'Absolutely.' There was something about the way Tim said 'Right' and 'Absolutely' that told Nat that Neil had definitely visited the strip joint more than once and had probably indulged in private dancers. Call it female intuition or plain old-fashioned suspicious mind but she mentally hung, drew and quartered Neil before Tim had managed to turn his scallops. She seethed, wondering why and when he'd visited strippers. Then it hit her, he was probably visiting strippers when she was checking out her old flames. Hell. What a mess.

'Can you pass me the pepper?' Tim said, vainly hoping that he might be able to change the subject. He could hear Karl and Jen arriving, there were happy shrieks being released in the hallway. He prayed that one or the other of them would wander through to the kitchen and rescue him.

Karl entered and commented, 'Jesus, I need a stiff one.' He poured himself a large G&T. 'So what's going on in here? You can cut the atmosphere with a knife. What secret shenigans have I stumbled on? Lovers' tiff?' Amused at the thought, he jokingly asked, 'Are you two secretly shagging?'

'Oh, grow up, Karl,' snapped Nat.

Natalie was pretty sure that if Tim knew Neil was visiting strippers, Karl knew it too. She felt angry and excluded and was therefore unprepared to participate in his playful banter as she might usually do. It irritated her that Neil was constantly harping on about wanting to start a family but at the same time had initiated a new hobby of ogling naked women. It wasn't responsible. Tim shot Karl a fractious and despairing look. Nat saw she could retrieve the answers she was looking for if she pushed home her advantage while Tim was too mortified to act.

'Tim was just trying to remember how many times it is, *exactly*, that you guys have been to Hush Hush this last month or so.' She spoke in a clear, confident voice. Tim, terrified, looked towards the doorway; Alison would kill him if she got wind of this. 'Is it two or three?' guessed Nat.

'Not me, babe. Just the once. It's your guy who's always there. Four times, he was bragging to me. You must be loaded,' said Karl calmly and with conviction. He too had a misplaced confidence in the transparency that existed between Nat and Neil; like Tim, he'd always admired that in his mate's relationship with his wife. He thought they were an enviable couple, but he was out of date. He poured himself another G&T and greedily gulped it back. Engrossed in his own concerns, Karl failed to notice that he had added to the spiky atmosphere in the kitchen.

'So what was all the shrieking about, in the hall just now?' asked Tim, who was very aware of the time bomb he had inadvertently helped to trigger.

'Oh yeah, you two need to congratulate me. Jen and I are getting married,' said Karl casually.

'What?' asked Tim.

'Wow,' said Nat.

'Yeah, what a wow.' Karl shrugged.

Nat was pleased no one asked, why? It was a reasonable question under the circumstances.

'Time was right,' added Karl, answering the unasked question.

What had made Karl cave in? Nat didn't want to view the engagement in those terms but she couldn't help it. Was Jen pregnant? Oh God, if she was, that would mean Neil would have new ammo. She knew he'd start to fantasise about him and Karl pushing trendy strollers through Ravenscourt Park and then, later, playing football and video games with their kids.

'You mean, she twisted your arm hard enough,' offered Tim.

'Yup.' Karl grinned. Nat noted that he didn't look unhappy with the development. It surprised her slightly that he was accepting his new affianced status with such serenity. Nat knew that Jen was a catch but Karl had always appeared relatively impervious to Jen's charms and generally unimpressed with the idea of commitment. What had changed?

'Hey, love, did you hear Jen and Karl's news?' asked Neil, bursting into the kitchen.

'What happened to your face?' Tim asked.

'Karl did it,' Neil answered bluntly.

'Yes, I want to have a word with you about that,' said Nat to Karl.

Neil hurried to change the subject. 'Not now. Have you heard their news? This calls for champagne. Should I go and get some?'

'We brought some with us,' said Jen with a giggle. She launched herself into the room and directly at Nat, left hand first. A beaming Alison trailed behind. It was amazing to Nat that Jen could wave her arm quite so energetically as the rock she was sporting was enormous.

'What a gorgeous ring! Congratulations,' said Nat, pulling Jen into a warm hug. Nat quickly calculated, if Jen was about to drink champagne, she couldn't be pregnant. Hurrah. And now with a wedding to plan, no one would talk about babies. Great news. For the first time that evening she thought she had a chance of enjoying herself with her friends, something that should be so natural and yet something that had been so difficult to secure of late.

Karl released the cork, creating a satisfying pop. He poured, everyone clinked glasses, giggled and took sips. The champagne kicked Nat's tonsils, she gulped, enjoying the chilly, addictive dryness; the effervescent bubbles tip-tapped on her tongue. Then she noticed Alison wasn't drinking.

'Not for me,' giggled Alison. 'I wasn't sure whether I was going to say anything tonight or not but since we're all here and celebrating, well . . . I'm pregnant!'

Wow. What a night.

30

Nat and Neil decided to walk home. They knew it would be tricky to persuade a cabby to drive them from one end of Chiswick to the other and, besides, they'd both drunk a stack and felt the chilly air might go some way towards sobering them up. Nat was aware that she was drinking too much lately. She felt relentlessly tired and drab. Even lifting her hand up to her neck to pull her scarf a fraction closer was an effort. Although, while regretting the certain onslaught of a vicious hangover, Nat in part felt grateful that she was drunk. She didn't want to be sober with Neil right now.

Nat recalled the last time the entire gang had been all together. It was a while back. Since Tim and Ali had been trying for a baby and Jen had been trying for a fiancé, they'd stopped spending so much time en masse. In fact, the last time they had met up as a complete crew was when they went to the Bluebird restaurant, when they'd been celebrating Neil's birthday on 26 August. She remembered the cab journey home that evening. She and Neil had been so cocky and self-assured about the strength, resilience and depth of their love. They were smug marrieds. Confident in their own relationship and choices, even somewhat condescending about their friends' relationships which appeared rather lacking by comparison; their friends had not seemed quite so sorted. It was painful to think about how much they'd taken for granted. They'd discussed Karl and Jen's relationship at length. Nat had wondered whether Karl was playing away, they'd commented on the unlikelihood of Karl ever proposing. They'd briefly talked about Ali and Tim trying for a baby. Nat had dismissed the subject quite sharply, preferring not to tumble into that particular conversational cavern. Now look at the pair of them. They walked along the street, silent and not touching; there was no sign of their previously vigorous and vocal love.

Neil had placed his arm round Nat, for a few fleeting seconds, but as they were both swaying from the effects of the alcohol, it hadn't been practical. That night at the Bluebird had been the night when Neil had asked for a baby and everything had started to unravel.

Natalie had received two texts during dinner. One from Alan Jones inquiring whether her hangover had faded yet and, if not, he recommended that she drink a hair of the dog, as he was. She thought it was pleasant of him to pretend they were now going to have some sort of buddy type relationship but she knew the idea was impossible. She couldn't imagine how he'd integrate into her life. Of all her exes, Alan was the least likely candidate for that. He knew too much about her. He knew more than Neil. She pressed delete. The second text was from Lee Mahony saying he was very sorry that she'd had to cancel this evening but he could meet up next Tuesday if she was free. She'd made this arrangement three weeks ago. Was it sensible to pursue it?

Lee Mahony. Her most passionate encounter. That's how she'd always referred to him when on the rare occasions she'd spoken of him to her girlfriends over the years. That's how she labelled him in her head, if ever he popped in there. She'd met him at a health care convention, years and years ago. The convention had been in Edinburgh. Many of her colleagues had seen the three-day event as nothing other than an excuse to try out a few decent malt whiskies or to stock up on cutprice cashmere jumpers. Nat resented their attitude and thought them immature. She had fully expected to attend every one of the modules and had signed up to listen to as many guest speakers as she could squeeze in. She considered the black tie welcome dinner (the highlight of the conference as far as most delegates were concerned) a bit of a time waster. She would have preferred to stay in her room reading up on myasthenia gravis, a little known autoimmune neuromuscular disorder, until she saw the seating plan and noticed that Professor Hans Coperberg, probably the world's most influential and controversial neuroscientist, was to be seated on the table right next to hers. She hoped to collar him over coffees, when most people were slipping off to the dance floor; she was sure someone as eminent and serious as Professor Coperberg would not strut his funky stuff.

The evening didn't pan out the way she planned.

Nat hadn't been able to get her nose out of the fascinating report on myasthenia gravis and so was late down to dinner. By the time she'd walked into the hotel dining room, it was clear that the majority of the delegates had enjoyed their fair share of cava cocktails. Daft, drunken men stood in self-conscious packs sneakily eyeing up women who were already laughing too loudly and indiscriminately. Nat blamed the black ties. Putting on a dinner jacket seemed to encourage every man into thinking that he was as irresistible and irresponsible as James Bond and convince every woman it was her patriotic duty to lie down and think of England. Nat prided herself on the fact that she was above such flights of fancy. She never mixed business with pleasure; which serious person did? It had therefore been especially annoying to her to notice that Professor Coperberg was lining up shots for his table. Disappointed, Nat found her table and name plate and sat down quickly. She planned to eat and retreat, asap.

He had been the first person she noticed. He had been the only person she noticed.

'I'm Lee Mahony, your future husband,' he'd said, leaning to reach for her hand. She politely held out hers but instead of shaking it, he'd held it to his lips and kissed her fingers. Right there, right then, in the middle of the table, in the middle of the conference. Was he insane? The touch of his lips on the ends of her fingers had set off a firecracker of excitement in her knickers. Twenty-four-year-old Natalie

Morgan had never experienced anything as brutally, brilliantly sexy before.

'Future husband, you say?' she mumbled.

'You can road-test me first. We'll have a drink and then get to bed early, eh?' His soft Irish lilt almost made his suggestion sound reasonable. Before Nat had been able to decide whether she was offended or delighted, Lee Mahony chuckled. 'Ah, getaway with you. I'm just laughing. I would never proposition a girl without knowing her name first. My ma brought me up well. What are you called?'

'Natalie Morgan.'

'Fine name,' he asserted, in what was a charming, irresistible tone. 'Want a drink? Wine? Red?' He was already pouring. Up until then Nat had always drunk white wine spritzers but she didn't say so.

Nat could still remember the way they flirted. It had been so audacious and exciting and blatant and brightening. They had moved up to his room before the pudding was served; they'd had sex before the band struck up a chord. All thoughts of collaring Professor Coperberg and quizzing him on his latest published paper had vanished from Nat's mind. Nat and Lee had sex for three solid days, punctuated by hilarious, shallow banter, six meal breaks and a spot of daytime TV watching. In a rare moment of indulgence and escapism, Nat rejected the convention programme and embraced the most fun she'd had, ever. They enjoyed the sort of sex that only strangers, living for the moment, can enjoy. It was wild, free, experimental and finite. Lee Mahony lived in Dublin and Nat lived in London, neither of them contemplated making the liaison last beyond the conference. Nat always believed theirs was such a passionate, tremendous encounter because it was left like a cliffhanger. They would never know what was next. They would never back way from the edge or plunge to their deaths. It had been beautiful, unfinished business that could only remain beautiful if it remained unfinished. Some years later Lee had moved to London and on doing so he had looked Nat up at her office. Whether he'd called looking for a bit of fun or with a view to developing a relationship, Nat never found out. She was seeing Neil by then and had found it easy enough to resist what had previously been irresistible. She'd moved on and had no desire to peek back over her shoulder. Until now.

A few weeks ago Nat had Googled Lee Mahony. He had been easy to track down. His quick mind and easy confidence had ensured a glittering career in the health sector. Plus his anarchic humour and ability to charm meant that he had an intriguing and informative Facebook site. Nat had read one or two articles about his recent work and then she'd sent him an email. They'd arranged to meet tonight, but Alison's dinner party had put an end to that plan. After her numerous fruitless meetings with her exes and last night's traumatic meeting with Alan Jones, Nat had wondered whether she ought to stay well away from her past but now that Alison had announced she was pregnant, Nat suddenly felt in need of a bit of indulgence and escapism and Lee was perfect for that. Of course she had no intention of sleeping with the man. God forbid! She didn't mean that sort of indulgence and escapism, the sort they'd had before. No, she just wanted to relax, flirt and have a bit of fun. So Nat had sneaked off to Ali and Tim's downstairs loo (fully furnished with scented candles and spare rolls) and texted back that, yes, she was free next Tuesday and looking forward to seeing him.

What was going on? She'd now been on six 'dates' with her exes and while she maintained to herself they were innocent meetings, the fact was, she'd failed to mention them to her husband. Indeed, she'd lied to him about her whereabouts on every occasion. Then tonight she'd discovered that he was regularly attending strip bars and keeping that a secret from her too. How come she hadn't noticed? And why hadn't he mentioned it? He'd always maintained those clubs were just a bit of fun. Had they become more than that? Wasn't he satisfied with her sexually? Probably not, thinking about it. It had been a while. Nat sighed and her tired breath hung around the freezing night air, causing a cloud.

Life wasn't a race. That was what her mum and dad were always saying to her, and she wanted to believe in the wisdom their age must offer, but if life was a race, even a go-kart race not an Olympic sprint, then she and Neil had just slipped behind on the happily married heat. She knew it and Neil had noticed they were lagging behind too, that was clear enough tonight. While she'd been quiet throughout dinner, leaving the burden of conversation to Jen and Ali, Neil had become motor mouth. He'd asked Ali a million questions about the pregnancy and her plans for the birth, and just about every day after until the kid hit puberty. Nat had noticed Tim was also uncomfortable with Neil's enthusiasm. Hell, it was understandable as Neil had even asked about the conception; he'd wanted to understand which were the most fertile days in a woman's cycle. Was he insane? Tim had muttered that he had been under the impression that Ali wasn't going to make an announcement until they'd had the twelve-week scan. There were risks, he said. Too right, Nat couldn't agree with him more. Why didn't people get that? Ever since Ali had blurted her news, Nat had felt a little sick as she always did when she heard someone she loved was pregnant. She couldn't quite fathom whether this time her nausea was rooted in her usual concern for their health or intensified by the fact that Ali and Tim announcing a pregnancy would inevitably lead to Neil making yet another bid for a baby of his own.

'Fabulous news about Tim and Alison, hey? Great. Really brilliant,' said Neil. He was wearing a sloppy grin, so loose that Nat thought it was poised to slip at any moment. He kicked a can that was lying in the street. Unfortunately it was still half full and instead of enacting the strike that secured the winning penalty in a cup final, beer spilt out and splashed all over Neil's suede shoes. It wasn't very cool. They'd known each other too long to care about being cool in front of one another; all Nat was thinking was whether the beer would stain so she was surprised that Neil looked suddenly embarrassed and uncomfortable. Her instinct, as ever, was to make him feel better.

'Absolutely. Lovely news. You'll probably get to be godfather,' she replied, trying to sound bright and cheerful. 'Wonderful news about Jen and Karl, too,' she added, hoping to steer the conversation away from baby talk.

'You think?' Neil sounded sceptical.

'Yes,' Nat replied with an enthusiasm she didn't really feel. Truthfully, she imagined that they would, in time, be going to Karl's second wedding, maybe even his third. Statistics said one in three marriages didn't make it and if that statistic was applied to their gang, then it was clear that Karl, the commitment phobe, was the horse most likely to fall at the first hurdle.

Wasn't it?

It was probably just the alcohol but suddenly a cold slither of fear darted up and down Nat's spine. One in three marriages didn't make it. What if she was wrong about Karl and Jen being in the position of weakest bet? What if she needed to look closer to home? Nat glanced at Neil, bundled up in a winter coat. She suddenly thought of his strong arms, hidden under the thick coat, and she felt a flutter of appreciation. He looked amazing – well, aside from the bruised cheek. Actually, he looked amazing even with the bruised cheek; he looked like a rough and ready hero. He was adorable and still very fanciable but there was something she couldn't hide from or ignore: he also looked sad. Worn. Tired. He was not happy. She was visiting exes and he was visiting strip joints. He wanted babies and she wanted none of it. Did that sound like a happy marriage?

Suddenly Nat wanted to have sex with Neil. Fast, urgent, healing sex. Thoughts of Michael Young, Alan Jones, Richard Clark, Matt Jackson, Daniel McEwan and Gary something or other swam round her head. Those men were smug, or gay, or dim or even very decent and lovely but just not her Neil. Suddenly, Nat wanted to grab hold of Neil very firmly and hold so, so tightly because she felt that perhaps Neil was slipping through her grip. She looked at Neil and knew that she loved him so much it hurt. A vicious, wrenching pain that she recognised. It was the pain of knowing something you have might not always be yours. Panicked and breathless, she wanted to exorcise that fear.

'Come on.' She tugged at his sleeve and started to run, yes, actually run up the high street towards home.

'What?' he asked, confused. Why was Nat running? It was icy and they were drunk. She might slip and fall. There was so much about her behaviour that was just plain odd at the moment.

'You'll see,' she called back over her shoulder. She wanted to shout out, 'I want you. I want you!' But even with lots of alcohol in her system she recognised that doing so would be a bit weirdo. Even though it was late, there were quite a few other people milling around the streets and while most of them were probably drunk too, she realised that some semblance of modesty was appropriate. Her hair was flowing out behind her. The light from the street lamp illuminated her, making her look like a pre-Raphaelite angel. In that second, Neil loved her so much it hurt. A fierce yanking pain that he identified as the pain of knowing something you have is under threat. He just wasn't sure what was threatening them. Him or her?

31

Her lips were warm and plump against his. Like the time they came home from his birthday celebrations, they were barely through the door before they were grabbing at one another. But this time it was Nat who took the lead. She urgently and incessantly kissed him, with an intensity that had been notably lacking of late. She ran her hands across and around his body as he closed the door behind them, blocking out the cold night. This time her mind did not inadvertently wander to calculations about whether they could manage a quickie, drink a pint of water and then still get to bed for about half past twelve; this time she stayed in the moment. She repeatedly kissed him. Hard and possessively. Neil was taken aback, but he was not about to look a gift horse in the mouth. He saw that this was the opportunity he needed. He kissed her back, cautiously at first, eyes open and staring at her, unsure where this passion had come from. But then he did, and always had, found her irresistible and soon started to return her deep and focused kisses.

His robust, tremendous response surprised her. It had been a long time since they'd kissed in such an adult and blatantly sexual way. Recently they'd settled for pecks on cheeks and foreheads and even if they had kissed one another's lips, it had been chaste to the point of cool.

It was astonishing to them both to register that they'd managed to have sex on loads of occasions over the years without igniting this particular needy, desperate and awesome wanting. Their kisses were as unpredictable and interesting as a first kiss between strangers but at the same time as sensual and assured as a kiss between age-old lovers. They fell back on the stairs and scrambled on all fours up them, not concerned about how silly or exposed this animal scamper made them appear. Once in the bedroom, Neil firmly pushed Nat back on the bed, then she hurriedly snatched at the belt on her dress as he yanked his T-shirt off in a messy, overexcited, uncoordinated movement. A quick flash of the smooth flesh of his abs reminded her how delicious he was to look at, to be with, to kiss and to have. How had she forgotten? Even for a short time? Why had she been wasting hours talking to other men?

Neil pulled open her dress, sending a shard of sexual tension reverberating through her body. He snapped off her skimpy knickers and then pushed his hand inside her bra, cupping her tit and smoothly massaging her nipple between his fingers. His urgency excited and delighted her and she grabbed at his body with an equal resolve and joy. Without completely leaving her (one hand was still clasped firmly to her tit), he edged over to the bedside drawer and in a familiar move he opened the drawer and reached around for a condom.

'Damn. None left. Hang on a minute, I think there's one in the bathroom.' Neil leapt from the bed and headed off to the bathroom.

Nat slipped out of her bra so that she was completely naked and lay back on the cool sheets. She tingled with happiness and gratitude. Hurrah, he hadn't ruined the moment by suggesting they have sex without protection. Yes, everything was perfect! She felt it. Or at least felt it could be again. They'd ride each other hard now and afterwards, straight afterwards, they'd talk about strippers and naked friends. They'd laugh at each other's foibles and get right back on track. She was sure of it.

Then he was back and without further delay he sank deep inside her. He thrust, pushed, scalded, seized and pulled, and she moaned, groaned, cried and yelped with a vivid and vital mix of desire and agony. It was frantic, rapid and staggering. Their lips meshed as they kissed deeply and forcefully. They could not identify where they each began and ended. For the first time in a long while they were as one. There were no unnerving silences or suspicious moments. There was no blame, guilt or threat. Her body accepted him as it had done many, many times before and he was willingly swallowed. They held one another's bodies and gazes. It was refreshingly shocking. It was critical. It was true. She sighed and shuddered. He moaned and shivered.

'Yes, yes, don't stop. Oh God.' She came.

'Oh, yes, more, more. Yes, Cindy!'

The name fell like a bomb from the sky. He paused, stranded in the moment when the only sound is the high-pitched whine as the bomb plummets towards its target. This was the whistling moment, before it detonates, when all anyone can do is steel themselves against the inevitable damage. Neil was paralysed. Of course he had not released the bomb on purpose, it was more like the stupidly named 'friendly fire', lethal, sickening, meaningless. He did not think to carry on muttering endearments, perhaps trying to interchange Cindy's name for his wife's in a vain attempt to pass off the word Cindy for Natalie; he did not possess the required amount of poise or cunning. Besides, he was swimming in a lusty stupor that caused a delay in his reactions. He wasn't in his right senses; that was why the wrong name had seeped out in the first place.

Neil felt Nat scramble from under him, her knees and elbows jabbed him as she squirmed away. He did not protest or try to pull her back to bed. He did not mutter that calling another woman's name did not mean what it seemed to mean. He watched her hurriedly pull on her bathroom robe and clasp it tightly around her.

'Who the fuck is Cindy?' she screamed, turning on him.

'She's a – she's no one,' he replied hopelessly.

'Who is she?' Nat demanded again.

'A friend.'

'A friend whose name you call out when you are making love to me? You bastard!' Nat felt as if she was starring in a low-budget film. Her husband had just called out another woman's name while they were making love. What did that mean? Of course it could only mean one thing. Why was she even asking what it meant? It was obvious. She swooped down and picked up Neil's jeans and T-shirt from the floor. She hurled them at him. Her action finally jarred him out of his stupor; he lifted his arms to protect his face from the accidental whip of his belt.

'Get out,' she yelled. She was unsure if she meant this or whether it was just the sort of thing she was expected to say. She was in too much shock to rationalise. She knew things were a mess but hadn't thought he'd actually be having an affair. She hadn't thought things were that bad.

'No, no, Cindy is not a friend, she's a stripper,' Neil tried to explain.

'A stripper!' Nat didn't know if this was better or worse. Did it matter?

'I've made friends with a stripper,' added Neil, trying and failing to be clear.

'That's what they're calling it now, are they? Friends?' Nat snarled. She reasoned that if he was admitting to being friends with a stripper, that meant he was sleeping with a stripper as it was unlikely he was spending time with a stripper and talking about the meaning of life. Neil disgusted her. She wanted him out of her sight. Now. Now and for ever. 'You're having an affair.' She stated the fact in order to get used to it. Neil was shagging someone else. He was screwing someone else. He was fucking someone else. The horrible thought flung itself around her head like a ball in a pinball machine, relentless, unstoppable. Suddenly something clicked in Nat's head and she realised that maybe, on some level, she'd been expecting this since Neil had come home with fake tan on his crotch. He'd confessed to visiting a stripper then and tonight she'd discovered that the visits were regular. That could only mean one thing. 'You bastard,' she screamed again, unable to articulate anything more crippling or reasonable.

'No. No, not an affair. Just one kiss.'

He was admitting to kissing someone else. A stripper. 'I don't believe you.'

'It's true. We're just friends.'

'Friends that kiss.'

'That was a mistake. I got carried away. Confused. Nothing happened because her husband interrupted us. It was him who gave me this.' Neil pointed to his face. He thought that by coming clean he might salvage the situation but it was a huge miscalculation. The truth sounded stranger than fiction and Nat did not believe him.

'Her husband?' She gasped in shock. They'd been caught at it by the stripper's husband. The thought was inconceivable. She'd lavished sympathy on him about that bruise. She'd rubbed arnica cream on it and now she discovered it had been delivered to Neil by a cuckolded husband. The bastard!

'We've been so weird recently. You know that.' Inadvisedly Neil started to justify his indiscretion.

'Oh, so this is my fault.' Nat had her hands on her hips now. She was adopting the pose that a million betrayed wives and lovers had adopted over the years. A pose that suggested resilience and was designed to disguise the agony of a breaking heart.

'No, I'm not saying that.' Neil got off the bed with the intention of taking Nat into his arms but she emitted vibes of distrust and resentment. Suddenly he was aware of his nakedness. He felt vulnerable, unsure how Nat's anger might manifest. She might very well kick him in the bollocks before he got the chance to explain himself; she was a feisty woman and wild when wounded. He scrambled into his jeans. 'I'm just trying to say that the thing between Cindy and me is not something terrible and sordid.' Neil glanced at Nat, she didn't look convinced. She looked as if she might kill him. It was understandable, he'd called out another woman's name during their best ever lovemaking and now he'd admitted that the other woman was a stripper whom he had kissed. He had to admit, it did sound *very* terrible and sordid. He wondered how he could explain Cindy. How he could convince Nat of his innocence. 'She has a little girl. I've met her daughter. I've bought her an ice cream.'

'Get out, Neil.' Nat delivered this line in a low, calm voice. Unlike the furious screeches, this tone could not be argued with.

Neil looked at his feet. He noticed some coins on the floor; they must have fallen from his jeans pocket. He saw that her bedtime reading book was lying on the rug, it was being used as a coffee coaster for an empty mug so there would no doubt be a circular stain on the cover now. He noticed Nat's pale blue panties were lying forlornly on the floor too, where he'd thrown them just minutes ago. Everything looked so normal, just the same as it always did and yet everything was different. Everything was ruined.

'I'm not going anywhere,' said Neil, trying to sound as confident as he needed to be, rather than as under-confident as he felt. He clawed around for a solution; he couldn't find one so he resorted to a complication. 'You weren't out with Becky last night. I saw her at the tube station. Where were you?' he demanded, aware that this was a stunning blow.

Nat blinked, astonished by the turn of the conversation. She had not felt she had the upper hand; indeed she was some way from it since her husband was sleeping with a stripper, but she thought she was at least unlikely to encounter any more shocks. Yet it turned out that she was wrong, Neil had another surprise up his sleeve. He knew she'd lied to him. She sighed. She had nothing to lose now, therefore no more reasons to hide.

'I met Alan Jones for a drink,' she admitted.

'Alan Jones?' It took Neil just a moment to place the name. As he did so, the lines on his furrowed brow seemed to slip to his mouth, weighing it into a nasty twisted grimace. 'Your ex?' he bellowed.

'Yes.'

'Are *you* having an affair, Natalie, with Alan Jones?'

'No.' Nat was using every fibre in her body to appear in control. She wanted to yell but did not dare. If she started to howl at him, or scream at him, she might never be able to stop until every window in the street was shattered. Her eerie composure further confounded Neil and caused him to roar louder.

'I think you are!'

'That's very predictable of you. I'm sure it would be very convenient for you if I was but I'm not. Of course that's bound to be the first thing you'd think of, considering your own position.' Neil was sleeping with someone else. He'd betrayed her. He was going to desert her. She'd lost him. The bleak thoughts tore at her gut.

'What am I supposed to think? You don't want a baby. You're never here. Even when you are here, you're not. Not really.'

'I've been seeing other people,' said Nat matter-of-factly, keen to deal a hurtful blow of her own while she was reeling from his killer punch.

'Fuck.' Neil slammed his hand into the bedroom wall. Crap, that hurt! Really, really stung. He had no idea it would hurt that much. He wasn't thinking about his hand. Well, yes, the hand hurt but not just the hand. His heart bled too. She was seeing other people! Not just one person but multiples.

'I'm not sleeping with them,' she said evenly. It was easier to take refuge in sarcasm than deal with the agony she felt.

'I'm not sleeping with Cindy!' yelled Neil. He realised he wasn't presenting his case in the most convincing manner. He sounded hysterical and irrational, the traits of a liar. He'd just punched the wall, the action of an idiot.

'Whatever.' Nat shrugged. Clearly she didn't believe him. But it scared him to see that she was so calm and untouched, almost as though she didn't care whether he was telling the truth or not. 'I'm not even kissing them,' she added slyly, somehow insinuating that kissing was now the accepted code for fucking someone's brains out in a gang bang.

'What then?' Neil challenged.

'I found an old address book, a couple of months ago. Packed full with the names of my exes. I've got into this habit of calling them up.'

'Why?'

Nat shrugged. She really didn't know right now. She couldn't explain. Something to do with checking Neil was her One. Well, she had her answer now, didn't she? It was loud and clear.

'Who have you met up with?' Neil demanded.

'Michael Young, Richard Clark, Matthew Jackson, Daniel McEwan, Gary—'

'You slept with all those men!'

'No. I told you. I didn't sleep with any of them. Stop going on about that. We just met up for a drink in a bar or a gallery. I went for supper with one or two of them. That's all.'

'You dated!' His tone made it clear she might as well have said she'd been having sex with these men. Neil thought he understood his wife and he jumped to the inevitable conclusion and asked in horror, 'Are you planning an escape route?'

'No. I'm trying to understand why I chose you,' Nat finally replied honestly and flatly.

Neil swayed, he thought his knees might give way beneath him and he'd fall like a discarded rag doll. He concentrated very hard on breathing deeply and then found the air to mutter, 'I'm not going anywhere.'

'Fine, then I'll go,' said Nat. Neil froze. In minutes she'd pulled on underwear, jeans and a top, shoved her feet into her trainers and banged the front door behind her.

The door banging seemed to pull Neil round. He rushed to the window and was relieved to see that, even in her fury, she'd paused to pull on a coat and pick up her bag; at least she wouldn't be cold and she'd have money to get a taxi to wherever it was she was going. He banged on the window.

'Don't go,' he yelled. Or maybe those words just stayed in his head because Nat didn't stop in her tracks or acknowledge him in any way.

He watched her brittle, determined figure march up the street and round the corner. He shook his head in case a thought happened to be hiding somewhere. Nothing. He simply didn't know what to do next.

32

Nat hurt so much that she thought her heart was bleeding. She leant against the damp, slimy wall of the house at the end of her street and felt the pain spread through her body. It seemed to squeeze the life out of every internal organ. She briefly wondered whether she should call for an ambulance. She'd had a crash, after all. Not a car crash but in some ways her crash was just as devastating, just as fatal. She and Neil had been on a collision course for some time now; she'd known it but she just hadn't wanted to think about it. All the insecurities she'd been swamped with when she was younger once again swirled around her and she thought she'd suffocate or drown in them. This was it. This was the disaster that she had always secretly anticipated. She hadn't known it would take this form. She'd thought that she could control events and protect herself against loss by not getting pregnant, not taking that particular risk, but no, she couldn't protect herself against loss. She'd lost Neil.

If these past weeks had shown her anything, they had shown her that she wanted Neil. Neil above all. Above the other men she'd dated and even those she'd never dated, above the men in the street that she'd walked past, the movie stars she'd fantasised about, the writers she'd admired, the band members who had sent flickers of lust through her knickers when she'd listened to their tracks. Above them all. They were nothing in comparison. Resting against the damp, inhospitable brick, Nat suddenly knew for certain Neil was her One.

Nat could hear neighbours hosting a dinner party. She listened to the sound of loud laughter and clinking glasses, good-time sounds. She felt a deep and terrible loneliness as she stood on the empty Chiswick street; it was a nasty, haunting feeling. She wondered what she could do next. Just what could she do? She considered hopping in a cab to Waterloo and catching a train to her parents', but she'd probably missed the last one and being alone on a station late at night was the last thing she needed right now. She couldn't face going back to Ali and Tim's, even though they lived within easy walking distance. Ali, snugly wrapped in her longed-for pregnancy, was the last person Nat could expect understanding from. Besides, Tim was Neil's oldest friend, she'd be putting him in a terrible position if she dashed round to his home to slag off Neil. Jen lived in Earl's Court; Nat could hop on a tube to hers but then wouldn't it be more likely that Jen had gone back to Karl's? Karl was only a ten-minute walk away. Unlike Tim, Karl would have no scruples about her dishing dirt on Neil. He'd listen to the angry trashing of his best pal just as though he was listening to the weather report; it would not embarrass him or challenge him morally and he would still be best pals with Neil on Monday morning. He'd probably award Neil a medal when he heard about him calling a stripper's name out during sex, Nat thought irritably. Yes, she'd go and find Jen at Karl's.

Nat ran through the street, relieved to have a direction to go in. She arrived at Karl's door breathless and covered in a cold sheen of sweat. She leant on the doorbell. Her insistent ringing was answered by Karl flinging the door wide open.

'Hi, babe.' He always called her babe. He called everyone babe. Karl immediately recognised a woman with hurt in her head. Even if she managed to keep her mouth clamped closed and resisted giving him the lowdown (unlikely, in his experience women liked to talk about pain), her distress splintered out from her eyes.

'I'm looking for Jen,' replied Nat hastily, pushing past him and bounding up the stairs to his first-floor flat. She was too distraught to manage to be civil, let alone consider that she was being actively rude; it was his flat, after all, she should probably have waited until he invited her in. Nat automatically headed towards the kitchen, Karl followed her.

'Not here.'

'She's not?' They stood in the cramped but surprisingly clean room and stared at one another. Nat was deflated. She'd run to Karl's expecting gallons of comfort to be sloshed on to her wounds. Karl couldn't do that, she needed Jen. 'Did you have a row?'

Karl glanced at her quizzically. He knew enough about women to understand why Nat had jumped to that conclusion, she and Neil must have had a row. Why else would she have run here in such a state looking for Jen? Nat was unlikely to be dashing here with a new idea for the bridesmaids' dresses. It must be quite a serious row as Nat wasn't usually the hysterical sort.

'No, no row,' he said smoothly. 'There's some bridal fair in Earl's Court exhibition centre tomorrow and she wanted to be outside queuing at about 8a.m. or something seriously mental. Not my thing. I told her I didn't want to be woken up that early so she went back to her place as it's practically on the doorstep.'

Nat wondered, not for the first time, why Jen put up with Karl's selfish behaviour. Was it true that love was blind or was it that Jen was hell bent on dashing up the aisle just to show her ex that she was desired? It wasn't a pleasant thought. Nat really needed to talk to Jen about this wedding. But she couldn't think about Jen's problems at the moment, especially as Jen was unlikely to think her engagement was a problem. Nat swept the thought away impatiently; she had her own problems to deal with right now, she definitely couldn't face any more.

'Want a cuppa since you're here?' Karl held up the kettle.

'During sex tonight Neil called out "Cindy",' said Nat flatly. She hadn't planned to say this but the thought had been banging its way around her head throughout her dash here and it just exploded into the kitchen.

'Fuck. Something stronger then,' replied Karl.

Karl was surprisingly sympathetic. Not an adjective Nat had ever associated with him before. When Nat refused to join him in drinking a neat whisky he insisted she at least have a measure in her coffee as he claimed it was good for shock. He made the coffee very sweet and led her into the sitting room. He almost lowered her on to the sofa because he noticed that she wasn't up to functioning on her own.

'OK, tell me all about it. Don't censor, pretend I'm Jen. I won't remember tomorrow anyway as I drank shedloads at Tim's gaff, and I'm pretty pissed.'

'Cindy is the stripper he's been visiting.'

'Yeah, I know.'

Nat was stung by Karl's nonchalance. Of course he knew more than she did, he'd covered for Neil only this evening when he backed up that ludicrous story to account for Neil's bruised face. No doubt Neil had been sharing all the nasty details with him for months now. She knew what she had to ask. 'Is he having an affair with her?'

'I don't know.' Karl shrugged. He answered the question he'd been asked without thinking about whether he should try to protect his mate or comfort Nat; both things could have been achieved had he said he definitely didn't think Neil was having an affair. But, Karl reasoned, it was possible that Neil was doing just that and frankly, Karl didn't think it was his job to protect his mate or comfort his mate's missus. If blokes got messed up in this sort of stuff they ought to be able to handle it, like he could. Neil was a prize twat to have called out the other bird's name while he was shagging Nat; that was just careless. That sort of thing let the brotherhood down.

'You'd tell me, right, if you knew for definite,' pushed Nat.

'Of course, if you wanted to know.'

Nat didn't know whether she believed Karl. He was more likely to cover for his mate, wasn't he? He didn't owe her any loyalty and honesty wasn't exactly his natural state. Nat thought she might as well leave. She'd finished her coffee, Jen wasn't here to sympathise with her and Karl couldn't do that job. She stood up but then it hit her, she didn't have anywhere to go. She glanced at her watch; it was nearly one in the morning. Even if she could still get a tube or hunt down a cab, she couldn't go and knock on anyone's door at this time of night. Karl read her mind.

'You can stay here. I'll take the couch.'

'Thanks.' She flopped back on to the sofa, infinitely grateful that she didn't have to go back out into the wretched, cold night. 'I don't want to go to bed yet, though,' she added. She knew she'd just lie awake all night, staring at Karl's ceiling, going over and over tonight's events. Could he be having an affair? Neil? Was it possible? Yes, of course it was. 'I think I will have a whisky now, if you'll join me by having another.'

'Oh yes. I'm always up for it.'

Karl went into the kitchen to get Nat a glass. She pulled her knees close to her chest and sat in a small ball at one end of the sofa. Oh God, his sofa smelt of sex! How was that even possible? What an off-putting thought. How many women had Karl seduced in this exact spot? Karl was such a grubby man and yet he was her only port in the storm. The thought depressed her. Sex seemed to be all around her. Illicit sex. Karl was a grubby man and Neil was Karl's best friend. Of course, Neil was having grubby, illicit sex.

Karl returned and sat next to her. Nat had always noted that while Karl was not a classically handsome man he put a lot of effort into countering the fact by wearing fashionable clothes, working out and getting hair cut at an expensive hair stylist. It cost a lot but it was worth it as his hair was floppy when floppy was required and spiky when that was in fashion. At the moment he was wearing it quite long and softly curled. It was his most effective look ever, as it gave the impression that he was somehow more artistic and deeper than was actually the case. You sort of forgot that his eyes were a little too close together, thought Nat. He smiled kindly at her and she felt mean about thinking so badly of him and his smelly sofa. The measures he poured were generous; they clinked glasses and knocked them back.

Karl had been a bit pissed off that Jen had insisted on going home tonight. For a start, it ruled out the possibility of a shag, which was unreasonable considering it was a Saturday *and* they'd only officially got engaged yesterday. He had been pretty confident that agreeing to buy the engagement ring would mean round-the-clock sex for a fortnight, minimum. And, the other thing was, he didn't like waking up alone on a Saturday morning; he had been considering whether he should make a booty call, when Nat had rung the doorbell.

Karl hadn't quite made up his mind how he was going to play it with his liaisons now that he was engaged. Would he knock it all on the head? After all, he'd had his fair share of totty over the years. Or would he carry on, just taking care to be uber discreet? They did say old habits died hard. Karl thought his individual skill with women was that he was careful to promise them absolutely nothing and he delivered on that admirably. His true genius lay in the fact that while maintaining a distance, he managed to make every woman he ever met feel amazingly special, thus answering the call of a particular twenty-first-century epidemic. Karl firmly believed that he should give every girl a whirl. Posh 'gals' did it for him, as did rough birds, he thought fat girls were enthusiastic and dirty, but then skinny women could be flipped around, so they were all good. Bright ladies were a challenge and the dim ones were a giggle. The only type of woman that Karl would pass up was the type of woman who cocked her head to one side and asked, 'How are you *feeling*?' with that painful sincerity they'd probably learnt from an American chat show host. He was more a doing sort of guy. The thing was, he didn't really feel ready to settle down. No matter what he'd told the others this evening, he didn't think the time was right. More, he didn't think the girl was right. But Jen had wanted it so much. She'd gone on and on and on and on, like some bloody Duracell bunny. She seemed to want it enough for the two of them. Karl necked another drink. Anyway, he didn't have to think about any of that now as Nat was fantastic, unexpected company; a booty call would not be required. He'd always had a soft spot for Nat. She was hot and bright but besides that he liked the fact that she so clearly disapproved of him and all he stood for and yet still seemed to find him amusing. There was nothing he liked more than good women finding his bad boy act irresistible.

Karl had often wondered what Nat would be like in the sack. He'd tried to get Neil to talk about it but he never would. He used to talk about the other women before Nat but not Nat, which suggested she must be something really special. A thought occurred to Karl: was it possible that he might still get to find out? He'd long since stopped hoping for that but with this turn of events, the opportunity might present itself. Karl, for all his faults, was a fair man. He'd always believed what was good for the goose was good for the gander. If Neil was shagging the stripper (and he might very well be) then Nat was owed a revenge fuck. He'd be doing them a service; it would even up the scoreboard. He wouldn't do anything particularly underhand to secure his chances; after all, Neil was a mate. He wouldn't say anything that wasn't true but Nat, once in possession of all the facts, might find she agreed with him. She might think she was entitled to a bit of off-piste. He poured them both another generous whisky.

'He *has* been acting a bit oddly recently,' said Karl thoughtfully. 'He goes for these long walks on company time. He told me he's spent almost two grand at Hush Hush. Is it like an addiction, do you think?'

'How could I have missed this?' Nat muttered. She let her head fall into her hands and stared at her shoes. Karl looked at the ceiling. He sensed that she was about to spill. Gaining her confidence was essential. He didn't push her. He had to let her come to him in her own time. Slowly, slowly catch the monkey. He stretched out his arm and gently stroked her back; he felt her shimmy under his touch. Mentally, he punched the air. Way to go, life in the old boy yet!

'He's a bloody fool,' said Karl as he pulled Nat into a friendly hug. She collapsed into his warmth, too drunk and too wrung-out to question the sagacity or significance of allowing Karl to hug her on his sex sofa, when they were alone in his flat, in the early hours of the morning. It was rather pleasant, actually, the first pleasant thing that had happened to her all night. So she didn't object when he held her a little too close and a little too long.

She sighed heavily, 'I haven't had my eye on the ball. I've been distracted with all this other stuff.'

'Such as?' Karl could smell a scandal.

'I have this old address book, a sort of Little Black Book, if you like,' admitted Nat.

'What?'

'I've been, erm, well, catching up with my exes.'

'Shag anyone?'

'No!'

'Sorry, didn't mean to be offensive but I thought that was the point of looking up exes.'

'Well, it isn't.'

'What is the point then?'

'It was . . . I just needed to . . .' Nat didn't know how to finish.

'What?'

'Check something.'

'What did you need to check?'

'You wouldn't understand.' She barely understood herself now.

'Try me.'

'Whether Neil was . . . well, whether he was . . . the right one.'

'Ah. The baby business,' said Karl with a knowing nod. Nat stared at Karl, somewhat taken aback by his perception. 'He wants a sprog and you don't want a sprog.' Nat nodded. That was it really, in a nutshell. That's where this had all started. 'I'm surprised Jen hasn't told me that's what you've been up to with this Little Black Book of yours,' mused Karl.

'She doesn't know.'

'You didn't tell her?'

'No.' God, her head was fuzzy. She had drunk far, far too much tonight. She needed to stop now or at least drink something a little less potent. She wondered if there was anything other than whisky; it was almost finished now anyway. Hadn't that bottle been three-quarters full when she arrived?

'I thought you two told each other everything,' said Karl, carefully slipping into gear.

'Not everything, no,' said Nat sadly.

'Wise. You know her. She can't keep a secret if her life depended on it. She's even shown me the wedding dress she wants. She's just not a secrets sort of girl.' Karl was revving up and he knew exactly where he was travelling to.

'Whereas—'

'You are a secrets sort of girl.' He was now checking in his wing mirror and rear view to see whether anyone else was about to make a manoeuvre.

'How do you know that?' asked Nat.

'Takes one to know one. And I'm a secrets sort of guy.' There was a silence that could be bitten. 'Another drink?' offered Karl, looking for a green light.

'OK,' agreed Nat, giving it to him, whether she was aware of it or not. They both silently watched the golden liquid dance into the glasses. Karl considered his next move. Nat considered her last one. 'You know what? I found that I didn't want any of them, my exes.' Nat saw this as reason to be hopeful. Karl immediately took the wind out of her sails.

'You know, the thing is, Nat, looking back isn't a problem. These blokes you've been knocking about with, well, they are just people you've already passed over. There's nothing enticing or exciting there. It's looking forward that's the issue. Things only get really tempting, dangerous, if you come across anyone new that you find interesting.'

The word interesting hung in the air like a shadow.

33

When she woke up, her throat felt sour and constricted and her head felt as if it had been turned inside out. She didn't dare move in case she vomited. For a fraction of a second, before she opened her eyes, she believed the worst thing she'd have to contend with that day was a vicious hangover but then she remembered . . . she'd left Neil. Fuck. Neil was having an affair. Fuck. Fuck. Before that realisation had a chance to strike its vicious blow, other thoughts started to punch their way into her consciousness. Fuck, fuck, fuck. No, no, no. Let it not be true, she begged. Begged who? Herself. There was no one else to blame. Let it be a bad dream, a vivid, cruel, careless dream. But even before Nat prised open her eyes, she knew this was not the case. The events of last night came crashing back to her in hopeless, overwhelming waves.

It was impossible for her to piece the night together coherently, she'd drunk far too much for that, all she had to work with were scalding images of flesh rubbing up against more flesh. She remembered the wrong lips, tongues, hands and fingers exploring her body. Horrified, she recalled the wrong man carrying her to bed. She squirmed with shame at the thought of Karl having her, taking possession of her. It had been a wild, animalistic deed; the sort of act that is fuelled by anger, whisky and confusion.

She turned her head to the side and was relieved to find that Karl was not there. Maybe he was in the bathroom or maybe he'd nipped out to buy a paper or some breakfast. She knew he wasn't the sort to have a full fridge, not unless Jen had stocked it. Oh God, Jen. Poor, poor Jen. What had she done? She had to get out of his bed, his room and his flat immediately. She lifted the alien duvet and the scent of last night's exertions drifted towards her. The distinct tang of sweat and a fainter, but just as recognisable, smell of sex assaulted her. She could taste his tongue. She really was going to be sick.

Quickly and quietly she leapt out of bed. She looked around for her clothes. Her knickers were still inside her trousers which made her think that he must have been in a hurry. She was still wearing her T-shirt, for which she was grateful. She supposed she must have put it back on last night after the sex, to keep warm, or maybe it had never come off and he'd just edged it out of the way when they were at it. She couldn't pursue that line of thought. All she knew was that she was grateful that by wearing a T-shirt, at least that removed the possibility that Karl had cupped her breast all night long as he spooned into her, just as Neil always did. Small consolation but, as irrational as it might be, Nat wanted to preserve that intimacy for just the two of them, no matter what. No matter that he was having an affair. No matter that she'd had a drunken mistaken shag. No matter what.

Nat swiftly retrieved her coat and bag which had been thrown on top of the dirty linen basket; she speedily slipped into her trainers and silently slipped down the stairs and out of the front door without pausing to say goodbye to Karl.

Once outside in the drizzle, Nat checked her watch. It was 8.40a.m. Nat longed to lie on the wet pavement, curl into a ball and howl but of course she could not. For a start, if Karl was in the bathroom or kitchen, then her howling outside his front door might just attract his attention. If he wasn't inside, and had just popped out to the local corner shop, he might return any second. She did not want to talk to him; about that much at least she was certain. Nat turned right and started to walk to the tube. It was imperative that she got away. Nat felt the seeds of a plan form in her mind. This time she knew where she had to go and what she needed. She needed her mum. She needed Nina.

The journey home to Guildford was the longest of Natalie's life. Throughout, nausea threatened to explode and she had to concentrate very hard on not allowing that to happen. Throwing up on a tube would be unforgivable but then so was sleeping with your husband's friend. Nat hated herself. She caught the District line from Turnham Green to Embankment and changed, then took the Northern line to Waterloo. At Waterloo, even before she bought a ticket, she searched out the public loos.

As she approached the station toilets, the sweet smells of croissants and strong coffee were shoved away by the disgusting smell of cheap disinfectant. The cheap disinfectant stench was all the more overpowering because everyone knows that it masks other, much worse, smells of London station life. Nat knew she was in serious danger of losing it when she discovered she needed twenty pence to get through the turnstile and into the loo, and all she could think to do was to kick the machine. The futile violence brought back the image of Neil thumping the wall the night before and she felt a pain as though he'd punched her. Oh God, just the night before? How could that be? How had so much happened in such a short time? She desperately rummaged through her purse and bag, hoping to unearth the correct change. By chance there was a loose coin hidden in the very bottom of her bag, nestled next to the damned address book.

Her freezing fingers were shaking as she urgently pushed the coin into the slot. She prayed that she would make it as far as the loo before she up-chucked. Nat barraged herself into a cubicle and then once again rummaged in her bag. She grabbed the small black book which she'd prized so highly over the past few weeks. It did not induce a voluntary gasp of excitement, just a long, low growl of anguish. Natalie hardly dared breathe in the skanky public conveniences so she did not sniff the book's cover, but even if she had, she knew it would have only smelt of leather, nothing more. The book could no longer evoke feelings of possibility or bright memories of her youth. Dusty angels and horny devils did not flutter out of the pages; instead, the book burnt her hands and she was scalded with shame, fear and a deep, deep dark sense of having completely and utterly fucked up. Nat shook and wept. She tore at the pages in the book and flung them down the loo. She wanted to pee on them, puke on them and, finally, flush them away. The vomit did not come and it took eight flushes of the loo before the pages finally disappeared down the pipes. Nat threw the leather cover in the disgusting bin intended for used sanitary protection. The attendant, suspecting God knows what (a suicide on her watch, someone shooting up or maybe just an act of vandalism), angrily banged on the door and threatened to call the police unless Nat came out of the cubicle immediately.

34

Neil had already called Nina and Brian. He hadn't wanted to alarm them but on the other hand he was terrified, clueless and panicked, so he did just that. He'd already repeatedly called Nat's phone but it was switched off and then he found it lying in the hall. It must have fallen out of her pocket, last night when she was scampering upstairs, desperate to make love to him. Oh God, how could that be less than a day ago? Neil called all of Nat's friends, one by one. He made up some daft story about her having said she was sleeping at a mate's but he couldn't remember who exactly and now he found he needed to talk to her about collecting the dry-cleaning. As it was 8a.m. on a Saturday when he called and the excuse was so pathetically flimsy, he didn't think it was likely anyone believed him, not for a moment, but he wasn't concerned about their gossip, he just wanted to find Nat.

He had to be more honest with Alison of course. To her he admitted that they'd had a row but he resisted going into detail. He just wanted to reach Nat and sort all this mess out as quickly as possible. He believed he could explain everything and in the cool, calm light of day Nat would be persuaded to believe that there was nothing going on between him and Cindy; at least nothing of any consequence. And now that he'd had time to think about it, he believed her that nothing was going on with any of her ex-boyfriends. So while their situation wasn't ideal, it wasn't dire either. Neil knew that Nat would be furious with him if he went into any sort of detail with her friends about their argument – over-sharing wasn't Nat's style – so he tried to keep his conversation with Ali brief even though she clearly had a thirst for particulars. Ali said she hadn't seen Nat or heard from her and suggested he call Jen. Jen hadn't seen or heard from her either; she suggested he call Brian and Nina. So when Nat arrived at her parents', she was greeted by Brian and Nina's anxious faces pressed against the window in anticipation.

'What's going on?' asked her dad.

'I need a shower,' replied Nat.

She showered but she was sure the stink of last night's vileness clung. Then she silently gulped back two large mugs of strong, orange tea while her parents fretfully hovered nearby. As Nat started to make her third cup of tea, Brian's impatience got the better of him.

'Well? Are you going to tell us what's going on?' he snapped. He was worried for his daughter but his concern came out as irritation. Nina shot her husband a warning look.

Nat didn't know where to begin. She stared at the small wooden kitchen table. The table had once been in her grandmother's home and had been brought to this kitchen when Grandma Morgan moved into a small assisted-care home. It was at this table, over many years, that Nat had sat to eat meals, do homework, complete jigsaws, decorate Easter eggs and do countless other harmless activities. She was unsure how she could spill her story over such an innocent. She looked around and saw familiar chipped mugs, a memorable blue glass vase, the eternally grubby black and white floor tiles and numerous well-thumbed recipe books. Surrounded by such well-known household items, she tried to search her brain for some sort of substance and meaning as she forced herself to think about the night before. Haphazard and horrible flashbacks battered her consciousness. Helplessly she grappled to understand what had happened but she couldn't make sense of anything.

Eventually she sighed and muttered, 'Neil and I are going through some difficulties.' Nat knew the explanation was woefully inadequate.

'He asked us to call him when you arrived,' said Nina gently. 'He wants to talk to you.'

'Don't do that,' pleaded Nat.

'We promised we would,' said Brian firmly. 'I think it would be for the best.'

'Not now,' begged Nat.

'Maybe she's not ready,' Nina said to Brian, throwing him a look beseeching him to tread carefully. He shot his wife a look that communicated his exasperation and frustration. He always believed that she was a little overprotective with Natalie, something she couldn't be accused of with the boys. He believed she was overcompensating for something that was beyond their control and he didn't agree with it.

'Do what the hell you like,' snapped Nat, knowing they probably would anyway. 'I'm going to bed.'

'Darling.'

'Yes?' Nat turned to look at Nina.

'You'll have to sleep in one of the boys' rooms. Shen Tu Weng is in the small front bedroom now.'

'Fine,' muttered Nat, too exhausted to care. In the last twenty-four hours she'd lost so much more than a childhood bedroom.

35

Despite her exhaustive antics the night before and her over-whelming fatigue with her situation in general, Nat did not fall asleep immediately, as she'd expected. She lay on her younger brother's bed and nervously anticipated Neil's inevitable arrival. She wondered what he'd say and what she could say to him. She dwelt endlessly on the events of the previous night. There had been so many grenades thrown her way (and she'd hurled a couple out of the trenches too), she didn't know how to process all that had happened. He was having an affair with a stripper. He'd said he wasn't but he'd called out the other woman's name while they were having sex and that had to be proof positive, hadn't it? Nat didn't know for sure. Last night she'd been so certain that he was betraying her but today she wondered whether she was right. She rolled on to her stomach and pulled the pillow over her head. The coolness did nothing to soothe her as she reasoned that it didn't matter anyway because now she'd slept with someone else too. Karl! Neil's friend. Her friend's fiancé. Why had she done that? It wasn't enough to blame the fact that she had been incredibly drunk, possibly drunker than she'd ever been in her life, that was a pathetic excuse. She hated herself. She'd never been unfaithful before, never, and now she was the worst type of person. Was it revenge? Was it inevitable after bumping into so many dead ends walking down memory lane? Had she always been secretly attracted to Karl? She really didn't think so. She wasn't even sure she liked Karl. Was she hoping to hurt Neil? Why had she put herself in such a position?

Babies. This all came down to Neil's desire for a baby and her horror of falling pregnant.

Last night Karl had been funny and he'd been kind to her. He had been so understanding; he really sympathised with the fact that she didn't want kids and he thought Neil was nuts to keep arguing about it. He agreed with her that she'd always made her position clear, he said he remembered her doing so on any number of occasions. Karl had been significantly more understanding than any of her exes had been and certainly more understanding than Neil. Karl said he really understood because he didn't have even the most fleeting desire to have kids either. Last night she'd thought that meant something. She was pretty certain (as they'd started in on the bottle of tequila) that it meant Karl was her One. She told herself Karl was the man she should have married.

He'd said, 'Yummy mummies are a myth. No, that's too kind, they're a lie.' He told her that he'd once picked up his sister's kids from the school gate and been shocked by what he saw, really quite devastated. He said he'd read *Grazia* and *Heat* (over Jen's shoulders) and he, too, had bought into the whole yummy mummy crap.

'Those pictures of Posh are to blame. I mean I'd give her one, and not only to say I've dribbled where David Beckham has, she's hot. And she's a mother, with a whole bunch of kids, isn't she? So I, too, believed a flat stomach was possible after a baby but it's a lie, Nat. I feel sorry for the poor bitches that are mums and read this propaganda, I do. It's *not* possible to be hot and a mother, at least not without a personal trainer, dietician and probably a decent surgeon. I think that pretending that it *is* possible amounts to a form of modern-day torture for normal women. Real women, specifically real mums, are . . . well, mummsie. I know I saw them at my nephew's school. They're not always, *invariably*, definitely fat, although the odds suggest that will be the case, but certainly they're tired and harassed looking and they all look more than a bit pissed off with the world. These might have been perfectly attractive women until they had kids but then they all seem to turn into women who resent midweek sex because it will steal precious moments of sleep and leave them craggy in the morning. I don't blame you for not wanting kids, Nat. I don't.'

Natalie hadn't bothered to point out that her objections to giving birth went deeper than vanity or interrupted sleep patterns. She knew that Karl was trying to be sympathetic and sympathy was what she'd wanted. So when he'd leant across the sofa, past the saucer that was doubling up as an ashtray (what was she doing smoking again?) and kissed her, she hadn't pulled away. If only it had been a terrible kiss then nothing more would have happened. But it wasn't a terrible kiss. There was definite chemistry. What a shame he was so expert! She'd felt the kiss stir a response deep down in the hot space where her legs met. She'd kissed him back hard and passionately.

She remembered draining the whisky bottle and starting in on the tequila. Its fiery roughness spilt down her throat as Karl's large hands spilt across her body. But then . . . then she wasn't sure. The alcohol consumption or her iron will had blanked out the details of the adultery. It was all too horrible to contemplate, too horrible to want to re-live. What had she done?

Nat must have fallen asleep eventually because a tap on the bedroom door jolted her awake. For a moment she was confused and skittish. She wasn't sure which was worse: her nightmare (about a five-foot baby coming out of her vadge and splitting her open into thousands of bloody pieces that looked a lot like confetti) or her reality, Neil standing in the doorway of the bedroom, head hung low and his hands dangling uselessly by his side.

'Can I come in?' he asked. Nat nodded although she wanted to push him back through the door and lock it for ever. She wanted to lock the door on Neil, Nina, Brian, Karl, Jen – on everyone and everything, actually. She wanted to hide away for ever as she was so ashamed and sad. 'I've got something for you,' said Neil.

He went back outside the room and re-emerged with a giant bouquet of flowers. Neil had agonised over which flowers he should bring her.

Something cheerful in yellow, perhaps? Were red roses a classic or a cliché? Would she like tulips? They were her favourite and they had a little private joke which they shared whenever he bought her tulips. He'd say while he always liked to see roses on the piano, he preferred two lips on his organ. So no then, not tulips, that joke would be excruciating under the circumstances of his wife thinking he was shagging a stripper. After an age he'd selected a dramatic arrangement of white roses and dark pink lilies. They were wrapped in cellophane and decorated with a fat, scarlet ribbon. Neil thought the bouquet was modern and flamboyant. He thought the flowers said sorry and that they would be an easy route into a hard conversation.

Nat stared at the enormous bouquet and thought it was inappropriate. You gave flowers if you were late for an anniversary dinner or if you'd got really drunk at a stag party. A bouquet did not reflect the seriousness of the situation they were in. Besides, the flowers looked somehow sexual as the lilies had petals with scarlet slashes that reminded her of probing tongues. Nat didn't want to think about sex; not the sex she'd had with Karl nor the sex Neil had had with Cindy, it was all too vile. She didn't take the flowers from Neil when he offered them and after a few moments of hesitation he placed the bouquet carefully on a bookshelf.

'I'm not having an affair, Nat,' said Neil. His voice was hoarse and oozed hurt. Nat felt guilt and regret flare in her stomach. She lay prone, staring at the ceiling, not daring to face her husband. He cautiously sat on the edge of the bed. His movements were tentative as he took care not to touch any part of her body as he knew she wasn't ready for that. Nat radiated a sense of separateness. It worried him that even while they were in the same room she was so far away. When Neil had first started dating Nat, all those years ago, he'd often had a vague impression that there was an invisible divide between them. She was unlike all the other women he'd dated as she did not rush to reveal every single thought and feeling that flittered through her mind; she was reserved and careful with what she shared. He'd found her slight detachment attractive, almost challenging. He wasn't sure whether it was motivated by aloofness or shyness and it didn't matter much either way because, naturally, over time the sense of her being separate disappeared as they became closer than he'd ever been to anyone before or since. Neil was alarmed to note that she'd reinstated the invisible barriers; it was a huge leap backwards. Together he thought they could sort things out; if he was left on his own to fix it then he was pretty sure he'd tangle things further. He knew he'd have to start the conversation. He just didn't know how to. He could hear the wind outside, shaking windows and bouncing around houses and cars. He heard some kids calling to one another as they raced round and round the cul-de-sac outside the Morgans' house. He could hear his wife's breathing and the screaming of his own thoughts.

'I've been very confused lately.' He coughed. 'We haven't been doing so well, have we?'

Ha, thought Nat, you don't know the half. But she couldn't bring herself to say so, not yet. It would all be over then, and while she realised their end was inevitable, she couldn't bear rushing towards it, she'd done enough of that already.

Neil continued, 'I've been acting stupidly. I shouldn't have been sneaking off to Hush Hush. I didn't know how to reach you, so I suppose I turned to Cindy as a bit of a prop.'

Nat's eyes slid from the ceiling over to where Neil sat in a pool of pain. The arnica cream hadn't been especially effective, the bruise on his jaw had spread and darkened and she noticed his knuckles were cut too. He looked a wreck. It hurt her to see him floundering, so she looked away quickly.

'She was just a fantasy figure.' Nat nodded ever so slightly, she could accept that might be true. Encouraged, Neil tried to be totally honest. 'But I don't mean that I fantasised about her tits and arse.' Nat looked sceptical. 'Well, not much,' he conceded. 'It was Heidi, her daughter.' He coughed, embarrassed. 'Cindy is so devoted to that kid, in her own way, despite not being archetypal mother material, and I became interested in them as a family. She told me stuff like Heidi has an intolerance to tomatoes and the fact that she chews her toenails.' Neil realised he was probably sounding weird. 'It's just the stuff everyone else our age talks about, Nat, kid stuff, and I liked being part of it. Can you understand what I'm saying?'

Yes, Nat understood. Neil fantasised about having a family; he wanted to be immersed in fetal scans, Calpol distribution and CBeebies viewing. She'd fantasised about carelessly dating men, being young again and never having to think about anything more long term than what she should order to eat for dinner. She understood but understanding terrified her. They were on separate paths.

'I so want a baby, Nat. I want a family, with you. And I don't understand why you won't talk about it. It's not fair that you just say it's off the agenda.'

'It's never been on the agenda,' said Nat quietly. She was despairing and deeply sorry that once again she had to reiterate her position on this of all things, and now of all times.

'I know. I know.' Neil didn't really want to get into the baby debate right this moment either. Of course he would have to tell her what he'd done last night. Wouldn't he? But not yet, his plan was to wait to see if his actions actually came to anything first. If there was a result then he could tell her. Right now, he had other deep and muddy waters to wade through first. 'Cindy was a bit of warmth.'

Just hearing the word warmth caused a pain that Nat thought must be the equivalent of something like a shard of glass being rammed into her flesh. She knew exactly what it meant when a man talked about warmth. This Cindy's hot tongue would have played with Neil's. Her hot, *hot* body would have performed for Neil. Nat had imagined that warmth between Neil and his stripper while she was with Karl last night. In fact, she hadn't been able to get the idea out of her head.

'I paid to see her naked. It was nothing more than that,' said Neil defensively. He wasn't sure whether he was being absolutely truthful. Now that his 'thing' with Cindy (a thing he struggled to categorise or define) might cost him his marriage, he was pretty sure it was nothing but over the past weeks it had sometimes seemed like the only good thing in his life. For this reason he felt a slight twinge of guilt when he added, 'It was a transaction.'

'Yet you met her kid,' Nat pointed out, puncturing his life raft.

'Yes,' Neil admitted because he could not deny beautiful Heidi.

'And you visited frequently.'

'Yes.'

'How often?'

'I forget.'

'Think about it. Work it out.' Nat needed the facts. She needed to get things straight in her head and she was pretty sure this might be the only time she'd get to ask these questions. Soon there would be no reason or motivation for them to talk to one another.

'I don't know,' Neil stalled.

'Six times? Seven?'

'Maybe seven times.'

'Ha.'

'What do you mean, ha?'

'Just a coincidence. I had seven dates with my exes.' She'd had six, actually. Plus Karl.

Suddenly Neil appeared animated. He sat straighter and said excitedly, 'Two wrongs could make a right, Nat! In this case they could, couldn't they? We could put this behind us. You said yourself that you hadn't slept with any of those guys and I believe you. I'm sorry I said I didn't yesterday, but I do now. You have to believe me too, Nat, *please.*'

Neil slipped off the bed and crouched down next to it so his head was only inches from his wife's. He stared at her profile and even though she was unusually pale today and had bags around her eyes which suggested a lack of sleep, he thought she was beautiful. She was still staring at the ceiling. He noticed a fat tear run down her cheek. He leant close to her and gently kissed it away. The phut sound sat between them, ephemeral and vulnerable. The tear tasted salty and familiar. He knew how his wife tasted and he loved it. He loved her. This was a mess. A terrible, terrible mess but he wanted to fix it. Would good intentions be enough?

'I'm so sorry,' he murmured. 'So very, very sorry. Let's put this behind us. We can, can't we? I won't go to see Cindy ever again, I promise. I really don't want to. It's you I want.'

Tears were beginning to fall thick and fast down Nat's face now. She could feel that the collar of her T-shirt was wet. She wanted to put this horror behind her too; she wanted to turn back the clock to Neil's birthday. She wanted all this misery and mayhem to vanish. She heard the old adage that her parents used to recite to her as a kid: 'I want never gets.' It had never seemed so true.

'But I did,' whispered Nat.

'Did what?'

'I slept with someone.' Nat's silent tears suddenly transformed into noisy sobs. 'I'm sorry, I'm sorry.' She turned towards her husband, hoping that he'd see the repentance in her face, but the room was empty. Neil had fled and in his haste he'd knocked the bouquet off the bookshelf and on to the floor.

36

At 6.40a.m. on Monday morning Nina and Brian were surprised to hear Nat in the bathroom; they both listened as she took a shower.

'Do you think she's planning on going to work?' Nina asked.

'Sounds like it,' guessed Brian.

'Do you think that's wise?'

'I don't know what to think. Neither of them has told us anything,' grumbled Brian. He was always more prone to being grumpy when he was worried.

'I'll get up and offer her breakfast. She hasn't eaten anything since she arrived here. She can't go to work on an empty stomach.'

Nina put the kettle on and poured out a bowl of muesli for her daughter. She put some wholemeal bread in the toaster, rummaged in the cupboard and found an assortment of sticky jars of marmalade, jam and honey. She placed them all on the table as she was unsure of her daughter's current preference with regard to condiments or anything much, now she came to think of it. The thought was a slightly melancholy one. There had been a time in Nina's life, years and years actually, when the preferences of any of her children were entirely known to her; food preferences, favourite TV shows, toy crazes, friends in and out of favour, she knew everything there was to know about them. She found it difficult watching them all grow up and move on, especially at times like this when one of them was so clearly floundering. Nina loved the idea that Nat was sleeping in the room next to hers, she loved all her children visiting and they were always welcome, she only wished it was under happier circumstances.

Nina waited for ten minutes and then couldn't wait any longer. She went upstairs and popped her head round the door of the bedroom Nat was using. She was sitting on the bed wrapped in a towel, her wet hair falling in tangles around her shoulders.

'Are you planning on going into work today, darling?'

'Well, I was.' Nat looked at her mother, her eyes brimming with tears. 'But I hadn't thought it through. I don't have any clothes. I don't even have a hairbrush or make-up. My laptop is in Chiswick,' Nat couldn't bring herself to say the words 'at home' but just the thought of Chiswick with all her comforts, most notably her husband, forced the brimming tears to overflow. She quickly wiped them away with the back of her hand. Nat was not one for crying. 'I haven't even got my phone; I left in such a hurry.'

'Hang on.' Nina disappeared into her bedroom and returned with a wicker basket the size of a shoebox. Triumphantly she sat down and showed the contents of the box to Nat. 'I read about this in *Good Housekeeping* or one of those magazines. There was an article that said it was always a good idea to keep spare toothbrushes, hairbrushes and toiletries etc. for forgetful guests.'

'And is that what I am?' asked Nat.

'Oh, darling, you know I only meant—'

'I know.' Nat put her hand on her mother's in a gesture that showed she understood Nina was doing her best under very difficult circumstances. 'These things will be really useful but I still need clothes.'

'You can borrow something of mine.'

Nat looked at her mother in mock horror. Nina had a penchant for wearing whispery, layered clothes often decorated with sequins or tiny mirrors. Nat couldn't see that sort of garb cutting it in her office. Nina allowed herself to smile, even amongst the gloom.

'Maybe not. I mean, clearly things are bad but that would just be a disaster, right?'

'Right.'

'I can drive you to Chiswick now and you can get changed there. We could pick up the laptop. You probably wouldn't be very late for work. If we set off soon then we'll be ahead of the worst of the traffic going into town.' Nina wondered if Neil would be at home. She hoped so. It was her opinion that they just needed to keep talking. They were a marvellous couple; they couldn't let things go wrong.

'Yes, I think that's the best idea. You don't mind coming with me?' asked Nat.

'No, darling,' replied Nina, who rather hoped her daughter might take advantage of their journey together to enlighten her as to what was going on.

37

Neil did not hear Nat come into the house to collect her belongings. He'd spent the previous afternoon and night drinking bottled beer and when it was time to go to bed he couldn't face sleeping in their room and so he'd opted to sleep on the floor in the spare room. He was surrounded by piles of ironing, defunct games consoles and boxes of Nat's work stuff; it was ridiculously uncomfortable but Neil didn't care. He'd drunk enough to guarantee that he'd sleep through his alarm, which he did.

Nat had been nervous about bumping into Neil. She'd carefully put her key in the lock and quietly, oh-so-gently pushed the front door open. She'd found a hold-all in the cupboard under the stairs and then calmly, silently and methodically collected together enough clothes for the week, her laptop, her phone, her make-up and other toiletries. She stood in the kitchen and changed out of her mother's three-tiered skirt and embroidered peasant blouse and put on a smart grey skirt and nipped-waist jacket, a pale blue blouse and high boots. She then wrote a note informing Neil that her dad would be back for the rest of her stuff the following weekend. Finally, she took her key off her Tiffany key ring (which Neil had bought her as a present to celebrate their last wedding anniversary) and she placed it on top of the kitchen unit, right next to the kettle; Neil wouldn't be able to miss it there. Nina watched her daughter perform these tasks and she thought that anyone else watching Nat might have believed they were watching a

woman who was calm, cool, collected and in control. Only Nina could
see the bloody turmoil in her daughter's eyes and around the corners
of her mouth where the grim, fake smile was stapled.

Neil woke up and was aware of a thread of saliva running from
his mouth on to a small pool on the laminated floor he'd slept on.
He checked his watch and saw that it was after midday. Good. He'd
wanted to sleep through the entire day and the next and the next if
he could. His head thumped but he'd had worse hangovers, the long
sleep had helped take the edge off that particular drama. The
thumping was more likely to do with the regret that was pounding
about his being. Slowly he sat up and stretched. Damn. The same
thoughts as the day before ambushed him. He'd been awake just a
matter of seconds and already he was thinking about Nat. But what
was he to think? She'd slept with someone else. She'd told him that
was the case. If she hadn't told him, he'd never have believed it. No,
never. No matter who had said the same thing. But this wasn't rumour
or gossip; this was a confession from her lips. Nat had slept with
someone else. When? How often? Was she in love with this someone
else? Well, she was a bitch and she could have him. He was welcome
to her, the stupid, silly, selfish bitch. It was done. It was over. He'd
move on.

Oh, but God, he loved her.

That would stop. He knew that. He'd been in love twice before
he'd been in love with Nat and then he'd stopped being in love with
those women. OK, he'd never loved them so much in the first place,
they weren't such deep or long-lasting relationships but his point was,
people got over stuff. Didn't they? Crap happens. He'd get over Natalie
Morgan, see if he wouldn't.

He stood up slowly and walked into the bathroom, put his head
round the door of their bedroom, walked downstairs, checked in the
living room and kitchen but they were all empty. She had not come
back. He'd thought perhaps she might and, if she had, he knew he'd
have taken her back. He was more sure of that than his thought that
she was someone he might get over. He had thought that maybe, if

they could contain this agony to just one weekend, it wouldn't have to spoil everything they had. Somehow they'd work round it. But now it was Monday, a fresh week, and the treachery and mistakes of the weekend had soiled the new week too. The thought terrified Neil. What if this mess couldn't be contained? What if they really had fucked up and they lost each other? What then?

No, it couldn't be so. Nat was a sensible woman. Far more sensible than he was. She wouldn't let this fall apart. But then, she'd slept with someone else. She'd told him so. When? How often? Was she in love with someone else? Well, she was a bitch and she could have him. Oh, God, he was going round in circles. Was he going mad?

He needed a plan. Neil thought about it for a minute or two as he peed and decided that his plan would be to make a cup of tea and then to call Nat again. A strong cup of tea, almost orange with tannin that hit the back of his throat was what he needed. He'd call Nat, she was bound to be at her parents', there was no way she'd have managed to go into work today after such a traumatic weekend. He'd give her a chance to explain. Maybe. Or at least he'd call her and tell her she was a bitch. Maybe. He wasn't sure but what he did know for certain was that he had to hear her voice again. This could not be it. But when he reached for the kettle he discovered the house key she'd left and the note telling him that she thought the situation was irretrievable. So he went back to bed instead.

38

Neil hadn't noticed it any other year but the whole purpose of Christmas was to torment the newly dumped. Christmas came with overwhelming expectations; everywhere he turned there was the hint of other people's hopes and unending promise of opportunity, happiness and intimacy. Everywhere he turned outside his own head, that is. Christmas was a time when families sat around hearths, couples dragged home Christmas trees and tear-jerking Nativity plays were performed in every school hall up and down the country. Neil couldn't wait for January, when things would get back to normal. When the sky would be eternally grey, only tat would be left in the shops and everyone would be battling with weight gain and credit card debts; only then could Neil hope that people might feel just a fraction of the misery he felt. He repeatedly reminded himself that Christmas was in reality often a day of family bickering, interrupted by the giving and receiving of unwanted, usually useless gifts; there was no real reason for the soap on a rope to exist. But he wasn't much consoled because somehow the Dickensian image of a more worthy and meaningful Christmas, filled with large and happy families, always niggled its way into his consciousness, and the truth was he longed for it.

He'd agreed to go to Fi and Ben's for Christmas Day because Fi had badgered him mercilessly. She loved it when it was her turn to host Christmas and she took her role as hostess very seriously; she'd insisted that Christmas would be entirely ruined if Neil didn't join in.

He would have been happy enough sitting around in a pool of stale self-indulgence (that smelt a little like a sewer) but Fi had visited Chiswick three weekends in a row in an effort to persuade him to join the rest of the family.

'Neil, we wouldn't be able to have a nice time if we knew you were all alone here,' she'd said the first week. 'My God, I think something in your fridge actually moved.' She emptied the fridge of rotting food and bought fresh fruit to put in the bowl on the dining-room table but while Neil was on some level grateful for his sister-in-law's attentions, he knew that the fruit would probably end up in a big black bin bag the next time she visited.

'Neil, the kids will miss you. It's bad enough that they haven't seen you for a few weeks as it is but they will be expecting you on Christmas Day as normal,' she'd said, the second time she visited.

The guilt card backfired when Neil replied, 'But it won't be as normal, will it? Natalie won't be there.'

'Well, no,' admitted Fi, somewhat embarrassed.

'Have you heard from her?' Neil asked. He tried to feign indifference but Fi could hear the tension in his voice. He was desperate for any scrap of information or news about his wife. Soon to be ex-wife.

'Yes, she did call,' replied Fi tentatively. The last thing she wanted was to end up in the middle of the two of them. Nat had asked the exact same question about Neil, she was clearly concerned about his welfare as she'd had reports from Karl and Tim that Neil was in a very bad way. But Fi was no go-between, she didn't have the patience or the time; she already had three kids, for goodness' sake, she didn't need two more and they *were* behaving like kids. Neil was lolling about the house, refusing to even go to work or so much as pop out with his mates for a pint. Worryingly, he was drinking plenty, though, on his own, while listening to Take That tracks. It wasn't as though Fi could even offer any advice. Neil would not explain what had gone wrong between him and Nat. All he said was that she was a bitch or sometimes a 'fucking treacherous bitch' but the exact reasons he'd labelled her as such were classified. It wasn't dignified, not at his age.

Weeks of nothing other than drinking and cussing and shunning the shower was unacceptable.

And Natalie was no better. She had gone to the other extreme; she was behaving as though nothing had changed at all. She was going to work every day and working a ten-hour day minimum (the only change being she had to commute in from her parents' in Guildford), she was still remembering birthdays and she'd telephoned to wish the kids good luck with their nursery Nativity play (Angus was a wise man, Sophia was a donkey, Fi thought they were both miscast). Nat hadn't whined, moaned or grieved for her relationship, at least not in public. The closest Nat would be drawn towards complaining about the situation was that she commented that her parents' rich food was making her put on weight and that the commute was tiring. To all intents and purposes, Nat didn't even appear ruffled by the fact that she and her husband had split but Fi knew this was not the case. It just couldn't be. However much Nat tried to disguise the fact, her voice had oozed concern when she'd asked Fi if Neil had plans for Christmas and whether he was eating properly or not. Fi thought that you could probably say he was eating properly if a diet of curries and takeaway pizzas, three times a day, constituted properly.

She tidied away the tin foil cartons and the cardboard pizza boxes.

'Do you recycle your cardboard?' she asked Neil.

'Used to,' he muttered. It appeared even recycling was beyond him now.

The week before Christmas, Fi arrived at Neil's with an arsenal. She brought baby Giles with her and the moment she was through the door she dropped him on to Neil's lap.

'He needs changing. Can you do it? I'm going to warm his bottle.'

Neil wasn't especially enthusiastic (but then she had asked him to change a nappy, she couldn't expect leaps of joy) but at least he got up off the sofa and took his nephew upstairs. When he returned with a more comfortable and smiling baby, Fi said, 'Your mum and dad are coming down for Christmas. If you don't join us, I'll bring them over here.' She glanced around the fleapit that had once been a tasteful

home and said, 'You don't want them to see this, do you, Neil?' Her
tone was no-nonsense and Neil recognised that he was beaten.

'OK. What time?'

'Noon.' Fi was building in a couple of spare hours. Lunch wasn't
likely to be served before 2p.m. but she felt there might be need for
a buffer. If Neil didn't show, she'd have time to drive over here and
haul him to Clapham before the turkey was carved. Besides, she rather
liked saying 'noon' as though she was demanding some sort of shoot-
out at the old chaparral, and in some ways she was.

39

Natalie was dreading dropping off Christmas presents at Ben and Fi's, the thought sent huge spasms of panic through her body but she knew she had to do it, she couldn't neglect the children. Her life was a hideous jumble but Angus, Sophia and Giles had no concept of secrets, deception, lap dancers or adultery – thank God – and so their worlds should not be disturbed by the adult disarray. She had done something terrible, she felt the weight of that every moment of every day, but she had a duty to carry on as normal, especially where the children, her family and friends were concerned. None of them deserved to be embroiled in this disaster that she'd brought upon herself and for that reason she had never so much as shed a tear in front of a single soul. Her pillow was often wet at night, though.

It was hardest to behave normally around Jen. For two weeks Nat had managed to avoid seeing or speaking to her directly; they'd simply swapped texts and voicemails as they played out an elaborate game of telephone tag. Jen's voicemails oozed concern and asked whether Nat wanted her to drive down to Guildford and Nat's voicemails were efficient and politely discouraging. Nat did not know what to do for the best. Should she tell Jen that she'd had sex with Karl? She had nothing to lose, other than face, but what about Jen? Nat now had the worst type of proof positive that Karl played away; surely Jen had a right to know exactly what sort of man she was planning on marrying.

But Nat could not forget that night, last September, when Jen burst into her dinner party and revealed her suspicions about Karl; Nat was almost certain that Jen had known the score back then but wanted to surge on regardless. If she told Jen she'd shagged her fiancé, she'd be forcing Jen to confront the facts. Did she have any right to do that? Was it her place? Karl clearly hadn't had a fit of conscience and he had not felt the need to talk about their drunken indiscretion with either Jen or Neil. Would she just be making more trouble by confessing? The whole thing was so bloody as it stood.

When it became impossible to delay any longer, Nat had agreed to meet up with Ali and Jen for a drink after work. At the beginning of the evening Jen had asked Nat how she was holding up.

'Fine.'

'Do you want to talk about it?'

'Not really.'

'Should we talk about something else?'

'Probably best.'

'My wedding plans might distract you.'

Ali had rolled her eyes and tutted but Nat had graciously agreed to hear all about the to-die-for dress, the stunning flowers, the delicious menu, the really quite original order of service, the fabulous shoes, the spoiling wedding list and the genius photographer. If Nat hadn't shagged Jen's fiancé she might not have been so obliging but as she had, she thought the least she could do was show a reasonable interest in the topic that was closest to Jen's heart.

Jen was having a fantastic time planning the wedding. She'd picked a date in early May. She'd been delighted to secure a beautiful country hotel, out in the lush Sussex countryside. It wasn't near her family home but it had been featured in *Brides* and *Setting Up Home* (Jen's bible). She'd opted to marry on a Tuesday because if she'd wanted a weekend wedding she would have had to wait up to three and a half years for a free date at the country hotel. When Ali had pointed out that not all her guests would be able to negotiate a holiday very easily in order to attend a weekday wedding, Jen had dismissed such qualms with an easy wave of her hand. 'Those who want to be there will make sure they are.'

'But your dad's a headmaster, he's not allowed to take time off during the week,' Ali cautioned.

'He can throw a sickie,' said Jen, determined not to have anything stand in the way of her speedy nuptials.

Nat kept quiet, she prayed a conference would crop up that might offer a legitimate excuse for missing the wedding because she was pretty certain she fell in the category of someone who did not want to be there. She managed to get through the evening by saying very little at all. Her friends thought her quietness understandable under the circumstances and it had never been Nat's way to blab in any case.

Nat participated in most of the usual Christmas preparations and managed to appear reasonably cheerful while doing so. She drove to B&Q with her dad to buy a tree and she helped her mother decorate it with the mish-mash of ancient baubles and ornaments that, as tradition dictated, adorned the Morgans' family tree every year. Nat tried not to think of last year when Neil had knocked over the tree after one too many glasses of port. The tree and Neil had both ended up splayed out on the sitting-room floor, baubles and tinsel scattered across the entire room. It hadn't been a problem; they'd all thought it was hilariously funny, probably because it wasn't just Neil who had been indulging in the port. Neil had emerged from the fray clutching their tatty angel and shouting, 'I have her, don't worry, the angel's safe. No need to panic.' Nat could almost hear him as she placed the angel at the top of the tree this year.

Nat ate her share of mince pies, she joined her parents on their trip to the cathedral to listen to beautiful, soul-piercing carol singers perform, she bought and wrapped lavish gifts for everyone as usual and she even bought Christmas cards but she didn't send them. When it came to it, she didn't know what to write. She couldn't sign them 'With love from Natalie' without adding 'and Neil'. But she had no right to send cards from Neil any more. In the end she gave the unopened packs of cards to her mother, who always forgot to buy any until it was too late to catch the post.

All those preparations had required Natalie to be disciplined, steely and aloof; a huge amount of determination had been necessary in order to avoid being sentimental about the lyrics of the Christmas songs (which were pumped out of every single sound system in every single store, in every single town). It took effort not to get maudlin after one too many at her office Christmas drinks party and an enormous amount of willpower to smile and endlessly reassure her friends and family that she was 'Fine!' when they asked. But that was nothing compared with the courage that was required when dropping off the presents at her in-laws'.

Nat wished she'd accepted her mum or dad's offer to come with her but she hadn't wanted to hijack their Christmas morning. She knew that they liked to visit neighbours for a glass of sherry while the turkey was cooking; she'd promised she'd be home in time for the carving. Two out of three of her brothers had turned up within the last week, which was rather unexpected but welcome. Nina was fussing about there being enough food and preparing everyone's favourites; she'd planned to cook nine vegetables, including sprouts (which, in fact, no one liked but it was traditional to put them on the table). Nina had been avidly rereading the old recipe books to get culinary ideas. To celebrate so many of her children being home (no matter what the circumstances) she'd planned an ambitious five-course meal.

As a starter Nina was preparing duck pâté served on toast, the bread was to be home-baked (well, bread-maker machine baked to be exact, but it was almost the same thing). Then a light lime sorbet to clear palates in preparation for the turkey. Nat thought that two courses of fowl would undoubtedly have led to one of Neil's habitual not-very-funny-but-you-can't-resist-laughing sort of jokes. If anyone had got snappy or grumpy at the table he would have said, 'Hey, Christmas is not a good time to be foul.' Besides the wide array of vegetables, Nina had prepared a rum and raisin gravy (her mother's recipe, not

one she'd found in a magazine), then there was to be bitter chocolate and orange cheesecake, mince pies and finally a wide variety of
cheese and biscuits. They ate Christmas pudding on Boxing Day; it
was Brian's idea of alternative. This meal demanded a huge amount
of cutting, chopping, sautéing and panicking and so Nat knew that a
trip to London on Christmas Day would be a nuisance for her parents.

A thought struck Nat. What if Neil's parents were visiting Ben and
Fi? It was likely. What if Neil himself was there? The thought was
chilling. Nat paused outside their house. She imagined that Neil would
have entertained the entire family with all the gory details of their
split, it would certainly be more entertaining than a traditional game
of charades. Eileen and Harold Preston would know that she'd refused
to furnish them with a grandchild, even though it had become Neil's
greatest desire, they'd know that she had then embarked on a series
of flirtations and they'd know that in the end she'd slept with someone
else. Oh God, the shame! Nat nearly turned back down the path.
Perhaps she could leave the kids' gifts on the doorstep. Maybe she
could just ring the bell, leave the gifts and then run away, like some
nineteenth-century women depositing illegitimate offspring with
distant, wealthy relatives. She glanced at the step. It was awash with
rain; the wrapping would get ruined.

Nat was pretty certain Neil would *not* have admitted to spending
nearly two thousand pounds at a strip joint or to kissing a stripper,
or having an affair with her, if that was what he had done. Had he?
Nat wished she could be sure. She thought he had. He said he hadn't
but the more she thought about it, the more likely it seemed that he
might have. Whatever. Nat shook her head in order to clear it. She
wasn't certain what to think about what may or may not have passed
between Neil and his stripper but then it hardly mattered now, it was
all history. Oh God! The worst thought suddenly slapped Nat. What
if Neil was still seeing the stripper? What if they had become an official item? She might have left her husband for Neil. Why wouldn't
she? Neil was gorgeous. Nat quickly adjusted that thought in her head
– at least, she used to think so. Neil might be playing dad to the

stripper's daughter. She might be inside Ben and Fi's house right this moment. She might be sitting in Nat's chair at the dining table. It was a vile, vile thought. Nat knew that she'd thrown away her marriage and she knew that there was no hope or chance of reconciliation but she wasn't ready for someone else to sit in her chair with Neil and the family that, up until so recently, had been her own.

Nat took a deep breath, gathered her courage and rang the doorbell. Fi had been looking out for Nat and she flung the door open almost immediately, before Nat had a chance to slip away. Fi imagined that this visit must be an ordeal for Nat but she reasoned many family visits were ordeals for many people over the Christmas period, it was almost traditional. She pulled Nat over the step, into the house and wrapped her in a big hug. Fi was flushed and jolly. Nat was unsure whether this was the sherry or the season. She had Giles on one hip and Sophia was dangling around her other leg.

'Aunty Nats!' cried Sophia in glee. She immediately swapped allegiance, deserting her mother's hemline in order to launch herself at Nat. Nat swooped down and picked up the little girl. She buried her face in Sophia's neck and inhaled. Sophia smelt wonderful. She smelt of chocolate (the kids had probably raided their selection boxes at about five this morning) and she smelt of home. Nat hadn't realised just how much she'd missed Neil's family until she was face to face with them again. Fi ushered Nat into the front room, where Ben, Angus and Harold were playing air hockey on an inconveniently large table.

'Father Christmas didn't check the room's dimensions,' explained Ben, raising his eyebrows and wrinkling his forehead in a parody of distress; he leant towards Nat and kissed her in greeting. Eileen was on the sofa with Fi's mother – Nat had met her once or twice before. Both ladies hugged Nat. Nat was relieved, Neil clearly hadn't dished the dirt; she was relieved *and* grateful. At least now she would be able to hand over the gifts, chat for ten minutes or so and then leave without too much trauma.

The house seemed to be swarming with Fi's siblings and nieces and nephews, various neighbours and friends. Nat stood by as the kids yanked off the wrapping from her gifts. They yelped their excitement and shouted, 'Just what I wanted' and 'Yes!' She was handed a drink, 'I'll have a juice, I'm driving,' and offered plate after plate of delicious nibbles.

'Caramelised onion tartlets with goat's cheese and thyme,' said Fi in a way that assured Nat she hadn't just read the name of the treat on the packaging. 'Bruschetta with tomato and basil,' she tempted. The choice was enormous. Nat wondered how anyone would have any room left for lunch. That said, she couldn't resist and helped herself to at least three Thai pork satay kebabs with coconut sauce and about half a dozen mini Yorkshire puddings with beef and horseradish.

'Maybe you could take something up to Neil,' suggested Fi.

'He's upstairs?'

'Yes.'

Nat wasn't sure where she'd thought he might be today. She hadn't wanted to think he might be home alone and yet discovering he was so nearby was upsetting too.

'He says he's setting up Angus's Scalextric but to be honest I think he's just keeping out of the way,' explained Fi.

Nat hesitated.

'It's Christmas, Nat, at least go and say hello. Surely that's not too much to ask.'

Reluctantly, Nat took the plate of food and trudged up the stairs.

40

Neil had showered that morning. Not so much because it was Christ's birthday but because Ben had said they'd have to drive to Clapham with the windows open if he didn't, and it was an extremely cold day; Neil thought there was a reasonable likelihood that he'd get pneumonia if they had to do that. Now that Nat was standing in the doorway to his nephew's bedroom, he was glad he'd showered; he only wished he'd shaved.

He looked up from the Scalextric set and Nat thought that his eyes seemed to bore a hole directly through her 'I'm doing OK' façade. On many occasions he would spot that she was bored in company, even when she had put on her best hostess act, and he would notice when she was upset by some belligerent git loudly expressing some prejudiced notion, even though she might have responded reasonably rather than confrontationally. Could he see through her show of calm now? Could he tell that she was struggling? Suffering? She hoped so and yet she hoped not.

'So you carried out your threat to grow a beard,' said Nat. Her voice was unusually squeaky. She coughed, like a teenage boy trying to bring her means of communication under control.

Neil fingered his chin. 'Not so much an active decision, more—'

'Neglect?'

'Suppose.' Neil shrugged.

He looked terrible. There was no getting away from the fact. He seemed to have shrunk. His skin (which was grey) appeared to hang from his bones, his hair was lank and his eyes had dimmed. Nat guessed that he wasn't having an affair with the stripper; there was nothing about this man that suggested new love or even a seductive liaison. He was heartbroken. Had the stripper dumped him?

'You're looking well,' Neil said snidely. Nat thought that 'well' was probably taking it a bit far. She didn't look quite as beat up as Neil did, her parents were making sure she ate regularly, she was groomed and clean, but if Neil looked closely he'd have noticed that her eyes had dimmed too.

'I'm getting up and going out in the world, if that's what you mean,' she replied defensively.

'Single life obviously suits you. Oops, what am I talking about? You're not single, are you? You've got a boyfriend.' Neil spat out the word 'boyfriend' with so much restrained aggression, it was as though he was cursing his own mother.

Nat wondered if she should explain that she didn't have a boyfriend. Her thing with Karl had been a one-off mistake. A terrible, terrible mistake. But then what would be the point? It would only open old wounds, perhaps create new ones. Fi had mentioned in passing that Karl had been visiting Neil reasonably regularly (Nat had assumed this good Samaritan act was motivated by guilt) but if she started talking about the person she'd had sex with, Neil was bound to demand exactly who that person was. By the look of him, he needed all the support he could muster, even despicable double-crossing support. Besides, Neil didn't want to talk. He'd made that much crystal clear. In the past seven weeks he hadn't once picked up the phone to her. He hadn't passed any comment on the fact that she'd left her key, and when her father had gone to collect her clothes, Neil had said he could take anything and everything, for all he cared. Nat had questioned Brian closely, and with reluctance Brian had admitted that Neil had not sent any message and, no, he had not inquired after her. His silence was thunderously loud. There was only one conclusion to be drawn: he didn't want her. He'd managed to turn off his emotions just as though he was turning off a tap. Well, how could she be surprised, considering everything? Nat tried to tell herself that this silence was best all round.

'You'd look better if you got dressed properly and had a bit of fresh air now and again, perhaps even went to work.' Nat sounded exasperated. It wasn't right that Neil had chosen to sit around and bemoan his circumstances indulgently. He was worrying everyone. Tim had called her a number of times and asked her to do something. But what? Even Karl had dropped her an email (cool and to the point, no mention of their night together) telling her that their manager was beginning to lose patience with Neil; a man in payroll whose wife had died of cancer hadn't taken this long off work. Nat understood the point Karl was making. But what could she do?

'You're going back to work on Tuesday, right?' she asked.

'Maybe.'

'Or are you going back after the New Year's bank hol?'

'Not sure.'

'You are planning on going back to work at some stage, though, aren't you, Neil?'

'Not sure.' On some level Neil was secretly enjoying this attention from Nat, although he would never admit to it. When Ben, Fi, Karl and Tim had all asked the same question, Neil had found their concern irritating and intrusive. Frankly, he wanted them all to sod off. He didn't want them popping by and insisting he open windows, put a load in the wash or some food in his belly. But he did rather like Nat taking an interest. He liked making her feel guilty. She fucking deserved to feel guilty, she'd crucified him. And besides the fact that she deserved to feel guilty, he liked her taking an interest in him (even a clearly exasperated one) because it reminded him of old times when he had been her constant focus and she had been his.

'What's the point of going back to work? Who cares?' he muttered.

Neil sounded like a sulky teenager and Nat wanted to throttle him. This was so typical of him; typical that he'd simply give up on everything. OK, so his marriage had gone AWOL, so had hers! It was the same marriage, incidentally, hadn't he noticed that? But she was still contributing to society; she was going to work, buying groceries, paying her mobile phone bill. People couldn't just cave in when things got tough, no matter how much they might want to. Her father never had. He'd been left with her as a teeny, tiny baby and she could bet her last quid that all he must have wanted to do, when her mother died, was crawl under the duvet and shut out the world, but he hadn't done that. Still, there was no point in her getting angry with Neil. Experience told her that would be fruitless and, besides, she was the last person with any right to do so. She accepted that this debacle was her fault, his reaction was his responsibility but she had instigated the disaster in the first place. She sighed deeply and tried to change the subject.

'What did you buy the kids for Christmas?' she asked brightly.

'I didn't get round to it,' replied Neil with a yawn.

'What?' Nat's patience and her intention not to get angry with Neil went up in smoke like a dry tinderbox.

'I couldn't face the shops and all that merriment. You might not have noticed, Nat, but I'm actually quite fucked up here.'

'Oh, I've noticed, Neil. I've noticed and so has half of London. What must Angus and Sophia think? Giles is too young to notice but couldn't you at least have bought them a selection box at the garage?'

'I suppose you selected amazing presents, did you?' It sounded like an accusation.

'Yes, actually, I did.' Nat had spent hours trying to decide between a Matchbox super blast fire truck and LeapFrog ClickStart My First Computer, for Angus. She saw it as a choice between fun or educational; put another way, Angus's favourite versus Ben and Fi's. The gigantic fire engine with lights, sounds, a moving hose and a function allowing kids to aim and shoot blue foam balls at the pretend blaze won out. Sophia had been easy, she got a dressing-up box complete with cow girl and princess outfits, and for Giles she'd had a small wooden bookcase carved in the shape of a lighthouse because his nursery had a nautical theme; it had been handmade by a local Guildford artist. She'd put hours into selecting their presents.

'You are so unfit,' Nat muttered. She hadn't meant to make that comment aloud. It was something that had played around in her head for days and she'd meant to keep that thought trapped in there for ever; it was the last thing she'd wanted to say and he was the last person she'd wanted to say it to.

'Unfit for what?' he demanded.

Nat bit down on her tongue. She literally put her hand across her mouth and tried to pull the words back into her mouth. But she couldn't. Despite the last few months, Nat and Neil were in the habit of being honest with each other. So she told him what she thought.

'This whole bloody mess started with you wanting a baby, Neil. And look at you. You are as self-indulgent as a teenager. You are a baby!'

'Fuck off, Nat.'

'Oh, very mature, very articulate.'

Nat suddenly felt light-headed. She sat down on the edge of the bed and put her head between her knees. For a moment neither of them said anything. Nat took in the room. She'd been in here a hundred times before but today seemed to be the first time she'd really noticed it. Angus's bedroom was like most four-year-olds' rooms – a tip. Fi and Ben had at some point poured great attention and love into preparing this room for their firstborn. This was clear because of the cheerful colour scheme and the careful selection of fabrics and fittings but Angus had stamped his own personality on to the room every time he stamped a biscuit underfoot or hid a small Lego model under the bed. Three of the walls were painted a vivid blue, Fi said the colour reminded her of the best type of summer skies, the fourth was a buttercup yellow. There were glow-in-the-dark stars stuck to the ceiling and the duvet cover and curtains also had stars all over them. There was an assortment of certificates Blu-tacked on to the cupboard doors, and propped behind clutter on the window sill and bookshelves. The certificates boasted achievements such as 'Showing a caring attitude towards friends in the playground' and 'Careful play in the sandpit'. There were drawings of dinosaurs and aliens scattered over the floor next to felt tip pens, cuddly toys, small plastic models of characters and monsters, books, badges, bouncy balls and stickers. There was also a huge number of scraps of paper that looked like rubbish to the untrained eye, but Nat knew that the pieces of paper were part of an elaborate imaginary game that Angus endlessly played out like some sort of soap opera. She'd noticed the chaos many times before but today she saw something else, she saw charm and individuality. The bed was unmade, the surfaces were dusty and there wasn't twenty centimetres squared of clear carpet space; instead, it was a dizzying, intoxicating centre of imaginative excellence. Nat tried to stay focused on a box of marbles in an attempt not to pass out.

'Should I get you some water?' asked Neil.

Nat knew she must look ghastly if he was offering to help her. 'Am I very green?' she asked.

'It's more that you're sort of transparent.'

'It's nothing to worry about. It's happened a few times recently.'

'Too many boozy nights,' muttered Neil nastily. He couldn't hide his fury or jealousy and his tone goaded her into saying the one thing she'd sworn she'd never say.

'I'm pregnant, Neil.'

41

'**P**regnant?'

Natalie was already regretting the confession, but she had been so hideously weary for weeks now and so utterly terrified for days that she was unable to think straight, it had just blurted out. If she'd thought for a moment about the consequences of her declaration, she would have cut out her tongue rather than mutter those two damning words but she was petrified, drained and lonely, and as such she was quite unable to think of consequences beyond throwing up on Angus's duvet.

Nat had known enough pregnant women to expect a bit of nausea in the mornings and maybe some tiredness; every pregnant woman she'd known had talked about both those things, but neither 'nausea' nor 'tiredness' came near the reality. Nausea was a polite word, one that suggested something bearable and acceptable. It was a viciously imperfect description of how Nat actually felt. She was *sick*. Sick, sick, sick. Entirely, utterly, right up to the back teeth sick. And not just in the mornings, oh no, the mornings were the times she might expect to vomit but the threat stayed with her all day. And the tiredness! Some days it felt as though someone had packed her body with wet sand as her limbs were so weighty and cumbersome. She was used to running up the escalators at work and on the underground; now it was all she could do to step into the elevator and lift her arm to press the button for the required floor.

At first Nat had thought the nausea and the exhaustion were part and parcel of her break-up with Neil. She'd known she was nervous and depressed so the symptoms were not unexpected. But then her period didn't arrive and she was one of those women who could set a clock by her cycle. She took a test. It was positive.

The irony of the word. Positive. How could *this* be positive? she'd wondered.

Nat forced herself to glance up at Neil. He looked as though someone had just sent an enormous electric charge through his body. He'd leapt to his feet and his entire body appeared rigid and fraught. His arms were spread wide and his fingers were splayed, his back, neck and legs were stiff and unyielding, even his hair seemed to stand on end; unbending and shocked.

'Is it mine?'

'Of course it's not yours! Are you mad?' He wasn't thinking straight. They'd always used condoms so how could it possibly be his? As much as either of them might want that to be the case, it simply wasn't. Another cold, hard fact. Nat's life was full of them. It was so unlucky. She'd only slept with Karl that once and while she couldn't even remember it, she had hoped that even in their horribly inebriated state they might have stopped and reached for a condom, that her habit of a lifetime would have made her insist on that at least, but apparently not. God, she was a fool.

Neil wondered if Nat had been pregnant that last time they had made love. The thought sliced him open. He had to admit that their lovemaking that night had had a new energy to it; Nat had been imbued with a different confidence and exhilaration. It was perfectly feasible to deduce that the energy and confidence had come from having another lover. Now, Neil felt sick too. He had his theory about who his wife had shagged, who had fucked up his life.

Neil had found Nat's mobile phone almost immediately after she'd left their home that hideous Friday night. He'd put it in his pocket with the intention of returning it to her when he delivered his bouquet and apologies. But when she'd boldly announced she had slept with someone else, he decided to hang on to it so that he could examine the call log and the text message records, like every other desperate and deceived partner had done for years and would always do. It was ignoble but he at least deserved to know who'd ruined his life. He'd scrolled through the names, shocked by the number of possible candidates, and was none the wiser. There were half a dozen men's numbers in the phone that he hadn't expected and a series of texts detailing times and places she had met them. Then he thought to check the last text she'd sent and it all became crystal clear.

Tsdy GR8. Again so srry bout 2nite.Ws looking frwrd! x.

A text to Lee Mahony. It was the exclamation mark and the kiss that upset him. He searched back and found Lee Mahony had sent three messages to Nat and she'd sent him one other. OK, so none of them were exactly pornographic but he was certain Lee Mahony was her lover. She'd probably run to him that very night they'd rowed. From the texts he'd learnt that they'd had plans to meet up and the invite to Ali's dinner party had screwed that up; that was probably why she'd been in such a mood all night. It made perfect sense. After all, she used to refer jokingly to Lee Mahony as her 'most passionate encounter', although she always added, 'until I met you, that is'. Neil was sickened to think that he'd always believed her because he'd always been so secure in her love. But no longer. Neil remembered bits and bobs about this Lee Mahony from the stories they'd swapped in the heady, early days when lovers compare and contrast their conquests of the past, to prove their desire and desirability. Lee Mahony was Irish. The Irish were known for their charm, thought Neil indignantly, suddenly believing the entire nation's gift of the gob was working against him. How was it that Nat had described him all those years ago? She'd said women could not resist Lee Mahony and the reason was that Lee Mahony could not resist women, he liked them all. Neil only remembered because at the time he thought this Lee guy sounded quite cool, the sort of man he might want to go for a pint with, secretly the sort of man he would have liked to be. No longer! Wanker!

Plus, out of all the names Nat had listed and all the dates she'd admitted to on that fateful night he'd called out Cindy's name, Lee Mahony's had been notably absent. Proof! She must have been protecting him. Even then. She'd talked about all the other names listed in her contacts: Alan Jones, Michael Young, Richard Clark, Matthew Jackson and Daniel McEwan. She'd given up their identities readily enough and she'd confidently denied having slept with any of them. But she had not admitted to Lee Mahony. Neil had thought and thought about why she'd confessed to sleeping with someone when she did, and he'd been able to draw only one conclusion: she wanted to be with this someone, she wanted to ditch him. Neil wanted to ask her how long she'd been sleeping with Lee Mahony and how often and how good it was. But he knew the answers would be a fatal blow. He couldn't do it.

'Fuck.' Neil wasn't sure who the expletive was aimed at. Natalie? Lee Mahony? Fate? Not the baby. Even in this moment of filthy, disgusting hurt and bewilderment, Neil couldn't help himself, he took a sneaky sideways glance at Nat's stomach. Was it curved? Even just a tiny amount? Or was he imagining that? To think there was a baby in Nat's stomach! Or womb, or were you supposed to say uterus, wasn't that the accepted word nowadays? He preferred womb, it was warmer, more feminine. The thought of a baby growing inside Nat was the most amazing miracle he could ever have dreamt of and yet, at the same time, it was the darkest, most cruel nightmare. 'Fuck!' he said again.

Nat flinched as the word shot across the room towards her. 'Not that any of this matters as it will all be over on Wednesday,' she said carefully.

'What?' Neil ran his hands through his hair with such violence that Nat thought he might yank out a chunk. 'You're having an abortion?'

Nat swallowed. 'Of course.'

'You can't!' Neil yelled. Neil had always believed in a woman's right to choose whether she complete a pregnancy or not. He believed that there were circumstances when bringing an unwanted baby into the world might be as big a crime as aborting a foetus. Women who were rape victims ought to have a right to choose, young girls who were barely out of their own childhoods had that right too, breadline mothers with more mouths to feed than they could physically or mentally manage perhaps, and women who had been told they would have babies with terrible illnesses or disabilities. But Nat? Did Nat have a right to choose? He supposed if he was going to be rational about this then, yes, Nat too had the right to choose. He understood that on an intellectual level but this had nothing to do with his intellect. His response was entirely emotional. 'You *can't*.'

'I can and I am,' said Nat, as though the decision had been easy for her. But it had not. Nat did not want a child. She knew that, she'd always known that. She did not want to be pregnant. A state she saw pretty much akin to a death sentence. But not wanting to be pregnant and terminating a pregnancy were two entirely separate things. She hadn't expected it to be so, but she'd discovered as much when she'd called the abortion clinic to try to make an appointment. The lady who had answered the phone had asked Nat if she wanted to take advantage of a counselling session. Nat had declined. Nat had also refused the invitation to read the literature on the development of the foetus. She knew what she wanted and she didn't want to be swayed. Gently, it had been pointed out to her that no one wanted to sway her; they just wanted her to have all the facts. But Nat did not want to dwell. This was a difficult decision to make on her own, pointed out the woman at the end of the phone. Then she'd asked if there was anyone Nat could talk to. The baby's father? Her mother? A friend? Was there anyone she might like to accompany her when she visited the doctor? Nat had said she'd think about it but she hadn't intended to do so. She was sure the best thing she could do was bury this reality away at the very back of her mind for all eternity; not to dwell on it, certainly not to share it. It was a surprise to her that, despite her firm intentions to keep this issue an absolute secret, she was talking to Neil about it. Neil of all people! She had to bring this conversation to a close.

'This is really none of your business, Neil,' said Nat. The truth of this statement pierced them both like an arrow. 'I shouldn't have told you. I have no idea why I did. I'm not thinking straight.'

'No, no you're not, so this is not the time to do anything rash,' said Neil desperately.

'Neil, it's not your baby,' she reminded him firmly.

He conceded the point. 'So what does the father say?' He couldn't bring himself to say Lee Mahony's name. Not here in his nephew's bedroom, it would be sullying.

'Nothing, he doesn't know, I haven't told him.' Nat found this conversation excruciating. More so because she knew she was throwing daggers at Neil.

'Hasn't he got a right to know?'

'He wouldn't be interested,' Nat said flatly. She was pretty sure this was the case. Besides, she wasn't interested in Karl. 'We're not an item, Neil.'

Neil was unsure whether Nat meant that as they were no longer an item, he had to back off and keep his nose out of her business, or did she mean that she and Lee Mahony were not an item? He felt a surge of hope flush through his body. If they weren't an item then . . . well, maybe . . . wouldn't there be a chance for . . . Neil wasn't able to complete his thought before Nat threw icy water on to his daydream by reiterating her initial position, a position that remained to him mystifying and indefensible. 'I don't want to be a mother and certainly not a single mother. I need you to forget we ever had this conversation.'

Nat stood up and left the room. As the door banged behind her, one of Angus's certificates fell off the door. Neil picked it up and stared and stared at it. It was a certificate to commend Angus for 'Showing a caring attitude towards friends in the playground'. Quite a skill, thought Neil.

42

Neil stayed in Angus's bedroom until his brother Ben threatened to physically carry him downstairs. Then he sat next to the Christmas tree (half hiding behind it) and remained mute for the rest of the day. His family threw sympathetic glances his way but they all realised that there was something profoundly closed and unusually distant about the expression he wore; even his mother did not dare to offer a 'penny for them' as she might usually have done. They suspected that he was picking over Christmases past, it was natural to remember happier times, and they tacitly agreed that silently indulging him for a little longer was reasonable. But who could have guessed how bleak and turbulent Neil's thoughts were? He could not make sense of his situation. He could not, no matter how desperately he tried, process what Nat had told him. The facts whirled around his head like clothes in a washing machine, tangled, misshapen and soggy.

He needed to talk to someone, but who? Family members were all too claustrophobically close. He knew if he told any one of them that Nat was pregnant and planning an abortion, and oh, by the way, it's not mine, he'd be opening the most gigantic Pandora's box and he would never get the lid back on. Neil couldn't face the inevitable slagging off of his wife (or should he say ex-wife now? He didn't know the etiquette), he couldn't bear the thought of wading through other people's hysteria and disbelief; he was only just coping with his own.

He was sure his family would all have strong views on the situation and they would all want to express them, and really, he just needed someone to listen. He thought of talking to Tim, who he trusted completely and who was capable of offering sound advice, as indeed he'd done often enough over many years. In many ways, Tim was like a brother to Neil but somehow that disqualified him too, Tim would be too staunchly loyal to be anything other than indignant and condemning, which left Karl. Karl was unlikely to respond hysterically; even if he were to be shocked by the events, he was too cool to let on. And if he had strong views and wanted to express them, the vocalisation was likely to take the form of the utterance of multiple, efficient expletives. Neil felt he could cope with a string of incredulous 'You are shitting me', 'the bitch' and 'no fucking way', which were likely to be Karl's immediate responses. Neil knew this was not a conversation he could have over his mobile. He'd have to wait until Karl was back in town. When would that be? He knew Karl was spending time at Jen's family home. He texted Karl and asked when he was coming back, and was relieved to receive a reply saying the twenty-eighth. He'd worried he might have to wait until the New Year and he couldn't afford to wait. There was no time to lose.

So on the twenty-eighth, Neil bought a six-pack, hunted out the chocolate orange that he'd snaffled out of Fi's fridge and set off to Karl's.

Karl was surprised to see Neil standing on his doorstep at nine in the morning. At first he thought Neil had come round to punch him, a thought he'd secretly harboured for seven weeks. So far his indiscretion with Nat had apparently gone undetected but still, Karl was nervous. Sometimes these things revisited you when you least expected them to, just when you'd stopped checking over your shoulder. He knew he'd been a plonker to fool around with Neil's wife. However tasty Nat was, it wasn't good form and he really wouldn't have done so normally (he hadn't in the seven years he'd known her, no matter how much he'd wanted to), it's just that on that particular night he'd drunk enough to sink a ship and truthfully he had been a bit unsettled by all this marriage stuff with Jen. He wasn't one for making excuses or over-analysing things, that was not his scene at all, but he was a bit freaked out by the fact that within moments of him handing over the money for the engagement ring, the wedding preparations had taken on a life force of their own. A force that was so overwhelming and all-consuming that Karl thought a Jedi Master might struggle to battle against it. He didn't feel in the slightest bit connected to the wedding and while he was the first to admit he wasn't exactly an archetypal romantic knight in shining armour, he had expected the woman he'd marry to be ga-ga about him. Was Jen? He wasn't sure. She was ga-ga about the wedding, definitely. But about *him* specifically? Take the ring, for example. They hadn't chosen it together; when Karl said yes, Jen admitted that she'd already selected one. It seemed all that was required of him was ready cash, when a shop assistant asked for it, and a ready smile, when anyone congratulated them. It bothered him. It hurt his pride and maybe somewhere a little deeper. So he hadn't been thinking straight that night Nat buzzed his bell.

With relief Karl noticed the beer and chocolate and thought it was unlikely that Neil had come to seek any sort of revenge. Once he was reassured on that front, Karl was genuinely chuffed to see his mate. For a start, Neil was out of his house and he was dressed in clean clothes, which hadn't been the case for weeks. Karl was not made of stone; he was worried about Neil because he'd really plummeted off the rails. Secondly, Karl was delighted to see Neil because he had neither beer nor chocolate in the house.

'Mate, good to see you.' Karl pulled Neil into a loose, back-slapping man-hug and led the way up to the flat.

Karl's flat was tastefully decorated. The walls were different shades of almost white, which made the most of the small place. Karl had funky black and white photos hanging everywhere; the best ones were displayed in the narrow, short corridor that led towards his bedroom. When he showed women these shots he often claimed to have taken them himself. He hadn't, they were all Habitat prints and their ubiquitous nature meant he occasionally got caught out on that particular lie but he didn't care, it rarely mattered. Claiming to be a photographer usually impressed at the pertinent moment, the moment he was leading the women down the corridor, and that was all he ever aimed to do. He had bought most of his furniture from Habitat too and last year he'd had an Ikea kitchen installed. It was grey lacquer and looked impressive. Jen did a good job at keeping the flat clean, or at least she used to. Neil noticed that the place was surprisingly dusty and there were coffee mug rings on every surface; it looked like it had before Nat facilitated Jen's stumbling into Karl's life.

'Is Jen about?' Neil asked, hoping he sounded nonchalant. In fact he desperately hoped that Jen was nowhere to be seen; there was no way he could talk about the things he needed to talk about with Karl if Jen was hanging around.

'She's at her mother's. We both spent Christmas Day, Boxing Day *and* Sunday at her folks' but, Jesus, mate,' Karl rolled his eyes with exasperation. 'I don't know how I'm going to do that every year. I came back here this morning and left her to it. She was on about us staying right through to New Year. Fuck that.'

'Difficult family?'

'No, not especially. They were totally normal. Bickering, which I put down to the fact it was Christmas, and nosey, which I put down to the fact that I'm fascinating. The problem was, they were just dead boring and farty.'

'You mean boring farts?'

'No. I mean they were so old they didn't have an embarrassment threshold and they didn't care about expressing their appreciation of the Christmas lunch the old-fashioned way. Seriously, all her family members look like and behave like Henry the Eighth, including her mother. I'm worried about that. They say take a good look at the mother because that's who you end up with.'

'Nat doesn't look like her mother,' pointed out Neil.

'No, she looks like her father, which still makes a better bet than

Jen's mum.' Karl cracked open one of the cans and asked, 'Do you want to watch the Boxing Day game? I recorded it.'

'Not really, Karl.'

'No? What then?'

Neil took a deep breath and then dived in. 'I need to talk to someone about something big.'

'Mate, I've seen yours, it's not that big,' joked Karl. He sensed an emotional onslaught and he was trying to head it off. Neil had been tough-going since he'd split with Nat. Karl had really tried to be sympathetic, way more so than he would have been with any other bloke who'd split from any other woman. He'd made a concession on account of having had a crack at Nat. Even though Neil hadn't found out about the incident and Karl had got away without a kicking (verbal, emotional or physical), hidden somewhere very deep inside, Karl felt inconvenient twinges of responsibility. If he'd stopped to think how floored Neil would be by losing Nat, he might have done things differently that night. He had, once or twice, asked himself if it would have been wiser to tell Nat that there was definitely nothing going on with Neil and the stripper, even though at the time he hadn't been a hundred per cent certain. Should he have called Neil and got him to come and pick Nat up? Could he have stemmed this disaster? Should he have been like the little Dutch boy who put his finger in the dam and saved an entire town from flood, instead of concentrating on getting into a completely different sort of hole?

Karl got his answer when Neil announced, 'Nat's pregnant.'

'Jesus!'

'It's not mine.'

'Nor mine,' blathered Karl.

'What?'

'Sorry, daft joke.' Jesus, Jesus, thought Karl. His legs turned to water. He staggered backwards and collapsed into his sofa. Neil took it as a cue and he sat down too.

'That night she left me, she went to meet this bloke Lee Mahony and it's his.'

'She did what?' asked Karl, confused.

'She had sex with him and it's his.'

'She said that?'

'Not exactly, no. Not in so many words. But I know she did,' insisted Neil. 'So, she thinks the baby is Lee Mahony's and of course it might be. Almost certainly is. It all depends on how many times they did it and did they do it before then, you know, dates and stuff. I don't know for sure. Was she having an affair for some time or did she just get angry that night and do it only the once? It affects the odds. I keep going over it and over it, trying to think it through.'

'Mate, I'm not following you.'

'Because if it was just that once, if it was just that night that she had sex with someone else, then it might still be mine.'

'How could it be yours?' asked Karl, bemused. He knew enough about Nat and Neil's private lives to know that they always used contraception.

'Because I put pinholes in the condom that we used when we had sex that night,' confessed Neil in a rush.

'Fucking hell,' replied Karl, which Neil thought was apt and covered it.

'But I can't tell her. She'll kill me. She didn't want a baby and now she doesn't want me either, so it's a double whammy if I tell her that the baby might be mine. It's only a slim chance anyway.' A chance Neil clutched at.

'But what the hell made you do a bloody irresponsible, utterly stupid thing like that?' demanded Karl, who was too dazed by the information overload to fully process everything yet.

'It was Cindy's idea.'

'The stripper?'

'Yes.'

'Genius mate, bloody genius. What were you thinking of, taking advice from a stripper who is no more than a kid herself?' snapped Karl angrily.

'She didn't advise me exactly, she inspired me. She said she stopped taking the pill to—' Neil stopped talking, he knew it sounded bad.

Karl finished the sentence for him. 'To trap some poor bastard into marrying her?'

'They were already married. Her husband just didn't want kids.'

'People have the right not to want kids,' bawled Karl, exasperated at this large-scale irresponsibility.

'And people have the right to want them!' yelled Neil, even more loudly. Neil knew what he'd done was wrong but he wanted his friend to understand his relentless, miserable desperation. 'I just got so pissed off that women hold all the fertility cards. It's not fair that it's them who decide when they want babies, or more importantly in our case, it's not fair that Nat decided she didn't want a baby. I deserved a say too.'

'They haven't always had the say. There were hundreds of thousands of years when they just got knocked up and had to get on with it. Contraception is a relatively new privilege. You can't blame them for being excited about it,' pointed out Karl. 'And Neil, mate, what you did is truly fucked up. This isn't like some April fool's day prank, this is massive.'

Neil shrugged moodily. He knew Karl was right. What he had done was massive. Making a baby was as big as it got, that had been his point all along. He knew it was desperately reckless to try to trick someone into a pregnancy.

'None of it matters anyway. She's aborting the baby. Today.' Saying the words made Neil feel shaky and sick. He was an idiot, a fucking idiot, he understood that now. The thought of Nat going under anaesthetic, having to deal with the trauma of an abortion, was too much for him to handle. Why hadn't he thought of that? He'd been so sure that if she fell pregnant she'd come round to his way of thinking. That's what he'd told himself when he'd drunkenly, impetuously put the pinpricks in the condom.

'Oh.'

'It might be my baby,' cried Neil in anguish.

'Or not,' pointed out Karl.

'I know. It's unlikely that she's fallen pregnant after a one off semi-protected occasion with me. Much more likely to be this bastard Lee Mahony's,' said Neil with a desolate groan.

'What were you saying about this Lee bloke?' Karl couldn't get his head around that bit of the story. Did this mean that Nat had had sex with Neil, then visited his place and then left his place in a hurry because she was nipping off to yet another bloke's place? That couldn't be right, could it? It was the behaviour of a nympho-maniac. She wasn't that sort of woman, was she? Karl couldn't slip the jigsaw pieces into place because Neil had another bombshell to drop.

'The thing is, mate, I don't care. My baby or not, I want it and I want her.'

'You're kidding.'

'Deadly serious.'

'You are so screwed up,' said Karl definitively.

'No, I'm really not. I have been. I now realise that sitting around for weeks, not even cleaning my teeth for days on end, that was screwed up and the holes in the condom, that was, well, wrong too, very desperate, underhand and impulsive, I see that. Plus, the whole stripper thing, well, that was one bloody silly, big mess. But *this*, Karl, wanting her and wanting the baby, irrespective of whose baby it is, *this* is my finest hour.'

'Getting sacked was stupid too,' added Karl.

'I'm sacked?'

'Didn't you get the letter?'

'No. Or maybe I did. I haven't been opening my post.'

'Oh.' Karl shrugged uncomfortably, that hadn't been the best way to break the news. 'Sorry, mate. They sent you warnings. You didn't turn up to work for six weeks and you didn't even get a doc's note. What were you thinking?'

'I wasn't thinking, I told you. I've messed lots of stuff up but none of that matters. All that matters is I want Nat and I want this baby.'

Karl considered. Was his mate certifiable or a hero? Was this his finest hour or just another form of delirium?

'But she's getting an abortion. She still doesn't want a sprog.'

'Yes, and because it's not mine I haven't got a leg to stand on. I reckon if it was my baby I'd at least get a say, wouldn't I? What are the rules on this stuff? Do dads have any rights?'

'Don't know. We'd have to Google it.' Karl was beginning to think that perhaps he could do something to salvage this situation. Maybe. But it would require him to be brave and utterly self-sacrificing, which was not his style. He needed to think carefully about what to do for the best. If he got involved now, confessed his part in this tragedy, might it not just further confuse things? He had to speak to Nat before he said too much to Neil. 'Do you think you could really do it, be a dad to someone else's kid and never resent the kid for it?'

'Of course. How can the child be in any way to blame for its parentage? I felt sure about it from the moment she told me she was pregnant but I didn't start shouting my mouth off. I took my time. I've given this a lot of thought. I've thought of nothing else since she told me.'

'And you'd not resent Nat either?'

'Do you know what? I had seven years with Nat and this will be my seventh week without her. Isn't it madness that it took the weeks *without* her to remind me how much I love her?'

He'd been paralysed without her. People didn't get that. They thought he was being a lazy git, or a self-indulgent git or just a plain awkward git but he was paralysed. Heartbroken. What an overused term that was. The word no longer touched the meaning but Neil was sure his heart had literally broken. He felt a relentless throbbing in his chest where it had once beaten. He thought his heart had shattered like glass and tiny shards were embedded in every aspect of his life because wherever he looked he found anguish, sorrow and grief. Shards of his heart lay within the folds of her few remaining clothes that were scattered on the bedroom floor or neatly hung in the wardrobe. He'd scooped up the clothes and sniffed at them, trying to find traces of her essence: her perfume, her deodorant, her toil, he didn't care which aspect of her he might inhale, he just wanted to hold something of her. He'd slept with her dressing gown for weeks and been bitterly disappointed when all traces of her had finally faded and been replaced by his own tangy smell. There were shards of his shattered heart inside the cupboards when he pulled out a mug that she'd decorated at a pottery class, and more hidden among the bottles on the window sill in the bathroom. Shards glinted amongst the pages of her books and magazines that were tightly squeezed on their bookshelves and newspaper racks. Shards in tunes, in movies, in the silver winter air; they were everywhere because she was nowhere. He missed her. He missed her more than he'd imagined it was possible for one human being to miss another. If he poked his head out of the window, he was tortured by imaginary sightings of her; if he poked about inside his head, he was tortured by vivid memories of her.

He thought back to their first date, the cinema trip to see *Kill Bill, Vol. 1*. That had been an amazing night, one of those nights that had its own momentum, its own time frame and rule book. Yes, he'd discovered that Nat's taste in movies was refreshingly wide (and perhaps in sexual experimentation, he'd never forget that comment she'd made about Uma Thurman, it was just so breathtakingly cool), but the thing that had won Neil hook, line and sinker that night happened even before the film had begun. They had been settled in the itchy blue seats, stuffing popcorn (that tasted suspiciously close to polystyrene) into their mouths when suddenly the music to announce the start of the programme had blared into the auditorium. Neil had never paid much attention to that jingle before; it was catchy although not what anyone would describe as seminal. But then Natalie had started to dance. She remained in her seat (thank God) but she'd done this little jive, a stationary boogie, so to speak. She was so uninhibited and joyful that Neil was completely unable to resist laughing, and the more he laughed, the more she danced, until he could no longer hold out and he had felt compelled to join in. They'd danced in their seats, candid and spontaneous. It was little things like that which really made a boy fall for a girl. A girl fall for a boy. Ever since then, Neil and Natalie had always boogied in their seats whenever they went to the movies. It was one of their things.

How would he ever be able to go to the movies again?

Neil took a deep breath and finally said what he really thought. 'You were wrong, Karl, sex isn't everything. Love is everything. I want her back even without the baby. Or any baby. I want a family, I do, but I want her more. She is the root to any family I might ever have. I see now, Nat alone is enough of a family for me. Karl, I seriously don't think I can, you know, not have her. I don't think I'd be able to, you know, *be.*'

'Right.' It was an uncomfortable moment. Karl thought about what he had done and not done. Neil thought about what he should have done and what he should not have done. The silence stretched.

After a Jurassic age, Karl said carefully, 'You can't give up, Neil.'

'What?'

'You should tell her. You should tell her what you've just told me.'

'It won't make any difference,' replied Neil despondently.

'It might. Tell her about the condom with the holes in it. Tell her you don't care who the father is. Tell her you don't even care if there are no babies. Tell her, Neil. Now. Tell her before it's too late.'

43

Nat wondered what to wear. She was worried about looking too affluent. Would the people at the clinic condemn her for not progressing with the pregnancy if it was clear she had the money to support a child? She worried that anything too bright, yellow, pink or red, looked too jubilant. She didn't feel at all jubilant, she felt wretched, gutted, punctured, so was it more appropriate to wear a dark colour? She didn't want to wear anything she particularly liked because she knew whatever she wore today she'd never want to see again. Why was it so hard? She was just getting dressed. She did it every day of her life. Why did she feel like stone? Nat closed her eyes and thrust her hands into her wardrobe; she'd wear the first thing she laid her hands on. There, a blue roll-neck, that would do.

Nat wandered down into her parents' kitchen at quarter to nine. Brian had already left the house, he had gone for one of his walks on the Downs and, even though it wasn't a Saturday, he'd taken his hessian bag and pointed stick. He'd noted, with some disgust, that there would likely be an increase in littering. A direct result of Boxing Day hikers, he reasoned; not regulars on the Downs and rather inconsiderate because of it. Natalie knew he would then have a well-deserved lunch in one of the pubs in the high street. He wouldn't be home until mid-afternoon. By which time it would all be over. Finished with. Behind her. That was the way to do it. The only way. And then she could get on with everything.

With what?

The thought was not a new one but every time it thrust its way into her head, Nat had shoved it away with equal force. Today she didn't have the required energy to fight against its bleakness; the truth was she had no idea what 'everything' was any more. It was no longer Neil or her home; she had her job still and that was vital to her but she was struggling with her relationships with pretty much all her friends and family. She'd distanced herself from Jen because of Karl and she'd distanced herself from Ali because of Ali's pregnancy. It was very hard being around Ali and listening to her constant updates about her fetus's development, morning sickness, birthing plans, cravings and fears about stretch marks. Nat wanted to shout out, 'I understand!' but did she? Ali was euphoric; Nat didn't understand that, she was terrified. It had been bitter-sweet seeing Neil's family on Christmas Day. Nat had not yet found the switch that she needed to turn off her emotions towards them. Would she ever? And as for her own mum and dad, well, she felt dreadful just catching sight of them. They crept around her, oozing concern but unable to find the way into a meaningful conversation. It wasn't their fault, it was hers; she'd blocked every attempt they'd made to talk about Neil. Her life had more holes in it than Swiss cheese.

For the first month after she split from Neil, Nat had thought it was enough (sometimes too much) just to put one foot in front of another, to simply exist. She had not allowed herself to think beyond the next tube journey, the next meeting, the next meal. Any longer-term vision required a Herculean effort that she was not capable of. And then she'd discovered she was pregnant.

For fifteen days now, she'd known there was another being in her body, that she was sharing her body. Her initial concern had been how to most efficiently put a stop to that being and how to hide its brief existence most thoroughly. But the more she tried *not* to think about the being, the more she found she *was* thinking about it. Maybe it was because she was being so sick and felt so tired; it was impossible to ignore a thing if it made its presence so inconvenient. She worried that her mother or Becky might notice her frequent visits to the loo to throw up or maybe they'd notice she'd put on a bit of weight because, although it wasn't always the case, Nat had started to thicken almost straight away. She hoped they'd think it was Christmas excess. She preferred to think of it as that too, it was an easier thing to believe because she could bring Christmas excess under control. And the pregnancy was just the same, of course. She could also bring that under control. Yes, she could, she could. She told herself this over and over again but she never sounded convincing.

In the end, Nat did have a quick peek at the literature the clinic had insisted she bring home with her after her initial consultation last week; she felt somehow compelled. The literature described the different stages of fetal development. Nat was somewhere between seven and eight weeks pregnant. That was nothing, she told herself. That meant nothing. Just a batch of cells, clustered together, hardly detectable.

It was madness to describe this batch of cells as a 'baby' or to talk of stretching, bending and unbending.

OK, so its embryonic tail has gone by eight weeks which makes it look ever so slightly less alien, and all organs, muscles, and nerves are beginning to function, noted Nat. That was something, she supposed, something quite remarkable; at least in a scientific sense but it still had no bearing on her emotional reality. But then, wow, she read that the hands could now bend at the wrist. Who would have known? And the eyelids are beginning to cover the eyes. Imagine that! Something so delicate as eyelids on something no bigger than a kidney bean.

Or not. Best not. Best not think, or imagine or wonder at all. Best plod on. Just plod on.

Nat needed breakfast. She found she needed to eat something about every two hours. She thought that Nina might have gone out into town; she'd been talking about returning a pair of trousers that Brian had bought her for Christmas, they were too long in the leg and she wanted something from the petite range. Nat was therefore surprised to see Nina at the kitchen table. She had a newspaper open in front of her but Nat didn't quite believe she was reading it.

'Oh, hello, I thought you'd gone into town.'

'No, dear, I was going to and then I thought I might take advantage of everyone else being out of the house in order to have a quiet word with you.' The quiet word she'd been trying to have for quite some time, the quiet word that Nat had avoided with the skill of a black belt martial arts master. 'I think it's time we had a chat.'

'Oh.' Nat did not want to encourage Nina to think that she might like such a chat but she dared not object either. Nat had holed up with her parents for weeks now and they had been remarkably reserved about cross-examining her about the split from Neil. Nat had known that probing questions were inevitable; rather like an outstanding fine, it was possible to avoid coughing up in the first instance but in the end you always had to pay big time. Nat used the excuse of putting the kettle on as a way of turning away from her mother.

'What do you want to talk about?' she asked. There were a million things in Nat's head that probably needed talking about but she didn't know how or even if she wanted to tackle any of them. Would she have the courage to tell her mother about sleeping with Karl? Could she explain that Neil had started to visit a stripper regularly and called out her name while they were making love? Could she justify not wanting children? That might be the trickiest of all the admissions.

'How pregnant are you exactly, darling?' Nina's question ricocheted around the kitchen; it hurtled about and gathered such a velocity that Nat was almost knocked on to her back.

'How did you know? she asked, turning to face Nina.

'I'm your mother. It's my business to know all about you. Besides, you left this in your jeans pocket and I found it when I was putting the washing on.'

Nina held up the leaflet on fetal development. Nat had been wondering where it had got to. She'd been looking for it last night as she'd wanted to check out when the fetus developed hair. She didn't know why she was interested; she'd told herself that it was just scientific curiosity.

'About eight weeks,' replied Nat.

'And can I take it from your face that you are not happy with the news?' asked Nina in a careful tone.

'I'm going to a clinic this morning to have an abortion. I booked it before Christmas,' said Nat, trying to keep her tone as efficient and detached as possible. 'It was very easy to get an appointment. Christmas isn't a busy time for this sort of thing.' Nat shrugged. She hoped to appear nonchalant; she struck Nina as bewildered and adrift.

'No, I don't imagine it is,' replied Nina.

'It's nothing for you to worry about. It will all be over very soon indeed,' said Nat determinedly

'I see.' Nina wanted to stand up from the kitchen table and slowly walk towards Nat, she wanted to wrap her arms round her daughter and comfort her but she knew Nat wasn't ready for that yet. She could see it in Nat's clenched neck and thin mouth. 'And have you made that decision because you've split up with Neil and you're worried about being a single mum?' Nina asked, carefully treading on eggshells.

'Oh God, you have no idea,' sighed Nat, pushing the heels of her hands into the sockets of her eyes and rubbing ferociously.

'Well, give me an idea then,' said Nina patiently.

Could she? Could she say it? It was so enormous. So shaming. So complicated.

'It's not Neil's baby.'

'Oh.' Nina's gasp was slight but significant. Nat snapped her head in her mother's direction and felt the full force of the condemnation radiating from the anxious and disappointed mother.

'I thought he was having an affair. Maybe he was. Who knows? He called out another woman's name during – well, when we were—'

Nina nodded. She wanted to tell Nat that Nat's generation hadn't invented sex and she could very well imagine which was the most inconvenient moment a husband might call out another woman's name, but this was not the time. She let Nat go on uninterrupted.

'She's a stripper. His other woman. So I ran into the arms, well, the bed I suppose, of someone else.' The sentences came out like the rat-tat-tat of a machine gun. Nina tried to absorb everything she was being told. 'But even if this baby was Neil's, I wouldn't want it. I wouldn't.' It struck Nat that she had just referred to a 'baby'; up until that moment she had called it a 'being', a 'fetus', or 'the pregnancy'.

Maybe it was the harsh nature of the confessions, or just her hormones, or the relief of talking about the issue, or the fact that she was about to abort her baby, Nat was unsure, but suddenly she burst into floods. The tears seemed to spray out of her eyes like a sprinkler on a summer lawn. The moment was almost comedic, despite the agony; it was certainly amazing. Nina didn't have a chance to process everything, she just acted on instinct. She acted as any mother would. She saw that this was the moment when Nat needed holding and she sprang to it.

Nina held her and rocked her gently in her arms for the longest time. She rubbed her back in an effort to soothe and in the hope that she could stop her crying. Eventually Nina led her little girl to the squishy, grubby two-seat sofa that was pushed up against the wall in the kitchen. She sat Nat down and even tucked a blanket round her legs, then she brewed tea and hunted out a packet of chocolate-covered HobNobs. As she passed her the mug, she kissed her daughter's forehead.

Nat gulped down the hot tea and ate the HobNobs in large bites. As the warmth and the chocolate started to take effect, she began to tell the story of the last few months of her marriage. She told of Neil's birthday celebrations and his sudden thought to start a family, she admitted to calling her exes in her address book and she gave her mother as much detail as she could about Neil's visits to Hush Hush. She concluded with her confession that she'd had drunken, unremarkable sex with someone she shouldn't have. Nina listened carefully and did not pass comment, she only interrupted to ask questions on timings or to contextualise conversations that were being relayed.

It was only when Nat concluded by saying, 'So there you have it. A mess, isn't it?' that Nina finally commented.

'Oh, my darling. Was I such a terrible substitute?'

Nat stared at her mother, unsure how she'd made the link. The jump. Nat had been careful not to say that her reluctance to have children was anything to do with her own mother's death and yet somehow Nina had guessed.

'No, no, Mum, no. You must never think that. You were perfect. Wonderful,' said Nat. She clasped her mum's hands in her own. She'd never noticed before that the skin on Nina's hands was thin and had the texture of greaseproof paper. Nat loved those hands, hands she'd thoughtlessly, constantly clasped as a child, hands that she was glad to reach for now. 'But what if there hadn't been you? Before you I was so lonely, Dad was so lonely. We were a disaster. I didn't want that for Neil or a child of mine. You were one in a million. But if you hadn't come along, then what?'

'Someone would have, your dad was a very attractive man, a catch, and you, you were a bonus! Sweetheart, you have to accept, your mum's death wasn't a hereditary condition, it was a terrible, terrible thing. An accident. A misfortune. But there is no reason to think you would suffer the same terrible fate,' said Nina calmly.

'But there was no reason to believe she would. And she did,' argued Nat bleakly.

'Have you explained this to Neil? Does he understand why you are so scared of having a baby?'

'No.'

'Why ever not?'

'It's our secret, it always has been. We didn't even tell my brothers.'

Nina was shocked. Might she have miscalculated? Might she have made a mistake?

'And anyway, I once tried to explain it to someone and he thought I was irrational, bordering on the insane actually. I didn't want Neil thinking that of me.'

'That other man, whoever he was, could not have loved you enough.

Neil loves you enough. He would have tried to understand. I promise you, he would,' said Nina confidently.

Nat wondered if this was true. Was there a time in the past few months when she could simply have talked about her fears to the man she loved above all else? Would he have been able to comprehend? For the first time it crossed her mind that maybe she should at least have given him the chance. Yes, maybe she should have. But.

'It doesn't matter, Mum. None of it matters now.' Nat glanced at her watch. 'It's time to go. If I miss my appointment then I'll lose more time, more days, and well, I don't want that.'

'I'll come with you.' Nina stood up. She wasn't a tall woman, outsiders would have considered her delicate, but Nat thought she was magnificent. Strong.

'I thought you'd hate the idea.'

'I do. That's my grandchild in your belly, Natalie. It is. No matter if I didn't push you out into this world, you could not have been more of a child of mine. I love you as much as I love your brothers. I don't agree with what you are doing. I'd like more time to talk to you about it, to make sure you never regret this decision or think you came to it too suddenly. I'd like the chance to help you bring this baby into the world but, darling, no matter what, *you* are my baby and I'm a hundred per cent with you. Now, tomorrow, the day after and for ever, I'll support you. I love you. Get your coat.'

44

Nina knew her daughter was a grown-up. Nat did a big-boots job, which involved huge budgets, important decisions, speaking at conferences and meeting some of the most influential business people in the world (it no doubt involved a lot more but Nina wasn't certain exactly what. The point was, she knew it was very impressive.) Nat owned a beautiful home (although admittedly wasn't living in it right now), she'd done nearly all the painting and decorating herself, she'd even tiled the bathroom floor and walls, something Nina wouldn't like to tackle. Nat had a clean driving licence, a National Trust membership and she bought wine, by the demi-crate, from Berry Bros and Rudd. She wasn't the nervous, panicky little girl Nina had met all those years ago. She was unequivocally grown up. Independent. And especially headstrong.

And yet Nina still believed Nat needed her.

Nat expertly wove her mother's aged, distinctly un-chic Volvo through the town traffic and out into the windy, narrow countryside roads. Nat had found a clinic that was not too far away; it would only take them half an hour to get there. They spent the journey in silence, each preferring to trawl through their own thoughts than listen to each other's. Nina stared out of the window. It was a relentlessly grey day: the people, houses, roads, cars, fields and sky were all a pitiless shade of grey. She took a sneaky sideways glance at Nat's belly, inside which lay a jewel of colour. Nat had an opportunity to bring a priceless, individual beam of colour into this world. A baby. A child. A person.

Nina had made a similar journey as this one herself, many years ago. When she was nineteen years old she'd aborted a baby of her own. She'd found herself pregnant after having sex for the first time, she never really understood how. By that, she didn't mean she was one of those green girls who thought she might get pregnant by sitting on the seat of a public loo (not that she would dream of sitting on the seat of a public loo, but that was for cleanliness reasons not fears of conception), Nina had understood all about the mechanics of sex and very much wanted to have it. She'd carefully selected a slightly more experienced suitor to do the deflowering (so as to maximise her chance of actually enjoying the occasion as she had heard some rather discouraging stories) but what she didn't understand was how *she* got pregnant. They had been careful, just not careful enough, as it happened. It was a definitive and age-old mistake. It only takes the once. She had been in the middle of her teacher training degree. She wasn't ready for that baby. She had an abortion. Those were the facts.

Nina had never regretted her decision. She did not allow herself that indulgence. It was done, for good or ill. If she owed that unwanted child anything, it was the guarantee that she would go on to live a good and full life, a life that perhaps would not have been possible if the baby had been born. Nina had been a mother four times since; each child was a privilege and she'd always made them her priority. She was a good mother. A good woman. And her abortion had allowed her to be those things.

Yet, she thought that Nat's case was different. She felt sure that Nat might regret aborting this baby. Nat would certainly regret never allowing any baby into her life, Nina was sure of that. Nina wanted to tell her daughter that being a mother was the most inspiring, elevating, natural and important thing she'd ever done but she knew the lofty words would fall on granite.

What to do?

Nina surreptitiously fingered her mobile which lay in her baggy, ancient leather satchel. She loathed texting. She could see it was useful as a means of keeping in touch with family who insisted on globe-trotting (as hers did) and she admitted it was handy to get a text confirming her dentist appointment, but she was not adept at sending texts and never wanted to be. Nina was old enough to be fond of conversation and sentimental about the time when people actually smiled at one another, rather than made do with sending and receiving silly pictures made up of semi-colons, dashes and the close bracket symbol. But she thought *this* might be the moment when she fully appreciated the usefulness of texts, now when she needed to practise a little skulduggery.

Yes, she could see that this might not be her business. Her daughter was independent and resolute. Perhaps she should respect that. But what if her daughter was simply misguided and terrified? Didn't she have a duty? Nina loved Nat so much that she could not stop herself from getting involved. Love demanded that sometimes. Love did not always make it possible to stand on the sidelines and quietly support. Sometimes love kicked you, in ungainly fashion, into the centre of a muddy, messy pitch. It was possible Nina would squelch about in the dirt, or be tackled to the ground, or be bruised in a scrum but that was all part of the game called love. Nat was not alone, she was part of a team and she needed to be reminded of that.

Carefully, Nina composed a text to her son-in-law, stating the address of the clinic and the words COME NOW. As she pressed the send button she prayed to God that she was doing the right thing. She also wondered why and how in the world she'd justified her interference by using a rugby analogy? She'd never really understood the game and liked it less!

45

'Turn the car round!'
  'What?'

'Turn the car round, we need to head back along the A3.' Neil reached for Karl's pristine road atlas and turned to the index. Neil and Karl were driving to Nat's parents' home when Neil received the text from Nina. 'Nina has texted me the address of the abortion clinic.'

'Oh, right.' Karl felt a bit sick. Nerves probably. 'What's the address? We can stick it in the satnav, it'll be quicker.' Karl figured it would be quicker because Neil was shaking so much he couldn't open the pages of the atlas very easily. 'Will we get there in time?'

'I don't know. I don't know when too late is!' Neil took some minutes to plug the address in the satnav. Karl diligently altered course and they drove on in silence until Neil's phone rang.

'It's Nina.' Neil pressed the receive button with fearful haste. What was she going to say?

'Darling, we're at the clinic. I've just popped outside because there is something I have to tell you.'

'Where's Nat?' Neil's only thought.

'She's putting her gown on,' said Nina gently. 'Neil, you need to understand something. I'm not Nat's biological mother.'

'What?' What was she talking about? Neil couldn't understand what Nina might possibly mean. Was she distancing herself from Nat because Nat was having an abortion? How perverse. That wasn't likely. That was not the Nina that Neil knew. The Nina who, on his wedding day, had pluckily pulled him aside and threatened to deliver all sorts of hell to his door if he ever hurt her baby. 'Her mother died in childbirth,' Nina explained.

Huge waves of nausea ran through Neil's body. He was suddenly drenched with a brutal understanding and icy fear.

'A hereditary condition?' he asked in a tight, slight voice.

'No. All Nat inherited was fear but that's still real, Neil. Very real. No one would insist a claustrophobic went pot-holing or an acrophobic went abseiling,' Nina said defensively. She wasn't sure where all these sporty analogies were suddenly coming from but she was scrambling around for ways to explain the impossible and any means would do.

Poor, poor Nat. How terrified she must have been. How much more terrified she must be now. Neil couldn't think why she'd never told him about her birth mother but now that Nina had, the last crazily confused months of his life became crystal clear. He hated Nat for not telling him, he wanted to scream at her for creating all this chaos and commotion. And he loved her, utterly, at the same time and wished he could hold her right now when she must be at her most bewildered and battered. 'I understand,' said Neil calmly.

'I hoped you would,' said Nina with a sigh of relief. 'I just needed you to know that much before you got here. And Neil, darling, be as quick as you can.'

46

Nat had not allowed Nina to go into the room with her. She'd asked her mother to wait in the corridor, it was enough that she knew she was there, close by. Nat didn't want the picture of the room to be imbedded on her mother's memory, as no doubt it would be on hers. No matter how uniformly impersonal the room was she knew it would always be distinct for her, and no matter how clean and neat it was, she knew it would always represent a huge, dirty mess.

The nurse who had showed her into her room was younger than Nat. She had an enviable air of competence about her. She was pleasant and efficient. She handed Nat a green hospital gown (just like the one Nat had worn when she'd had her appendix out two years ago). She squeezed Nat's arm in a gesture of sympathy and understanding and instructed her to put the gown on and then just lie down on the bed.

'A doctor will come and see you before we move you into surgery. Try and get some rest.'

Nat obediently lay on the bed but resting was beyond her.

47

Neil had never seen traffic like it. There had been tailbacks all along the A3 so they'd taken a chance and followed an alternative route, nipping through a series of small villages. Under other circumstances, Neil would have commented how picturesque these villages were; a few months back, if he'd been travelling with Nat, he might have even chanced his hand and commented that these were the perfect sorts of places to bring up kids. God, he'd been a tosser. He'd put her under so much pressure, constantly going on and on about starting a family. He'd more or less demanded it, then whined about it, threatened, cajoled, sulked about it and ultimately even tried to trick her into it. He should have approached the whole thing differently, he should have found out why she didn't want a family. They could have talked about her fears; they could have had counselling or some such bollocks. He'd have tried anything that might have helped soothe her. Neil longed to turn back time and yet he also desperately wanted to press fast forward. He looked out of the window but could see nothing other than an endless chain of red brake lights. Why were they standing still now? What could possibly be delaying them? They had been stuck behind a gritting machine and a tractor already today, what else could go wrong? As if reading his mind, Karl explained.

'We're only about a mile and a half away. It's just after this little town. I think the traffic jam is down to shoppers trying to get parked.'

'Fucking sale shoppers, I hate them,' Neil snarled, banging his hand on the dashboard.

'Nearly there, mate. We're doing our best. We can't do more than we are doing,' reasoned Karl. 'Why don't you call Nina again and see what's going on?'

'I tried, went straight through to voicemail. Her phone's switched off, I think. You have to switch your phone off when you're in a hospital, don't you?'

Karl hated hospitals. No one had said anything about hospitals when he signed up to this. He'd offered to drive Neil round to Nat's parents' gaff, which would have been trial enough, and then Neil had said they had to go directly to a clinic, which was a step further than he wanted to go, and now Neil was talking about *hospitals*. Hospitals made him squeamish. He really didn't fancy talking to Nat in a hospital. They had that funny smell about them, didn't they? Illness and sorrow. Still, he had no choice, he realised that. A man had to do what a man had to do. In the meantime, of course, he could always try and hide in a joke.

'They make you switch your phone off on aeroplanes too. Maybe she's had a change of plan and nipped to the Caribbean instead.'

'Shut up, Karl,' said Neil and Karl thought it was probably best if he did.

Neil's phone suddenly rang and he nearly dropped it as he scrabbled to press the receive call button.

'Neil, darling, how far away are you?' Nina asked. The concern was audible.

'Not far but the traffic is at a standstill.'

'I just wanted to call you, darling, to warn you that you might be too late. I think she's already gone into surgery. I'm sorry.' Her voice was tired and forlorn.

'Stop the car!'

'What?'

'Pull over, Karl. I need to get out.'

Neil flung open the door even though the car was still moving. 'Where you going, mate?' yelled Karl.

'This is too slow. I'm going to run. She's gone into surgery.'

'We're too late?' asked Karl, his face distorting with genuine regret.

'No, I'm not too late,' said Neil. 'I'm going to my wife. She'll need me when she comes round. I'm going to bring her home. I might not be too late for that.'

Neil started to run up the road. Karl leant out of the window and called after him.

'Mate, I'll follow up in the car. It may have escaped your notice but you don't have a white charger. You're going to need my Toyota.' Karl thought Neil was likely to head off in the wrong direction or collapse with a stitch; it would undoubtedly be wiser and more rational to have stayed put, no matter how slow they were travelling; it was bloody cold out there but even so, Karl was really proud of him.

48

The pain in his chest was unlike anything he'd ever experienced, it felt as though his lungs and ribs were trying to pound their way out of his body. His breathing was shallow and he felt dizzy and sick. The agony of his effort stretched through every one of his muscles in his stomach, back, legs and arse. The pain was worse than the pain when he had been punched in the face by Cindy's husband or when he'd punched the wall that night he was rowing with Nat. It was relentless and it got worse with every step he took. Up until the split he had played football in the park, every weekend, and Neil was used to running around a pitch for ninety minutes at a time. But his fitness levels had quickly fallen well below par, having existed on a diet of self-pity and pizza for so long.

By the time Neil arrived at the clinic, he was breathless and sweaty. He considered he must look a bit like Chris Moyles climbing up Mount Kilimanjaro to raise money for Comic Relief but not as noble. He burst into the reception with such force that the receptionist fingered the button that summoned the security guard. If Nat hadn't rushed so willingly to Neil's side, he'd probably have been forcibly ejected.

'Neil, what are you doing here?'

'I've come to tell you . . .' God, it hurt to speak. He had this great speech he wanted to make; he'd been playing it over and over in his head as he'd run here and in his head it sounded like something as impressive and motivational as Barack Obama might utter but in reality, between gasps, it wasn't cutting it.

'I'll get you some water,' Nat said, quickly turning to the water cooler.

No, no, it was all wrong. Neil didn't want it like this. He wanted to look after Nat, not the other way round. Why didn't Nina or the receptionist get him some water if someone had to? Instead they were just staring at him, with something like amazement (and not in a good way). They shouldn't be letting Nat dash around, not straight after her procedure, it wasn't right. If he'd had the breath he'd have complained. Neil flopped into a chair, accepting at once both the indignity of his unfitness and the plastic cup of water. He gulped it back and then waited to catch his breath.

'Nat, I have some things I need to say. Please listen to them. Please don't interrupt because they'd be really difficult things to say even if I had enough breath to make me audible.' Nat nodded. 'I know there is no baby.'

'Neil—'

'You agreed, no interruptions.' Neil placed his finger on her lips. She didn't move it. Oh, the joy. The joy of touching her again. He considered leaving his finger up against her soft, swollen lips throughout his speech but then thought it might distract him. Reluctantly he took it away. 'Even though this is now academic, it's still extremely important. I need you to know that I'd have been its dad. Even if I wasn't. Although I might have been.'

'Why would you imagine that you might have been, Neil?' Nat wasn't keeping her promise of keeping quiet but Neil was pleased to note her tone was tender not aggressive.

'I put pinpricks in the condom that last night we were together,' Neil said quickly.

'You what?' Nat looked stunned.

'Can we do this outside?' Neil looked left and right and saw Nina and the receptionist stare at him, aghast, jaws hanging open. Nat ignored his request.

'You irresponsible, stupid—' This time Neil clamped his entire hand over Nat's mouth, he didn't think a tender finger would do the job. Her eyes continued to screech at him.

'I know, I know. Big mistake. Wrong. Desperate. But you slept with Lee Mahony.'

Nat bit hard down on Neil's hand; he had no choice but to pull away. 'I did no such thing! I slept with him!' Nat pointed an accuser's finger at Karl, who had just sneaked in the door. He hadn't parked his car in the car park, he'd abandoned it in front of the building, not caring if he got a ticket. He thought now it might be a good thing to jump back in it and flee. Infinitely preferable to playing a part in this drama but he knew he could not run. Not on this occasion.

'Karl!' shouted Neil in disbelief. 'You slept with Karl?'

'Yes,' admitted Nat.

'No,' insisted Karl.

Nat and Neil both turned to glare at Karl. It was unclear which of them had the most ferocious inclination to rip him limb from limb.

'Karl, there is no point in denying it now. We might as well have everything out in the open,' said Nat with a deep sigh.

'We didn't have sex,' Karl insisted.

'What?'

'We fooled around.' Karl coughed and stared at the floor. He wasn't sure who he was most embarrassed to be making this confession in front of, Nat, her husband or her mother. He hoped to hell Nat didn't ask how far they'd fooled around. He really didn't think he could say the necessary words in front of someone who had a bus pass. 'Nat, you started to cry, you said you couldn't do it to Neil. Well, actually, you said you couldn't do it to the nasty bastard but I knew who you meant. Then you passed out. I slept on the couch. Don't you remember?'

No, Nat did not remember. She had woken up in Karl's bed and thought the worst. What else would anyone think of Karl? She remembered flashbacks of flesh and lips, she had never been able to remember coherent details, she'd never wanted to, and then she found out she was pregnant, which seemed to confirm things.

'Oh my God.' Any one of them might have said it but it was Neil. He had worked out that the baby, the baby that was no more, was his after all. His minuscule moment of pure, unadulterated delight was blasted apart by a searing grief. His vision blurred with tears. He wiped them away and tried to stay focused. 'It doesn't matter,' he insisted bravely. 'None of it matters. It's all finished with. I set off today with the intention of telling you I'd be the father, if you let me, no matter whose the baby was.' Nat gasped, desperate to interrupt but Neil was determined to woo her. 'But I also wanted to tell you that even without a baby, without the chance of there ever being a baby, I'd like to be your husband again, if you'd let me. I'd like it more than anything on earth, Nat. That's what I wanted to say. Nat, can we start again, please?'

'But Neil, there *is* a baby. Your baby. Our baby. I couldn't go through with the abortion. We're going to have a baby.'

49

As Natalie had lain on the hospital bed, wrapped in nothing other than a starchy, arse-exposing gown and a paper hair net, she had thought about her mothers. Both of them. She thought of Nina, sitting in the sterile corridor, no doubt half crazed with worry. Poor Nina. She thought how much it must be costing Nina to come here with her and support her even when she did not agree with her decision. Nat could almost feel the waves of sympathy and stress oozing through the walls. How selfless and brave and uncompromisingly maternal Nina was. It struck Nat that Nina would make a great grandma. Nana Nina had a ring to it.

And Nat thought of Christina. Christina had been a cheerful-looking woman. She looked distinctly cheeky and carefree, with bright green, laughing eyes and a wide, honest forehead. She had dimples. Nat knew this from studying photos, as there used to be pictures of Christina around Brian's home but over the years the photos of Christina had slowly disappeared. There hadn't been a dramatic moment when Nina had swept away all evidence of her predecessor, that wasn't Nina's style at all. Over time the photos had simply, quite naturally, been replaced as newer shots, capturing important family moments such as the boys' christenings or Nat's first pony gymkhana, had been displayed. One photo had been removed when its frame broke (although Brian had had the intention of getting it replaced, he'd never got round to it), another was taken down when a wall was repainted and it never found its way back up. Brian carefully kept all these photos, preserved in a big red box that sat at the bottom of his wardrobe and he enjoyed looking through them from time to time. He'd encouraged Nat to keep one for herself as he thought that keeping a picture of her mother by her bed might be a comfort to a young girl. Nat had accepted the photo but did not keep it by her bed. She found it difficult to relate to the woman in the photo, a woman she didn't know, a woman she'd hacked down in her prime. Nat tucked the picture away between the pages of a *Jackie Annual* and she'd rarely looked at it. She tried never to think about it.

But, lying in the rigid hospital bed, staring at the ceiling, Nat found she couldn't get Christina's cheeky, cheerful, carefree grin out of her head. Would her baby inherit that beam? And those dimples? Was that possible? Nat had not even glanced at a photo of Christina for many years but she found the image was indelible. Nat wished for the millionth time that her mother had lived and that she'd shared the secret that lay behind that seismic grin which must have given her such confidence in the world.

Suddenly, from nowhere, like an angel's kiss, it struck Nat what Christina's secret might have been. Christina was loved. Christina loved in return. She loved Brian, her parents and her many friends too, no doubt. For once, Nat did not shun thoughts of her mother but instead she pursued them. She wondered if Christina had ever tasted buttered toast on a cold winter afternoon? Yes, probably, almost certainly. Had she felt sunlight flood through a window and warm her back? Yes. And she'd have read funny books and watched moving films. She'd have had a favourite colour and a favourite outfit. She'd have smelt waxy lilies and French coffee. She might have rolled down the side of a grassy hill, giggling until she thought she might be sick. She'd have watched sunsets and sunrises and marvelled at them. Boys would have made her cry and she'd have hurt one or two herself, no doubt. She'd have panicked about exams, carefully saved money, carelessly spent money. She'd probably got drunk on occasion and sung at the top of her lungs, maybe tunelessly, like Nat did.

Christina had lived.

Loved and lived. And if she'd lived a little longer, no doubt she'd have loved her daughter more than anything, Nat was sure of it.

But she hadn't lived until a ripe old age, which was a tragedy. Nat had been at this point in her reasoning when she heard Nina cough. She'd crept into Nat's hospital room even though Nat had instructed otherwise. Nina sat down next to Nat and firmly took hold of her hand. She said nothing at all, which was the most articulate and absolute show of her love. Nina was there. By her side. Splendid, wonderful Nina. She had always timed her entrances to perfection.

Nat had gazed out of the hospital window at the cold, wet, uninspiring January afternoon and yet her mind was clear as a summer day. Both mothers deserved a more fitting tribute than Nat's fear. Such love and devotion could not be met with dread and trepidation. Nat understood that she deserved a life full of careless, dimpled grins, a life devoid of fear.

EPILOGUE

'Nat, look at this.' Neil was waving a heavy-looking cream envelope. Nat gave him a fraction of her attention but largely she was concentrating on scraping the last of the raspberry jam out of the jar and on to her third slice of toast. The bump was ravenous this morning.

'What is it?'

'An invite to Jen's wedding.'

'But—'

'Not Jen and Karl's, obviously.'

Nat blushed inwardly. Although Neil had been very forgiving and understanding about her indiscretion with Karl, as she had about his indiscretion with Cindy, she still found the whole thing embarrassing. They'd both forced themselves to put the messy past away and concentrate on their bright future instead. Nat had gone so far as to encourage Neil to post Mrs Flippy back to the nursery, as neither of them could stand the idea of Heidi missing her comforter, and Neil had helped Nat word her note to Jen, confessing and apologising for the drunken fumble with Karl. Both of them were inordinately pleased that was all it had been but they both understood that for Jen the news would be devastating.

Nat had wondered for a long time what she ought to do for the best. Should she tell Jen at all or was it Karl's business to do so? Once she had decided for sure that her need to confess was nothing to do with easing her own conscience and everything to do with saving Jen (and Karl, come to that) from a disastrous marriage, Nat had compiled a note. There had been sixteen drafts written before Nat was content that she'd struck the correct tone – remorseful but not vengeful and aware but not dramatic. Neil hadn't seen Karl for a few months now, not since that day at the clinic. It was possible that one day they'd find a way to allow him back into their lives but right now Neil didn't know when or how. Karl wasn't godfather material, that much was clear.

'She's marrying Christopher Shaw,' said Neil.

'Who?'

'Her ex. Don't you remember? She'd not long split up from him when you met her.'

'Yes, it's ringing bells. Alarm bells.'

'Karl always said that she hadn't got over him. My God, they're getting married in May.'

Nat grabbed the invite from Neil. 'Wow, it's the same date, same venue, just different groom. Don't laugh.' Nat flicked through the papers that came with the invite. There were directions to the church and the reception, a list of suggested hotels for guests to stay in, a gift list and a suggested car pool list. Eventually Nat found what she was looking for – Jen had included a private note among the trail of logistics.

Dear Nat,

How's the bump?! Bet you're getting big now, hey?

I just wanted you to know that I did appreciate your note. It was very brave of you to send it and I realise that it can't have been an easy letter to write. As it happens it was the wake-up call I needed. When I went home for Christmas with Karl I bumped into my ex, Christopher. Do you remember me talking about him? I probably would have resisted the overwhelming chemistry between us but for the fact of your letter arriving when it did. It turns out that Chris had not married his girlfriend as I'd been informed, it turns out that he'd put that rumour about to make me jealous (sweet boy!). Karl

*had gone home to watch the football on his flat screen and so (well,
to cut a long story short) I enclose an invite to our wedding for you
and Neil! Crazy, huh?*

*I'm so glad you two sorted things out, you are made for each
other! I imagine by the time of the wedding you'll have quite a
sizable bump but you can get really pretty maternity frocks to
disguise that, you know, so don't worry!*

*I hope you understand why I couldn't ask you to be bridesmaid.
Rest assured it is absolutely nothing to do with you snogging my ex,
I just think pregnant bridesmaids spoil the photos.*

*I do hope that you come to the wedding and that you don't think
too badly of me. I just can't explain the pull of an ex.*

Lots of love,

Jen

Nat passed the note to Neil, who read it carefully.

'Shall we go?' he asked.

'I do love a wedding,' replied Nat and she kissed Neil on the cheek.
'OK. Let's go.'

'Great. I'll put in a holiday form today. It's quite timely because
I'm meeting my boss to discuss maternity leave so I might as well get
all requests on the table.'

'But you're happy with the arrangement?' Neil asked, wrapping his
arms round his wife and pulling her into a tight and warm hug. She
could smell Weetabix on his breath and suddenly had an urge to eat
one herself, perhaps with yogurt and honey and raisins.

'Damn right. I'll take the statutory and then you take over.'

Neil kissed the top of his wife's head and reached down towards
the bump. 'My pleasure,' he muttered into her hair, 'my pleasure.'

Tina Nina Rose has arrived at 3.35am!
7 lb 5 oz. Mother and baby perfect!
Dad fainted but doing OK now!

ACKNOWLEDGEMENTS

Thank you, over and over again, to my fantastic editor Jane Morpeth and the entire team at Headline for the most splendid welcome imaginable. I'm so delighted to be working with such an incredible, impressive and enthusiastic bunch. I am thoroughly grateful for, and appreciative of, the talent and dedication of every last one of you! With such a wealth of flair and forte it is almost impossible to begin to name names but I would like to give a particular shout out to Georgina Moore and James Horobin.

Thank you, Jonny Geller, for your endless support over the last ten years. Thank you for your wisdom, patience, encouragement and sense of humour. I'm scratching the surface here.

Thank you to all my readers. Each and every one of you is so lovely, glamorous, smart, wise, beautiful, perceptive, witty, humorous, sensitive and insightful.

Thank you, Jimmy, for everything. For all things. Without you I'd never have managed to write ten books in ten years; I probably wouldn't have managed to write ten books in one hundred years. You are my inspiration, my insight and my purpose. Thank you.

Finally I'd like to warmly acknowledge Rob and Becky Booker for their very generous support of Sparks, the children's medical research charity. The remit of Sparks is to fund research across the entire spectrum of paediatric medicine. Their goal is for all babies to be born healthy and stay healthy.

To learn more about Sparks visit www.sparks.org.uk